P9-DCM-361

RECKLESS DESIRE

When Joaquin looked down at Flame's sweet expression, he dared not go further with his caresses. He had only meant to kiss her, to hold her—how had he nearly taken her like this, like wild creatures whose passion for each other knew no limits except the depths of their own desire? He pulled her close to his heart and held her tenderly until her breathing was steady and even once more.

"Joaquin, why did you stop?" Flame stood with her head against his shoulder.

"I am your guardian, Flame. I am supposed to protect you from reckless young men, but I fear your greatest danger lies in my arms."

Flame tried to understand his words but could not. What danger did he mean? What possible danger could there be in his love? She looked up at him—loving him so tenderly—and wondered if the danger he spoke of was his own lust. . . .

PASSIONATE ROMANCE BY PHOEBE CONN

CAPTIVE HEART (1569, $3.95)

The lovely slavegirl Celiese, secretly sent in her mistress's place to wed the much-feared Mylan, found not the cruel savage she expected but a magnificently handsome warrior. With the fire of his touch and his slow, wanton kisses he would take her to ecstasy's searing heights — and would forever possess her CAPTIVE HEART.

ECSTASY'S PARADISE (1460, $3.75)

Meeting the woman he was to escort to her future husband, sea captain Phillip Bradford was astounded. The Swedish beauty was the woman of his dreams, his fantasy come true. But how could he deliver her to another man's bed when he wanted her to warm his own?

SAVAGE FIRE (1397, $3.75)

Innocent, blonde Elizabeth, knowing it was wrong to meet the powerful Seneca warrior Rising Eagle, went to him anyway when the sky darkened. When he drew her into his arms and held her delicate mouth captive beneath his own, she knew they'd never separate — even though their two worlds would try to tear them apart!

LOVE'S ELUSIVE FLAME (1267, $3.75)

Enraptured by his ardent kisses and tantalizing caresses, golden-haired Flame had found the man of her dreams in the handsome rogue Joaquin. But if he wanted her completely she would have to be his only woman — and he had always taken women whenever he wanted, and not one had ever refused him or pretended to try!

Available wherever paperbacks are sold, or order direct from the Publisher. Send cover price plus 50¢ per copy for mailing and handling to Zebra Books, 475 Park Avenue South, New York, N.Y. 10016. DO NOT SEND CASH.

Love's Elusive Flame

PHOEBE CONN

ZEBRA BOOKS
KENSINGTON PUBLISHING CORP.

ZEBRA BOOKS

are published by

KENSINGTON PUBLISHING CORP.
475 Park Avenue South
New York, N.Y. 10016

Copyright © 1983 by Phoebe Conn

All rights reserved. No part of this book may be reproduced in
any form or by any means without the prior written consent of
the Publisher, excepting brief quotes used in reviews.

Third printing: April 1985

Printed in the United States of America

Prologue

Celeste stretched languidly with a supple feline grace, then rested her slender arm on Joaquin's shoulder as he slept. Her fingertips slid through the tangle of dark curls which covered his bronze chest as she relaxed against him, drinking in his warmth. She could remember distinctly each time he'd come to see her, every memory separate from the rest. She had been in the company of a state senator the night they had first met, quite briefly at a formal reception. The senator was merely one of her many influential clients, a man who paid her well just to accompany him around San Francisco. She had been bored and restless that night when suddenly Joaquin Villarreal had appeared by some wonderful chance and her life had taken on an excitement it had previously lacked. She had found him more than merely handsome: his appeal was almost magnetic, a tangible force, an attraction she couldn't resist. He had done little more than nod when they were introduced, but when the senator had taken her home she had found the fascinating stranger waiting inside. He'd said not one word that night—she hadn't been certain he even spoke English—but he had made love to her as no other man ever had. He had held her so tenderly in his embrace, kissed her as if he really loved her. When she had awakened the next morning to find him gone and only his money left behind she had wept bitterly at that cruel disappointment.

She was far wiser now. She knew she was not the only woman he saw in San Francisco, dared not even hope she might be his favorite, but she looked forward to his infrequent visits with an eagerness she couldn't hide. He had been with her several times before she realized what he did was no more than a clever trick of technique. He brought forth emotion as no other man could, but it was a sport for Joaquin, nothing more. He had no feelings for her, none, she was certain he was not even capable of love, but what he did offer was so unique and pleasant she counted his attentions as a blessing and hid her sorrow that she meant so little to him. She made no demands whatsoever upon his time for she knew should she make even so slight a mistake as to inquire when she might see him again he would never return. A man like Joaquin Villarreal would never be owned by any woman and she was wise enough to have recognized that immediately.

Joaquin brought Celeste's hand to his lips then turned on his side to face her. His smile was playful, his dark eyes shining with a teasing gleam. "Were you trying to wake me?"

Celeste tossed her raven-hued curls and her bright blue eyes sparkled as she replied in a seductive whisper, "I do not ever complain that you neglect me, Joaquin, why would I wish to wake you?"

"I do not want you to be lonely when all you need do is ask."

"I should ask you, Joaquin?" Celeste traced a line down the taut muscles of his flat stomach as she spoke, her touch light, enticing.

Joaquin caught her hands in his, forcing her back upon the pillows where he held her easily with a light pressure upon her wrists. "Yes, I want to hear you ask

6

me, Celeste."

"Why? You know I want you, surely that is no secret. You are as fine a stallion as that black devil you ride."

"Then ask."

"Make me."

Celeste's playful challenge was all Joaquin needed for encouragement. He lowered his mouth to her throat and began to kiss her smooth silken skin. As his lips strayed lower to the pink tip of her ample breast he felt her breath quicken and chuckled, "You are too easy now, Celeste, but I enjoy you still." He released her wrists to caress her perfumed body with the most tantalizing of touches, then let his kiss work its magic upon her again until she begged him to stop, calling his name in hoarse sobs. He moved upon her then, let his own desires lead him further into the ecstasy he so easily gave to her. When finally they lay nestled again in each other's arms they were exhausted by pleasure, so warm and content neither cared to speak.

At last Celeste reached up to brush Joaquin's shiny black hair away from his eyes as she whispered her question: "Have you ever been in love, Joaquin, truly in love?"

"Love is for parents and their children, Celeste, for them and for fools."

"I know you are no fool, Joaquin, so therefore you must not have ever really cared for a woman."

"Why, Celeste, I have never loved any woman more than I love you." Joaquin kissed her lips lightly, then sat up, a sly smile curving his handsome mouth as he glanced down at her.

"Which is not at all. I know you well, Señor Villarreal, too well for you to fool me with your riddles."

Joaquin laughed, his amusement genuine. "You should know better than to ask me such foolish ques-

7

tions then. We please each other greatly and that is enough, do not ask more of me.''

"No, I will not. What I do ask of you is more than enough, thank you.'' Celeste giggled coyly as Joaquin leaned down to kiss her good-bye. She made no secret of watching him dress, did not avert her eyes. His body was perfect, strong and lean with the unusual height of the Spanish race. She had never met a more fascinating man—or a more puzzling one.

As Joaquin left her apartment he forgot Celeste immediately, but her question remained in his mind. He had always scoffed at the notion of love: it was a ridiculous idea, too silly to merit a grown man's contemplation . . . yet he could not help but think of it now. He considered himself far too smart, too clever to ever fall under any woman's spell; he had certainly never met any woman so beautiful or charming that he had been unable to resist her efforts to tame him. No, he had always been free to take women as he wanted them, whenever he wanted them, and no woman had ever refused him or even pretended to try. That he was almost unbelievably rich did not hurt his cause—that he knew; but San Francisco was filled with wealthy men who apparently had no idea how to please a woman. Poor creatures, he thought sadly, when they were so easy to please, why did so few men bother to learn how to do it? He laughed out loud as he strolled toward the docks. Women provided no challenge at all for him anymore, but as long as the pleasure was still there he would not complain too loudly.

As he walked up the gangplank of his sleek China clipper he paused to look out over the crowded bay. There was something in the wind which called to him, spoke to him so clearly he could not draw away. It was a memory, one which tantalized his senses as seductively as the most exotic perfume, but then it was gone, lost in

8

the mist of his past. He heard it again, a happy child's sparkling laugh which had been carried far out over the water. The sound touched him with a longing he could neither name nor place as he turned away. His own words came back to him then with the clear ring of a prophecy: love was for parents to lavish upon their children. But he was unlikely to ever have a child. . . .

Pushing all further thought of love from his mind he leapt aboard the graceful ship and strode off to find the captain.

One

Flame held the soft ruffled skirt of her new yellow silk gown above her tiny feet as she ran up the stairs. "Grandmother, Grandmother, it was the most wonderful party!" She burst into the elderly woman's bedroom and ran across the thick carpet to the four-poster bed.

At seventy-two years of age Fanny Bellefontaine needed little sleep, she always waited up to talk and her blue eyes sparkled with pleasure as she looked up at her beautiful granddaughter. "My goodness child, calm down. What was so special about tonight, was this party so different from all the others?" Fanny closed the book of poems she had been reading and smiled at Flame. Although baptized Linda, she had always been called Flame, a pet name of her father's, for her hair was a rich golden red which fell in long curls clear past her waist when she let it down. Fanny always said hair of that remarkable shade would have been an asset to any young woman but for Flame it was only one of her many blessings. Her deep green eyes were filled with mischief, glowing like priceless emeralds in the dim light which filled the spacious bedroom. Her dark eyelashes were so long and thick they cast shadows upon her flushed cheeks. It was her skin Fanny envied most, a creamy pale ivory so delicate and lovely no one could ever see Flame without wanting to reach out and caress her.

"Oh the orchestra was superb and we danced and danced till I'm afraid my new slippers are nearly worn out!"

"You did not want to stop dancing to rest, my love?" Fanny lifted her wrinkled hand to caress her granddaughter's cheek wistfully. "I can still remember the delights of being young and pretty, but it is not wise to overdo. You might become ill from so much excitement."

Flame took the older woman's hands in hers, giving them an affectionate squeeze. "I am far too happy to become ill, I love dancing so much, you know that."

"Who attended the party, anyone special, anyone new?"

"Yes, Laura Martin's brother brought three friends from his West Point class who are staying here with them while they are on leave."

"Lieutenants, soon to be posted to California, no doubt?" Fanny frowned. "You know I heartily disapprove of the military. Certainly no common soldier, granted these men are officers, will ever be worthy of you, Flame. I really must be more careful about the invitations I allow you to accept. I know this party was well chaperoned, but still—"

"Grandmother, please. The men are going to California, to the Presidio of Monterey, but you should see them. They looked so dashing in their uniforms and they dance so well too."

"Was one of them dark, the man for whom you've been waiting? Perhaps I should not encourage your fantasies but there is no harm in your being romantic at your age, my dearest. You'll learn the truth about life and men soon enough when you marry. At least I certainly did."

11

Flame shook her head, sending her gleaming curls flying. "Oh grandmother, maybe it is all just a silly dream which means nothing, but it is always so real, I can see him so clearly."

"I loved dreams when I was a girl—they were so full of promise then. My dreams are like dust now. . . . Please tell me about your man once more, I love to hear that dream."

Flame licked her lips thoughtfully for a moment and then began. "He is very tall, and dark, a Frenchman perhaps, like Papa, or a Spaniard, and so very handsome his smile reaches clear inside me, all the way to my heart. He has laughing eyes which are so deep a brown they seem black, and in my dream he is always smiling at me with a look I simply can't resist. But I've dreamed of him only, we've never actually met. Whenever I go out I look for him, I always do, but he's never there, never. Do you think it's possible I'm just remembering Papa?"

Fanny looked away for an instant and in her mind's eye she saw her daughter's husband again. André Lannier had been handsome all right, far too handsome in her opinion. "Perhaps, sweetheart. He's a very handsome man, or he was when last I saw him. I thought now that the railroad extends to California he might consider returning to Philadelphia to visit us. He has not been back once since he brought you here to me when you were four."

"Oh, do you think he might come to see me? I'd give anything to see him again! I'm sixteen now, Grandmother, if he won't come here I could take Lottie and go to visit him!" Flame's pretty eyes shined with delight at that thought.

"Never, Flame, don't even suggest such an outrageous thing. I won't hear of it and neither would your father. Ladies of your breeding will never travel alone." Fanny's mouth was set in a firm line. "What nonsense, I scarcely permit you to leave my sight, a trip to California is impossible!"

"But Grandmother, I'd love to see California again. I can remember so little of Daddy and his ranch and Lieutenant Bradley says that—"

"Flame, I've told you repeatedly to call your father Papa . . . it sounds so much more refined. And now, who is this Bradley?"

"He's one of the lieutenants I told you about, one of Richard Martin's friends. He's going to Monterey next month and he tells the most wonderful stories about California."

"Before he's even been there? Sounds like a remarkable man to me. Not tall and dark though?"

"No, not at all, he's very blond with deep blue eyes, but he knows men who've just returned from California so his information is reliable even if he hasn't been there yet himself."

"Tell me something more about this Lieutenant Bradley. Who are his people? You must learn to make discreet inquiries about families, Flame—sometimes a younger son does inherit his family's wealth after all."

Flame threw up her hands in frustration. "I didn't ask him! I'm nowhere near ready to marry, there's so much to do and see and now that the railroad goes all the way across the nation—"

"Now Flame, enough of that, you will stay here in Philadelphia until you are suitably married. I raised you to be a proper bride and I'll see to it you have a husband who can not only appreciate your beauty but afford your tastes as well. If he wishes to take you to Paris, or even to California, then he most certainly may do so, but until then forget your silly dreams of seeing the world."

Flame stared closely at her grandmother for a long

moment before replying soberly, "What if I never marry? Maybe I won't ever find the man I can love. Maybe love will always be like the stranger in my dream, a vision only, never real. What if the man I was destined to marry died in the war and it is only his spirit which calls to me in my dreams?"

"Flame, really, you become more unmanageable each day. Many fine men died for the North as well as the South during the war, but thank the good Lord many more did not. I am almost positive very few Spaniards were lost. Let's be sensible for a few minutes—if you can force yourself. Was Alex Richmond there tonight? You know I consider him a fine prospect for you, he's from a respected family. He is most desirable as a husband, so I hope you did not neglect him in your foolish infatuation with these lieutenants who will soon be gone."

Flame exploded in a fiery burst of anger. "I detest that man! How many times must I tell you before you believe me? He is no better than a rake, no woman is safe with him and I hate him!"

"Perhaps he is too forward simply because he cares for you, my dear. It is sad that so wealthy a young man appears to have so little breeding but I'm prepared to make allowances for him if he finds it difficult to control his feelings for you."

"It's not only me though, it's all the girls—Mary Louise, Elizabeth, Margaret—all of them say exactly the same thing."

"Well, it sounds as though he needs a good talking to. I'll speak to his mother the first chance I have."

"No! Please don't do that, then the Richmonds will think I'm interested in Alex and it will only encourage him to be all the more amorous, and I can't stand to have him touch me now. Dancing with him is horrid the way he holds me so tightly and I won't even repeat

14

the things he says they are so disgusting!''

"Don't fret about him then, Flame." Fanny smiled to herself. "I find it difficult to believe young Alex could be all that obnoxious. His appearance is pleasant enough and he is so extraordinarily rich."

Flame straightened her posture and placed her hands on her hips in a defiant pose as she glared down at the petite lace-clad figure in the large bed. "Grandmother, promise me you'll say nothing to his mother, not one word. No matter how much money the Richmonds possess it will never be enough to make up for the lack of character in that snake they call their son!"

Fanny made no attempt to stifle her yawn. "Go to bed, Flame, we'll discuss your beaux another time—I'm really quite sleepy. Now good night."

Flame gave up with a strangled cry of frustration, "Good night, Grandmother." She bent down to kiss the woman's wrinkled cheek then crossed the hall to her own room where she immediately began to undress, carelessly tossing her beautiful silk gown over the back of a chair. Lottie came in to help her get ready for bed and to brush out her long red hair, but Flame could scarcely sit still while the poor servant girl tried to work.

"Oh Lottie, I just love parties, I had so much fun dancing with Lieutenant Bradley. I don't care what grandmother says about military men, she's wrong."

"Miss Flame, you mustn't say things like that." Lottie stepped back a moment, awed by her beautiful young mistress' clear defiance. "I just know Mrs. Bellefontaine is right about most everything, she must be right about military men too."

"Oh go to bed, Lottie. I'll brush my own hair tonight, get going!" Flame yanked the brush from the maid's trembling hand and waited until the frightened girl left the room. She brushed her hair only a few strokes, however, before she grew bored with the tiresome task and stretched out upon her bed. She wasn't in the least bit tired, not at all sleepy after such a wonderful night. She closed her eyes, sighing contentedly as she thought about the young men with whom she'd danced. Even Alex was handsome in his way; it was just his personality that was so repugnant to her. He was rough and crude, totally lacking in the charm so many other men displayed. But where was her Spaniard, the man who appeared only in her dreams? Was it a dream, or a memory, a man she'd met long ago whose face still haunted her dreams? If he were a memory then he must have been a delightful man for her to recall his face still. She could remember her father's face, but just dimly, but no, this man was different, a tall man like Papa, but different nonetheless.

Flame couldn't remember her mother's face at all and that thought saddened her greatly. She remembered her soft dresses and sweet perfume, but not her lovely face. Her grandmother had a miniature of Deborah painted before she'd married and gone to California: it showed a beautiful young woman with creamy skin and gorgeous golden hair. Flame thought she looked more like the portrait with each passing year, and yet there was something of her father in her too. Her spirit and defiance were his traits, surely, for they seemed so lacking in the sweet face of her mother which smiled out from the tiny portrait.

When Alex first began to call on her Flame was merely annoyed, but when he persisted in visiting her as often as decency allowed she rebelled. "Grandmother, I can't abide Alex Richmond! Why must I tolerate his insistent attentions?"

Fanny Bellefontaine lay her embroidery aside. "Is there some problem with his manners? He is not being too forward, is he?"

"No, it isn't that. His manners have been perfect—

16

too perfect in fact. I cannot complain that he has not been a gentleman, it's just the way he looks at me. I swear he almost drools, it's just disgusting."

"There seems to be no pleasing you, Flame, you are spoiled because of your beauty but it's time you learned to be realistic. I shall not live forever, nor do I wish to, but I do plan to see you married suitably and soon. Alex is twenty-six, old enough to take a wife and he's doing extremely well, you know he will inherit his family's bank in time."

Flame held her breath, not liking the direction their conversation was taking. "Must I again repeat the reasons for my violent objection to Alex Richmond?"

Fanny ignored the high-spirited girl's outburst. "All men are the same in their desires, Flame. All the young men have exactly the same thoughts in their heads when they look at you, so it makes no difference which one becomes your husband. The only important consideration is that he should be from the same social standing in the community. The Richmonds are a respected family, it would be difficult to find a more suitable husband for you."

"Husband! I am barely sixteen years old!" Flame clenched her fists defiantly at her sides. "How can you say all men are the same? I remember Papa, he was so handsome, and he was—"

"Yes, Flame, André was charming and handsome, but he was wild all the same. I'll never forgive him for taking Deborah to California to live, taking her away from all her family and friends who loved her. She should never have been expected to live like some indigent pioneer!"

"That's not true and you know it, Grandmother. Papa's ranch is large and successful, look at the lovely presents he sends me, he's rich! I'm sure Mother wanted to go with him because she loved him. He was

17

all that mattered to her, not the people she left behind here in Philadelphia!''

"Your dear mother is dead all the same, Flame."

"But she was ill. Daddy, oh, Papa, could hardly have kept her from becoming ill. It wasn't his fault she died."

"Sweetheart, it is not my purpose to malign your father in your eyes. I know you adore him regardless of how long it has been since you saw the man or how infrequently his letters arrive. André is really not the topic of our conversation. All I am asking is that you continue to be pleasant to Alex. That's a simple thing, just be polite as a lady always is. You may change your mind about him in time."

Flame knew better than to argue any more that afternoon, but when they were invited to the Richmond home for dinner two weeks later she wasn't at all pleased. She complained bitterly the entire time she dressed, thinking the evening only another in a long series of bothersome social obligations her grandmother had accepted on her behalf. The evening was pleasant enough, however, Flame had to admit that: for once Alex didn't leer at her and his conversation and conduct were almost charmingly polite. When he escorted them to their door he eagerly accepted Fanny's invitation to come inside, but then the woman excused herself, pleading the fatigue of old age, and left an embarrassed Flame alone in the parlor with the young man.

Alex moved quickly to sit close beside Flame on the velvet loveseat, his knees brushing hers. "How long have we known each other, Flame?" He reached for her hand as he spoke, squeezing her fingers between his.

Flame fought the revulsion which his cold clammy touch brought for as long as she could but finally had to

18

yank her hand from his. "I think I've always known you, haven't I? Our families have been acquainted since I was small."

The young man grinned, showing off slightly crooked teeth. "Yes, since you came here from California. You were just a little girl then, about four, but I was in my teens and remember you well. Your grandmother brought you over to meet my mother. You were dressed in blue like some exquisite French doll."

Well I'm no empty-headed doll, Flame thought angrily. She yawned and didn't cover her mouth. "Forgive me, Alex, I'm very tired. Let's talk another time." She stood quickly and smoothed the folds of her green satin skirt as she walked toward the front door, eager to see him gone.

Alex overtook Flame in an instant. He put his arms around her slim waist to catch her in a tight embrace. "I'm in no hurry to leave."

"Alex, please, let me go!" Flame pounded on his hands but he only laughed at her feisty defense and held her that much more tightly.

"What's the matter, Flame? You won't still try and fight me once we're married, will you?"

His taunting words shocked Flame so much that she ceased to struggle for an instant, and Alex seized that opportunity to turn her around to face him. His mouth bruised hers with a wet sticky kiss, and though she shoved against his chest with all her strength he just moved his hand to her bodice, grasping her high firm breast in a rude caress. Flame struck out at him then with both fists finding their mark.

Alex released her, swearing as he stepped back. He pulled his handkerchief from his pocket and tried to stem the flow of blood from his battered nose. "We'll see how long you fight me after we're married, Flame!" He sneered at her in disgust, his pale blue eyes

19

filled with loathing. "You may have won this time, girl, but never again!"

"What nonsense is that? I'll never marry the likes of you, I despise you!" Flame stamped her foot and threw open the front door. "Go home and don't ever bother to come back here ever again!"

Alex laughed at her anger. "It's all been arranged, Flame, I spoke with your grandmother tonight while you were with my mother after dinner. She has given her consent and you'll be my wife within the month!"

"Never!" Flame screamed at him, shrieking the word so loudly the young man jumped back in surprise.

He grabbed her, putting his hands around her slender throat to pull her face to his, kissing her again in the same brutal way. When he released her she stumbled backwards but swiftly regained her balance and yelled at him again. "Never! I'd kill myself before I'd marry you!"

"I think not, my dear." Alex glared down at the petite beauty, quite proud of the masterful way he'd taught her who would be the boss. "I'll beat you if I have to, but you'll be an obedient wife if it kills you!" He giggled at his own grizzly joke. "Yes, beating you will be such pleasure, I can imagine how good your smooth white skin will look streaked with trickles of blood! It's a very exciting thought . . . do you want to feel what you do to me?"

As Alex grabbed Flame's hand she gave him a savage shove to push him through the open door, then locked it quickly behind him. She could scarcely draw a breath she was so badly frightened and ran shrieking as she climbed the stairs to her grandmother's room. "Grandmother, what have you done? I'll never marry that fiend, never, do you hear me!"

Fanny only smiled and answered patiently, "Dear child, go to bed, you're overwrought. We'll discuss the arrangements for your marriage in the morning.''

"No, we will discuss Alex right this minute because I'll never marry him, I won't do it!"

Now Fanny grew alarmed. "Perhaps I misjudged your dislike for the young man, but that's so silly. All men are basically the same, dear, with the same lustful tastes. Just go on to bed, the matter is settled. You will wed Alex Richmond, and soon.''

"Never, you can't make me do it! I'll scream and scream, I'll never say the words, you won't even get me in the door of the church! I'd kill myself before I'd let that man touch me ever again!''

Lottie came running into Mrs. Bellefontaine's bedroom horrified by the shrill sound of her mistress' voice. She stood staring dumbly, not comprehending what terrible thing could have upset even such a high-strung girl as Flame to such a degree.

"Put this child to bed please, Lottie. She is throwing a tantrum, behaving like a two-year-old tonight, so I shall have to treat her as one. Lock her in her room and bring me the key.''

Lottie's eyes widened in alarm. "Yes, Ma'am, but how do I get her into her room?'' The frightened girl's voice quivered as she spoke.

Flame tossed her curls defiantly. "Oh stop sniveling, Lottie, I'll walk into my room. But mark my words, Grandmother, you'll not live long enough to see me married to Alex Richmond!'' Flame turned and left the room to walk into her own. She threw herself across her bed as she heard Lottie turn the key in the lock but she was too outraged by her grandmother's treachery to weep. She'd run away, leave as soon as she could possibly get enough money together for train fare. She racked her brain frantically for a solution to her problem—then an idea so simple it was amazingly easy came to her mind. She'd go home to California, to her father! She sat up, delighted with her plan. Of course her father would be overjoyed to see her, and *he'd* never force her to marry a man she despised. She'd seen a place while out shopping, a small shop that bought jewelry and other items of value: She'd sell everything she could to raise the money she needed. As soon as possible she was going to California!

When Flame awoke the next morning the house was strangely quiet. There was none of the early morning clatter the servants always made. She sat up as she heard the key turn in the lock, but instead of Lottie bringing in her breakfast it was Dr. Devereaux, her grandmother's physician, who looked in. "Are you awake, child?"

"Yes, Dr. Devereaux, what is it? Is Grandmother ill?"

The grey-haired gentlemen shook his head as he slowly approached her bed, "I'm sorry, Flame. She passed away during the night. She died peacefully, without suffering . . . she simply did not awaken this morning."

Instantly Flame's angry words of the previous night rang in her ears. She had been right after all: her grandmother hadn't lived to see her married. She clasped her hands tightly over her mouth to muffle the sound as she began to scream. The kindly doctor rushed to her side, pulled her close to his chest and patted her back soothingly until she relaxed against him, sobbing pathetically for the woman who had loved her, the woman who had been the only family she had ever really known.

The days before the funeral passed swiftly. So many friends came to the house, ladies who had known Fanny Bellefontaine all their lives came to pay their respects and talk in hushed voices of their memories, often forgetting they had come to console Flame as they

22

chatted. Flame nodded and smiled as best she could, but she hated every minute, for she wanted only to get away, to leave Philadelphia with all possible haste and go home to her father. When she found herself alone for a few minutes one afternoon she gathered up her jewelry and went hurriedly to a gem shop she'd seen. The proprietor was pleased to buy her jewels, he said they were exquisite and gave her what she considered to be a fair price. Next she went to the railroad station to purchase two tickets, then returned home to complete her plans.

The Richmonds insisted upon driving Flame home from the funeral in their elegant carriage; she thanked them graciously and invited them to come in for tea. She sat across from them in the parlor, averting her eyes demurely while her fingers fidgeted nervously with the satin ribbons which trimmed her new black dress. She couldn't bear to look at Alex; being in the same room with him made her sick to her stomach and she hoped her guests would remember her grief and leave quickly.

The elder Mr. Richmond cleared his throat with an anxious cough before he spoke. "Ah, Linda, now that your grandmother has been laid to rest, we must turn our thoughts to far more practical matters. You cannot continue to live here alone, and you know it was Fanny's last wish that you and Alex marry. I think everyone will understand your haste to wed after this saddness, the bans will be read for the first time this Sunday and the wedding ceremony will take place next month."

Flame continued to stare fixedly at the floor, letting them think she was overcome with emotion, as indeed she was—if not with the one they imagined. If she argued they might become suspicious, insist she move into their home, where it would be that much more dif-

23

ficult to escape, so she nodded agreeably. "Yes, Mr. Richmond, that is so very kind of you, so thoughtful of you to consider my welfare now that I am alone." She dabbed away her tears with her lace-trimmed handkerchief and was relieved when the Richmonds seemed to believe the matter was settled and prepared to leave.

Alex lingered briefly as his parents departed. "Perhaps you would allow me to take you out for a ride in my carriage tomorrow. The air would be good for you, Flame, you look very pale. I know just the spot where we might go, not too distant and yet quite secluded, where we might become better acquainted without attracting undue attention."

Flame wasn't fooled by Alex' pleasant words. She needed more time though, she had to get away before anyone found out she had gone. "That sounds very nice, Alex, it would be so enjoyable to go out, but could we wait a few days? I'm really not up to it yet." She brought her handkerchief to her eyes again as she whispered tearfully.

"As you wish. I will call for you at the end of the week then."

"Yes, thank you, Alex." Flame waited at the window to be certain the Richmonds had left, then ran up the stairs, unbuttoning her stiff black dress as she went. "Lottie! Come quickly! We haven't a second to lose, the train leaves within the hour!" She had timed everything perfectly, their trunks were already at the station and when the train left Philadelphia that afternoon Flame Lannier and her maid were aboard. The well dressed young woman sat calmly, watching the sights of the city pass by, and she prayed it would be several days before her absence was noted. She'd given the other servants the rest of the week off so no one would be in the house to notice she had gone. By the time Alex came to call for her and realized what she had done it would be too late, she'd be too far away to catch. She had sent a wire to her father apprising him of the date and time of her arrival in San Francisco. Surely he'd be thrilled to see her, and all her troubles would be over. She hugged Lottie and exclaimed in delight, "We're going home, Lottie! Thank God we are finally going home to California!"

Two

The journey by train from Philadelphia to Chicago proved to be too much for Lottie. She was unbearably homesick and wept unceasingly for the entire trip. Flame wished a hundred times she had left her maid at home: the young girl was simply a nuisance, and she'd made the trip which would have been such an adventure tedious in the extreme.

By the time they reached Chicago, Flame had had enough of the miserable servant's company. "Lottie, we have to change trains soon to board the Golden Gate Special for San Francisco, I think it would be best for both of us if I called the conductor now and arranged for your fare back home."

"But Miss Flame, you'd be all alone then!" Lottie's tear-filled eyes overflowed again as she imagined the dire consequences for a single woman traveling across the country unescorted.

I am already alone, Flame thought sadly. She reached out and patted the girl's knee, "No, Lottie, it has been much nicer here on the train than I ever expected. We have not been bothered once, nor will I be when I continue alone. I have noticed several young mothers with small children who will most probably appreciate my help—surely a crowd of little ones will be enough to discourage any man's attentions. Now the matter is settled. I will write a letter for you to present to Grandmother's lawyer, he is paying all the servants now and will continue to pay your salary until you find another position. I'll give you a nice reference too."

"Mrs. Bellefontaine would never have allowed you to travel alone, Miss Flame, you know that."

"Times have changed, Lottie, do you know there are groups working for woman's suffrage? Why only last year there was a convention in Cleveland of the National Woman's Suffrage Party. How are women ever to be independent if we're afraid to sit on the train alone? I swear there are times when I just hate being a woman, it is so confining! Now I'm calling the conductor, you're going home, so stop crying this instant."

The Golden Gate Special featured Pullman Palace cars whose elegance well matched their name. Flame was entranced by the decor of her luxurious car. The mahogany paneling was carved as intricately as a Chinese puzzle box and the velour furnishings were as expensive as those in her grandmother's parlor. Each car seemed to be more magnificent than the next, as each had its own distinctive beauty and name. But not even the gracious rococo setting could distract Flame from the splendor of the passing landscape. To be able to cross the whole country and to enjoy it all in comfort with such a spectacular view was an endless delight for her. She was free at last to enjoy life as she had longed to do, free just to relax without being bothered to follow her grandmother's strict rules of behavior and etiquette although she had to admit she had not once violated them. She was pleasant and charming company for her fellow travelers and thanked God each hour for her escape from the horrible Alex Richmond, for surely nothing which awaited her in California could ever be as awful as marriage to him would have been.

When Flame stepped out upon the platform at the San Francisco depot she was dressed in one of her most fashionable outfits. The deep green shade brought out the rich color of her eyes as well as the bustle and slim skirt enhanced her graceful figure. It had been twelve years since her father had seen her and she wanted him to be proud of his only child. She tried to remember how handsome he was but as she searched the faces of the gathering crowd she saw no one who resembled her father. As the minutes passed she grew increasingly anxious. What if he hadn't received her wire? She knew not a soul in San Francisco and had very little money left—if her father were not coming to meet her whatever could she do? She blinked back her tears and tried to be more patient, reminding herself he would be there soon, he just had to be.

Rafael Ramirez stood at the edge of the crowd scanning the faces of the departing travelers. His instructions from Joaquin had been very specific: he was to meet Miss Lannier, and see that she returned to Philadelphia immediately. He found her easily enough but she was far more lovely than he'd thought possible, certainly several years older than Joaquin had thought. Impatient to complete his errand he approached her swiftly. "Miss Lannier, I'm Rafael Ramirez, your father's attorney."

Flame returned the well dressed young man's smile with an enthusiasm she couldn't hide. He was not the man from her dream, but the resemblance was so close she felt as if she knew him already. "Oh, I am so happy to meet you, Mr. Ramirez. But why didn't my father come to meet me himself?"

"That is a rather long story, Miss Lannier. It would be best if we left your luggage here for the time being while we go to my office where we might talk in private. Now where is your maid? Your wire mentioned she was traveling with you."

"I had to send Lottie back home. She was more of a

28

nuisance than I could bear.''

"You traveled all alone?'' Rafael's handsome features were scarcely marred by his frown, but he was astonished. To consider sending her back home in the company of a maid had been bad enough, but to send her home alone was unthinkable.

Flame read his expression accurately and hurried to reassure him. ''Yes, and as you can see I arrived quite unharmed. Now please tell me why my father sent you instead of coming to greet me himself. It has been twelve years and I'm so anxious to see him again.''

Rafael reached out to take Flame's arm gently. ''If you'll just come with me, Miss Lannier, I have my carriage waiting. My office is not far.''

Flame shook her head and pulled her arm free of his grasp. ''No, wait! I don't even know you, Mr. Ramirez. How do I know for certain you even know my father! I'd rather not go to your office—I'll just wait right here until my father comes to get me himself.''

Rafael looked down at Flame's defiant expression and smiled slowly. ''I assure you I am indeed exactly who I say I am. Now come with me.'' He again reached for Flame's arm but she eluded his grasp deftly.

''No! I won't go with you until you tell me where my father is and why he isn't here himself! What business could he possibly have that is more important than meeting me?''

Rafael sighed in frustration. ''I had hoped to tell you in private, not here in this public walkway, Miss Lannier, but if you insist then I have no choice. Your father is dead. He died almost a month ago in a fire which destroyed his home.'' He watched as Flame's expression changed swiftly from defiance to horror. For an instant he thought she might faint, and when he reached out to hold her this time she did not draw away.

"No! Oh no! That can't be true!" Flame searched Rafael's face for some trace of insincerity, some clue that he was lying, but his expression was an honest one, his gaze devoid of treachery.

Not wishing to prolong what he considered to be an entirely unnecessary public scene Rafael took Flame's arm in a firm grip and led her to his coach before she could argue. She sat in a daze during the short trip and did not protest when he led her to a comfortable chair in his oak-paneled office. She had grown pale, but didn't cry; she only stared at the handsome attorney as if she simply could not accept his shocking news as fact.

"It is my fault you have made this trip unnecessarily. I was in Los Angeles when the tragedy occurred and had to wait until I had returned to my office to find your grandmother's address. I wrote to her only last week but obviously you were already on your way here by then. Perhaps it would be best if you planned to leave for Philadelphia tomorrow when the train begins its return trip East."

Flame was not listening to the young man. No, it was not possible—how could her father be dead? Surely he wasn't, not after she'd waited so many years and come so many miles to see him! It wasn't fair! Fate could not possibly be so cruel!

Rafael leaned forward and took her small gloved hand in his. "Miss Lannier, I had no idea you were traveling alone. We must find someone to travel with you when you go home. I will not send you back to Philadelphia unaccompanied."

His words finally reached her and Flame disagreed violently as she yanked her hand from his. "No! California is my home! I've come home at last and I have no intention of leaving!"

"But Miss Lannier, your expectations are totally unrealistic. There is no way you can remain here in

California now."

"What of my father's estate? You said you were his attorney, surely you must be a clever man, since my father was wealthy didn't he leave something to me?"

"He left everything to you, Miss Lannier." Rafael paused long enough to wish most desperately that Joaquin were there to help him. "You own a ranch, cattle, horses . . . your father's holdings were extensive, but you don't want to live on a cattle ranch. Surely you belong in a city like Philadelphia, where—"

Flame interrupted him immediately. "Mr. Ramirez, are you perhaps deaf? I have come home! How far away is my father's ranch? How long will it take me to get there? I just want to go home."

Rafael was at the limit of his patience. He had expected a child he could easily direct back to Philadelphia, not this young woman whose tongue was as sharp as her wits! "No, damn it, I am not deaf, are you? Your home is gone, burned to the ground, Miss Lannier. Your home is gone!"

Flame was startled by the man's angry outburst: his temper was obviously as bad as her own. "Mr. Ramirez, are you by any chance from Spain?"

"What?" Rafael was taken back by her question; it was so terribly irrelevant to their argument he could not help but laugh. "What has my ancestry to do with what we are discussing?"

"Nothing actually, just a point of curiosity. I have never met a Spaniard and thought perhaps you were one. You are dark and Rafael Ramirez sounds like a Spanish name to me."

"Miss Lannier, let us decide what we are going to do about you first. Then I will be happy to regale you with stories about my family for as long as you care to listen."

"That seems fair. When may I leave for my ranch?"

31

Flame sat back in her chair, but her expression was still determined.

"I'm certain your grandmother will not allow you to reside here now that your father is deceased. I will have to follow her wishes."

"I attended my grandmother's funeral the day I left Philadelphia. I have no reason to return there: I have no one, Mr. Ramirez, to care for me on either side of the continent, so I much prefer to remain here in California."

Rafael was stunned by her announcement. "I had no idea Mrs. Bellefontaine had died. I received no word, no wire . . . why was no message sent to your father about this?"

Flame glanced down while she composed a lucid reply. She was afraid to tell Rafael the truth about why she had left her grandmother's home so swiftly. Perhaps he would consider her engagement reason enough to send her back, and she couldn't risk that. She had planned to tell her father the truth of course, but this man was a stranger, and although he seemed to be a pleasant one, he had no reason to be on her side. "I simply planned to tell him myself, but since he is dead, I am on my own." Flame was surprised she could make such a statement with a large degree of composure, but the freedom of being independent far outweighed the worry of being alone in the world.

Rafael got up from his chair and circled his desk to open the top drawer, from which he withdrew a thick envelope. "That is not the case, Miss Lannier. Your father appointed a guardian in his will, and so it appears that you do have someone who will be responsible for you after all."

"A guardian? Who is it?" Flame was alarmed. A guardian meant only one thing to her now: someone to meddle in her life just when she had thought she was going to be free.

"His name is Joaquin Villarreal. His ranch borders your father's—your ranch. He is down at the port today or he would have come with me to meet you himself. One of his ships docked last night and he will be occupied for several days before he will be able to return to his home."

"Villarreal, that's a beautiful name. Is it not Spanish?"

Rafael finally gave in to his frustration, "Miss Lannier, Joaquin Villarreal and I are both native-born Californians. Our names are indeed Spanish: our blood is as pure as the day our great-grandfathers left Castile. Our first language was Spanish and we speak it still when we are together. We were known as Californios rather than Spaniards until California had the misfortune to become part of the United States. Now does that satisfy your incessant curiosity?"

Flame leaned back and stared at the handsome man's flashing eyes. "Why are you so angry? Are you ashamed of your heritage for some reason?"

"Ashamed! Of course not, I am extremely proud of my heritage. It is all the United States has left me."

Flame was eager to hear more. Rafael Ramirez was one of the most intriguing men she had ever met and his story interested her greatly. "My command of California history is minimal, Mr. Ramirez. What did the United States do to you, to the Californios? You must have been only a boy when California became a state in 1850."

Rafael was surprised to realize that Flame's question was asked from genuine interest. "I am sorry, this is no time for me to parade my complaints."

"You have another appointment, a client perhaps, who is coming here shortly?"

"No, my afternoon is entirely free. Why do you

33

ask?''

"Mr. Ramirez, I have just completed an extremely long train trip and you tell me I'll have to travel an additional four days to reach my ranch where I'll find I have no house . . . if I could just sit here in this chair all afternoon while you recite your complaints I'd be most content. Now please tell me what happened to you.''

Rafael returned to his chair and regarded Flame more critically. A beautiful woman who could think was a rare creature indeed; what would be the harm in indulging her? His gaze strayed over her lovely skin and delicate features, but it was her hair he liked most, an absolutely glorious shade, neither red nor blonde, but a golden haze which he longed to reach out and touch. With considerable effort he tried to remind himself of what she had asked. "Since my story is also Joaquin's I will relate it. It might help you to understand the man your father asked to become your guardian. When what is now California belonged to Spain, our great-grandfathers were the recipients of large parcels of land, land grants given by the governor to encourage settlement in what was then largely untamed wilderness. When Mexico gained its independence from Spain in 1821, California came under Mexican rule. But Mexico City is nearly as distant as Spain in our minds and the life here changed not at all. When the United States gained possession of California from Mexico a treaty was signed, the Treaty of Guadalupe Hidalgo by name. The original version of the treaty guaranteed the Californios clear possession of their land whether their titles were held from Spanish or Mexican grants. However, that clause was deleted from the final version of the treaty. Can you guess why?''

Rafael's bitter expression left little room for doubt.

"You mean there was a deliberate plan to rob you of your land?"

"Nicely put. Yes, in 1851 a Land Commission was established in San Francisco and each person holding a Spanish or Mexican title had to furnish proof of the validity of his claim."

"But was there any proof, deeds, whatever for grants that were by that time so old?"

"No, of course not. That was the whole point. The grants were based on landmarks, groves of trees, rocks, roads which were hardly more than trails, all of which changed over time. Each ranchero knew the boundaries of his own land, but when cattle were out grazing it made little difference where they wandered, there were no fences."

"So the boundaries were difficult to prove?" Flame was totally absorbed in Rafael's story; she listened carefully to his every word.

"Not impossible. It could be done, but litigation went on for years, attorneys' fees were steep, many unscrupulous men defrauded their clients. Rancheros had to borrow money at high interest rates to finance their court battles . . . it was a losing proposition from the beginning. My father was left with his house and not much more, then he proceeded to gamble away even that."

"But what of the Villarreals? You said the man has ships as well as a ranch near mine? They did not suffer as your family did?"

"No, they did not. Joaquin's father was the most suspicious man who ever lived. He knew there would be trouble and he had everything ready when he went before the Land Commission, so his title was upheld. Joaquin's ranch is the original size, nearly half a million acres."

Flame's beautiful green eyes widened in surprise

35

when he named the large figure. "Isn't that an enormous amount of land?"

"Yes, it most certainly is, but it is what I would have had if my father had not been such a gentleman he could not believe the government of the United States capable of such underhanded work."

"But why was it done, Rafael, why?" It had seemed natural to Flame to address him by his first name. She pronounced it as he did, with three distinct syllables. He smiled when she said it but she didn't understand why.

"The Gold Rush had increased the population of California so enormously that it was difficult for men who had farmed small parcels of land in the East to comprehend why we needed so much more for our cattle. The government wanted our large land holdings divided up, and they succeeded to a great degree in their aims."

Flame's expression grew thoughtful as she sat back in her chair. "Is that how my father was able to buy his ranch? He bought land where the original title could not be proven?"

"Yes, that is correct." Rafael folded his arms across his chest and waited for the question he was sure would follow.

"Is my land now what was once yours?" Flame's eyes filled with sadness as she looked at her new friend.

"Yes, but I no longer consider it mine. Your ranch is only a small part of what was once ours. Many people now own what was my home."

Flame's eyes filled with tears she could not hold back. "Oh Rafael, this is terrible! I don't want to live on land that was stolen from you!"

Rafael viewed Flame's anguish and shook his head in disbelief. "Miss Lannier, why would you weep over my loss when you did not shed one tear for your own father?''

Flame took out her handkerchief and wiped her eyes. She sniffed shyly and tried to explain: ''Rafael, I can barely recall my father's face. He seldom wrote to me—he sent gifts, but presents mean little to a child who longs for love. I am so disappointed I'll never know my father—meeting him again had been my fondest wish—but truly, I know you this minute far better than I ever knew him. But if my tears embarrass you forgive me.''

''Your tears do not embarrass me, Miss Lannier. I cannot recall a woman ever caring so much for my feelings and I am touched, but let me assure you I was your father's friend. I bore him no animosity whatsoever that my lack of fortune was his stroke of good luck. As you pointed out, I was a boy when all this transpired. I am content with my life and do not begrudge you your land in the least. I'll take you back to get your luggage and you will stay at my house tonight. Tomorrow we will begin our journey to Joaquin's ranch. I think you will find his home extremely comfortable until he returns, and then the two of you can make plans for your future.''

''Your house? Is that proper? Perhaps I should go to a hotel.'' Flame was uncertain what to expect: Rafael seemed to be a gentleman, but her grandmother had warned her about men's desires too many times for her to be trusting. Then she remembered she had little in the way of finances to cover her lodgings. ''Whatever you think would be best.''

''I have a housekeeper, Miss Lannier. You will be quite safe with me, far safer than you would be in even San Francisco's finest hotel. Now come along.'' Rafael stood up and extended his hand and Flame took it readily; she was tired and glad to allow him to lead her wherever he wished to go.

Three

Rafael had their driver stop the carriage on the rise so Flame might see the Villarreal ranch for the first time from the best perspective. "Well, what do you think of your new home?"

Flame took his hand lightly and stepped out upon the grass-covered hill. "That is a house, Rafael? It looks more like a whole city to me!" Flame smiled as she looked up at him, her eyes wide with excitement.

"It is a large ranch. Joaquin is very progressive in his thoughts, as was his father. Miguel had barns and stables when other rancheros still let their stock run loose. The house itself is quite old, but it has been renovated frequently. You will find all the comforts of my home in the city at your disposal here also."

Flame stared intently at the buildings below. The house was immense. Built of adobe brick that was whitewashed each year, it gleamed in the late afternoon sun with a bright sparkle. The red tile roof added the only color to the house itself, but even from where they stood the flowers in the patio and surrounding gardens provided a riot of color. Blossoms of every variety seemed to grow in profusion, giving the stark house a welcoming charm.

Rafael gestured as he explained, "Originally, the house was built in a square enclosing an open courtyard. A patio and wings have been added over the years so the house now spreads out in four directions. Rather than a cube it now resembles an H on its side."

"It looks far more like a fortress than a home. If my father brought me here, I'm afraid I do not remember it."

"It did serve as a fort at one time. The walls are nearly four feet in thickness. The Indians in this area were not all that friendly when our great-grandfathers first settled here."

Flame inclined her head with an impish tilt as she glanced up at her friend. "You mean they didn't like men from Spain stealing their land any better than you liked men from the East coming here to take that same land away from you?"

"You are very astute, Flame." Rafael frowned impatiently. His opinion of her hadn't altered one bit during their four-day journey: Flame Lannier was as bright as she was beautiful, and she said whatever came into her head without any regard for the consequences. "I suggest, however, that you make no comments of that sort to your guardian. He is neither liberal nor tolerant where questions of his ranch and his right to his land are concerned."

"You make him sound very dull, Rafael."

"Joaquin dull? Never!" Rafael couldn't help but laugh at the thought.

"What is so terribly funny, Mr. Ramirez? I don't see anything humorous about having such a stuffy, dull man for a guardian!" Flame stamped her foot angrily to make him stop his ridiculous laughter.

"Just wait until you meet Joaquin, then tell me what you think of him. Now do you see the other buildings surrounding the house? There are the barns of course, a blacksmith's forge, a slaughterhouse, a—"

Flame nodded as she tried to listen to Rafael's description. She could recall her father's ranch only

39

dimly, but it had been nothing like the magnificent one in the valley below. She turned quickly to touch Rafael's sleeve. "Would you please take me to see my father's grave?"

Her request did not surprise Rafael, but as usual her abrupt change of subject caught him off guard. He sighed with the hopelessness of his task. "I did not mean to bore you. Perhaps you will be more interested in learning of the ranch and how it functions after you have been here for a while."

"Yes, of course I will. I'm sure it's all fascinating and you explain everything so clearly too, but could we please go now? Is it far?"

"No, but you want to go now? You do not wish to stop here first and unpack your things, or rest? We can visit the grave in the morning."

"No, I want to go and visit his grave first, please. Where is he buried, at our ranch or in a churchyard?"

"At his ranch, beside your mother. Come, let us go quickly, before it becomes too dark to see." Rafael helped her back into the carriage, slammed the door soundly, then climbed up beside the startled driver to give him their change in directions.

When Rafael saw the pain fill Flame's expression he realized he had been foolish not to warn her, for her former home was little more than ashes and rubble and the sight of the burned-out ruins had obviously upset her. "Joaquin meant to raze the house completely. I'm sorry the job wasn't done before today. Come with me, the graves are over here, beneath the trees."

Flame turned away from the remains of her home. That it was gone saddened her greatly; that her dear father had died there grieved her even more. She took Rafael's arm as they walked through the wrought iron gate into the small graveyard. There were flowers blooming in abundance along the fence which enclosed the grassy area; the hallowed ground had obviously received the expert care of the finest of gardeners over the years. A wooden cross marked the new mound where her father lay buried, but a beautifully carved marble tombstone sat at the end of her mother's grave.

"Joaquin has commissioned a tombstone for André, your father. It will be completed soon, one to match your mother's." The tall man frowned as he tried to hurry Flame. "I am sorry, I dislike visiting cemeteries. Death in any form angers me, and André's death was particularly senseless."

Fascinated by her mother's tombstone, Flame only nodded absently as she leaned down to trace the incised dates with her fingertips. "She was only twenty-two years old when she died, Rafael. She was so very young." But as she read further her breath caught in her throat with a hoarse rasp, and, feeling faint, she reached for his hand.

"What is it, Flame, are you ill? Let us go, you are too tired after our long trip for this sadness."

Flame lifted her trembling hand to point. "Look what it says: there is a child buried with her, a boy? I had a baby brother?"

Rafael was astonished by her question. "You do not know how your mother died, Flame? She died in childbirth . . . her son appears to have lived only briefly from the dates. What were you told?"

Flame began to weep softly, and could not seem to stop. "Lies, only lies!" This was much too sad to bear, her beautiful mother and tiny brother dead and she had not even known of the child's existence. When Rafael gathered her into his arms she put her face against his soft woolen jacket and continued to cry. She wept all the way back to the Villarreal ranch, nearly hysterical with grief for her loved ones. That they had been so long dead lessened her pain not one bit.

Rafael was beside himself too. Women never cried with him; he had no experience at all in soothing unhappy ladies, and he felt totally inadequate as Flame clung to him. He deeply wanted to console her, but he couldn't decide if he should pat her shoulder or stroke her brilliant curls or hold her in his arms. . . . It was not that he lacked sympathy or warmth, only that he had great difficulty in expressing his emotions. He knew only one way to comfort a woman, and such intimate behavior seemed totally inappropriate with Flame. When the carriage came to rest he spoke softly: "I sent word we were coming today. Maria, Joaquin's housekeeper, will have your room ready. Come inside and rest before dinner and you will feel better." As he helped her down from the carriage they were immediately surrounded by the household staff as well as numerous vaqueros who had been close by.

Flame wiped her eyes and tried to smile; all the faces were so curious, but open and friendly. Everyone chattered rapidly in Spanish with Rafael and she was swept along into the house before she could even say hello. One of the younger servants reached out to touch her golden hair and Flame realized as she looked about the gathering crowd that everyone there was dark. Some appeared to be as Spanish in nature as Rafael, while others were of smaller, stockier builds, obviously Indians. There was no one like her, however, not one person with fair skin and light eyes, and Flame worried for the first time about what her guardian would think of her. If she were as different from him as she was from the rest of his household she was dreadfully afraid they were going to find themselves too dissimilar to ever be friends.

As they passed through the Villarreal house Flame was surprised to find it furnished in so spare a fashion. The heavy carved furniture was more functional than beautiful and nowhere was a woman's delicate touch evident. She found her room comfortable and spacious but the Spartan decor was so different from her cluttered bedroom in her grandmother's home that she nearly wept again with homesickness. There was a large wardrobe which easily held all her dresses, an ornately carved six drawer dresser with a fine mirror, an immense four poster bed and one high-backed chair. There were no paintings, no tapestries, nothing to relieve the monotony of the bare white walls, but the views from the two iron-barred windows were breathtakingly beautiful. Flame thought only about how lovely the countryside was and knew in time she would come to regard her sparsely furnished room as home. At least that was her fondest hope.

The young girls who unpacked her trunk spoke only Spanish, but Flame understood their delight in her pretty clothes with no need for a translation. They were charming girls, happy, with laughing brown eyes and long black hair braided neatly and tied with ribbons. Flame was certain they were happy to have her arrive, for she would surely prove to be an exciting diversion from their usual household tasks. The girls giggled as they left her room and Flame could not help but think how different they were from her grandmother's servants, and she hoped her maid had found her way home safely.

That the dining table was set with the whitest of Irish linen, English bone china, delicate Venetian crystal and ornate Spanish sterling was another astonishment to Flame. The fine old silver glowed in the dim light of the lamps and the serving girls brought in their food with far more grace than she had ever seen in Philadelphia. She smiled at Rafael as she placed her linen napkin in her lap. "Is this some special occasion?"

"Yes, this is your welcome to the Villarreal ranch,

but Joaquin dines with the same elegance each evening. You will not find him to be an unschooled country farmer, Flame.''

Flame was hurt by the disapproving tone of his voice and rushed to clarify her question. ''Oh no, I didn't mean that, but the table is so beautiful and this house so plain.''

''Plain? Well, surely brocade draperies and silk wallpaper would be out of place here, and rugs have never been considered conducive to good health, so that is why you see only the bare wooden floor. But I think the house is perfect and so does its owner . . . but then it is what we have learned to love all our lives. I hope you will not find the house too austere after you become accustomed to living here for awhile.''

''I am sure that it is only because everything is so new to me that it seems strange. Did all the homes of the Californios contain churches like this one does? I have never before been in a home which had its very own church.''

''It is a chapel only, Flame, and yes, it was always the custom to include a chapel in our homes. The whole household gathers for prayers each day in the morning before breakfast.''

''I see.'' Flame's expression grew thoughtful. She had never been particularly religious, and the habit of daily devotions was foreign to her, like so many other things in that home. As she glanced down at her plate she realized how hungry she was after the day's long ride. She lifted her fork to taste her dinner only to find her mouth suddenly aflame as the spicy sauce on the beef scalded her tongue. She dropped her fork with a cry of pain, and though she quickly took a drink of wine that only served to spread the fire all the way down her throat.

Rafael lost no time in sprinting into the kitchen, from

which he swiftly returned with a tall glass of milk. "Here, drink this quickly, Flame."

Flame would have tried any remedy to end her suffering by that time, but to her immense relief the cool white liquid ended her discomfort immediately. Tears ran down her cheeks as she looked up at him. "What did they put in my food, Rafael? Is someone trying to poison me?"

"Of course not—here, let me taste a bite of your dinner." Rafael found Flame's meal no different from his own. "You are simply unaccustomed to the chilis and spices we use here, that is the only problem. I should have thought about this and asked Maria to prepare you something more bland. Excuse me, I'll see what I can find for you now."

"No, please, I don't want to be a burden. I don't want to complain about my first meal here, that would be too rude."

"Flame, you cannot eat your dinner without crying, now don't be silly, I don't want to dine with a woman who is in tears the entire time!" Rafael strode out of the room and when he returned with a variety of cheeses and fruits Flame was most grateful.

"Thank you for being so considerate. I am sorry to be such a bother to you, Rafael."

"It is nothing, Maria will prepare your food separately from now on. I don't expect you to like her cooking immediately but you will learn to enjoy it in time."

Flame watched closely as Rafael began to eat his dinner with no apparent pain. "It does not seem as though the meal is too highly seasoned for you."

"No, but I have grown up eating food prepared in this manner."

"Surely babies do not eat this!"

"No, not tiny ones, but children do not seem to find our food disagreeable."

45

Flame merely shook her head in wonder. Everything was so strange to her—the starkness of the house, the language of its inhabitants, the uniqueness of the food—would she ever really belong there or would she remain an uncomfortable stranger? "Does Mr. Villarreal speak English, Rafael?"

"Yes, as well as you or I, Flame, but I must remind you again to exercise caution in what you say. It will not be pleasant for you if you make Joaquin angry."

"Doesn't he like to discuss things, talk over issues?" Flame sliced a peach and found it to be delicious. The ranch grew an abundance of produce, to judge from the variety on the platter Rafael had presented. At least she wouldn't starve, she thought to herself with a smile.

"Yes, he most certainly does, but never with pretty young women."

Flame blushed deeply; she was surprised by Rafael's unexpected compliment, but when she glanced up at him it was obvious he was merely stating a fact, not flirting. "You mean he thinks women have no brains, that we are not worth talking to? If that is so perhaps it will be amusing to see how many topics I can make him discuss with me where he has never done so with a woman before."

"Believe me, Joaquin is very much aware of a woman's assets, Flame. Just don't provoke him, that's all. Now would you like more wine, the grapes are grown here on the ranch and Joaquin's wines are always among the finest."

Rafael's level gaze left her with no choice, the subject was closed. So she turned to another. "I know you worked for my father, but you work for Mr. Villarreal too, don't you. Aren't you also his attorney?"

"Yes, I work almost exclusively for Joaquin. We learned all too well that the government will cheat us unless we fully understand its laws. That is why I became an attorney, to protect what is left to us."

Flame could not help but wonder about the man. His features were so fine, his posture so proud, she could not imagine him working for anyone but himself. "You are not just an employee of Mr. Villarreal's are you, Rafael? You must be much more, I can see that by just looking at you. Aren't you his friend too, a close friend?"

Rafael studied Flame's expression for a moment and his glance was not friendly. "You continually amaze me, Flame, for you see things which others do not. Perhaps you realize what you have just asked me and perhaps your question is a more innocent one than I think it is. Joaquin and I are closer than most brothers; that he pays me a salary is the least important part of our relationship. He is the best friend I shall ever hope to have and I am his, but we are both men, Flame, in every way we are men."

Puzzled by Rafael's remarks Flame did not speak again. Whatever was he talking about? Then with sudden insight she knew—she had only heard of such things, whispers, innuendos, but she knew they existed. Is that what he thought she was asking? She was so terribly embarrassed she hoped to disappear from the room without a trace, vanish rather than have to face him again. Rafael was somewhat aloof, rather stern too, but she had not thought him anything other than normal in every way, and what he had read into her question appalled her.

An amused smile curved Rafael's lips as he saw Flame's consternation and rightly read its cause. So that had not been her question after all. He should have known better than to suspect such an impertinent inquiry from such a sweet young woman. He began to chuckle.

"Rafael?" Flame was completely exasperated now:

he had seldom shown such good humor before and now it was totally without reason. Was the man crazy?

"It is nothing, Flame, I was merely wondering what you will think of your guardian when you meet him. Come, let us go into the library for a moment if you are finished eating. Joaquin has a large selection of books, perhaps you will find something to keep you amused."

Flame took Rafael's arm and hoped she would indeed find the most interesting of novels to read. She vowed to keep her mouth shut in the future and thought perhaps she and her guardian would get along well together after all.

Rafael began the next morning to teach Flame how to ride. Flame promptly informed him she had ridden ponies as a child and already knew how to ride. She could handle the gentle mares he selected for her with ease, so rather than giving her lessons as he had been prepared to do, Rafael simply took Flame to explore the endless trails of the Villarreal ranch while she practiced the skills she had learned as a small girl.

Flame reined in her horse at the top of the ridge and waited for Rafael to join her. The colors of the lush foliage which stretched before them were of such an amazing variety, the shades ranged from the palest of grey-greens in the mesquite bushes to the brightest of yellow-oranges in the wild poppies which grew in profusion along the slopes of the valley. Never had she seen such a spectacular landscape, "Oh Rafael, I love it here, the land is so lovely, I'll never tire of just looking at it."

Rafael smiled at her innocent enthusiasm. "You sound remarkably like Joaquin, but I like San Francisco myself. I much prefer the city to this rustic environment."

Flame lifted her hand to shade her eyes from the sun as she talked with her companion. Rafael still intrigued her. He had an almost feline grace, tall and lean—yet very strong, for he had lifted her on several occasions as if she were a mere child. But his manner toward her was always polite in the extreme; he never flirted with her, nor teased her as men usually did; he seemed most often to speak to her as if he were a professor and she his pupil. He had taken her into town on Sunday so she could attend the protestant church, but he had remained outside with the carriage rather than enter the small frame church himself. While he seemed to like her company, his conduct was that of a very proper gentleman. He might have been showing her grandmother around the ranch for all he seemed to notice her charms. Flame felt a pang of regret as she thought of Fanny and the last angry words they'd shared. It was such a bitter parting after all those years of love, and Flame would have given anything to take back that last night. She hadn't even kissed her grandmother good night . . . on that night, of all nights, she wished she'd kissed the dear little woman good night. Then she realized that had Fanny not tried to force her to marry Alex Richmond she might not have been inspired to return to California, and she loved California so. She was enraptured with the exquisite beauty of her home state and thought suddenly of the sea. "Rafael, let's ride down to the ocean again, may we go that way, please?"

"Of course, whatever you wish, Flame." Yet the man continued to gaze out at the countryside, a scowl drawing his brows into a firm line, and he made no move to lead the way.

"Rafael, what's the matter?" Flame was puzzled by his serious expression. "Would you rather we went straight back to the house instead? I've been taking up so much of your time and I know you have far more important things to do."

"No, that is not true, I was just thinking." He

paused to consider his words carefully, then continued in the same somber tone. "Joaquin should arrive home soon and when he does I will have no excuse to remain here. I'll have to return to San Francisco immediately—and I will not be able to stay here to help you, Flame. You will be on your own then, and I am afraid I have failed to impress upon you how careful you will have to be."

"But Rafael, if my father asked Mr. Villarreal to be my guardian, if they were such close friends, won't he at least make some effort to like me?"

"Of course he will like you, what man would not? It is only that he takes his responsibilities very seriously and will want to do what he feels is best for you."

"Without ever consulting me, you mean?" Flame was growing more unhappy each second. "I've no hope of being allowed to continue to live my own life as I have since you brought me here?"

"Have these past few days been all that good for you?" Rafael smiled slyly, finding it difficult to believe the sophisticated young lady he'd met at the depot could be the same one who faced him now. She resembled a young boy when she was dressed to ride, but he remembered all too well what a lovely woman she truly was.

"Yes, I love it here!"

"Good. Do not give Joaquin any unnecessary problems and you'll continue to be happy here. Now let's go towards the sea." Rafael spurred his mount and Flame's horse followed closely behind. He was an excellent rider: despite his protests of preferring the city he was as at home on horseback as the vaqueros who tended the ranch's stock.

Flame smiled to herself as they rode along. Was it possible Rafael was becoming interested in her? He had seemed genuinely concerned for her welfare and she

50

was very pleased indeed. When they reached the cliffs, they had to dismount and walk their horses, carefully threading their way down the narrow rocky path to the shore. The day had grown warm but the Pacific was as chilly as she'd found it on her previous visit. "Does the ocean water ever get warm, Rafael?"

"Really warm? No, never. In the late summer it will be warmer than today, but never truly warm as it is in the tropics. Joaquin and I used to swim all the time when we were younger, I can't recall the last time we did though. We have become too busy, too serious in the last years to enjoy such simple pleasure as an afternoon at the water's edge."

Flame stepped back to avoid being soaked by the onrushing tide and reached for Rafael's arm to keep from stumbling. When she felt his muscles stiffen she moved away quickly. She had always been relaxed around men, comfortable in their company rather than shy as so many of her girlfriends were. She would touch a man she liked as she spoke to him, no more than the lightest of caresses, but caresses all the same. A reassurance perhaps that the man was real, a flesh and blood creature, not merely a phantom who existed only in the mind as her father had, as he always would now. But she drew back instantly, confused. Rafael had flinched when she'd touched him, made no move to catch her in his arms, and that rejection hurt her terribly. She couldn't bear any type of rebuff, even the slightest disapproval caused her pain, so she withdrew now, shut him out as she remounted the small black mare and headed her out into the shallow surf.

There were no ships upon the horizon. That her guardian owned ships in which to transport his hides in addition to his magnificent ranch amazed Flame still. He sounded like such an awesome personality she could scarcely imagine what he would expect from her. She

51

hoped he would be too busy to care about what she did. She could easily be content to spend the rest of her life riding his pretty horses by the edge of the sea. Forgetting her injured feelings in the beauty of the surroundings she called over her shoulder, "Come on, Rafael, let's race back to the point!" She galloped away from him, her horse's flying hooves kicking the salt spray all over him as he leapt upon his horse's back in an effort to catch her.

Four

Flame drew the nimble mare to a halt while she retied the ends of her scarf more securely. The morning was such a glorious one she was glad she'd decided not to delay any longer waiting for Rafael to rise. The breeze held the tantalizing scent of the sea and she wished she knew where the Villarreal land ended and her own ranch began. Perhaps she had crossed the unmarked boundary already without realizing it. It was still difficult for her to believe she owned a ranch; even if it were not nearly so large in size as Villarreal's it was a marvelous expanse of Calfornia all the same.

She giggled out loud as she glanced down at her makeshift attire. Rafael's pants were comfortable; she had no idea where Maria had borrowed the shirt but the muslin was soft and cool. At least the boots were her own, as was the green silk scarf which covered her hair. She had to admit that for a young lady who had always been dressed in the finest of gowns she had certainly lost her interest in clothes rapidly! Yet she could not recall ever being so at peace with herself, so delightfully happy just to enjoy life and its endless beauty.

Flame's carefree reverie ended abruptly as she lifted her gaze again to the surrounding hills where she was startled to see a lone rider observing her closely. The man and his immense black horse were silhouetted against the brightness of the morning sun and a sudden chill surged down Flame's spine despite the warmth of the day. She knew the rider had not been on the ridge just moments before. The ranch employed vaqueros too numerous to count but there were no cattle grazing in this narrow valley, so the man had no business being there unless he'd simply been following her. That frightening realization was enough to inspire Flame to return to the safety of the ranch house with all possible haste. She spurred the agile horse with an anxious jab of her heels and pushed the animal to the limit of its endurance as they sped away across the flat central plain of the valley.

Flame had covered no more than fifty yards when she heard the man shout as he urged his horse to greater speed. So he was following her after all and wanted to make a race of it! The thunder of the powerful animal's hoofbeats grew louder as the rider closed the distance between them, and Flame cursed her own folly for having ridden so far away any bandit or felon could accost her unseen. As she glanced over her shoulder her breath caught in her throat, strangling her with fear, for the black horse was nearly even with her mare's flying tail. Flame pulled her mount sharply to the right, veering away into a thick stand of oaks in a last desperate attempt to elude the stranger. Her evasive action had little effect, however, for the rider swiftly drew alongside her and reaching out for her slender waist forcefully pulled her from her saddle and carried her along at his side as he rode under the trees before drawing his mount to a bone-jarring halt.

"Let me go, put me down!" Flame beat on her captor's hands and to her surprise he did as she asked, dropping her soundly to the tall grass where she landed in a startled heap. Before she could scramble to her feet and run he was on top of her, grabbing her wrists and tossing her easily upon her back.

"Let me go!" Flame tried to bite the villain, to kick him, but he held her so easily in his strong grip that her efforts at regaining her freedom were futile. "Villarreal will kill you for this, if you so much as touch me he'll tear out your heart and feed it to the crows!"

The stranger merely laughed at her angry threat. He grasped both her wrists in one of his hands and tossed his hat on the grass. He was a handsome man and obviously knew it, for his grin was obnoxiously confident. His even white teeth sparkled against the deep bronze of his skin and the thick black hair which fell across his forehead gleamed with copper highlights. "Villarreal will have to catch me first, won't he?"

Flame's eyes widened in terror for she recognized the man instantly once he'd discarded his broad-brimmed hat. He was the man from her dream, the very one she'd longed to meet—but dear God, the dream had been a warning of danger, not a promise of love after all! "If Villarreal doesn't horsewhip you for this outrage then I will! Now turn me loose!"

The man's voice was low, no more than a whisper as he responded, "I mean you no harm, girl, now stop fighting." He leaned down then and kissed her pink-tinged lips, a man's kiss, full of desire, like no kiss Flame had ever been given. When he lifted his head to smile at her again she only gazed up at him, too astonished by his unexpected affection to struggle or to speak.

"That's better." He stretched out beside her but didn't slacken his hold on her wrists. His mouth covered hers again and his tongue slipped between her lips to drink in the delights of her small moist mouth now that she had ceased to resist him.

Flame felt herself being drawn into him, powerless to resist. She had no will of her own when he touched her so tenderly, simply none. His kiss seemed to last forever, gentle, demanding, teasing; she had no desire to fight his enticing affection, she only wanted more. She felt his fingers slowly unbutton her blouse and could not stifle a low moan as his warm lips caressed the tip of her breast, bringing a new burst of sensual pleasure. She wanted to touch him, to learn the secrets of his muscular body as he was learning hers. She pleaded with him softly, "Please, let my hands loose, I won't fight you."

The man laughed, then hugged her happily as he pulled her into his arms. "I thought you were Indian by the way you ride, but you're obviously not, nor Mexican either by the fairness of your skin."

True to her word, Flame slipped her small hands beneath his shirt and caressed his strong back. His skin felt like silk, smooth over the rippling muscles of his shoulders. She unbuttoned his shirt quickly, wanting to feel the warmth of his bare flesh next to hers.

The man responded eagerly to Flame's enchanting touch. He began to kiss her lips once more, playfully biting her then brushing her mouth lightly with his. Flame clung to him, pulling his head down to hers, and returned his kiss with a sweetness and passion all her own, for this was no clumsy boy whose touch revolted her but a man so tender she was overcome with desire.

The stranger continued to caress Flame's slender body slowly, his hand returning to the soft fullness of her breast before reaching for the buckle which secured her belt. She laced her fingers in his quickly to stop him and he did not persist in his efforts to undress her, but drew her closer as he deepened his kiss until she could no longer see or think she was so lost in the exquisite pleasure he gave. When he felt her enticing response he withdrew his hand from hers to stroke her cheek gently before pulling away her scarf. His gesture released cascades of golden curls which nearly blinded him with their brilliant sheen, and he sprang away from her with a hoarse cry: "Flame? Oh my God, Flame!" He stared down at her his dark eyes wide with the wonder of his startling discovery.

Flame blinked as she tried to focus her passion dazed eyes on the man's handsome face. How did he happened to know her name, and what possible difference did that make? She licked her lips slowly while she tried unsuccessfully to steady her breathing but her words escaped her lips in a breathless rasp: "Does my name matter so greatly to you?"

"Dear God yes, why didn't you tell me your name?" The man was having no more success controlling his emotions than she had with hers, for his breathing was also far from even.

The delightful stranger's obvious panic only amused Flame. Perhaps he was afraid she really would have him whipped, but she'd no desire to see him suffer any punishment now and smiled sweetly as she teased him. "I don't recall your asking my name, but why would you shrink in terror from my name when you didn't blink an eye at Villarreal's?"

"I *am* Villarreal, damn it!"

Flame closed her eyes as she sank back upon the cool grass. "Oh no."

"Oh yes." Joaquin got to his feet and leaned against a nearby oak tree. He stared down at Flame but she made no move to straighten her clothing before she rolled over on her stomach and began to cry. Her sobs racked her slender body and Joaquin longed to go to her, to take her back into his arms and finish what they had begun, but he shook his head to clear his mind of such dangerous thoughts and turned away, steeling himself to ignore her tears. He hastily rebuttoned his shirt and shoved it back under his belt. He had been as lost as she was in their loving games and that surprising fact amazed him as greatly as did her unexpected identity. How had she managed to distract him so completely as other women could not? When he had thought he knew it all, was it possible so young a girl knew even more?

Flame was so ashamed she couldn't stop crying. Her whole body ached with the unsatisfied desire he'd aroused, but that torment was slight compared to her mental anguish. Never had she willingly allowed any man to have more than a kiss upon her cheek but she had nearly given herself, and eagerly too, to a complete stranger! That he was to be her guardian and now knew she possessed absolutely no morals humiliated her so, horribly she wanted to die. What would he think of her, a woman so wanton she'd gladly make love to any affectionate stranger who rode by? She sobbed on and on. Thank God her dear father was dead and would never hear of her shame, at least she had disgraced only herself and not his fine name too.

Finally Joaquin grew worried. Flame was obviously becoming hysterical and he could bear no more. He knelt down beside her and began to stoke her golden hair softly as he called to her in a gentle, mellow tone. "Flame, please don't cry, there's no reason for you to be so unhappy. I remember when you were a little girl and your father would bring you along when he came to visit us. I would pick you up and carry you on my shoulders. Do you remember, Flame? I used to lead your pony around the yard, you always looked so pretty, like a little princess. I've never forgotten your beautiful red hair, you were a precious child, Flame, and you're an even more beautiful woman. Now stop crying and smile for me."

Flame wiped her eyes on her sleeve but she couldn't see through the tears which filled her long thick lashes. She attempted to smile bravely but she didn't tell him she had remembered him too—all the years she had remembered him and loved him, not even recalling his name.

"There, that's better, now here's my handkerchief, dry your eyes and we'll talk." He sat down next to her, so close his knee brushed her thigh, and she began to weep all over again. Her whole body felt warm and she could not have been more ashamed.

"Flame, you've no reason to carry on so, I didn't rape you!"

She looked up at him, her green eyes flashing with the fiery light of emeralds. "It wouldn't have been rape, Joaquin, you know that."

Joaquin frowned impatiently. "Is that what is bothering you? You are ashamed of your own passion? How are women raised to be so frightened of their own desires?" He was tremendously annoyed by the obvious error in her upbringing. "No, it wouldn't have been rape, you are right, but it didn't happen so there's not the slightest cause for all those tears. You've a woman's body and a woman's emotions, that's only natural and I can assure you your husband will be greatly pleased by both those assets."

His words, although meant as encouragement, burned clear through Flame's conscience. Husband, what husband? She only wanted to die of shame, not to contemplate marriage!

Joaquin mistook her silence for composure and continued to discuss their plight. "I should be the one sitting here in tears, not you, Flame. I promised your father I'd look after you and you're not safe with me for five minutes. Do you imagine I routinely accost young women I see riding across my land?"

Flame frowned . . . what had her grandmother always said about men? "Don't you? I thought all men were interested in the same thing, that's what my grandmother always taught me."

Joaquin began to chuckle. He had a rich, deep laugh, almost infectiously pleasant, and Flame could not help but smile. "Your grandmother was an expert on men?"

"She was married three times!"

"Oh well, that explains it then, she was most definitely an expert with all that experience!" Joaquin shook his head and continued to enjoy her unintentional joke. "I will admit only this, my men occasionally invite women to meet them for an evening's amusement. I mistook you for such a visitor and wanted only to speak to you for a moment to ascertain which men had hired you, as that is a practice I forbid. I was a fool not to recognize you immediately, however, for you are far too lovely a girl to ever sell herself to vaqueros! Unfortunately, I failed to draw any reasonable conclusion once I'd seen how pretty you are."

"Thank you." Flame dabbed the remainder of her tears from her eyes on his soft linen handkerchief, then studied his face closely. It was incredible how well she had remembered him, every detail of his face was as she had dreamed it. His features were perfect, even and strong, just like the rest of his superb body. She blushed deeply at that thought and glanced away before he could see the color flood her cheeks. "How did my father happen to ask you to be my guardian. How could he have known he was going to die so suddenly?"

"He didn't know when he asked me, it was several years ago. He'd been ill; I only agreed to humor him. I never thought I'd ever really have to be responsible for you. I didn't think you'd ever want to leave Philadelphia or that he would die so young . . . he was no more than ten years my senior, you know."

Flame sat up and began to rebutton her blouse, her self-consciousness forgotten for the moment. "How old are you, Joaquin?"

He grinned at her, a rakish lopsided grin which charmed her instantly. "I'm thirty-one, but I thought you were much younger than you obviously are. I'd planned to send you up to San Francisco, to Santa Teresa Convent, I'm not sure that's appropriate now though."

Flame was terrified by his words and reacted quickly. "A convent! But I don't want to be a nun, I'm not even Catholic! Please don't send me to a convent, please don't send me there!" Big tears rolled down her flushed cheeks as she begged him to reconsider her fate.

Joaquin swore softly under his breath, not at all pleased to see tears again gushing from her jade-green eyes. "Flame, it's a school for girls, I didn't think you'd want to join their order! Christ! I thought you were only fifteen, sixteen at the most, how old are you? We couldn't find anyone who knew for certain and all your father's papers were lost in the fire."

Flame searched her mind frantically for an age, any age which would keep her out of the convent. She had no idea what a convent would be like, very like a prison she feared. How did women ever get out of convents anyway? She'd heard of women entering convents, never exiting them—maybe it was impossible to leave once you went in. She had to appear older than sixteen to him, she knew that already from his own words. Surely eighteen would be old enough. "I was eighteen last month." She held her breath but relaxed when he didn't question her lie.

"Well, you're definitely too old for Santa Teresa's then. Lord, what am I going to do with you, Flame?"

Flame's answer came swiftly to her mind. "You were certain what you wished to do with me before you knew my name, Joaquin."

"Flame!" Joaquin leapt to his feet then reached down to pull her up beside him. He was quite tall, well over six feet in height and she had to crane her neck to look up at him. "Look, none of that ever happened, do you understand? I never touched you, never kissed you, absolutely none of it happened. Now promise me you'll never speak of it again." Joaquin frowned angrily but when she turned to look up at him his knees grew weak. Flame had brushed her golden hair back from her forehead and her enormous green eyes were regarding him with a curious stare. Her dark lashes were so long and thick they didn't seem real and yet he knew for a fact they were. Her features were so lovely, delicate and sweet but his eyes strayed down the gentle curves of her lithe young body before returning to her face. When he spoke the hoarseness in his voice shocked him. "Will you give me your promise?"

Flame smiled slowly. "Whom would I tell, Joaquin?"

"Promise me!" He was becoming more irate each second, his lips were set in a thin line and the muscles tense along his jaw. As he frowned angrily his dark eyes were barely visible under their thick fringe of black lashes.

Flame was surprised to find she had such power over the man's emotions and continued to probe the depth of his reaction. "No, tell me who isn't supposed to know. If you are my guardian, surely no one will question your conduct where I'm concerned."

Joaquin could no longer hold back his unruly temper and began to swear in one long stream of incredibly foul epithets all uttered in fluid Spanish until he had exhausted every filthy expression he'd ever heard at the ranch or at sea.

"If you expect me to understand you, Joaquin, you really must speak to me in English." Flame laid her hands gently upon his broad chest and stepped closer, but he took her hands in his and shoved her away.

"Don't touch me either, Flame, you must never touch me ever again!" He turned his back on her and scanned the horizon with a watchful eye while he struggled to get control of himself again. "Who let you come out riding all alone? Have you been out each day like this, all by yourself?"

"No Rafael has always been with me, but he was still in bed and I didn't want to wait for him it was such a lovely morning."

Joaquin turned slowly to face her. "How did you know he was still in his bed, did you go into his room and look for yourself?"

Flame was stunned by the question. Did he think just because she had been willing to give herself to him she had done it before? That she frequented men's bedrooms at all hours of the day and night? She chose her words carefully to deliberately repay the hurt he'd just given her. "I'd rather not say. I promised Rafael never to speak of what has happened between us, and I'll make you the same promise now, just as you asked."

Joaquin's mouth fell open, "Madre de Dios! You've been with Rafael? You mean he's—"

Flame interrupted quickly. "A promise is a promise, Joaquin, I am very discreet. You would not want me to tell him what happened between us today, would you? I'm sure Rafael is as fine a gentleman as you and would never speak about me either, just as you will not." She bent down and handed him his hat, with one easy gesture ending their conversation.

Joaquin was beside himself. He had thought becoming responsible for his friend's daughter would be no more than a slight annoyance he could easily avoid by sending her away to school. That's what he had meant to do, just send her away to school and forget about her, but he had expected his ward to be a child, not this vixen. This beauty was another story altogether. "Do you always dress like a boy? Couldn't you at least find some ladylike attire to wear when you ride?"

"You seemed to have had no trouble discerning my sex, Joaquin."

"I explained what I thought!" He was shocked by her ready retort—how could she have been in tears as if she were so damn innocent when she had a tongue like that in her head?

Flame looked down at her unusual assortment of borrowed clothes. "I can't ride in a dress, I never learned to use a side saddle and you don't even have one in your tack room anyway. Rafael was kind enough to lend me these pants, he's not nearly so well built as you and—"

"My God, those are Rafael's pants!"

Flame was fast losing her patience too, "Do you honestly believe I took them off Rafael while he was wearing them? I plan to have some made for me, I know the fit of these is not all that good, but I didn't expect to see anyone this morning. I didn't even know you had come home."

"I arrived quite late, after both you and Rafael had gone to bed. Now that I am home, however, we will have to think of somewhere for you to go."

His accusing words hurt Flame terribly. "Go? Well, I had not planned to stay indefinitely, Joaquin, I had no idea my father had died before I left Philadelphia, I only came to California to be with him. He was all the family I had, I never would have come had I known he was dead, I only wanted to see him again."

Joaquin apologized hurriedly. "I'm sorry, that was most ungracious and I did not mean to be unsympathetic about the loss of your father. You don't have to go, not ever if you don't want to, but we really should make some plans for your future. Since school is not an option, perhaps it would be best if you just returned to Philadelphia as soon as possible."

Flame stepped back, her bright eyes filled with sudden terror. Philadelphia meant only one thing to her now, Alex Richmond with his sickening kisses and disgusting threats. If Joaquin learned of her engagement, would he force her to return to that hateful man just so he'd not be bothered with her himself? She was horrified by that possibility. "No! I'll never go back there, never!"

Joaquin was astonished by the violence of Flame's reaction to what he'd thought was a sensible alternative. "What is it? What's wrong with that city? Aren't all your friends there?"

Flame shook her head, sending her golden curls flying about her head in wild disarray. "No, my friends mean nothing to me anymore. You can't force me to go back there."

Joaquin gave up in frustration. "For God's sake calm down! I'll not send you where you've no desire to go. Since you're eighteen you'll doubtless marry soon and have no need for a guardian anyway."

"Marry!" Flame shrieked the word. "I have no wish to get married, none at all!" She clenched her fists at her sides and stamped her foot to emphasize that point, but as she looked up into his warm brown eyes she knew her words were untrue. She wanted *him* for a husband, but this was no time to say so.

"You had no suitors in Philadelphia? A young woman as pretty as you must have had plenty of men interested in her. I can't believe you haven't received any proposals of marriage."

"I refused them all!" Flame could scarcely explain that she'd been too young to receive any proposals now that she had him convinced she was eighteen. She had refused Alex most definitely—that was at least the truth—and that fact helped to ease her conscience somewhat.

Joaquin looked at the defiant tilt of her chin and

shrugged. "Why, weren't the men handsome enough, or rich enough? What didn't please you?"

Flame took a deep breath as she stared up at her guardian, unable to reply. How could she tell him the truth—that she had been waiting for a man she saw only in her dreams? She had been waiting her whole life to find him. "Oh, they were fine, handsome and rich, whatever men are supposed to be, but I didn't love them, not any of them, not even in the smallest amount did I love them."

"You believe in love then, Flame?" Joaquin dusted off his hat and placed it on the back of his head as he spoke. "Love is so important to you that you'll not marry without it?"

"No, of course not. I'd never marry a man I didn't really and truly love. But what of you, Joaquin: why have you no wife?"

Joaquin chuckled as if her question were too ridiculous to merit a serious response. "I don't want the bother of a wife yet, Flame. Women are all such an awful bother."

Flame felt her cheeks redden again, "I see, well, I'll try not to cause you any further trouble."

"Damn it, Flame, I didn't mean you. You'll be no great trouble to me."

"Well, I'm afraid I'm going to be a problem right now."

Joaquin was confused by her remark. "A problem? In what way?"

"I don't see my horse, do you? Your stallion is right here, but my horse has gone. Will you let me ride home behind you?"

Joaquin turned to look across the valley. Flame was correct, her horse had vanished, returned to the comforts of the stables rather than wait for her. "Ill-trained beast, I'll see you're given a better mount in the future.

66

But don't ever come out alone again, Flame, it is far too dangerous."

"Are there that many more men like you around your ranch?"

Joaquin caught himself before he could begin to swear again, but it took a great deal of effort to exercise such self-control. He knew he had a terrible temper, it had gotten him into trouble on more than one occasion, but never had he met a woman who provoked him so continually as this beauty did.

Flame read his expression and understood his angry scowl, but she continued to taunt him: "You must admit your conduct was something less than gentlemanly, no matter who you thought I was." Flame was learning to enjoy teasing him; she had always been a flirt, and he responded with such outrage at her jests she couldn't resist baiting him.

"Do you want to walk all the way back home? Keep that up and you can get yourself back to my house!"

"Whatever you wish." Flame left him and began to stroll away, turning back briefly to call over her shoulder, "If you'll please tell Rafael I'm walking home I'm sure he'll come and get me." She continued to walk then without looking back.

Joaquin threw his hat to the ground and yelled after her, "Damn it, I did not tell you to walk home, now come back here!"

Flame smiled sweetly as she approached him. "Perhaps I misunderstood your meaning, Joaquin."

Joaquin found his anger dissipating rapidly as he gazed into her deep green eyes. Their color was marvelous, as lush as the plants which filled the valley with vibrant beauty, and he could not even recall why he'd raised his voice. The woman confused him completely with her spiteful taunts, all spoken from behind an irresistibly innocent expression. "Wait until I get up on

Diablo, then I'll pull you up behind me.'' He whistled to the stallion then sprang easily upon the horse's back, but when he extended his hand Flame hesitated to take it. "What's the matter, Flame, I won't drop you.''

"What shall we say happened, Joaquin? Surely someone will ask how we happened to return together. We should have some story ready.''

Joaquin sighed impatiently. "We'll simply say your horse threw you and I came along as you were walking home.''

Flame put her small hand in his and he swung her up behind his saddle. "Put your arms around me and hold on, you won't fall.''

"Joaquin, does everyone know what happens to pretty young girls you find walking alone across your property?''

"Oh Christ! Will you never cease? I'm beginning to think you would have been happier had I not recognized you when I did!''

Flame didn't answer—she couldn't. She still wanted him every bit as much as she had when he'd held her in his arms and kissed her into an abandon she hadn't even known existed. She merely tightened her hold around his waist and lay her head against his warm back. "Am I holding on too tightly, Joaquin?''

"No, that's fine.'' Joaquin frowned unhappily as they rode along; he was horribly uncomfortable with Flame wrapped around him so tightly he could scarcely breathe. Her small hands rested on his ribs with the lightest of touches but still he was all too aware of her slender arms and soft round breasts against his back. Lord in heaven, what was he going to do with her? She was no child he could board away at school, not in any way, she was a woman, an all-too-beautiful young woman. Far too lovely for him to ignore, but what other choice did he have? Then he remembered what

68

she had said to him: he could never have been accused of rape for she had been more than willing. She was the most affectionate and loving woman he'd ever held in his arms, and he cursed softly under his breath as he dug his heels deep into Diablo's sides, sending the horse home at a faster pace. If he had made love to her he'd have had to marry her. There would have been no other option available to him. That he had escaped being forced into marriage by such a few minutes' time by the rare good fortune that Flame possessed hair of such a distinctive shade terrified him. All he needed was a wife! Then he remembered the easy way she had lain in his arms, a gorgeous, eighteen-year-old wife; his whole body ached with the agony of that thought and he tucked Flame's hand in his as they continued toward his home. He'd send her away, and soon, the very minute he could think of someplace to send her!

Flame relaxed against Joaquin's broad back. She could hear his heart beating, feel it throbbing steadily beneath her ear, and she was filled with happiness. He didn't seem to think badly of her after all. Perhaps, just perhaps, he might kiss her again soon. She said his name over and over again softly, she was so glad to know his name, Joaquin Villarreal, it rolled off her tongue like a poem, some wonderful romantic poem. She felt her cheeks burn as she thought of what had almost happened, they had come so close, what if he had made love to her? Would he have just ridden away, thinking they'd never meet again? That would have been some parting, she thought, only to find themselves facing each other over the dinner table that evening. She began to giggle and couldn't stop. He would have died of embarrassment when he found out who she was, but she would have been only happy to learn his name. Joaquin Villarreal. She loved his name and she knew she loved him too—but then, she always had.

Five

The very minute Rafael left the ranch Joaquin summoned Flame into his study and proceeded to make their relationship clear. He was prepared to be responsible for her well-being, to provide her with a home until she married, and in return he demanded complete obedience to his wishes where she was concerned. He leaned back against his desk and crossed his arms over his chest as he spoke. His pose was casual but his words were all harsh.

Flame would not have believed Joaquin could speak to her so coldly, as if their intimacy of the day before had simply not occurred. She looked down at the small violets woven into the fabric of her muslin dress and concentrated on the delicacy of the charming print rather than on the grim tone of her guardian's voice. He was leaving her no room for hope, none, he would be the most stern and strict of parents, and he was warning her in very explicit terms never to disobey him. Rafael had warned her frequently enough to be circumspect in her actions and words with Joaquin, never to run the risk of provoking his anger, but she was still surprised to hear the man himself tell her the same thing.

She glanced up at him through her long thick lashes and thought only of how warm his lips had been upon her skin, how sweet the taste of his kiss. Her fingertips could still feel the strength of his muscular body, the smoothness of his bronze skin. His shirt was open at the neck revealing the tangle of dark hair which she knew tapered into a thin line as it grew down the hard muscles of his stomach. She blushed as she looked down at the tiny violets once more—no, she would never be able to regard Joaquin as anything other than the most attractive and affectionate of men. A man who had taught her how to return his delicious kiss and respond to his tantalizing caress, how could he possibly expect her to pretend it hadn't happened? Perhaps he was an expert at pretense, but she was not. The eyes she lifted to meet his level gaze were filled with love.

"I must apologize for the fact there are no young girls on the household staff with sufficient command of English to serve as your maid. I expect, however, that you will master Spanish quickly and in the meantime Maria will see to your needs herself. She has more than enough chores as my housekeeper so please keep your requests to a minimum. I won't change Rafael's directions on the preparation of your food since my friend has complete authority in my absence and his word is to be respected, but I consider your dislike for our favorite foods and requirement for a separate menu an unwarranted nuisance. I will, unfortunately, also have to permit you to continue to ride dressed as a boy. Since Rafael allowed it the damage is already done, but I'll caution you again never to go out riding alone. I will expect your presence at the dinner table each evening but other than at that time do not come looking for me nor disturb me with questions as I am too busy to be bothered with trivial concerns when I'm working. While José is a competent foreman, I am the owner of this ranch and take an active part in seeing that it runs smoothly, so you will seldom find me at home except in the evenings. Rafael may have let you behave as you

71

pleased, Flame, but I am not nearly so tolerant as he. I expect you to be in chapel each morning for prayers and—''

Flame interrupted him quickly: ''Joaquin, perhaps you didn't realize I am not Catholic, but I don't know your prayers nor have I any wish to learn them.'' She sat up straight in her chair and clasped her hands tightly in her lap. The matter was settled in her mind, she had taken all she could of his overbearing attitude. The Villarreal ranch was fast proving to be more of a prison than she'd feared a convent would be!

''Perhaps you misunderstood me. You are part of my household now and you will do as I say. You will pray with us every morning. You will learn our prayers soon enough, children can recite them so they will be no challenge for you to master.''

''No, I will not.'' Flame stared down at her hands and would not lift her gaze; she was simply too angry to risk looking up at him.

''My orders are never disobeyed. Never.'' Joaquin glared down at the lovely girl and shook his head in disbelief. ''Tomorrow morning you will be in the chapel on time, do you understand me, Miss Lannier?''

Flame leapt to her feet, her green eyes blazing as she yelled at him, ''Why do you pretend not to understand me? No! I will not go, my faith is not yours and I will not pray with you! I am not a vaquero you can send to tend your cattle nor a sailor you can command this way and that on board one of your ships! My father asked you to be my guardian, not my jailor!''

Joaquin clenched his fists at his sides. Women never treated him this way, they were always eager to please him, to cater to his every whim. In all his life he could not recall anyone daring to cross him the way Flame was, and he knew she would do it continually. He was furious, so mad he could barely see, so he left the room rather than let her take any pride in how badly she had upset him.

The next morning Joaquin stepped into the chapel and waited only a few seconds. Flame was not there and he knew she would not be coming, not that morning nor any other, and he would not allow her to defy his command. He strode down the hall and threw open her door, awakening her instantly from her slumber. Before she could protest he scooped her up from the bed and carried her into the chapel where he set her down gently by his side. "You will kneel here beside me and repeat the prayers, is that clear? Every morning you are late I will carry you in here myself, now here!" He thrust a rosary into her hands and fumbling with his own began to recite his devotions for the day.

Flame said not a word. She wanted to die of shame. The room was filled with the household servants and others from the ranch, all praying in soft low voices along with Joaquin. She could not hold back her tears but wept soundlessly, the tears falling to dampen the smooth wooden beads in her hands. Joaquin was so close she could not even think; she closed her eyes and tried to catch her breath but could not. She was so terribly hurt by his rudeness, she'd never pray with him, he couldn't force her to pray. She was a guest in his home, not a slave to be commanded, to drop to her knees at her master's whim. Her arm brushed against her guardian's and she felt him draw away quickly, but not quickly enough, and something made her move closer still, leaning her slight weight against his side.

Joaquin looked down at Flame and frowned impatiently. What was the girl doing now? Her slender body was pressed so closely to his he could scarcely breathe. Abruptly, he ceased to speak, leaving the others to intone the prayers without him. He moved over to give her more room but she moved right along with him, giving him not a second's respite from the enticing touch of her soft slender body.

Somehow Joaquin managed to gather the willpower to finish his devotions, but he left the chapel at close to a run the second he was through. Flame continued to kneel alone while the chapel emptied, a sly smile curving her pretty mouth. If he wanted to drag her in again she'd do that to him every time. He could pretend all he wanted that he was her guardian and knew what was best but he'd never fool her—he was a man and she was a woman and they would never get along until he would admit the truth of that simple fact. If only he'd stop hiding the delight she already knew he felt at her touch then they would get along just fine.

The next morning Joaquin caught Flame as she slipped out the back door. "You will not leave my house until after chapel and not before, Flame. You may go riding all day if you like but not until after we pray together." He held her wrist so tightly she could not even hope to pull free as he brought her into the dimly lit room, but this time he was wise enough to push her down to kneel at least two feet from his side. He had not spoken one sentence, however, before she brushed up against him. Her body was not touching his but she was so very close, no more than a hair's breadth away, and her effect upon his senses was the same. He again found himself leaving at the first possible moment.

Flame waited in her room the next morning all dressed and ready for Joaquin to come. She would never go willingly, and he knew it as he escorted her down the hall. He showed her to a pew in the back of the room before taking a place in the front. He thought that would solve his problem with her outrageous behavior but he could not resist looking back toward her row and was furious to see she had gone, left the moment his back was turned. He left then himself, unmindful of the amused stares of the others in the small congregation.

Flame heard Joaquin coming and did not turn away. She smiled up at him as if there were no reason for her to expect any but the warmest of greetings.

"Why did you leave? I cannot trust you unless I can see you, is that it?" He scowled down at her, the muscles tensing along his jaw as he clenched his teeth angrily.

Flame tossed her beautiful curls as she shook her head. "Why no, I know only one prayer, I said it. You demanded only that I pray with you and I did. Was there a time requirement of some sort you failed to mention?"

Joaquin lost his temper completely, swearing as usual in Spanish but she understood his meaning all the same. "I want you to remain the entire time I am in the chapel, is that clear enough for you? If you know only one prayer then say it fifty times! Father León will be here this afternoon, he can begin your instruction and hear your confession then."

"My what?" Flame was appalled. The man really expected her to just take up Catholicism because he demanded it? "Joaquin, I have absolutely nothing to confess, nothing!"

"There's your pride for one thing!" He shouted right back at her, his anger not lessening one bit.

"My pride is a small fault compared to yours. I am the most humble of God's servants compared to you, Joaquin!"

"Damn it, Flame!"

"No, just stop swearing at me and listen! I do not wish to become Catholic, not now, not ever! Can't you leave my faith alone? I have lost everything, everyone I loved—must I lose my religion too? There is a Protes-

75

tant church in the town. I want to attend church there."

Joaquin tried to hold his tongue while he thought of some logical reason why she could not do as she asked. "Flame, there is only one God. Is my religion so different, so abhorrent to you? You cannot give me even the slightest respect on this point, you can not follow my wishes because I ask this small thing from you?"

Flame looked away from him, trying to collect her thoughts too. "First of all, you did not ask, you demanded that I change my faith and secondly, even if you had asked me politely my answer would still be no! I am not your slave, Joaquin, I am not and I will never give in to you when you yell at me as though I were!"

She had told him far more than she realized and Joaquin's expression softened as he began to smile. "It would please me if you would but speak to my friend, the priest, when he comes to our home. Is that better?"

Flame stared up at him and could not reply. How had he done that, changed so completely in an instant from a hateful tyrant to the tender lover she knew him to be? "Would you let me ask the priest his opinion, Joaquin? If I were to ask him for his advice would you abide by his decision if I will?"

Now Joaquin grew even more confused. Surely Father León would tell her to respect his wishes, but she must realize that too. Did she only want to save face? That was a desire he could readily understand. "Yes, whatever he decides will be agreeable to me, Flame."

"What am I supposed to do, kneel and kiss his ring, or what?"

Joaquin chuckled as he answered, "No, that's a bishop, not a simple village priest like Father León. Treat him as you would any older gentleman."

Flame could not keep the sparkle from brightening her eyes. "Surely, not just any older gentleman, Joaquin.''

''Flame, don't you dare flirt with him, don't you dare do that to him!''

''Is that what I do, flirt? You are an older gentleman, aren't you?'' Flame's expression was bewitching, alluring, she was flirting openly with Joaquin and made no attempt to disguise it.

''No, I am not!''

''Not a gentleman? Why, Joaquin, you'll admit that now yourself?''

''Damn it, Flame, you know what I mean, I'm not old!'' He was sick of her teasing, she was too cute by far.

Flame perplexed him all the more as her gaze swept his lean form with unabashed admiration. ''Oh, I have already noticed that, Joaquin, believe me I have.''

When the good priest arrived, Joaquin sent immediately for Flame but he had no idea what to expect from her. She had pulled her hair back from her face and caught it with a ribbon; in her pale blue cotton dress she looked so sweet and young he could not help but stare. She appeared so innocent and docile, not at all like the young woman he knew so well, fought with every damn day of his life now. When he left her alone with the priest he was worried, somehow he didn't think things were going to work out as he'd hoped they would.

Flame's youthful appearance was no accident. She had spent the better part of an hour in front of her mirror to bring out the child she usually suppressed. Convincing Joaquin she was eighteen had been easy enough, but she knew the priest would think her no more than twelve that day. ''Father León, may I have your promise Joaquin will never learn of the secrets I reveal to you this afternoon?'' Flame leaned close, touching the man's sleeve as she whispered.

The kindly cleric smiled. ''Of course, my dear, I

77

hold all confessions in the strictest of confidence. Have no fears that your guardian will ever hear anything you wish to confide in me.''

Flame's speech and gestures were carefully rehearsed, but it was truth which made itself plain in the guileless expression which lit her pretty eyes. ''I am not a Catholic, nor do I wish to become one in spite of Joaquin's desire for me to take his faith. I have gone to the Protestant church in town and would like to become a member of that congregation. The simple truth is that I cannot kneel beside Joaquin and think of any thought other than how dearly I love him.''

The priest gasped in horror. ''But dear girl—''

''Yes, I know. I am young and he is my guardian, but I have fallen in love with him and cannot pray for the strength which I need to resist such temptation when he is by my side. I have refused to pray with him but he does not suspect my reason is other than a religious one. But surely a child should not kneel beside her guardian and pray for him to make love to her.''

The tears on her long lashes broke the old man's heart and he took her hands in his. ''I had no idea, simply none. You realize such a thing is a sin?''

''Of course, lust is the word, isn't it? I know what it means, but you know the chapel here, it is dark and cool, the candles have such a sweet perfume and Joaquin's voice is like music. I cannot pray there, I cannot. I can think only of the love which is forbidden.'' Flame lowered her eyes and awaited his response. Joaquin would wring her neck if he heard this, she thought, but it was the truth, every last word.

The priest sat back and fingered the rosary which hung from his belt. ''We believe ours to be the true faith and I can advocate no other, dear child, but in this case I feel you are right to resist Joaquin's request that you attend his devotions or practice our faith when

78

your mind is so, shall we say, preoccupied? I will tell him to release you from all further attendance at chapel here and to see that you are allowed to go to the church of your choice as often as you desire.''

Flame squealed in delight and hugged the astonished priest before she ran from the room. She hated to fight with Joaquin, it pained her dreadfully to constantly oppose him, but she had won again, she was free to do as she pleased and it was a wonderful feeling. Joaquin, however, did not concur.

''You told her what?'' Joaquin could not believe his ears. He had been so certain of Father León's decision he was dumbfounded.

''The girl has a great spiritual quality, my son. Let her go to whatever church she chooses. It is not your decision but God's and he will call her to our beliefs if he so desires.''

''But—'' Joaquin gestured helplessly, frustrated beyond words by his friend's action.

''No, Joaquin, you told me to decide this issue since you two could not, and I have done so. The matter is now settled. Do not bother the child any further on this point.''

Flame was far too clever a young woman to gloat. She never spoke of the chapel again, but Joaquin could not drive her memory from his mind. He could not kneel without feeling the soft touch of her body next to his own and it drove him to distraction. Her words came back to him again and again: if he would but ask, ask as a gentleman should, then she would follow his lead; but he could not ask. The words stuck in his throat whenever he saw her, he continued to yell when he should have been polite, but he could not help himself nor comprehend why the beautiful girl was such an unending torment to him.

Dinner was no longer a particularly pleasant time for

Joaquin: he could scarcely relax with Flame at his table. He tried to converse politely but it was nearly impossible to avoid arguments, since she never agreed with any of his opinions and never missed an opportunity to say so. To make matters worse, she was logical and precise in her debates, never giving him the slightest reason to dismiss her arguments as the foolish opinions of a silly young girl. Frequently he had guests, other rancheros traveling to San Francisco or Los Angeles, businessmen hoping to convince him to invest in their enterprise—even Newton Booth, the governor of California, had been entertained at the ranch. Flame's behavior at those times astonished Joaquin, for she was the soul of tact whenever there were guests present. She was so charming and pretty everyone loved her immediately and complimented Joaquin on his good fortune at having become responsible for so delightful a young woman. Joaquin could only smile and nod at their praise, but as soon as he was alone he would explode in his usual burst of bitter oaths, cursing the day he'd given André Lannier his word he'd look after Flame.

When they dined alone, Joaquin had grown so silent that sometimes the only words he spoke were the grace before they ate. When he knew Flame would argue with some point he wished to make he would wait until they were almost finished eating before he brought up the subject. On this particular night he had done that very thing. "I want you to braid your hair like the other women here at the ranch, Flame. There's no reason why you should go about with your long red hair blowing wildly all about. It distracts my men too much."

Flame put down her fork and tried not to get angry . . . she tried, but she did not succeed. "Joaquin, the other women here have very beautiful hair. It is exactly like yours, dark, shiny and also quite straight, which mine is not. It is much too difficult to braid my hair, it is too thick and curly to look pretty in braids.''

Joaquin spoke without glancing up from his meal. ''I don't care how it looks, just braid it tomorrow. You may wear it as you please when you are in the house, but braid it before you leave to go out riding.''

''Don't you understand me, Joaquin? It is too hard to do, I can't do it myself. Even Lottie, my maid at home, could not braid my hair.''

''Don't be ridiculous, Flame, you can do it and you will, now don't argue with me any more about it.''

Flame shook her head. ''I won't argue, I'll make you a wager. I'll wear my hair in braids if you can braid it, otherwise I will not. Is that a bet?''

''I am no lady's maid!'' Joaquin threw down his knife in disgust, then had to reach under the table to retrieve it when it fell to the floor.

''You know how to braid hair, don't you? You've done a horse's mane?''

''You think I can't do it, is that it?'' Joaquin flashed her a murderous look that should have warned her but didn't.

''I know you can't do it.'' Flame spoke with calm assurance.

''Go and get your hairbrush for me then.''

''Right now? Don't you want to finish your dinner first?''

''I *am* finished. How you expect me to have any appetite when I have to listen to your incessant arguing I don't know! Just go and fetch your brush and we'll settle this right now!'' Joaquin was angry: surely it wasn't impossible to braid Flame's hair. If any man could do it he knew he could. Her hair could be no more coarse than a horse's mane, and that he could braid handily.

When Flame returned Joaquin moved their chairs so she could sit in front of him. ''Do you want to make a bet as to time, Flame? Don't you want to make this a

81

challenge for me?''

"It will be enough of a challenge, Joaquin. Take all the time you need, all night if you wish." Flame sat down with her back to him and handed him her silver-handled hairbrush.

As soon as Joaquin touched Flame's hair he knew he'd made a serious mistake. First of all, he was seated much too close to her and the fragrance of her sweet perfume was terribly distracting, as were her lovely white shoulders. In his haste to teach her a lesson he had forgotten why he never touched her, and it was a struggle for him to keep his mind on his task when all he really wanted to do was bury his face in her beautiful red hair and kiss the gentle curve of her slender throat. While she sat relaxed in her chair Joaquin began to curse his own stupidity, but he had no choice but to try and accomplish what he had boasted so arrogantly he could do. Separating the long curly locks into groups to braid proved nearly impossible—if he began near her scalp he found the ends in tangles, but when he brushed out the ends first he could still not separate the hair into three parts to braid.

Flame began to giggle, she couldn't help herself but she had warned him. She put her hands over her mouth to stifle her laughter but her shaking shoulders gave her away.

"You think this is funny?" Joaquin threw her brush to the floor and began using only fingers to yank her golden curls into sections.

"Ouch, be careful, Joaquin, you're hurting me!" Flame put her hands over his but he pushed them away.

"That wasn't part of this bet, was it? There was nothing said about pain!" Joaquin pulled her hair as tightly as he could and began to braid it. If the ends tangled then he just yanked them apart. It took him considerable time and a great deal of effort but he did manage to braid Flame's hair as he had promised. He sat back and viewed his handiwork and had to admit even to himself that her hair was a mess. Curls and wisps stuck out all over and her hair now looked more suitable for a grotesque scarecrow than for the lovely young woman she was.

Joaquin's voice held no trace of pride as he moved his chair back to the table. "You must admit that I did it. You'll have to say I won this time." When Flame made no obnoxious retort Joaquin stepped around to face her and was shocked to find her in tears. Had she been crying all the time he'd been so rough with her and he'd not even noticed? He knelt down beside her and took her small hands in his. "Flame, I am so sorry, I didn't know I was hurting you and I did, didn't I?"

"You knew exactly what you were doing, don't lie to me! You said there was no mention of pain, you were trying to hurt me just as badly as you could and you did, well you did braid my hair, you won!"

Joaquin was overcome with remorse. He retrieved her brush and handed it back to her. "I never lie to anyone, Flame, and I'd certainly never lie to you. You were right, your hair looks awful and I don't want you to even attempt to wear it in braids. Wear a scarf or a hat and that will do the job, and I want you to believe me when I say I'm very sorry that I lost my temper and hurt you. I didn't mean to do that." But as he looked down he saw there was hair all over the floor, in his haste to take out the tangles he'd simply yanked out handfuls of hair and he was horrified he hadn't realized how badly that must have hurt her.

Flame's long eyelashes were spiked with tears as she looked up at her guardian. She hesitated while she studied his expression and decided it was an honest one. "Truly, you really didn't mean to hurt me?"

"No, of course not. Why would I want to hurt you, Flame?"

The young woman rose to her feet and answered him as she moved gracefully through the door. "Only you know the answer to that question, Joaquin. I certainly don't understand why you hate me so."

Flame was gone before Joaquin could reply. Stunned, he sank back down into his chair. Hatred was what she thought he felt when he saw her, touched her, smelled her delightful perfume? He had no choice but to hide his feelings, none whatsoever, and now Flame saw only hatred when he'd fought so hard merely to keep her from seeing the depth of his desire. . . .

Six

Flame's life began to take on a peaceful routine in the days that followed her bitter confrontation with Joaquin over the braids. She followed his orders carefully and never went about the ranch without first tying up her bright curls and covering them with a scarf. She spent nearly every morning out riding. The terrain was spectacular in all directions whether she went by the sea or toward the mountains. She never grew bored with riding: she chose from among several different mounts and took different trails each day, and that variety kept her days from seeming monotonous.

Joaquin never allowed her to ride alone and she didn't argue. She readily understood the reason for his concern, for she knew if he could overtake her while she was out riding then it would be possible for another man to do the same. She always had a vaquero by her side, lean, taciturn men who spoke only Spanish and wouldn't have cared to converse with her in English had they shared that tongue. Flame didn't mind. They made her nervous at first, but she soon grew accustomed to their silent presence, and finally she forgot them entirely she was so lost in the beauty of her own freedom as she explored her new home each dawn.

Each man rode with Flame for only a few days at a time since none enjoyed the task and Joaquin wanted to make certain none ever did. Maria complained constantly that Flame should have a female chaperon also but there were no women on the ranch who cared to ride as much as Flame did so the pretty young woman and her male escort went out alone each day.

On Sundays, Flame was taken to church in one of the buggies since Joaquin refused to permit her to ride into town dressed in pants and Flame didn't want to anyway. She enjoyed going to the small church; the people were polite, if somewhat aloof, but the young men and women her age were few. Except for Suzanna Lewis, the minister's daughter, she had made no real friends among the congregation.

As the two young women moved gracefully down the steps at the front of the church Flame reached for Suzanna's hand and smiled warmly. "Why don't you come home with me today? You could have dinner with us, then I'll bring you back late this afternoon. Please say you'll come, it would be such fun." Flame's invitation was issued graciously but met with a quick refusal.

"Oh, Flame, I could never go with you! Joaquin would be at dinner wouldn't he?" Suzanna's pale blue eyes grew enormous as she thought of having to speak to the handsome man.

"Of course he'll be there, it is his home. Is there some reason you don't like him?" Flame was puzzled— Joaquin had so little to do with the small farming community she could see no reason why anyone would dislike him.

"Father always says he's, well, I shouldn't gossip, but Father would never allow me to go to his ranch."

"And why not? Tell me this instant what your father says or I'll not speak to you ever again!" Flame reached out to give her friend's thin shoulders a gentle shake to emphasize her point. If there were gossip about Joaquin, she wanted to hear it instantly.

Suzanna wrung her hands nervously. She admired

86

Flame enormously, her new friend was so pretty, her clothes the finest she'd ever seen—she just adored her, and looked forward to seeing her each Sunday with a delight she couldn't hide. "He says that Joaquin never wanted a town here, that he won't help any of the merchants by buying their things. Oh you must know how he is—he's like a king and his ranch is his kingdom and we're all just serfs to him, not worth his trouble to know."

Flame stared at Suzanna for a long moment, then nodded in agreement. "Yes, that's probably true, but don't you understand his family has been here for generations? All of California used to belong to men like Joaquin. It was their home, and so many were cheated out of everything they owned just so men who'd come from back East could have small farms. No wonder he isn't friendly to the townspeople!"

Suzanna stared wide-eyed at her beautiful friend. "Why, Flame, you're on his side, aren't you?"

"Of course I am, he's right!" Flame had to laugh when she realized she was defending her guardian for a change. "Oh let's not argue over things we can't change, Suzanna. Joaquin has his ranch, and the town and the farmers look prosperous enough to me. There's no reason for you to hate Joaquin just because he's rich."

Suzanna blushed deeply, then giggled too. "No, you're right, but what is he really like, Flame? I've seen him so seldom but I swear he does look like a king, he is so handsome and that black stallion he rides is so wild!"

Flame sighed and scuffed the toe of her slipper in the sparce grass which covered the churchyard, but despite her attempt to stall for time she could think of no simple way to describe the man she loved. "Joaquin is easily the best and worst of all men. I'll say no more. Now do you think your father would let you come visit me sometime when Joaquin is away? He travels frequently from what I've heard. Would you be able to come for a visit then?''

"Yes, I think so, if my brother were to come with me. I'm sure if Joaquin weren't going to be home I could convince Father to let me go home with you. He is very happy that you're so faithful in your attendance here and that we've become friends.''

"Thank you for telling me that, Suzanna, I like your father very much too. Your whole family has been very sweet to me." As Flame turned she saw Jimmy Lewis duck around the corner of the small frame structure. He'd been watching them again, she was certain. Jimmy was the shyest boy she'd ever met, he never did more than stammer hello, but she was wise enough to know he liked her as much as or more than his sister did.

The matter of a visit settled, the girls continued to chat until Flame had to return home. She liked Suzanna and was sorry she couldn't see more of her, or anyone else her age for that matter. She was terribly lonely. Before coming to California she'd been so popular, had so many good friends, that to suddenly find herself with only one she could seldom see was heartbreaking for her.

The next morning Flame was surprised to see one of the younger vaqueros ready to accompany her on her ride. She had talked to him a few times, once she'd heard him play his guitar. She hardly knew him, but he was young and spoke English so she was delighted to see him. That his greeting and glance seemed a bit too familiar worried her only briefly.

Miguel followed Flame at a discreet distance until they were out of sight of the ranch house, then he brought his mount up beside hers and tipped his hat. "Good morning, señorita.''

"Good morning, Miguel, how are you?" Flame smiled prettily as she greeted the friendly young man.

"I am fine, señorita, where do you wish to ride today?"

"Toward the hills I thought, do you mind going that way?"

"As you wish, señorita, perhaps I know trails which you do not." Miguel flashed a charming grin and gestured east.

"Would you lead the way then, please?" Flame continued to chat with him for several minutes before he moved his horse ahead of hers and picked up their pace to a brisk canter. She was grateful for pleasant company for a change, someone young and friendly, and she looked forward to spending the morning with him. He led the way up an unfamiliar path which ended in a grove of oak trees where he dismounted with an agile leap and let his horse graze in the tall grass.

Flame slipped down from her saddle and gazed about the small clearing. "This is a beautiful spot, Miguel, so lush and green. Are the mountains always so pretty?" Flame did not realize how close he'd come until a twig snapped under his boot, but when she tried to move back he grabbed her around the waist, trying eagerly to kiss her pink-tinged lips. She pushed against him and turned her head away. "Miguel, stop it! I'll leave this instant if you don't behave as you should!"

Miguel only laughed at her threat, "No, señorita, you will not leave here for a long while. You usually ride all morning so we have plenty of time to get to know each other better."

"I think I know you as well as I care to, now good day." Flame shoved him away and reached for her horse's reins but the dark eyed man stepped quickly to block her way.

"Why are you so unfriendly today, little one? You

have always smiled at me before. I know what you want, now come here." He lunged to catch her again, grabbing her wrists—but he had forgotten her feet, and she kicked him in the shins with a swift blow that sent a sharp pain clear up his leg.

"Puta! Am I not good enough for you after Villarreal?"

Flame struggled against his rough grasp as she shouted, "Let me go! Let me go!" She kicked him again and broke free, running to her horse in a dash for safety, but he was right behind her, his fingers ripping her blouse as his hand failed to catch her shoulder.

"I'll show you, you damn bitch!" Miguel shrieked as he spun Flame around and threw her to the ground. He fell upon her, ripping the rest of her blouse to shreds before he tried to force her legs apart with his knee. His hands were rough, his touch rude as he caressed her exposed flesh before he reached to unfasten her belt.

Flame screamed but there was no one to come to her rescue and the piercing sound echoed against the surrounding trees like the mournful cry of a coyote baying at the moon. In desperation she grabbed a handful of dirt and hurled it in Miguel's face, effectively blinding him. She scrambled away while he fought to regain his vision, but this time she was in the saddle and gone before he got to his feet and came after her.

Joaquin had just turned the corner of the barn when Flame rode into the yard. He took one look at her disheveled appearance before running to her side. He swung her down easily from her horse, his face black with rage. "Tell me who it was, Flame. Who did this to you?"

Flame struggled to catch her breath but the tears which streamed down her cheeks choked her with hoarse sobs. "Miguel Torres, he tried to—"

"I can damn well see what he tried to do! Where

90

were you?''

Joaquin listened closely and recognized the location easily from her description but before he could saddle Diablo and leave Miguel appeared on the horizon. "Go on into the house, Flame, I'll take care of him, well go!'' He gave her a shove to set her in motion then stepped back into the shadows to wait for the vaquero. The young man rode up in front of the bunk house but Joaquin was upon him, yanking him from his saddle before he could dismount on his own. He dragged the hapless youth out into the yard and began to methodically beat him senseless.

Flame ran into the house, too sick with shame to watch. Miguel had thought her friendly. Had he thought she meant to encourage his attentions just because she smiled? She threw herself across her bed and sobbed. Joaquin was going to beat the boy to death, she knew he would, and she was sick with fear. She was still crying as though her heart were broken when her guardian came in to see her. He sat down on the edge of her bed and touched her back which was now barely covered by her shredded blouse.

"Did you kill him?" Flame looked up at him through her tears. He still looked so angry she was afraid he might hit her too.

"Not quite, but had he raped you I certainly would have. You are my responsibility, Flame, and I'll not let anyone harm you.''

Flame's eyes filled with sadness. A responsibility? Was she no more to him than that, a tiresome responsibility? "You would have killed him?" Flame could scarcely form the question, it terrified her so.

"Of course. And if there is another man on this ranch who didn't realize that before today he knows it now. I have killed men before, Flame, with my fists, my knife . . . I've shot more than one man but

91

whether or not they died I'm not certain."

"Joaquin!" Flame was horrified by his accounting of such grim deeds.

"It's true, I have not led the peaceful life you have observed here all that long. I spent five years at sea, which were pure hell, and most of the worst fights I've ever been in were during that time."

Flame touched his bruised knuckles lightly but he didn't flinch. "You've hurt yourself too."

"It's nothing. But I am curious, Flame. José told me he found out Miguel had paid another man to take his place with you today. Why would he do that? Did he have some reason to think perhaps you'd be open to his advances?"

Flame's cheeks burned with shame. He thought she had invited the attack, somehow encouraged Miguel's assault? She turned away quickly, unable to face him. Did he really think the way she had behaved with him was the way she behaved with all men?

"Flame, you answer me!"

"I hardly knew him, Joaquin."

"But you did know him? How could you have met him?"

"We were never introduced, I've just seen him around from time to time. He was always polite to me, talked to me, I listened to him play his guitar one night. I never did more than that, just smile and say a few words. So few of your men know English, Joaquin, I only wanted to talk to Miguel, he had no reason to try what he did."

"Good Lord, Flame, you just smiled and chatted politely, is that all? Well, take a good look in your mirror when you stop crying. You are undoubtedly the most beautiful woman the men here have ever seen and I know exactly how you smile and talk. No wonder he thought you liked him. These men aren't used to sophisticated young ladies like you, to them a smile means an invitation for only one thing, and you nearly got what you were asking for. You were damn lucky you got away. You may not be so fortunate the next time you tease one of the men.''

Flame was livid now. He had no right to make her feel guilty for being friendly—she wouldn't take his insults. She sat up quickly, her eyes blazing angrily as she spoke. ''It wasn't my fault, Joaquin, don't you dare try and blame me. This was all Miguel's idea. He thought I was your woman and one more man wouldn't make any difference to me!''

''What!'' Joaquin was clearly stunned by her words. He grabbed her shoulders and shook her. ''What are you saying?''

''Your vaqueros think I'm your whore, that's what puta means isn't it?''

Joaquin released Flame instantly as he leapt to his feet. ''I don't want to ever hear you talk like that ever again. If my men think I'd want some girl who dresses like a boy and runs around wild most of the day then they're mistaken! From now on I'll assign the vaqueros who'll ride with you or you'll stay home, do you understand? You're too damn much trouble for me, Flame Lannier, and I won't have you speaking even one word to any of my men ever again. If I see you so much as smile at any of them ever again you'll regret it!''

''Why? Will you beat me the way you beat Miguel? At least he was honest about what he wanted from me!''

''And I'm not, is that what you mean?'' Joaquin was shaking with rage. ''Never in all my life have I so much as slapped a woman, Flame, let alone beat one, but so help me if I catch you flirting with one of the vaqueros I may start with you!'' Joaquin slammed the door as he went out then leaned back against it to catch his breath.

Dear God, what was he going to do with that woman? Could she see how badly he wanted her? Had that been what she'd meant about being honest with her? He began to chuckle as he strode off down the hall. Surely she didn't honestly think he could beat her, that was preposterous! It was difficult enough to keep his hands off her she was so lovely, but he would never ever want to beat her.

Seven

Flame saw the new mare as soon as she came out to the yard. She had never seen a more beautiful horse, dark like the night but dotted with white flecks as if she'd been left out in the snow. Joaquin was leading her into the small corral at the side of the barn.

"Where did you get such a magnificent horse, Joaquin? I've never seen one like her. Is she some type of pinto, an Indian pony?" Flame climbed up on the rails of the corral, her feet on the bottom rung, her arms over the top in order to have a better view of the intriguing animal.

Joaquin could not help but smile at Flame's enthusiasm. She was so like a child at times—unfortunately, not nearly often enough. "Well, some might say that she is an Indian pony. The Nez Perce raise these horses, but she is descended from horses the Spaniards brought to New Spain, or Mexico if you prefer."

"Does that kind of horse have a name then?"

"Yes, she is an Appaloosa, named for the Palouse River where the Nez Perce live."

"There is no Spanish word for the horse then, no special name? I remember you told me pinto was from the Spanish word pintado which means painted. You see, I am trying to learn Spanish, I really am."

Joaquin laughed at her boast. He doubted she knew more than a dozen words at the most, but he would have to disappoint her now. "If there ever were a name for these animals in the old world I do not know it. I bought her from a man who was using her as a pack mule. She is worthless except as a brood mare but I thought her far too pretty to suffer such a fate."

"Why Joaquin, I had no idea you were even capable of such sweet thoughts! But why do you consider her worthless? Couldn't I ride her?"

"No, she has been too badly abused. She'd only throw you, so I'll not let you even attempt to ride her and that's final."

"Abused? You mean beaten, treated cruelly?"

"Yes, horses can be ruined rather easily, Flame. They are useless if they do not trust their master. This poor mare was broken with too rough a hand. See how she shies away from me now and I have not harmed her. No, she would not be good for riding, but perhaps her colts will be."

"I can't believe she can't learn, Joaquin. Surely if we treated her with kindness she would come to trust us. Couldn't we win her over with love?"

"We?" Joaquin glanced up at her in disbelief, "Since when have you begun to train horses, Flame? I doubt you would have the patience to train even a willing horse, you could never gentle this mare." Joaquin moved to tie the mare's halter to the corral, then fixed hobbles to her back legs.

"Why are you doing that to her?" Flame asked curiously.

"So she can't kick Diablo." Joaquin brushed off his pants as he came through the gate, closing it behind him.

Flame didn't understand. "Why would she wish to kick him?"

Joaquin shook his head wearily. Flame was not usually so dense. "Why don't you just stand there and watch, I'm letting Diablo in now.'' He grinned down at her, amused to see by her sudden blush that she at last understood what was about to happen.

"You mean she'd not be willing? You would turn the stallion loose on her and she would have no way to fight him?''

"I don't want her to fight him, damn it, she is worthless to me unless she bears strong foals.''

"But she is an Appaloosa, that makes her special. Is there no stallion of her kind to sire her colts?''

"None near here, Flame, and Diablo will be more than willing. An Appaloosa stallion isn't required.''

Flame looked at the beautiful mare and thought of Joaquin's powerful black stallion with growing dread. "How would Diablo treat a mare if she were free, part of his herd. Surely no one comes to hobble mares when they roam free.''

Joaquin sighed with growing impatience. "Flame, Diablo is a valuable horse, far too valuable an animal to risk injury from a reluctant mare's hooves. These are not wild horses—they're mine, and I want to see they are treated well.''

"I still think we should find an Appaloosa stallion, Joaquin. Diablo is all wrong for her. Their colts would have none of her beauty and none of his strength. Don't do this to her, give her to me instead.''

Joaquin was astonished by her request. "Flame, you don't want this horse, believe me you don't. She'd give you nothing but trouble. If you want a horse of your own I'll give you another, I have hundreds, but not this mare, the answer's no.''

Nothing was ever settled from Flame's point of view until she had her way and she was not about to give in so easily. She got down from the fence and glared up at her guardian with her hands on her hips ready for a fight. "How much did you pay for her, Joaquin? I'll double that amount. I don't want her as a gift, I'll be happy to buy her from you.''

Joaquin scowled down at her, growing more irritated by the second. ''Why is it you never believe a word I say? Do you hate me so much that you will argue with anything I tell you just for the sheer sport of it?''

''Oh, Joaquin, I could never hate you, don't you know that? But is it my fault you're always wrong?''

''I am wrong?!''

''Always, Joaquin. Now how much do you want for this mare, name any figure and I will give you the money gladly.'' Flame knew she had absolutely no money, but surely she must have some somewhere . . . her father's estate had been large so Joaquin must have her money someplace.

''No, I will not take your money. She will be a gift from me to you, and I hope you learn every damn time she throws you how right I was and how wrong you are!''

Flame threw her arms around his neck to hug him warmly. ''Thank you, you won't be sorry, you'll see! She'll be a wonderful horse, as dear to me as Diablo is to you.''

It took every bit of Joaquin's self-control to ignore the sensation of Flame's luscious body which was pressed so closely against his. Her perfume was delightful, her joy so enticing he could barely take her arms from about his neck to push her away. ''I'll tell José to give her a stall in the barn but the mare will be your responsibility alone. You will clean out her stall and take care of her feed or she will starve. And I won't take her back when you decide you're bored with her either. You'll have to find a new owner for her yourself. I mean it, Flame, don't come to me with your complaints. I've already warned you how foolish this is and you've chosen to disregard my advice—she is your problem from now on, no longer mine." He strode off angrily before she could reply but she was too happy to argue and turned back to the mare to open the gate.

"I'll never do this to you, never, do you understand me, girl? I'll find you a stallion, an Appaloosa, or you'll never have a colt." She bent down and removed the hobbles, then led the mare out to the pasture and released her, turned her loose to run through the tall grass, beautiful and free, bending to the command of no man, exactly the life Flame longed to have for herself.

Joaquin repeated his instructions to José. "I swear if I ever have the misfortune to own a horse as willful as that woman I will destroy him gladly."

Jose dug the toe of his boot in the dirt as he responded, a low chuckle escaping from his lips. "How would you describe Diablo, Joaquin? That beast is so wild he will permit no other man to touch him yet he would carry you as far as you would go. How can you have such a gift as to bring the strongest of stallions to bow to your will without breaking his spirit and not realize the heart of a woman is a far greater prize?"

Joaquin stared at his foreman in surprise. He could not recall hearing such an eloquent speech from the man before. "It is not the same, José. Animals can be won with gentleness and patience but Flame has more spirit than any beast and I could never live so long as to win her with patience."

"You are wrong and were I a younger man I would show you myself how easily she could be tamed."

"I am her guardian, José. I know how to charm a woman only too well, but this is not the same."

"You fool only yourself then, Joaquin. She is a woman like any other, and it pains me to see how you treat her. You have tried to crush her spirit, when that would destroy her very soul. You do not understand her and you have not even tried. Perhaps you should send her away, find her a husband who would give her the love she is crying out to receive."

Joaquin could not keep the bitterness out of his voice. "Who would take such a defiant creature? I would not wish her on any of my friends."

"It is a pity Rafael did not remain here longer. You would have seen then how to treat her. He never raised his voice to her once and she smiled at him the whole day long."

"I know what he did, he gave her free run of the ranch, let her behave just as she pleased."

"What did she do that was forbidden? Nothing that I can recall, but she was happy then."

Joaquin swore, then caught himself, "But I am responsible for her, I cannot permit her to run wild, she must do as I say!"

José laughed at his employer's anger. "Let her go, Joaquin, let her be free and she will surprise you, I promise you that."

"She surprises me enough already, I can stand no more!" He turned to look at her as she stood watching her mare. Her golden hair blew back from her face and his breath caught in his throat. She was more beautiful each time he saw her, more lovely each day, but he had to make her obey him, he had to. "Maybe she will learn this time, José. She'll never train that mare."

"We will have to wait and see, Joaquin. Let's just wait and see." It was not that he would disobey Joaquin openly, but he had not been told not to help her and he smiled to himself. Flame would tame the mare, he knew she would, and then what would Joaquin say?

The next morning Flame found her mare's stall already swept out and filled with fresh straw. She had not dreaded that task but was surprised to find it done. When José came into the barn she called to him,

"Who has cleaned her stall, José? I don't mind the job, really I don't."

José smiled and led Flame over to a barrel and motioned for her to be seated. "Joaquin means well, señorita, but he does not always realize the implications of his decisions. Now I have two young boys whose job it is to keep our stables as clean as Joaquin would have them. They hope to become trainers someday and I teach them all I can as they work, but if they were to see a pretty young woman performing their labors they would lose all pride in their work. I cannot allow you to clean out stalls here, but Joaquin need not know. I will not tell him if you do not, he will realize soon enough the mistake of his order and change it, then we will all pretend to be impressed by his wisdom."

"José! Do you do this all the time? You do as you please while Joaquin believes you are following his orders to the letter?" Flame could not keep from laughing it amused her so to know someone else defied Joaquin as often as she did.

"Always, but you must not tell him."

"Oh, I won't, don't worry, but if he should come in and see one of the boys in her stall he will know all the same. If I came in very early I could still do it and the boys wouldn't know, they might each think the other had done the work."

José frowned sullenly. "You would go to such lengths to follow Joaquin's command?"

"I am so tired of fighting with him, José. I don't mind doing this. I will come earlier tomorrow and do the job myself, then everyone will be happy."

The foreman shoved his hands into his back pockets as he leaned back against the wall. "I had not expected you to be so willing to follow Joaquin's words in this. I have said too much."

"I'll never tell him what you've told me. I'm very

101

good at keeping secrets, you'll see. You can trust me."

"Good, now how do you plan to train your mare? Do you know anything about horses other than how to ride them?"

Flame shook her head sadly. She had remembered her scarf but it barely covered her pretty curls. "No, nothing at all." She blushed as she recalled what Joaquin had wanted her to witness the previous afternoon. "I thought I'd just turn her loose for awhile. Maybe she can forget what happened to her before and I can tame her as if she'd never known another hand. Joaquin says she's ruined but that can't be true, can it, José?"

José shrugged. "We will see. Try your way with her, it may work. But brush her coat each day, bring her treats—I will show you where Joaquin keeps the special food which makes Diablo's coat so shiny. Then when you decide to ride the horse she will know you well."

"Thank you, José, I want this to work. I hope it will, she is too pretty to waste."

"She would not have been wasted, señorita. She would have liked Diablo, all the mares do."

Flame shook her head angrily as she rose to her feet. "If she would have liked him so much Joaquin wouldn't have had to tie her, hobble her hind legs. I couldn't stand that, I just couldn't. I want an Appaloosa stallion and I'll set her free with him."

"Horses are not people, señorita."

José continued to observe closely as Flame worked with her mare, he spoke to her frequently in the following days with the most subtle of hints, and she understood. He would teach her how to train a horse and Joaquin would never know, he would never guess she was using any technique other than her own intuition as her guide.

Flame had never been given to introspection. She

seldom made any plans beyond the next hour and thinking about any subject in depth was foreign to her. She was so bright she could see in an instant what it took others hours to figure out, but that did not always work to her advantage. As she spent her time at the edge of the pasture just watching her sleek mare graze contentedly she could not help but let her mind wander—to imagine, to dream and to worry over the past as well as the future. How would things have been different had she found her father alive and as delighted to see her as she had hoped that he would be? Would Joaquin have come to call, brought her flowers, presents? Would he have fallen in love with her had she been living in her father's house and not his? She wiped away a tear and hugged her knees as she sat in the tall grass. Nothing was ever as she dreamed it would be . . . perhaps she was too old for dreams. She loved her pretty mare already, lavished the attention upon the horse which she would have joyfully given Joaquin had he only loved her as she loved him.

Joaquin pretended a total lack of interest in Flame's endeavor but in truth he was greatly intrigued. He had never seen Flame put so much as a blanket on her mare let alone a saddle. Had she no intention of riding her horse at all? When his curiosity finally got the better of him he walked out to the pasture and called out to her, "What are you waiting for, Flame, do you plan to sit there until the mare is too old to throw you?"

Flame ignored his taunts. She didn't even turn her head as he continued to tease her, remarking at great length upon her lack of methods. When she wouldn't fight with him he was puzzled; he leapt over the fence and walked to her side.

"Flame, are you all right?"

"Yes, I'm quite well thank you, and you?"

Joaquin sat down beside her and grinned. "I'm fine,

as a matter of fact. Are you making any progress at all with your mare?''

''Yes, she's coming along nicely.''

''Is she really now? How can you tell?'' He could not remember ever seeing Flame in so subdued a mood. She had been sitting for hours while the horse grazed in the lush field.

''I can tell.'' Flame turned her full attention to Joaquin. She rested her chin on her arms and smiled. ''I will ride her when she's ready and not a day before.''

''Let me know so I may come out here to carry you back into the house. I certainly hope you receive no broken bones. I have been thrown often enough not to envy you your fate.''

''But my fate is not yours, Joaquin.''

Joaquin forgot his usual caution as he looked into her eyes. They were such a deep shade of green, like the sea, and he thought what a lovely mermaid she would make with her golden hair, a perfect mermaid luring unwary sailors to their deaths. At that morbid thought he caught himself quickly and reached out to touch her cheek. ''You are getting freckles, you should wear a hat if you're going to sit out here in the sun all day.''

''Are my freckles really so unattractive?'' Flame had already noticed she was the only person on the ranch with them, the others all had Joaquin's bronze skin which deepened in the sun but apparently never freckled.

''No, Flame, they do not harm your looks in the least.'' He looked away for a minute as if embarrassed. ''I've been meaning to tell José to see that your mare's stall is cleaned for you. That's no job for a lady and I shouldn't have told you to do it yourself.''

''It's no trouble for me, Joaquin, I do not mind. It is not such hard work.'' Flame could not recall talking with her guardian in such a relaxed fashion since the morning they'd met, but the afternoon was so pretty and warm, she hoped their conversation would never have to end.

"But I do, you'll do it no longer."

"If you insist. I was only following your wishes, Joaquin." Flame's playful smile did not amuse him.

"For once! Is that all you'll do for me, only the most menial of tasks?"

Flame paused only a moment, then told him the truth, "I think I would gladly do anything you asked of me, Joaquin, but you do not ever ask."

Joaquin was not pleased by her words. He'd been careless and she was getting too close, sharing her feelings with him as he refused to do with her. He shut out any further such confidence by pointing toward her mare. "What do you call your horse? Does she have a name?"

His abrupt change of mood was not lost on Flame; she was sorry but not really surprised. "I'd give her a Spanish name, but I know so few, so I call her Lady. She *is* one, don't you think? Such a very elegant animal, but that is the way I see her. Perhaps you disagree."

"No. Lady is a fine name. I told you I thought she was pretty—why do you think I might have changed my mind?"

"You did not describe her temperament in very complimentary terms as I recall."

"Don't remind me. I hate to think of you lying out here with a broken neck." Joaquin scowled as if that were a real possibility.

"So do I! It won't happen, she won't throw me, you'll see soon enough. Are you sure there's no Appaloosa stallion you know of near by that I might purchase?"

"Good lord, now you want to buy a stallion? You are

105

going to persist in this fantasy of yours that you can train horses, aren't you?''

"It's no mere fantasy, I still own a ranch don't I? Isn't my father's ranch now mine? Can't I have even two horses on it if I wish? You don't expect me to live here forever do you? Surely you can't want me underfoot forever?'' Flame's anger was plain in her hostile expression as well as her tone.

"Now Flame, there's no reason for you to get mad at me. Why is it we cannot talk for more than five minutes without your starting a fight with me?'' He reached out and took her hand in his. Her skin was of the palest golden hue next to the deep bronze of his. She struggled to pull away but he held her hand tightly. "Look at us, Flame, are we so different, like Lady and Diablo, not of the same kind? Would you be happier here if I were some damn Viking, fair haired and blue eyed? Would my home please you then?''

Flame looked down at their hands but could hardly respond as the warmth from his body moved from her fingertips up her arm, flooding her whole being with desire as his touch always did—yet her hand in his was as cold as ice. "A Viking, Joaquin? What made you think of them? There are no Vikings in my family. My people were all English or French, not blue-eyed blondes at all. My father was dark like you, wasn't he? I have always thought you the handsomest of men, but truly I fear we are not of the same kind. Perhaps no man and woman ever are. That is why we argue isn't it, Joaquin? We are simply a man and a woman who belong together but you will not admit that, nor let it be.''

As she glanced up at him she found his expression impossible to read: his eyes were too dark, his face too stern. But he did not move to leave her side—he sat with her, her hand in his for several minutes more, before he got to his feet to return to his work.

"Be very careful with Lady, Flame, for if she hurts you I'll destroy her, I'll shoot her myself, I swear I will."

Flame stared after him too frightened to speak. He'd kill her mare? Why would he go to such extremes for revenge when he cared so little for her? She got more and more angry. If Lady threw her a thousand times she'd never tell Joaquin.

Joaquin's dark mood had not lifted by dinnertime that night. He was not one bit happier than when he'd left Flame that afternoon. He knew she was right, their problem was an extremely simple one. He wanted her as any man would crave such a lovely young woman and he wouldn't admit that to her . . . he barely admitted it to himself. They'd never get along, it was pointless to try, because he intended to remain as her guardian, a gentleman who had her best interests in mind and nothing more.

While the noonday meal was traditionally the main one, Joaquin was so often away from his house at that time of the day that the evening meal had become the more formal one in his home. He had dressed for dinner, even when he dined alone, but since Flame had come to live in his house he found himself going to extra lengths to appear as refined a gentleman as she was a lady. She had an extensive wardrobe, all exquisite and expensive gowns, and while she might dress as a boy to ride or work with Lady each evening she appeared at his table as beautifully groomed and dressed as any woman he'd ever known.

If Joaquin were usually aloof, he was more so that night. He did converse politely as any gracious host would, but he showed Flame none of the charm he used so frequently and successfully on every other beautiful woman he'd ever met. So they sat that evening, an ex-

107

quisitely lovely young woman and a devilishly handsome man trying their best to be only polite strangers while both struggled against the torment of their own desires. Flame wanted so much from Joaquin, all he could possibly give, and yet he held back, unwilling to risk even the mildest of flirtations. He knew what he wanted: he wanted her off his ranch, out of his life which had become unbearably complicated since she had arrived. He was in control of all facets of his life save one: he could not control Flame, he could not dominate her in any way, and that was driving him to distraction.

Early the next morning Flame took Lady out of the barn before anyone else awoke. She led her mare to the farthest corner of the pasture and turned her loose to shake out the early morning stiffness from her legs. Lady followed Flame around like a puppy now, nuzzling her back pockets looking for the treats her mistress always carried. She had responded eagerly to Flame's loving attention by becoming more gentle and affectionate each day. When Flame grabbed her mane she did not even flinch, nor did she bolt when the slender girl leapt upon her back. Flame sat astride the mare holding her breath and praying the ground was soft, but Lady didn't seem to notice the slight weight upon her back. After a few minutes Flame slid off and hugged Lady's neck excitedly. She hadn't been thrown, but perhaps Lady would object far more to a bridle and saddle than to being ridden bareback. Encouraged by her success, Flame returned to the barn for a bridle. Lady eyed her suspiciously this time and trotted away to avoid being caught but when Flame stood patiently waiting the mare approached her curiously and allowed her to slip the bit between her teeth, then stood quietly as Flame secured the bridle's buckles.

Taking a deep breath Flame again climbed upon the horse's back, and when the mare did not object she rode her around the pasture, letting her stop to graze whenever she wished to pause. "You are a fine horse, I knew you were and I'll bet you're fast too, aren't you my Lady?" Not wishing to press her luck, Flame soon dismounted and removed the bridle so Lady might enjoy her customary morning freedom to roam the lush pasture alone.

The next morning Flame followed the same routine. She wanted to be certain the mare would not throw her before she tried putting a saddle on her back. As long as Joaquin were still in his bed she felt confident, for he could not punish Lady for misdeeds he hadn't seen. After several mornings of leisurely rides around the pasture at dawn José met Flame as she replaced the bridle on its wooden peg in the tack room.

"I've seen you ride the horse, señorita; let's try a saddle today and I will ride with you. Let us take her out of the pasture and see what happens."

Flame glanced toward the house anxiously. "Does Joaquin know what I've been doing too? I didn't want him to find out yet."

"No, he doesn't know, but let's go out riding now before he finds us here still discussing the matter." José went out and led the mare into her stall and to their surprise she appeared to be the most willing of mounts. "You have tamed her well, señorita. She will not throw you today. Let's go."

When Flame put her foot in the stirrup Lady turned her head to look back at her mistress with a puzzled eye but made no attempt to buck her off. José was so impressed by the mare's fine manners he took Flame much farther than he had planned, enjoying the crisp morning air and their two fine mounts as much as she did.

As Flame glanced toward the horizon she saw a cloud of dust and a flash of gleaming black hide and knew it had to be Joaquin. He'd probably be furious she'd ridden her horse without his knowledge and she was afraid he'd be angry with José for accompanying her too.

"Señorita, just smile as though we ride together each day." José had time to offer no more advice as Joaquin drew up beside them.

Following José's suggestion, Flame greeted her guardian warmly. "Good morning, Joaquin. Lovely morning for a ride, isn't it?"

"I was afraid you'd taken Lady out alone, but since José is with you I will cease to worry."

"There's no reason for you to worry at all, my horse is quite docile as you can see." Flame stroked Lady's soft shiny neck and smiled prettily.

"So you have actually done it, Flame. And she did not throw you, not even once?"

"Let me say, not yet. But she is fine horse, just as I knew she would be. She only needed someone to believe in her as you believe in Diablo. She is fast, really fast too."

Joaquin opened his mouth to make a taunting reply but thought better of it. "I'm proud of you then. Good day." He touched his hat in a brief salute then turned Diablo toward the east and was gone in an instant.

"I don't believe it, José, he didn't yell at me, not once!"

José laughed at her astonishment. "Let us return home, señorita. I think maybe you could train a man as well as a horse if you but tried." He spurred his horse as he turned away, leaving Flame to stare after him in wonder.

"Train, Joaquin?" What a challenge that would be, she thought. But it would be impossible, he never wanted to please her as Lady did. Then she giggled and

110

could hardly contain her mirth for she was certain he wouldn't care at all for the treats that had made Lady look forward to her company! Lost in thought as they rode home Flame did not see the rabbit dart past until after Lady did. The mare veered sharply to the right, pitching Flame off into the dirt where she lay shaken soundly and badly hurt.

José made no attempt to catch Lady as she streaked by but leapt from his saddle and ran to Flame. She was dirty and crying, holding her hands which had been cruelly cut when she'd tried to break her fall.

"Do not cry, little one. Can you stand up—are only your hands injured?" José was frantic: he'd let her ride the mare and kept a close watch but the rabbit had jumped from its hole before he'd had a chance to warn Flame. He lifted her to her feet but she collapsed against him, too shaken and frightened to walk alone.

José tried to again to reassure Flame, allowing none of his panic to be heard in his voice. "You will be all right, señorita, I will take you home swiftly."

Flame cried all the harder then, she was in such pain from her torn hands but she was far more concerned by what Joaquin's reaction would surely be. "José, don't tell Joaquin what happened, please don't! It was all my fault and not Lady's. I wasn't paying attention, it was my own fault that I'm hurt."

"Let us see to your wounds before we worry about what to tell him." José pulled her up in front of his saddle and put his arms around her waist. She was trembling all over like a motherless fawn and he swore at his own stupidity which had allowed him to be so careless that such an accident had occurred. When they reached the house he carried her into her room then quickly summoned the housekeeper.

Maria talked in a low soothing voice while she worked. The cuts on Flame's hands were deep and would leave scars no matter what she did, but fortunately the gash on her right hand had missed extending to the veins at her wrist. Maria held Flame's hands submerged in a bowl of warm water and hoped that would soak out all the dirt—an infection would be dreadful and she feared the worst even though her words were reassuring. "Do not cry, child. As soon as your hands are clean I will apply some medicines to the cuts, they will stop the pain. Now don't cry, you will make yourself more ill if you do."

In spite of the sympathy she was receiving Flame sobbed on. She cared little that her hands were ruined: her grandmother would have been livid to see her precious grandchild's palms torn to shreds but Flame's only concern was Joaquin's threat. "José, please take Lady and hide her somewhere so Joaquin can't find her. He said he'd shoot her if I got hurt. This wasn't her fault, it was my inattentiveness alone, please help me to hide her. Perhaps if you took her to my ranch and turned her loose there she could escape him."

José was appalled. What had Joaquin done now? Didn't he understand the most basic of emotions? The girl adored him, it was plain to every eye on the ranch but Joaquin's. That man seemed to enjoy torturing the lovely girl with endless threats. "I will see she is safe from harm, do not worry, señorita."

Joaquin leaned back against the bedroom door and watched the scene at Flame's bedside. So she'd been thrown after all. He'd obviously been too quick in his praise, but she didn't appear badly hurt from what he could see. He had just turned to leave when he heard her speak his name in a broken sob and remained to listen. He could not make himself leave then as he realized Flame wasn't crying because she was hurt but because she was terrified of him! He had no idea he had ever intimidated her even to the smallest degree but she

112

was apparently nearly paralyzed with fear now. He felt sick—she had stood up to him all this time, ignored his abuse on so many occasions, and had she always been afraid? He had regarded her as annoyingly obnoxious but that she was afraid of him and defied him all the same showed such courage he could not help but be impressed. When she at last seemed reassured by José's kind promises he walked toward her bed.

"You may leave now, Maria. I will take care of Flame while we talk. I'll speak to you later, José, and I want to find Lady in her stall. Just leave us please." Neither José nor Maria wanted to leave until they realized Joaquin, far from being angry, stood smiling quite warmly at Flame. Then, exchanging knowing glances, the two good friends left quickly.

As soon as they were alone Joaquin took Flame's hands in his and turned them over. Her wounds were far worse than he had anticipated but he tried to hide his shock to keep from frightening her. "Next time you ride Lady wear leather gloves. That will afford your hands some protection when you fall. At least you did not cut your face."

"Next time? Oh Joaquin, then you won't destroy her?" Flame's green eyes were enormous as she looked up at him, her lashes were spiked with tears making them appear even more long and dark than usual.

"Not if what you say is really true. If it was your fault and not hers, I can scarcely punish the mare for her owner's lack of common sense. Now tell me exactly what happened after I left you."

"We were returning home. I was just daydreaming I guess; a rabbit frightened Lady and I fell. But had I been paying strict attention as I should have been it never would have happened. It was entirely my own fault that I fell."

"No, it was mine. I should never have let you talk

113

me into giving her to you in the first place. She's going to do this to you time and again, Flame.''

''I've ridden her all week, Joaquin, she does not shy away without reason, she is a good horse, truly she is.''

Joaquin frowned thoughtfully as he began to apply the salve Maria had made to Flame's cuts. ''When have you been riding her? I've not seen you on her back.''

Flame hesitated to tell him the truth, but knew she must. ''Each morning, I've ridden her bareback in the pasture. I've been going out early before you were awake.''

''Is it even light then? What were you doing, just trying to keep me from stopping you?''

''She is my horse, Joaquin, and I had every right to ride her whenever I chose, but I didn't want to make you angry. I know it was dangerous of me to ride her alone, but it was worth the risk.''

''Surely your poor hands would not agree. How am I ever to find a husband for you when you let your fine skin get covered with freckles and have hands which would make those of my vaqueros look refined?''

Joaquin could not have said anything which would have startled Flame more. ''But I want no husband! Do not tease me, Joaquin, I am not ready to marry—and when I am, I will find my own man. You need not look for one for me.''

''Perhaps you are still too young, but you must think of the future. You do think of it at times, don't you?''

''Yes, of course, but of marriage, never!'' Flame watched his face closely as he bandaged her hands. When he was smiling no man had ever been more handsome. His eyes sparkled with a laughing fire when he looked up at her again and she blushed deeply, certain he could read her thoughts. She had already found the only man she'd ever want to marry: she'd become

114

his wife or stay single forever.

"How are you going to find your man when you have so little opportunity to meet anyone here? I have been most remiss—I think I should give a party. We used to have parties all the time, my father entertained constantly, but that was when I was young, when our life was so pleasant and simple. That was before you were even born, Flame."

"Before California became a state you mean?"

"Yes, when we were allowed to live here as we pleased. California belonged to Mexico then, to us, and things were so much better for us, we were free to live our lives and run our ranches as we chose. Now nothing is as it used to be. That life is gone forever, Flame, but I will always miss it."

Flame was touched by Joaquin's wistful words and when she spoke her voice was barely a whisper. "But we can never go back, Joaquin, we simply can't. I think so often of how different things would have been had I come to see my father just a few weeks earlier . . . he might not have died as he did had I been here."

"Or you might have died with him. Did that thought ever occur to you?" Joaquin was surprised how that thought saddened him, but that wave of emotion did not show in his expression. He merely looked calm, intent upon her reply.

Flame shuddered at his gruesome question. "Then we'd all be dead, all the Lanniers would be gone."

"I'm sorry. I didn't mean to depress you. I am serious about helping you meet people; when you are well I will invite all my friends to come. You'll like them and I'm sure they will like you." Joaquin winked at her and hoped with all his heart that at least one man would like her enough to propose marriage so he could return to the calm, orderly life he'd known before her arrival.

"Would Rafael come if you gave a party?"

115

"Yes, of course he would. Do you want to see him again?" Joaquin finished tying the bandage at her left wrist then leaned back in his chair. Her question had surprised him. When he'd thought of a husband he hadn't even considered Rafael. Why was she so damn fond of him?

"Yes, I *would* like to see him again. He was very sweet to me and taught me so many things about California and my new home."

"He was nicer to you than I am, is that what you mean?" The antagonism was right back in his voice, replacing the affectionate tone he'd used while he tended her wounds.

"Oh Joaquin, I don't feel well enough to fight with you today. You can be so sweet when you want to be . . . thank you for taking care of my hands. That was the nicest thing you've ever done for me, but I would rather rest now than argue with you."

As he stood to leave Joaquin remembered the medicines and stopped to pick them up. "Maria's mother was an Indian—she learned all their ways. She is a wizard at preparing medicines from herbs. Your hands will heal quickly and I hope the scars will not be bad."

"I'm not worried. Scars do not upset me." Flame lay back against her pillows and yawned sleepily. She ached all over and was filled with a tiredness too great to fight any longer.

"You rest then. Only your hands were harmed, you suffered no other injuries?"

"Everything hurts, Joaquin. I have never been so bruised."

"Will you admit now that I was right?" He knew his question was a foolish one but he couldn't resist asking it—she might possibly admit defeat in her present mood.

"No, and it would take worse than this to change my

116

mind." Flame lifted her chin proudly.

"I will tell Maria to mix up more of her potions then, for I fear you are in for a lot of cuts and bruises."

"It would not be so bad if you would continue to be my doctor." Flame smiled up at him as she drifted off to sleep. "You are a wonderful doctor, Joaquin, so very gentle, thank you."

"You're welcome, now go to sleep, Flame, I think you are becoming delirious. I am no doctor and I'll let Maria care for you the next time you're thrown."

Flame hastened to disagree: "But I wasn't thrown, I fell."

"Whatever. . . . Save your pride if you must, but we both know the truth about what happened. But I am curious, was your daydream worth all this pain?"

A lovely smile curved across Flame's pretty mouth as she replied, "Yes, it was a wonderful dream, but I will not let my mind wander again. I will pay strict attention tomorrow."

"Surely you don't plan to ride Lady tomorrow, not with those hands!"

"Yes I will, I will ride her, you'll see."

"Flame, can't you give up now? Doesn't what happened today make you want to quit all this foolishness?"

Flame sat up in her bed and glared angrily at him. "Have you ever in all your life quit on anything, Joaquin?"

"No, of course not, and you wouldn't either would you? I should have known. Just go to sleep and tomorrow I'll make it a point to see the bandages are ready. Sweet dreams."

Joaquin closed her bedroom door quietly, returned Maria's supplies to the kitchen, then went outside to find his foreman. He listened patiently as José gave his account of what had happened, a version that was identical to Flame's. "That's what she told me too, José, but daydreaming? Whatever could she have been thinking about with such concentration?"

"I can think of only one thing that interests pretty young women, Joaquin, and you must know what that is."

"Men, you mean? There are no young men around here worth dreaming about, José."

"There is one." José grinned as he saw from his boss's startled expression that at last he understood, then he broke out in loud laughter.

"That's enough, José, you must have some work to do, go and see to it!" Joaquin tried to ignore José's taunt but he couldn't. Damn it all, how was he to get rid of Flame? He went into the barn and saddled Lady again and was surprised that in spite of his heavier weight the mare was still swift. She gave him no problems as he rode her that afternoon and when he returned her to the barn he was satisfied she was as good a mount as Flame had claimed.

The next morning he watched the lovely golden-haired girl ride out with José. The pain had been so clear in her expression and still she had gone riding. Joaquin shook his head in dismay and strode back into his house. Flame would be well worth the trouble it would take to tame her, but since he'd not take on the challenge himself he prayed one of his friends would. Then a thought crossed his mind like a sudden shadow obscures the moon: any man but Rafael. He would never give her to him.

Eight

Flame was overjoyed to see Rafael again. She hadn't been at all sure he would come despite Joaquin's repeated assurances that he would. Rafael was so serious—she was certain he wasn't the type to enjoy parties. But Flame was mistaken, for Rafael Ramirez loved parties of every sort . . . but then he would have come to see her no matter what the excuse had been.

Joaquin walked off in disgust when Flame threw herself into his old friend's arms. He was mad at her again for her affectionate, endearing ways and if he'd only admitted to himself, he was jealous too. So he strode off sulking as he went to greet the next arrivals, saddened when Flame gave to another man the affection he refused to allow her to give to him.

"I was so afraid you wouldn't be able to come, Rafael, I've missed you so dreadfully."

Rafael laughed as Flame hugged him warmly but the squeeze he gave her in return was only a brotherly one. "What have you been doing, Flame? Have you gotten accustomed to your new home?"

Flame's enthusiastic gaze darkened instantly and she turned away to hide her disappointment as they walked into the house. "I love California, the ranch is so very beautiful, and I have my own horse now, an Appaloosa mare who is a delight to ride."

Rafael caught her hand quickly. "Wait, Flame, that

wasn't the intent of my question. Are you happy here, content?''

Flame moved away from him, afraid to reply until she realized she'd never fool him and shouldn't even try. "Joaquin hates me, Rafael. He doesn't want me here, but when I ask to go to my own home, to rebuild my father's house, he refuses to allow it.''

"As well he should. You don't want to live all alone. You could never manage a ranch by yourself, Flame."

"Why not? It would be better than listening to Joaquin criticize me from dawn to dusk. I'm not wanted here, Rafael, not at all. I've been so terribly lonely and I thought you might never come back to see me."

"You've made no friends?''

"Only one, Suzanna Lewis, do you remember her, the minister's daughter? Joaquin said I might invite her to come for the party this weekend but her father wouldn't allow it. He refuses to let her visit me here so we can talk only after church on Sundays. I've met no one else my age since I arrived.''

"That's why Joaquin has invited everyone here this weekend, isn't it? We have many relatives and friends, dozens of them. You needn't be so alone, Flame. Now try not to be so critical of Joaquin, I know he means well.''

"I don't belong here, Rafael. Just look at me—do I resemble any of your relatives, even one?''

Rafael smiled. Flame was gorgeous all the time, but especially so when she was angry. Her eyes glowed with a green brilliance and her once ivory skin had turned to a pale gold from the California sunshine. "Why would you wish to resemble us, Flame? You are so beautiful just as you are, perfection.''

Flame's pretty mouth fell open in surprise. "Why Rafael, are you trying to flirt with me?''

"Do you wish me to?''

"What do you think?" Flame stepped closer to her friend, then lay her head against his chest as her arms encircled his waist. "Please hold me for a moment, Rafael, just hold me." Flame wanted reassurance his words were true. Since she had so few friends, his compassion meant a great deal to her.

Rafael was more shocked than he'd thought possible, but she'd caught him completely off guard. The sweet perfume of her golden hair assailed his senses, creating a longing he couldn't deny and which she would soon know about if he didn't put more space between them. He took her hands from around his body and directed her toward a chair. "Sit down, Flame. Tell me what is wrong."

"Everything. This wasn't my dream, Rafael. I only wanted to come home, to be happy in my father's house, to live my own life without being forced into situations I could neither handle nor control."

"What are you talking about, Flame, what situations?" Rafael wiped his forehead with his handkerchief and prayed Flame would not notice his discomfort or have any idea of its real cause.

Flame had no desire to even think of Alex Richmond, let alone repeat that ghastly story. "It's not important now, my grandmother had made plans for my life in which I had no say, but Joaquin is every bit as bad, he's far worse than she was actually."

"Now, Flame, Joaquin never expected to be responsible for you. This has probably been a far greater shock to him than to you."

"That is impossible!" Flame hadn't meant to be so rude and was instantly sorry. "Forgive me, Rafael, but what am I to do?"

"Let's enjoy ourselves this weekend, Flame. Joaquin gives wonderful parties, just relax and have a good time. Everyone will love you, I know they will."

"There are so many guests here already, Rafael, how many did Joaquin invite?"

"Probably he did not even count, but he'll keep everyone busy. The men like to have races and there are a lot of games we used to play on horseback which I am certain someone will insist we play again."

"What of the women—none of them like to ride with the men, to join in the fun?" Flame had not even bothered to ask Joaquin if she might not race Lady, she knew what his response would be without having to ask.

"Certainly not. The sports are much too dangerous, as you will see—but don't worry, they're exciting to watch and there will be dancing at night. I'm sure you must like to dance, don't you?"

"Yes, I love to dance, but I'm afraid I won't know any of the dances you do here. I asked Joaquin to teach me some but he refused, as always. He refuses every request I make."

Rafael ignored her sarcasm. "We will all teach you then. I will probably be lucky to have even one dance with you."

Flame grew puzzled. "Do you like to dance, Rafael?"

"Why yes, of course, why wouldn't I?"

"I know you don't like me to touch you, you always push me away when I do, as you did just now. How can you bear to dance?"

Her question stunned him, was that what she thought of him? That he couldn't bear her touch when the lightest caress of her hand set his blood on fire? He was so digusted with himself he turned away, unable to respond.

"Rafael?" Flame waited for him to speak but when he did she was astonished by his anger.

"You are mistaken, Flame. I like your touch, I like

everything about you. You mean more to me than you'll ever know. I realize women find me a trifle stiff, I do not have Joaquin's easy affection, but that does not mean that I don't care for you!''

"You think Joaquin is affectionate?'' As soon as she'd asked her question the beauty of the morning they'd met came back to her with sparkling clarity. Yes, Joaquin was marvelously affectionate when he wanted to be, only now he didn't want her!

"Flame, will you stop to think for a moment, he is your guardian. That is a different relationship, he would not treat you as he does other women.'' Rafael was totally frustrated now, he had told her how he felt about her and she had promptly changed the subject to Joaquin as if he did not even exist!

"But I am a woman, don't you see that I am either? He is my guardian and you are too shy. Is there never going to be a man who will love me as I want to be loved?''

As Flame ran from the room Rafael had no desire to follow. If he had been too formal, too proper a gentleman, it was only out of respect for her. Whatever did the girl want from him? He had offered affection, she had said that's what she wanted but she ignored his feelings for her. Rafael swore as he got to his feet— there was no way to please a woman, none, and he had been a fool to try.

Her eyes filled with tears, Flame did not even see Joaquin moving down the hall until it was too late. He grabbed her shoulders quickly to keep her from falling but his touch was far from gentle and his words were harsh. "Ah, here you are, Flame, walking gracefully through my home like the perfect lady you always are.''

Flame was ready to kick her guardian in his blasted shins when she realized he was not alone. A tall raven-haired young woman stood by his side and her expression was anything but friendly.

"So this is your little waif. I think she's rather cute, Joaquin. She has a pathetic quality about her that is almost endearing, pobrecita."

"Pathetic! This must be one of your relatives, Joaquin. Surely you don't have such tactless friends!" Flame pushed herself away from him and stood in a defiant pose ready to slap the obnoxious brunette should she dare insult her again.

Joaquin's mellow laugh distracted Flame momentarily and she looked up to see him grin. "This is my cousin, Maria Elena, I thought she and her two sisters would be most comfortable in your room while they are here."

"Really, and where did you plan to put me? Not in your room I hope!"

"Lord no! Your room is large enough for twice that amount, Flame. You won't even be crowded, and I thought you would like having their company. Try and make my cousins feel at home while they are here. Now where is Rafael?"

"He was in your study a moment ago, shall I call him for you?"

"No, I'll find him myself while you show Maria Elena where to put her belongings." Joaquin moved on down the hall, leaving Flame to cope with his cousin on her own.

"My room is just down this way. Do you and your sisters have much luggage to bring in?"

"Enough." Maria Elena had disliked Flame on sight, she was far too beautiful not to be considered a rival and Maria Elena wanted no competition when it came to the men she wanted. She observed Flame closely as they walked along but she could find no flaw. The girl's petite figure was perfect, her skin lovely and her hair so glorious a shade Maria Elena knew all the men would be enchanted by her. She surveyed her bedroom with a jaundiced eye. "This is your room, Flame? I'm surprised Joaquin didn't give you one of the nicer bedrooms."

Flame recognized jealousy when she heard it and ignored the haughty girl's taunt. "This one is more than adequate for my needs."

Maria Elena walked around the room slowly, then stopped at the dresser to look over Flame's silver-handled hairbrush. "You must find it difficult to live here with Joaquin. Isn't he very strict with you?"

"Why no, he is the most generous and sympathetic of guardians. My own father could not love me more and I couldn't be happier than I am living here with him." Flame could scarcely keep her face straight as she complimented Joaquin but it was worth it to see the effect her words had on Maria Elena: the girl looked ready to choke.

"Is that the truth? I never would have realized it of Joaquin, he hardly seems the fatherly type. What do you think of Rafael? Do you find him sympathetic also?"

Flame smiled warmly at the prying girl. "Rafael is a wonderful man as you probably know, he is so warm and affectionate." She stopped and adjusted her bodice with a knowing glance. "Almost too affectionate I could say, but you must know how charming and loving he is."

Maria Elena stared at Flame and as her shock at the meaning of the stunning girl's comments spread through her she gasped, "Rafael? Surely he has always behaved as a gentleman toward you!"

"Oh forgive me, Maria Elena, I see you do not know Rafael nearly as well as I thought you might. But believe me, he is well worth the trouble of getting to know." Flame walked to the door then turned back for a moment. "Put your things wherever you like, I'll go and find your sisters." She slammed the door as she went out. Why in heaven's name would Joaquin have given her such a bitch for a roommate? She hoped the sisters were an improvement but they could hardly be any worse! She laughed to herself as she went outside— Maria Elena had believed every word she had said, what a fool.

Dolores and Lorena at seventeen and eighteen were both older than Flame but they were cute and friendly, with none of their older sister's spiteful disposition. Unfortunately, neither could speak more than the briefest of sentences in English and Maria Elena seemed only too happy to converse entirely in Spanish, effectively leaving Flame out of their conversations. Even though the others fell asleep quickly, Flame could not. She had never spent a night with another person in her room, let alone in her bed, and although her bed was large the three extra girls made it crowded. When she could stand no more she took her pillow and left her room.

Once out in the hall Flame hesitated. If Rafael were in the same room he had occupied before he had a small couch he might let her have for the night. She tiptoed down the hall and was just ready to knock at his door when Joaquin came out of his room. He was handsomely dressed in the grey wool suit he'd worn for dinner, he was about to join several of his friends in a game of cards and wasn't at all pleased to discover Flame wandering about his house in her nightgown.

"Why are you out of your room at this hour, Flame?"

"Oh Joaquin, I can't sleep with those other girls in my bed. Perhaps you are all used to large families but I am not and I can't get to sleep."

"So you planned to spend the night in Rafael's bed? My God, Flame, do you never consider your actions

126

before you take them? Go back to your own room this instant!''

''No, I won't go back in there. I'll sleep in the barn with Lady if I have to but my room is too crowded and I'll not go back there.'' Flame clutched her pillow tightly as she argued with Joaquin but it scarcely hid the alluring curves of her figure which were readily apparent under her sheer nightgown.

If the erotic nature of her pose escaped Flame's notice it most certainly wasn't lost on Joaquin and he gestured quickly, ''Get in here then!'' He opened his door and waited for her to proceed him into his room. ''You take my bed for the time being and I will sleep elsewhere.''

''You have a large bed, Joaquin, there is more than enough room for both of us, I will be happy to share it with you.'' Flame smiled sweetly at her guardian as she turned back the covers.

''Flame, so help me, one of these days I'm simply going to wring your pretty neck and be done with you! Now go to sleep, I'll see you in the morning.'' Joaquin slammed his door as he left but Flame only laughed at his anger. His bed was very comfortable and she was asleep in seconds.

Joaquin returned just before dawn and stood looking down at Flame. She seemed so small as she lay curled up in his large bed that he hesitated to wake her. A smile played across his lips as he wondered how much effort it would take to wake her—did she wake up suddenly or would it take some time to remove her from his bed? He sat down beside her and traced a line down her cheek with his fingertips and although she smiled slightly she did not stir. Joaquin looked at her sweet mouth and leaned down to kiss her lightly. Flame turned over but was still sound asleep. The game was proving far too intriguing for Joaquin to stop now so he began to push her hair gently away from her face and leaned down again to kiss her. This time he put far more pressure on her lips before moving away.

Flame often dreamed of Joaquin, he filled her thoughts during the day so completely it was not surprising that his image also filled her nights. She recognized his kiss even when she was sound asleep and could not help smiling as she whispered his name softly.

Joaquin sat up quickly. What had possessed him to kiss Flame? Even in her dreams she had known it was he and he stood quickly then leaned down to shake her shoulder roughly. "Wake up, Flame, I want you to go back to your own bed now. All I need is gossip that you share my bed, now hurry up!"

Half asleep, Flame returned to her own bed and lay down on the narrow portion that was left to her. Her head had not touched the pillow, however, before Maria Elena's vicious whisper reached her ears.

"You just wait until I tell Joaquin about you! You weren't in your bed all night! You just wait until he hears about that, you little tramp!"

Flame turned her head and smiled. "Who's bed do you think I've been in!" Flame shut her eyes and tried to recapture the dream she'd been having before Joaquin had awakened her. It had been so real, it had seemed as if he'd kissed her and she loved his kiss so. But it had only been a dream, just a dream, and she was asleep again before she realized this time it had been real.

Sleep eluded Maria Elena. She was so shocked she couldn't bear it—first Rafael and now Joaquin! Tears began to fill her eyes as she realized her jealousy had far more grounds than she'd thought possible when she'd first met the stunning red-haired girl. As Flame slept peacefully Maria Elena lay in torment until the rest of the household began to stir, her mind filled with dire

128

thoughts supplied by her own wicked imagination and Flame's taunting innuendos. She hated Flame then as much as she had ever hated anyone and vowed to get even with her the first chance she had.

In spite of his bitter disappointment the previous afternoon, Rafael found himself waiting for Flame that morning. "Come with me, Flame, I will take you on my horse out to where the races will be run." He was dressed in a similar fashion as the other young men, in the same styles the rancheros had worn for generations. The outside seams of his black wool trousers were laced with silver cord from hip to knee but then allowed to flare out revealing the bright red lining. His serape was a snowy white banded with red at each end. Flame thought him quite a dashing figure and gave him her hand. He removed his sash which he then knotted to form a loop which he hung over his saddle horn for her foot. "You sit in front of me and I'll hold you. Just place your foot in the loop and it will be like riding side-saddle which I know you hate but you have no choice today." His smile was engaging even if his words were teasing and Flame quickly joined him on the back of his mount. The other young men all seemed to have found partners to escort in the same manner but when Flame saw Maria Elena with Joaquin her good spirits disappeared.

"Rafael, is Maria Elena only a cousin, or is she something more to Joaquin? Is she his girl too?" She was almost afraid to hear his answer but had to know.

"She is a cousin, that is true, but men have been known to marry their cousins in the past."

"Oh." Flame leaned back against Rafael's shoulder and tried to think. "Is it all arranged, settled perhaps? He plans to marry her?"

"No, Joaquin has no plans to marry that I know of, but what Maria Elena may be planning could be some-

thing else again. She is very pretty don't you think?"
Rafael smiled down at Flame but he could tell by her
downcast expression that she was miserable. "Flame,
she is not nearly so pretty as you."

"Thank you." Flame tried to return his smile and as
they rode along in silence she remembered the races. "I
didn't think you would want to take part today, Rafael,
but since you are dressed as the others, are you going to
race?"

"I still own the clothes if no longer a ranch, but truly
I hate doing this now."

Flame turned to glance up at his face and was surprised by his bitter scowl, his anger was too fierce to ignore. We are a fine pair she thought, a woman who
wants to be with another man and a man who does not
want to be here at all! "This hurts you doesn't it? Joaquin talks about how things were when he was a child,
so much better than now in his view. Do you think that
too?"

"No, I would go crazy if I did, but the past is no
more and I can no longer pretend to be a ranchero. Joaquin is not pretending, this is his life and he wants it.
You are very perceptive at times, Flame. Yes, this
hurts me, it hurts very much."

Flame covered his hands with hers. "Then let's not
go with the others, I'll get Lady and we'll go riding by
ourselves. We can talk about whatever we want. We
need pay no attention to what the others are doing."

Rafael shook his head emphatically. "No, Joaquin
wants everyone to meet you, Flame. I cannot take up
all of your time, no matter how much I would like to do
so."

"You said the sports were too dangerous for women.
Does that mean they are hazardous for the men as
well?"

"Yes, we will be fortunate indeed if no one is seriously injured today.''

"Rafael, you don't want to do this and yet you will even though it is dangerous? Why?''

"I have no choice, Flame, none.''

"That can't be true. Surely you may refuse to participate.''

"And appear to be a coward? I would never do that, not in front of you, my Flame.''

Flame's pretty eyes swept his somber expression slowly before she replied. He looked different that day—it wasn't just his clothes, but the look deep in his eyes which was new. She had enough sadness in her own life to read his despair with ease. "I'm so sorry for the way I treated you yesterday. You were not being shy with me at all and I was unforgivably rude to you. I am so pleased that you like me and I would never think you a coward. If you must do anything today then do it for your own pride, but not to impress me. I don't want to see you hurt, please don't risk your life on my account. I will go back home right now, I won't even watch. If all this is only to gain my respect you needn't bother, for you already have it.''

"We are nearly there, Flame, and neither of us is turning back. Do not worry, I will not be hurt, I am almost as fine a rider as Joaquin. In spite of my dislike for these childish games I am quite good. You must wait and see.''

When they arrived at the chosen site Flame slid down from Rafael's horse and walked over to join the other young women. They were all chattering excitedly in Spanish and Flame soon gave up trying to understand them. Very few seemed to speak English and those who did refused like Maria Elena to do so. Flame was alone for no more than a few seconds before she found herself surrounded with more attentive company than she had thought possible. Not every man participated in every

131

race and she never had fewer than three young men smiling and talking with her in a most charming fashion. They were all dark like Joaquin and Rafael, with black laughing eyes and white teeth which sparkled as they grinned. Flame had never met more handsome or charming young men and she had a wonderful time although she knew the outcome of not a single race.

Joaquin pushed his hat back on his head and glared. Flame had not so much as glanced in his direction all morning. She seemed to be having such a good time talking to Gabriel Alvarado—perhaps his plan was working as well as he had hoped, but still, he was disappointed to find she had not even taken the time to tell him good morning. He began to swear as he recalled the way Maria Elena had spoken to him, she was apparently furious with him and wouldn't even explain why!

"Joaquin, tienes los gallos?"

Flame turned when she heard her guardian's name being called and wondered what on earth the men planned to do with roosters. "Gabriel, did he ask Joaquin for roosters? I'm just learning Spanish and I get most things hopelessly confused. I must have misunderstood what he said."

"No, señorita, you understood the man, come and watch. This is an exciting game." Gabriel led Flame to where the crowd had begun to gather. José had buried a rooster in the sand so only his head and neck were exposed.

"What ever are they going to do with that poor bird, Gabriel?" Flame had to stand on her tiptoes to see through the people in front of her, but she could think of no sport that required a half buried rooster.

"The goal is to ride by as fast as one can, lean down and pull the rooster out of the sand and carry him to the finish line." Gabriel gestured as he spoke, directing

132

Flame's attention to a group of riders some distance away.

"You're not serious!"

"But I am, it is an old game, carrera del gallo, but it is a difficult one. If a man grabs too soon or too late he may fall."

Flame turned away quickly and hid her eyes. "I don't think I want to watch."

Gabriel laughed at her fear. "Everyone will expect you to watch, señorita. We only do this to impress the women, you must know that."

Flame peeked up at him through her fingers. "Will Joaquin do it?"

Gabriel shrugged, "Only if no one else can succeed. He can do it too easily, it is no sport for him and he is too polite a host to shame his guests in such a fashion."

"There is a trick to it then?"

"Yes, the timing is the key, but you will be more impressed later when Joaquin will cape the bull. You see the longhorn in the corral?"

"Good lord, you mean bullfighting?" Flames eyes widened in terror: the ferocious beast was pawing the ground sullenly, obviously in no mood to be teased.

"Señorita, you must not be so frightened, it is merely for fun, we find it amusing and the bull is not harmed."

"But surely there are other less dangerous amusements!" Flame looked up at Gabriel more closely, then realized with a start that his eyes were green, almost the same shade as hers. "Why Gabriel, your eyes are like mine!"

"Yes, it would appear so. Not all of us are dark. Flame; not all the Californios look the same. My mother is as fair as you are."

"Well, you may not all look the same, but you are all exceedingly handsome." Flame was charmed by the at-

133

tentive young man whose gaze was so like her own. She was about to speak again when the crowd began to roar as the first rider to try for the rooster came by. He came close but missed the bird by at least a foot and although he didn't fall he was met with jeers from those at the end of the route. The next four riders had no better luck and Flame relaxed a bit. None had fallen and if the men could take the ridicule then perhaps there was nothing so hazardous in the game except for the danger to the poor rooster.

Gabriel took her arm and motioned toward the next rider. "Now you will see how it should be done. They have talked Rafael into having a turn. I think he is even better than Joaquin—he has a smoother style. Just watch."

Flame's heart caught in her throat. She knew Rafael's horse to be fast, surely too swift for this sport. He could fall and be killed so quickly, and all for a silly contest she knew he didn't even want to enter. She clutched Gabriel's arm, too terrified to turn away yet too horrified to watch.

Gabriel's description had been accurate, even in the saddle Rafael possessed the grace of a mountain cat. As his mount thundered past the crowd he leaned down and scooped up the rooster easily from the sand, returned instantly to his saddle with the squawking bird still held tightly in his right hand, then streaked on to the end of the course.

Flame nearly fainted with relief. She pushed to the back of the crowd and ran down to the end of the race course where Rafael was being congratulated by the group of men on horseback. She ran between their horses up to Rafael and touched his knee to get his attention. Her eyes shone brightly as she smiled up at him. "That was wonderful, Rafael, truly it was, but I was so frightened for you!" The men laughed at her remarks and began to tease Rafael but Flame ignored them and waited patiently for him to speak.

Rafael tossed the enraged cock to one of his companions, then jumped down from his horse. "I told you I was good, you did not believe me?"

"Yes, I believed you but please don't do anything else. I can't bear to watch when I'm so frightened you will be hurt, or worse."

"But you did watch me, Flame, you did watch me just now, didn't you?"

"Yes, and I would have come to you now no matter what the outcome. I'm glad you succeeded, but I would not have laughed had you failed."

Rafael frowned as he turned to remount his horse. "Perhaps you have been too busy this morning to have noticed, but I am a grown man and not a boy and I do not often fail. I will not fail today, do not worry about me any longer. My safety is not your concern."

Flame watched in silence as Rafael leapt upon his horse and sped away. She thought he would be pleased with her praise and couldn't understand his anger. She knew only too well he was a grown man, in his thirties while she was but sixteen. She fought back her tears as she turned but found Gabriel Alvarado blocking her way.

"Be careful with that one, señorita. My father says he is the most dangerous of men, one with nothing to risk but his life. Do you know him well? I saw you with him this morning. Does Joaquin approve of him as your escort?"

"What are you talking about, Gabriel? Rafael is an attorney and a successful one. I've been in his office in San Francisco. He is no reckless fool. Why would Joaquin object to him? They are close friends."

"Just be careful, that is all. Joaquin is going to fight the bull, do you want to come and see?"

"No!" Flame's disgust was clear in her horrified expression.

"You may not want to, but you will." Gabriel offered his arm and Flame took it after a brief hesitation.

"By all means, Joaquin is a grown man and can take care of himself, why should I worry over him?"

"He will not kill the bull, señorita, that is not the sport here, only to attract the bull to his cape and then to maneuver his horse out of the way of the horns."

Flame halted abruptly. "Fight the bull on horseback, on Diablo, that's what he'll do?"

"Yes, but Joaquin always wins, a bull has never touched him. Diablo is swift and has great stamina, it is hardly a fair contest."

"The bull has such sharp horns, Gabriel." Flame leaned against the corral and watched as the crowd drifted over to form a ring around the circular enclosure. The bull looked enormous and his long horns wickedly sharp.

Gabriel pointed to a large group of mounted riders near the gate, yelling insults to one another in a boisterous but friendly manner. "The men on horseback will try and catch the bull when Joaquin gives the signal to open the gate. They'll try and catch him by the tail and flip him into the air."

"Gabriel, will you please stop, I don't believe any of this."

"You will, just watch, they are ready to begin, here is Joaquin." Gabriel nodded toward the gate and Flame turned to look.

Joaquin rode Diablo so easily there seemed to be no distinction between the man and the magnificent black stallion. He had such great skill, but Flame thought only of how handsome he looked, so tall and proud . . . but she was afraid for him, really afraid: why would he risk his life and that of his fine horse for these few minutes of glory? Then following Joaquin four other horsemen entered the corral but they moved back against the sides out of Joaquin's way. Flame's glance swept over the men, then stopped. The last man to enter the ring was Rafael.

"Oh no." Flame couldn't bear this, not both of them.

"Señorita? They are only to assist should something go wrong, should Joaquin fall from his horse." Gabriel whispered so as not to disturb the concentration of those around them.

"He will not fall." Flame gripped the rough rail of the corral and hoped she would not faint. She imagined little bits of Joaquin flying in all directions as the bull gored him and shuddered violently, yet she couldn't turn away. If Joaquin wanted to kill himself she wanted to be there to see him do it.

The corrida de toros was the favorite sport of the crowd and except for the soft thud of Diablo's hooves upon the dirt there was not another sound as all ears strained to hear, every eye focused on the massive bull, waiting for him to charge. Joaquin rode Diablo up to the belligerent beast, closer and closer until at last he spun the horse around sending Diablo's long tail flying across the surprised bull's nose. The bull sprang after Diablo and Joaquin scarcely needed the red cape to attract his attention. He turned Diablo into a tight figure eight pattern and the bull appeared to be gaining ground but it was only an illusion, the bull could have run for hours and got no closer to Diablo than the coarse strands of his flying tail. The game continued for a short time with the bull stopping as he pawed the ground then Joaquin would come back, inch closer until the bull would give chase but then Diablo would spring from his path and with agile steps he avoided the bull's sharp horns at each turn. Then without warning

137

the bull's tactics changed swiftly, he stood snorting one moment then exploded in a wild burst of speed at an angle after the man and horse who were tormenting him. Diablo had great speed, but it was not enough and disaster seemed imminent as the bull charged them, his head down, horns aimed for Diablo's gleaming black hide and Joaquin's knee. Someone screamed and Flame wanted only to close her eyes to force away the ghastly scene which was sure to happen from her mind. She didn't see Rafael dash by until his cape caught the bull's horns snapping the animal's neck sharply to the left giving Joaquin the extra seconds he needed to escape unharmed. Suddenly the excitment of the corrida turned to terror and people began to yell for the men to open the gate but Joaquin waved them off.

"He can't continue, not after that!" Flame could not believe what she saw, yet it was plain Joaquin had no intention of quitting as yet.

"I would not, señorita, but I am not Joaquin Villarreal and he has barely begun. Rafael saved him that time, as you said he is a good friend to have, but you must agree now that he is reckless."

"Brave, or heroic yes, but reckless no." Flame was so lost in the game being played before her eyes she cared little what Gabriel thought. Again and again Joaquin approached the savage bull but the animal's reactions were unpredictable. He would ignore Joaquin for minutes at a time only to explode in another blinding flash when next the urge struck him. At last the bull began to tire and Joaquin toyed with him, leading him around in graceful figures which Diablo's hooves traced in the dirt until at last Joaquin gave the signal to open the gate. The crowd of riders let out great whoops and shouts as they dashed off in mad pursuit of the bull who made a drive for freedom with the considerable strength still left in his powerful hulk.

While the crowd applauded and cheered for Joaquin, Flame could not. When he glanced around the corral he spotted her brilliant red hair easily but her head was down, resting upon her arms, she had not been watching at all that he could tell. Had she seen any of it? He waited for her to come to congratulate him as he had seen her go to Rafael but she made no move to do so. When Gabriel led her away from the corral she went without a backward glance and Joaquin cursed as he leapt from Diablo's back. He wanted to make certain the stallion had not been touched by the bull's horns and ran his fingertips over the horse's sweat-drenched hide but he was frowning angrily all the while. He knew Flame had not been pleased and he was disappointed not to have impressed her, not to have heard her voice raised in a cheer for him.

Rafael dismounted also and led his horse over to the side of the corral where Joaquin stood. "It was a bad bull, my friend, he came too close to goring Diablo and he would have had your right leg as well."

"Had it not been for you, Rafael, you have saved my life. I will not do this again, the prospect of losing a leg was too real to be lightly regarded. This was a warning and I will heed it. This was my last corrida."

"We are getting old, Joaquin, we are becoming cautious and therefore old, we should quit now before our caution makes us vulnerable. No one will ever call you a coward after what you have done here today, you need prove yourself never again."

Joaquin straightened up and put his hand on Rafael's shoulder. "I do not thank you often enough for all you do for me, thank you for being here today to help me."

Rafael made a slight bow. "It was worth the trip, Joaquin, if you were not injured."

"Except for my pride!" Joaquin dusted off his pants

and grinned at his friend. "But pride is a small thing when the choice was a leg and the life of the finest horse in all of California!" The two old friends led their mounts out of the corral but each looked for Flame without success. She had already returned to the house where she was violently ill and then fell sound asleep in the middle of her bed and not even the return of her new roommates woke her.

The musicians were beginning to play and still there was no sign of Flame, Joaquin searched the faces in the gathering without success, she was simply not there. He hadn't seen her since he'd come back to the house late that afternoon and he could not imagine what was keeping her from joining the party. It was after all in her honor and he knew she had the good sense to know she was supposed to attend. When he saw Maria Elena nearby he walked to her side to inquire, "Have you seen Flame? Is she still getting dressed?" Joaquin had spent a good deal of time getting ready for the party himself that evening so he could appreciate a woman's need for more time. The silver trim on his elegant suit shone as the result of many hours of polishing, several he had put in himself when Maria had grown too busy to complete the job and he would trust the work to no one else. He was satisfied he looked his best, he had never been more lean and fit and the excitment which lit his dark eyes made his deeply tanned skin glow with health. He had grown accustomed to being handsome in his early teens and no longer considered his appearance a particular point of pride, but he knew it had its uses, especially on a night like this one when beautiful young women were in plentiful supply. But damn it all, where was Flame?

"She was still asleep when we left her room, perhaps she still is, Joaquin. I think it must have been the sun, she is such a pale little thing, I don't believe she had the strength to watch you all day as the rest of us did."

"You did not try to awaken her, to help her to dress?"

"Of course not, I am not her maid." Maria Elena smiled coyly at her handsome cousin as she ran her fingers down the silken braid which trimmed his jacket. "Let her sleep, we do not need her here tonight."

Joaquin pushed her hands away rudely and strode off through the guests back into his house. When there was no answer at Flame's door he turned the knob and peered in. She was still sleeping just as Maria Elena had said. "Flame?" He called her name again and when she did not respond entered the room pausing to close the door behind him before he lit the lamp beside her bed. Even in the dim light he could see the streaks her tears had made as they had run down her cheeks. Had she taken ill? He longed to lean down and kiss her as he had done before dawn but put his hand on her shoulder and shook her gently instead. "Flame, wake up, it's late." He was greatly relieved when she began to stir, slowly at first, stretching as she yawned, but then she was wide awake with her luminous green eyes staring up at him in surprise.

"Are you all right? You've already missed dinner and have little time to dress before the dancing begins. I kept expecting you to appear at any moment. Were you so tired you would have slept the night through had I not come for you?"

Flame sat up and pushed her long hair away from her face but she didn't answer, merely stared at the man she loved as if she wished to memorize each detail of his face. His smile was so pleasant, she wanted only to reach out and hug him, to hold him and tell him how frightened she had been and how happy she was to find him safe. Yet she dared say nothing and so just sat looking up at him until he began to laugh.

"What is it, Flame, what's the matter, didn't you enjoy yourself today?"

"No! Not one bit, how can you laugh when you were almost killed? How could you call that mere sport when the bull came so close to killing you?"

"As you can see I am quite well, the bull did not give me so much as a scratch in spite of your fears."

"Only because Rafael saved your neck! You came too close to death today, Joaquin, for me to have enjoyed the sight." Flame shuddered again as she thought of the tragedy which had been so narrowly averted.

"Is that what upset you? You were worried about me." Joaquin reached out and traced the line her tears had made on her freckled cheeks. "Or perhaps it was Rafael you were more concerned about."

"You are both fools! I wish you had never invited your friends to come here, they are a bloodthirsty lot but I am not." She knew she hadn't answered his question but what was the point, he didn't want to hear her say she loved him, and that hurt all the more. He might have died that day and she would never have had the chance to tell him how very much she loved him. Her eyes began to fill with tears again and she tried to brush them away before he could see.

"Flame?" Joaquin lifted her chin with his fingertips and looked down at her pretty face with a puzzled expression on his own. "Don't weep for me when I am still alive and well."

Flame pushed his hand away quickly, embarrassed that he had understood her so well even without her offering an explanation. "You frightened me, Joaquin, you really did. I was so afraid I would lose you."

"I have never encountered such a bad bull, he was not so erratic when I chose him. Perhaps the crowd upset him, I had few problems with him when we practiced during the week."

142

"Joaquin, you have been in that ring working with that blasted bull all week!" Flame's eyes widened in terror, if she had seen him in the corral with a bull she never would have left the house that day.

"Yes, of course, I do not do this so often that I can trust Diablo not to leap the fence at the first sight of the bull. He needs the practice far more than I."

"He shows more sense than you if he knows he should jump the fence rather than risk his hide! If you care nothing for your own skin you should at least consider his. He is a magnificent stallion, much too fine to risk so foolishly."

Joaquin smiled slyly as he agreed with her. "Yes, you are right, I will not do it ever again."

"What, are you agreeing with me?" Flame was astonished, but she had no hope that Joaquin would make any decision simply to please her.

"Yes I am, but think how rich you'd be if that bull had gotten me, since I have no other children you are my heir."

Flame shook her bright curls as she argued with his logic. "I am no child of yours, Joaquin Villarreal, and I don't want a cent of your fortune. It is not something to make light of. Do not tease me like that."

"I am not teasing you—ask Rafael, you will inherit everything when I die. Now enough of this morbid conversation, you are not too upset to dance are you? Many men will be disappointed if you are."

"And you?" When Flame smiled up at him coyly he began to laugh again.

"Yes, I most of all. Now hurry up and dress, I can not stall the musicians much longer."

"All right, I'll hurry." Then Flame remembered and called after him, "May I sleep in your bed again tonight?"

Joaquin paused, resting his hand on the door handle.

"Flame, did you tell Maria Elena about that, is that why she is so angry with me?"

Flame's voice was a coquettish purr as she responded innocently, "What was I to say when she threatened to tell you I had not been in my own bed most of the night?"

"So you told her I already knew where you'd been, didn't you?"

"It seemed to be the only way I could save my reputation, Joaquin. She had already called me a tramp, but I did not say you were in your bed with me, that was her own conclusion."

"Let's just hope she's so mad she won't spread such gossip, Flame. You'd better pray she keeps her mouth shut about this."

"Why do you fear what she says? Are you hers to command?"

Joaquin could not let that taunt go by and returned to face her. "No, I am not hers but neither am I yours, Flame, try and remember that, and no, you sleep in your own bed tonight, you may not have mine ever again!"

Flame did not reply, for his curt rebuff had hurt her too badly. As soon as he had slammed her door she summoned Maria to bring water for her bath then went to her wardrobe for the dress she planned to wear. Joaquin had never seen it but it was one of her favorites and she had saved it for a special occasion. The dress was French like so many of her fashions and made of delicate handmade lace, the style was flattering but it was the unusual color which made the gown her favorite for it was midnight black. With her creamy skin and golden hair she was a most exotic figure as she emerged from the house to join in the dancing. She had taken only two steps past the door before she was greeted by several young men who had obviously been waiting for

144

her arrival. In spite of her worries, she found the dances fun and quite easy to learn once she'd mastered the basic steps. She was an exceptionally fine dancer, so graceful and light of step that she escaped no one's notice as she danced with a succession of partners. Not all the young women were so popular as she and they soon began to sulk and make spiteful remarks amongst themselves but Flame heard not a word of their malicious taunts nor would she have cared if she had.

Gabriel Alvarado watched as Flame danced with one of his cousins, he was fascinated by the young woman and turned to his companion, "What do you think of her, Luis, why does Joaquin not keep such a treasure for himself?"

"That has puzzled me too, but perhaps he has already made that decision and wants only to provide her with an evening's amusement."

"I would keep that beauty under lock and key if she were mine."

"It is unlikely she will ever be yours, Gabriel, Joaquin is no fool, he will keep her, you will see." The young man's despondent expression made Luis laugh. "Maybe I am wrong, have you seen him with her, even once during the day or this evening? I have not seen him dance with her once and she is such a delight as a partner I cannot understand why he has not asked her."

"Maybe he is a greater fool than we thought." Gabriel began to chuckle and winked when he caught Flame's eye. If Joaquin were a fool he was not and he quickly cut in on her partner and danced with Flame again himself.

Joaquin held his glass tightly in his hand and tried to hold his temper with as much success. He had wanted Flame to have a good time but surely there was some limit to her endurance! She had danced every dance since she had come outside and there was no shortage of partners waiting at the end of each number to claim her for the next. Only when the musicians paused for a break did she stop and then Joaquin had barely been able to see her through the throng of men which encircled her. She was a beauty and her smile pleasant to all that was true but Joaquin was outraged all the same. She hadn't even looked his way once the entire evening! And that dress! He had been shocked by her choice of gown, unmarried women in his family never wore black, but somehow Flame managed to look charmingly innocent in a dress he knew would have been at home in Celeste's closet. The gown was daring and sophisticated, but on Flame it merely enhanced her beauty as all her clothes did, he could not take his eyes off her and grew more desperate each second.

"It is a pity you had no time to teach Flame some of the dances, Joaquin, otherwise she might have been more popular."

Joaquin turned quickly at Rafael's jest. "How in heaven's name could she be any more popular?"

"Ask them to play El Jarabe, after she watches Maria Elena dance once I'll wager she can do it better."

"Maria Elena is a cow compared to Flame!" Joaquin's outburst gave his feelings away too clearly and he took a quick drink and hoped Rafael did not understand the full import of his words.

"Why, Joaquin, if she heard you say that your cousin would slit your throat." Rafael continued to chuckle. "It is no bet then since we both chose Flame."

"I don't want any contests between those two tonight, Rafael, there is enough going on between them as it is. I should never have put Maria Elena in Flame's room, that was lunacy!"

"Yes it was, you really should learn to think more carefully before you make your decisions, my friend.

But do not worry, tomorrow we will all depart and you will have no more problems.''

"Not unless Flame leaves tomorrow also!'' Joaquin went to get another drink while Rafael continued to laugh. He was having a wonderful time even if his host was not. But Rafael had no reason to worry, he'd seen Flame looking in his direction but he didn't plan to dance with her just yet, he'd wait, until the last dance perhaps. Then he would claim her, by then perhaps she would be able to tell the difference between men and boys.

At least an hour had passed before Flame realized Joaquin was not ever going to ask her to dance. If he were going to ignore her so openly then she would give him back the same, and while she smiled prettily and chatted attentively with all her partners she made it a point to keep her back turned toward her guardian. She didn't need to see him, she knew only too well how splendid he looked, he was easily the handsomest man in a group where none was less than good looking and her heart ached with longing for him. If only he would ask her to dance just once, but she knew he was angry with her again, but was it her fault his cousin was so nasty?

The last dance of the evening was the Varsoviana, a graceful blending of waltz steps with lilting music and when Rafael had appeared at her side none of the other men wished to challenge him for the privilege of her company. He led her out onto the dance floor as if she were his alone.

Flame relaxed in Rafael's arms and smiled as she looked up at him. "The answer is yes, Rafael.''

"I am delighted to hear it, but I seem to have forgotten the question.''

"I noticed a long time ago that you are a grown man, and a very handsome and brave one I might add.''

147

"Thank you, I did not mean to be so rude to you this morning, I should not have said such an insolent thing to you." While his words were spoken politely, his meaning was all too clear, he had meant every word he had ever said to her.

"No, you shouldn't have, but you did so, I have answered, and now we may be friends again." Flame closed her eyes as they danced, Rafael was a wonderful partner, and her body followed his lead gracefully, she could have danced with him forever and was sad when the music at last came to an end. "Must we go in now, Rafael, I'm not in the least bit tired, are you?"

"It is after midnight, Flame, and today I am feeling my age, my day was not nearly so relaxing as yours I'm sorry to say." But in spite of his words he kept her hand in his and began walking away from the house toward the gardens.

Joaquin turned in time to see them step out of the lantern's glow into the shadows and he choked back an oath. What was Flame up to now! He began to regret telling her she couldn't have his bed, at least then he would have known where she was all night!

"Tell me honestly, Rafael, do you think I'll ever be able to master the Spanish language? I try so hard but my progress is minimal, I was disappointed so few of the girls here knew English. I'm afraid I haven't been able to make a single friend."

"More speak English than you realize, Flame, but they are a jealous group and not nearly so friendly to newcomers as they should be. They will grow accustomed to your presence though and make friends with you before long. Do not worry about them, it is their loss they do not know you."

Flame smiled shyly as she glanced up at her friend. "I did not really know you until today either, did I, Rafael? You do not give yourself enough credit, you are

148

every bit as fine a horseman as Joaquin and I think you probably save his life far more often than he saves yours.''

"That is only because my life does not require such frequent saving as his does, Flame!''

Flame laughed with him as they strolled through the gardens, then something that Joaquin had said returned to her mind. "Am I really Joaquin's heir?''

"Did he tell you that you were?''

"Yes he did, but I don't really believe him, is it true?''

"If Joaquin said it, then it must be true, Flame.''

"Why won't you give me a straight answer, is it true or not?''

Rafael stopped walking abruptly and pulled Flame around to face him. "Must we begin again? I am not playing with you, Flame, I have no desire to flirt with you, that is not my purpose at all. If Joaquin tells you something then believe him and do not badger me about it!''

Flame glared up at the tall man. "I am not badgering you! He told me to ask you if I didn't believe him and I don't!''

"Did he? That is a different matter then.''

"Forget that I asked any questions. I am not Joaquin's child and I refuse to be his heir. I am not anyone's child any longer. I wasn't trying to flirt with you, I know you well enough to understand you are far too serious a man for such ridiculous pastimes. I know you don't want that from me, but what is it that you do expect?''

"Only this, my Flame.'' Rafael's fingertips tilted her mouth up to meet his as he began to kiss her, and when she relaxed in his arms he grew more ardent until he was certain she knew exactly what he wanted.

Flame was startled by his affection but only for a mo-

149

ment, his kiss was not unlike Joaquin's but different too. He held her so tightly she could not have escaped his embrace had she even wanted to. He moved his hand slowly down her back to rest upon her hips then pressed her close so she could not mistake his need for her and the heat from his loins began to spread through her own. Flame grew weak as she clung to Rafael and Gabriel's warning rang in her ears, she had asked for love and Rafael was gladly supplying it, but the boldness of his gesture shocked her. She could scarcely draw a breath as he continued to kiss her, but when at last he released her she looked up at him and smiled unsteadily then more warmly. She put her arms around his neck and drew his mouth back down to hers, he had frightened her, but she enjoyed his kiss more. She savored his taste and feel for as long as she could but she knew she didn't love him, at least not the way she loved Joaquin but he could not read her thoughts in her delicious kiss nor understand as she hugged his neck how much she longed for another's love.

Rafael stepped back as he took her hands in his. "I am going to take you inside while I still can." He led her back into the light of the lanterns and as luck would have it Joaquin overtook them, he scowled down at Flame and then proceeded them into his house without bothering to wish either of them a good night.

When Maria Elena saw Flame come in with Rafael she was beside herself with jealousy. Flame was the most brazen flirt she had ever met, but that the girl could keep two men like Joaquin and Rafael on the string made her livid. How did she do it? Surely one man must know of her escapades with the other? How could the girl share Joaquin's bed last night and tonight be with Rafael? When she got into bed with her sisters Flame had still not returned to her room and Maria Elena lay awake trying to think of new insults to hurl when the tramp finally did appear. Fortunately, she was so tired she soon fell fast asleep so when Flame came to bed she found her room quiet and was soon enjoying a peaceful sleep on the edge of the large bed her roommates had left free for her.

Nine

Rafael spent the better part of the morning with Joaquin in his study. The last of the guests had left for home and the two men had turned their attention to the shipping contracts Rafael had brought for Joaquin to sign. Once that chore was completed the attorney changed the subject to a more pressing one. "This weekend was a success, don't you think? However, you were rather obvious in your motives. I doubt a man left here without knowing why he was invited."

Joaquin grinned widely as he shrugged his shoulders. "I merely wanted Flame to meet my friends, some of my family. I had no special reason other than that for inviting them here."

"Really? Then where were all the young men who have wives and children, Joaquin? There was not one such man here. Are you so eager to see Flame married? Is she all that much trouble for you?"

"Yes, damn it, she is no end of trouble to me. I look forward to the hour she leaves my house with great anticipation!" Joaquin's good humor vanished as he recalled the pain she'd caused him the previous evening.

Rafael leaned back in his chair and waited a long moment, carefully considering his words before he spoke. "All right then, I will take her home with me now. You want a husband for her and I would be delighted to have her as my wife."

"What!" Joaquin was astounded, certain he could not have understood his friend's offer. "Since when have you wanted a wife?"

"Since the afternoon I met her at the railroad depot. This is no spur-of-the-moment decision, Joaquin. I want her for my wife, you will give your permission, won't you? I don't think you will refuse if both you and Flame are so miserable with your present arrangement."

Joaquin stood up slowly and walked around to the front of his desk. "I had hoped my friends would like Flame, but I really wasn't prepared for everyone to adore her as they obviously did. I don't know what to say to you, I—"

"You must realize it will be only a matter of days before you receive other inquiries and invitations for her. Everyone did love her, Joaquin, they all did, or perhaps it would be more accurate to say all the men did. The women were all too envious of her beauty and charm to like her."

"I didn't notice. Were the girls rude to Flame?"

"I swear you notice nothing, Joaquin. Yes, they were all very rude to her but you were more rude to her yourself. Did you think the way you ignored Flame would be lost on all of us? You danced several times with each of your female guests, but not even once with Flame. Did you mean to deliberately snub her, to hurt her feelings? If so you succeeded well. Is that how you treat her most of the time, Joaquin, you simply ignore her?"

Joaquin only scowled. He'd been furious with Flame, she was an outrageous flirt, she certainly didn't need his attentions with all the other men fighting over her. Just thinking of her enormous popularity with his friends brought back every bit of his anger and he clenched his fists tightly at his sides.

Finally Rafael grew impatient. "Well, will you give your permission or not, Joaquin? I want her to leave with me today. I will invite you to the wedding, you will be my best man won't you?"

Joaquin knew he'd have to give some reply and responded with the first excuse which came to his mind. "She is too young to marry, Rafael, much too young."

"Why would you say that? She is eighteen, she will be at least nineteen before our first child can be born."

Joaquin turned away quickly when he knew his expression would tell Rafael far too much. He shut his eyes tightly and tried to suppress the erotic images, which flooded his mind for he could not bear the thought of Flame's exquisite body lying pinned beneath Rafael's. It made him sick to think of his friend making love to her and he nearly strangled on the jealousy which tightened his throat in a hard knot. Dear God, what had he done? "She is a child herself in too many ways, certainly not ready for the responsibilities of motherhood, Rafael. You do not know her as well as I do and I simply cannot let her marry as yet."

"You say you want her out of your house in one breath and then tell me she is too young to leave in the next? Make up your mind, Joaquin."

"It is made up! I will not give my permission for her to marry now and that's final!" Joaquin walked to the window and gazed out at the familiar landscape to avoid facing his friend but the anger in his voice was unmistakable.

"Is that your real reason, or do you object to me personally? It was my father who gambled away our ranch, not me. Is it because I have no property that you will not accept me as her husband?" Rafael flecked a speck of lint from his trousers, his voice calm as he tried to analyze his friend's refusal.

"No, of course not. I know you would not gamble

154

away her inheritance, it is not that at all. You are my best friend as well as my attorney, I have always trusted you with my life as well as my fortune, you know that.''

''You want a wealthier man perhaps? The Alvarados can almost match your fortune, and Gabriel did seem to be taken with Flame . . . would you prefer him?''

''No! It has nothing to do with money, Rafael, nor the man. I know Flame liked Gabriel, she spent enough time with him, but I would refuse him also, she is simply too young to marry now.''

''All right, I can wait, when may I expect to make her my wife? Do you want me to wait a year, or two? How long? I have no objection to a long engagement if Flame does not.''

''No, you must not speak to Flame about this yet, not yet.'' Joaquin turned back to face his friend squarely. ''She would be livid if she even suspected we have been discussing her marriage without her being present. She has very definite ideas about finding her own husband. Don't press me for a date, just wait a while longer, then you can ask her first and then come to me. We can't ever let her know it was the other way around.''

Rafael rose to his feet with deliberate slowness and replaced his chair in its original position beside the massive desk. ''I am not a patient man, Joaquin. I will not wait long, especially not when I know full well others will soon be asking for her hand. I do not intend to lose her while another ignores your conditions.''

''Do not worry, I will refuse anyone who proposes marriage, my friend. You will be able to ask her first, but I cannot guarantee her acceptance. I never know what to expect from that woman, never.''

''That is because you do not even attempt to understand her as I do. She will make a fine wife for me, Joaquin. I know she is young and often thoughtless but she is more frequently sweet. I will teach her how to please me and she will be happy. Do not concern yourself with her future. Now when will you be coming up to San Francisco? There are many things which need your attention, far more than I could bring with me. It is not like you to stay away for so long.''

''There are things here which are pressing also. I do not enjoy traversing the state endlessly but I will make an effort to come up soon.''

''I know you do not enjoy the journey but you have always enjoyed your stay.'' Rafael's sly expression left little doubt as to his meaning.

''Perhaps I am too old now to spend so much time whoring!'' Joaquin's mood had not improved a bit. He realized with a start that what he had said was true. He didn't want any of the women who'd become rich off his money alone—not Celeste, not any of them. They didn't appeal to him in the slightest anymore.

''Somehow I never thought you would ever be that old, my friend. But no matter, I will try and keep your business affairs in order until you arrive, your other 'affairs' are your own concern. Do you mind if I bid Flame farewell before I go?''

Joaquin had not forgotten Rafael had taken Flame out to the garden the previous night and could not keep from asking, ''Rafael, I know you spent at least some time alone with Flame last night and—''

''Very little time, Joaquin, and she is not a woman I would want to take hurriedly in the bushes. I understand your concern—Flame is a sweet girl. I would never take advantage of her innocence . . . is that your worry?''

''I know you to be a gentleman, but Flame is, well, frankly so flirtatious a creature than I think maybe you are the one who should be careful. Tell her good-bye in any manner you wish, but do not tell her about our conversation.''

"I won't, if that is your desire. Good-bye, Joaquin.''
Rafael extended his hand and Joaquin shook it warmly,
but he sank back down into his chair the minute Rafael
had left the room.

He held his head in his hands and cursed. Dear God,
not Rafael, any man but not Rafael, he simply could
not bear that thought. He sat back and began to go over
the guest list in his mind, but as he considered each
man who had met Flame that weekend he found none
of them acceptable either. The possibility of her marrying anyone he knew revolted him completely, his imagination was simply too vivid and the pictures his
mind conjured up turned his stomach. He could still remember how Flame's slender body had fit so perfectly
in his arms, how sweet and loving she had been, how
smooth her soft white breasts had felt to his lips. How
had he ever been so stupid as to think he could send her
away, give her up to any other man? God in heaven
what was he going to do with her now? He searched his
mind frantically for some alternative, but his problems
continued to compound. Rafael had been correct in his
prediction for he had already received inquiries, not
even discreet ones, as to the extent of Flame's inheritance and property. Very natural questions which
might proceed a marriage proposal but he had been
extremely vague in his responses. When invitations arrived for her he would give every excuse he could con-
trive from the heat of the summer to his own pressing
business schedule which would prohibit him from making any social engagements for her until the fall. Then
he'd stall and hope the winter was an unusually harsh
one that would keep everyone confined in his own
home until very late spring! That would give him
nearly a year, in a year's time almost anything could
happen and he prayed he could find a way out of his

torment with that much time on his side.

Rafael leaned back against one of the posts which supported the veranda that ran the length of the front of the house and wrapped Flame in his embrace, pressing her close. He wound his fingers in her golden curls and smiled as he remembered his hesitance to even touch her only a few days before. Everything had changed between them now and when he brought his mouth down upon hers she opened her lips readily, allowing him the access to her sweet warm mouth which he had longed to have.

Flame relaxed in Rafael's embrace, her small hands caressing his chest, feeling his strength, the tension in his muscles as he drew her closer. She cared not at all that anyone might see them, his kiss was too delicious for her to pretend shyness when she felt only growing desire. She didn't want him to ever stop and was sorry when at last he lifted his lips from hers.

"I must go, Flame, but I will see you again soon, I promise you it will not be long before I return." He leapt upon his horse and then touching the brim of his hat lightly had departed before she could even whisper good-bye.

Flame's lips continued to burn with the heat of Rafael's kisses as she watched him ride away. He had kissed her as passionately as he had the night before and if it had occurred to him that she knew how to return such a kiss because another man had taught her he had not mentioned it. For all of her insistence that she wanted to be treated as a woman, Flame knew she had begun something with Rafael which she was never going to be able to complete. Now that he was gone she was frightened. She knew he was not a man who would allow a woman to trifle with his emotions, he would expect more from her the next time they met and she had

158

no more to give.

It must be a sin to kiss one man when I am so in love with another, she worried, but she had enjoyed his kiss, needed his affectionate embrace despite the shame she felt now. She had encouraged his affection, demanded it when she could not honestly return it. She had laughed at Rafael for his reserved behavior and he had changed his manner to suit her request. She had never dreamed he possessed so passionate a nature and now was dreadfully sorry she had aroused it. Perhaps when the priest came next she could seek his advice, she had bragged to Joaquin about having no sins, but surely this was a terrible thing she had done and her conscience would give her no peace if she did not confide her anguish in someone.

When she returned to her room she had no desire to dress and go riding, so she lay down upon her bed and tried to think calmly of what options she might possibly have left open to her. In spite of her love for Joaquin, she knew he cared nothing for her, which he had made all too clear again by refusing to dance with her when he had danced with every other woman who had been there for the party. That neglect hurt badly. To think he had done that deliberately, shut her out of his life as if she didn't exist just to punish her again. Life in his home was becoming more impossible each day, but if Joaquin would never permit her to rebuild her father's home, then she'd have to stay with him forever unless she married and went to live in her husband's home. Was it possible Rafael might propose marriage? He seemed no more interested in having a wife and family than Joaquin but perhaps he would change his mind in time. She bit her lip to hold back her tears. Would it be better to never marry and stay in a house with a man who hated her, or to marry a man she didn't love just to escape? She put her hand to her lips and closed her eyes as she recalled Rafael's kiss. It was so pleasant—wouldn't his loving be nice too? Her whole body still felt warm from his embrace and she blushed as she thought how easy it had been to return his kiss as she had. Her body responded readily to his even if her heart did not, why was that? Did she need love so desperately that she would accept any man's attentions? Would she have felt the same way if Gabriel or one of the others she had just met had kissed her? She wished her grandmother had told her more about men, about love. She was so dreadfully ignorant when it came to understanding how to accomplish that act. She wasn't at all sure how to go about it but surely Rafael must know how and would teach her. His touch was gentle and his manner usually charming, if he asked her to marry him she would say yes and try to be a good wife, the best she could be, and if Joaquin's image remained in her heart Rafael would never suspect. She could not stop her tears at that wretched thought and wept bitterly for the man she loved so dearly who cared not a bit for her.

Father León was quite pleased when Flame came to find him as he sat resting in the patio. He had just finished eating a light lunch and was enjoying the afternoon sun, but he much preferred the company of the charming young woman to his own. He noticed immediately how different her appearance was that day. She seemed so much older, more mature than on their previous meeting, but he thought perhaps he hadn't remembered her all that clearly.

"I wanted to thank you for helping me the last time I needed your assistance, Father. May I speak with you for a moment today?"

"Why of course, child, sit here with me." The cleric patted the bench at his side and Flame joined him. "How have you been doing, my dear? You look well."

"My health is excellent, it is other things which trouble me now." Hesitantly Flame tried to describe her torment. "Father, you know I love Joaquin, I have confided that secret in no one else."

"My dear, really, you must not allow yourself to dwell on such improper thoughts."

Flame closed her eyes as she sighed. "Please, won't you just listen to me for a moment? There is no one else I might tell and the pain of my loneliness is more than I can bear."

"Forgive me if I sounded harsh, what is troubling you?" The priest leaned forward, alarmed by her desperate tone.

"I love Joaquin, Father León, I love him dearly and I always will. He means the world to me, but I know he cares nothing for me. My presence here is a burden to him and he wishes me gone."

"My dear—"

"No, it is true! But I want to leave him, I must. If another man were to ask me to marry him, a man I liked, a good friend, would it be a sin for me to marry him knowing each time he kissed me, made love to me, I would be longing for Joaquin? That no matter who made love to me, it would always be Joaquin in my heart? Would that be an evil thing for me to do?"

Father León stared at Flame and gasped in horror. How did such a sweet child continually have such complicated problems? When he took her hand he found her trembling almost uncontrollably. "Let us think for a moment, Flame. Perhaps you can answer your own question. What if Joaquin were to marry you, knowing how much you loved him, but while he loved another woman. Each time he touched you he would think of her. Could you bear that?"

"But Rafael will never know. I'll never give him the slightest cause to suspect I love Joaquin and not him."

"You are speaking of Rafael Ramirez?" The priest gasped in alarm.

"Yes, do you know him?"

The priest wiped his forehead quickly and regretted his decision to take a place in the sun. The warmth of the day had ceased to be relaxing and was now making him even more uncomfortable. "I know him well and he is not a man who could be fooled for long, and the fury of his anger when he discovered what you'd done to him would be horrible indeed. Rafael is capable of any revenge, Flame, and he would take it."

It was now Flame's turn to stare in surprise. "Rafael? You are the second person to warn me of danger in a man who has shown me only kindness and compassion. I am not afraid of Rafael, he would never harm me."

"Well, perhaps he won't ever guess the truth, but think again of how you would feel in such a situation, if Joaquin were married to you but loved another."

Flame needed no more than a moment to formulate her response. "I would be so happy to give Joaquin pleasure I would not mind that he thought of someone else. I would feel his love, not her, and I would know only joy in his arms. Even if he called me by her name I would do whatever he asked because I love him so."

Now the priest was appalled, his hope at making her see the folly of the action she contemplated had backfired. He tried once more, "But that is your choice, would it be Rafael's?"

Flame shook her head quickly as she grasped his meaning. "You mean I should tell Rafael before I marry him that I love Joaquin?"

" Secrets harm all relationships, they would ruin a marriage, especially a secret so immense as the one you think you could carry. If this question has troubled you now, believe me, it will be nothing compared to what you will suffer if you marry a man you don't love."

"No, I can not do what you ask, I could never tell Rafael that I don't love him, that would be too cruel."

"He will be able to tell anyway, Flame, when he kisses you, or when—"

"No, that's not true, he can't tell! Oh what must you think of me, Father? Rafael has kissed me, he has and I want him when he does, I want his kisses but I still love Joaquin. What is the matter with me, why am I so weak that a man has only to kiss me and I am his?"

The priest was afraid to hear the answer to his next question but could not stop himself from asking, "Child, Rafael is a very sophisticated man, a very worldly one, but he has not taken advantage of your innocence has he?"

Flame blushed deeply as she reassured the kindly man. "No, he would never force me, take me against my will, he has not done that." Her mouth felt dry as she remembered Rafael's passion filled embrace. Would he stop at kisses the next time they were alone? Gabriel had warned her, now the priest, but he had warned her himself that he was a man. Was that what he had meant? She knew he was strong, if he so desired he could force her to submit to him, once he'd made love to her she would have no choice but to marry him. She grew faint with fear and gripped the priest's pudgy arm. "What shall I do?"

"I suggest you do nothing at all, child, do not worry any further about these matters, you are too young to marry now. Put these thoughts from your mind, do not marry a man you don't love, you are far too lovely to worry over love, it will come to you soon. Be more patient and you will see, love will find you."

"Is that really true?" Flame didn't stop to realize that love had already found her in the person of Rafael and had terrified her.

"Yes, I know it is, you will have a husband who adores you as you will him if you will be but a little more patient. Give the man time to find you, Flame, give him a little more time."

The priest was speaking in platitudes but Flame thought only of Joaquin. Perhaps if she but gave him more time he would grow to love her. She smiled as she stood up to leave. "Thank you so much, Father León, you have been so helpful."

"Do not spend any more time brooding, dear. Spend your time outdoors, riding, working in the gardens, or read—Joaquin has more books than anyone could read in a lifetime. But do not allow your mind to dwell on sadness. And the next time you see Rafael be honest about your feelings for him, for both your sakes." The cleric smiled as Flame walked away. Had he really been of some help, he wondered? He had never felt so inadequate, but surely the girl would soon meet a man who could please her without presenting so many problems. Then he thought again of Rafael and shuddered. How had such a sweet girl gotten involved with so ruthless a man as he?

Ten

Flame loved Joaquin's library, it held the most wonderful assortment of books she'd ever seen. The older volumes were all in Spanish, beautifully bound in tooled leather, but the newer books were in English, much to her delight. There were books on every conceivable topic and novels of the most imaginative sort. Some books like Shakespeare's plays and the Greek myths were well worn, but the newer volumes had all been read too. Had Joaquin read all the marvelous books, she wondered? Her only problem with the library was the complete lack of order in which the books were displayed. With bookcases extending to the ceiling on three walls there was an enormous amount of books, but why were they arranged in no order at all? Whoever had begun the collection must have simply walked in, unpacked his books, placed them at random upon the shelves and then walked out. The next person had apparently followed that example. After one particularly frustrating afternoon in which Flame had spent more than an hour searching for a book of poems she'd read only the week before an idea came to her. She would set up the library as a real library should be kept, with novels arranged alphabetically by the author's last name and the other books arranged by subject. The more she thought about the idea the better she liked it. It would be just what Father Leon had suggested, something worthwhile to keep her mind off her problems with love.

The project took nearly two weeks to complete since she worked only a few hours each afternoon. She dusted all the books, swept out the shelves and then sorted the books into the categories that seemed best to her. She was nearly finished with the last bookcase when Joaquin walked into the room to locate a book he needed. He walked past her with only the briefest of nods and then walked to the far wall to reach for the book he wanted. He looked at the shelf in amazement then turned back to frown at her.

"What in God's name have you done with my books!"

Flame had never considered her pursuit any but the most useful and said so. "There was no order of any kind that I could see. You have so many nice books and they really should have been classified long ago. I've simply arranged them for you in a logical way. Now it is easy to find whatever you want, before it was impossible."

"Impossible for you maybe!" Joaquin's hostile expression began to deepen.

"You mean you could find books with no trouble?" Flame was puzzled. "Had you simply memorized the location of each and every one?"

"Yes! Now look at this, how am I supposed to find anything?" He gestured impatiently toward the newly dusted and arranged rows.

Flame explained her system in a few sentences. It was logical, and she liked it, but although she promptly handed him the book he'd wanted, Joaquin was still not pleased. "I don't recall your asking my permission for this project. Did that detail slip your mind?"

"Ask permission? Well I'm sorry. I live here too and I only thought you'd be happy to have your library arranged so nicely.''

"No, you didn't think, not for one second did you think about my feelings. This is my house and these are my books. I want you to put everything right back the way you found it.''

Flame was crushed by his order. "But why? That makes no sense, Joaquin.''

"Must I explain again, this is my house and it will stay as I have it. You are never to touch any of my things ever again, do you understand me?'' Joaquin's dark eyes glowed with the cold sparkle of obsidian as he glared down at her.

Flame's stare grew as cold as his. "Yes, I understand you. If you want the books replaced the way they were you'll have to do it yourself. There's no way I could ever do it since they were in no order at all!'' She turned and left the room, too hurt at his rejection of her efforts to remain another second in his presence. She had worked so hard to please him and as usual she had failed.

Joaquin leaned back against the wall and swore angrily. Damn it all, he hadn't meant to yell at her. She was right, the room had been a mess. He should have done something about rearranging the books years ago, he'd just never had the time. Despite his boast, most of the time he couldn't find what he wanted anyway. Why couldn't he have just thanked her without behaving like an overbearing jackass? This wasn't working at all, he couldn't watch her each day as she laughed and smiled and moved through his house with such ease and not want her, not ache to have her. He slammed his fist down on the small table at his side and cursed again. Never in his whole life had he wanted a woman so badly and if that torment weren't bad enough, this was the one woman in the world he couldn't have! He knew why they couldn't get along, what was tearing them apart, he wanted her and he had no way to satisfy the desire that grew stronger within him each day. He was her guardian, and guardians were supposed to be responsible for their children, not seduce them! He slumped down in a chair and put his head in his hands. Hell, it wasn't incest that disturbed him, he knew they weren't related, it was that there was only one way he was ever going to have Flame and that was to marry her, to make her his wife and keep her with him forever, and he had never wanted a wife. His father had done far too thorough a job in raising him in the Villarreal tradition for that. Women were for pleasure, to use and discard, one had to have a wife eventually in order to produce an heir, but that was a matter of continuing the family name—pride and tradition, certainly not love. Love did not exist, it was an illusion, an unnecessary one his father had often boasted, but Joaquin's emotions tore away at him now. Flame would not marry without love, she had told him so, but their relationship was closer to all-out war than affection! Joaquin sat for more than an hour trying to think but could not decide which would be worse, living forever without Flame, or making that lovely creature his bride and trying to live in harmony with her. It was a dilemma Joaquin could not resolve for he was trying to make a rational decision for once in his life when all he really had to do was follow his heart, and tragically, he had never even admitted to himself that he had one.

Flame refused to cry over Joaquin's angry outburst, she just refused to be so weak. He could be such a bully at times but she'd never give in to him. He could yell all he liked but she'd not replace one book where it had been before, even if she could remember where the books had orginally been, which she couldn't.

She was so restless she couldn't bear the prospect of sitting in the parlor before dinner. She could imagine what Joaquin would be like during the meal, he'd probably just scowl at her and not say a word. Nothing she did ever pleased him. He'd never mentioned the morning they'd first met or what had nearly happened between them. That had been so spontaneous, so sweet, she had hoped he would come to love her as she loved him. But being patient wasn't going to help, it was hopeless, he didn't even like her. He never smiled and would probably never kiss her again. She was right back where she had been the day after the party, trying to decide whether or not to marry just to get out of his accursed house where he expected to be treated like a king who never gave any thought to the comfort of those around him. It made her head ache to worry so. There seemed to be no way she could ever be happy. She could remain with Joaquin and be miserable, or marry Rafael and be miserable, and undoubtedly make him miserable too!

Flame left the house and strolled aimlessly near the vineyard while she pondered her problems. She hadn't meant to stray but as the shadows lengthened she realized she'd gone too far and turned back toward the house at a run. All she needed was to be late for dinner. Joaquin had probably already given her food to one of his dogs!

Miguel crouched down in the shadows. He could scarcely believe his luck. The señorita had walked by within an arm's reach of him and when she returned he'd grab her before she could scream. He held his pistol lightly in his hand ready to strike her when she reappeared.

Flame held her skirt above her feet as she ran along, so intent upon reaching the house swiftly she never saw Miguel step out from between the rows of vines. She saw only a bright flash and felt the blinding pain as his pistol came down on the side of her skull. When she hit

169

the dirt with a sickening thud everything had already turned black.

Miguel dragged Flame's limp form back along the narrow path between the vines. His plan was working perfectly, he'd hide the girl and then wait for his real prey, the man he despised, Joaquin Villarreal. Dusk had covered the valley by the time he reached his horse and his deed went unseen. He slung Flame across his saddle and rode away toward the cliffs. A rude laugh escaped his lips. "Ay, Senor Villarreal, yo tengo su muñeca! Your little doll is mine!" He licked his lips hungrily. It was too dark for a search party to be effective, so maybe there would be time for him to do more than just look at the beautiful young woman who had cost him his job.

Miguel pulled Flame from off his horse and half dragged, half carried her into the small opening in the face of the cliff. He pulled her to the back of the narrow cave, making his way by the light of the lantern he'd left earlier. He lay Flame down upon the sand and unbuttoned her bodice to fondle her soft breasts, but when she did not stir he grew frightened. Had he hit her too hard and killed her? He put his ear to her breast and was relieved to hear her heart beating steadily. With a wicked grunt he lowered his mouth and took a firm pink nipple in his teeth. Flame moaned softly under that pain but did not become fully conscious and Miguel grew tired of his sport.

"You are no fun like this, señorita. I want a woman, not a rag doll." He sat back, watching her breathe in and out slowly as she slept too deeply to be awakened. He would wait until she was wide awake. He wanted to hear her scream when next he touched her smooth skin. He wanted to make her pay for that beating he had taken, pay and pay dearly. He bound her hands and feet with rope before hauling her further up on the stretch of sand. He left then, he'd not spend the night in so dark and dank a cave, she would sleep alone that night, and with continued luck he would kill that bastard Villarreal and rape his woman as often as he pleased. He nearly shrieked with demented laughter. Maybe he'd take the puta to Mexico, that was a long trip and what a companion she would make! Once there he would sell her, he knew men who would pay for a white woman such as this one, offer any price. He cursed to himself—he'd have to be more careful, scars would reduce her price and he couldn't have that, he wanted all he could get for Villarreal's whore.

As Miguel slept on the cliffs above, the tide began to rise in the narrow cave. The sand where Flame lay soon became damp with water which rose slightly higher with each advancing wave. The sea lapped around the hem of her dress, then soaked her skirt. Soon it was seeping under her bodice and inching toward her throat.

When the freezing cold salt water reached her face Flame awoke slowly. The pain in her head was too intense to allow her to move with any rapidity. She blinked her eyes repeatedly but still couldn't see. The atmosphere at the back of the cave was so thick with mist she could scarcely breathe and she struggled to catch her breath, strained with each painful gasp. She was so cold, drenched clear through by the icy water, and she ached all over, but when she tried to sit up her bound wrists and ankles held her back.

No experience of her brief life had prepared Flame for this terror. Where is God's name was she? Down by the edge of the sea obviously, but how had she gotten there? Why was it so dark and who had tied her up? The water level kept rising and she pushed herself further back but met the sharp edges of the rocks each way she turned. If the cave completely filled with water at high tide she would have no chance to survive. Something scurried over her hand, a crab or some other small creature, and she began to sob. How had she come to be in such a dreadful place all alone? Then she grew more terrified still: what if her captors never returned for her, or worse yet, what would they do when they did?

Maria looked in on Joaquin before going to bed. He was seated in the parlor reading a book and she apologized for disturbing him. "I am sorry, Joaquin, but the girl has not come home. Even if she were mad at you and refused to eat any dinner where could she be at this late hour?"

Joaquin slammed his book shut; he'd been unable to concentrate on it anyway. He'd rehearsed apologies for an hour before dinner and Flame hadn't bothered to appear to hear them, he was even more furious at her for hiding this way. "She's probably sitting not ten feet from the door, just pouting. I told you we had another argument and she's just trying to get even with me. I'll leave the doors unlatched so she can come in when she's tired of her silly game but I'll not wait up for her."

The next morning Joaquin walked by Flame's room and knocked. Hearing no answer he opened the door and looked in. Had she come home and left again early to go riding? When he found Lady in the pasture his anger grew. Damn the girl anyway, how long would she pursue such a childish course? He turned toward the mountains, looked at the low lying hills dotted with oak trees, and swore. He'd not give her the satisfaction of looking for her. When she got hungry she'd come home. He strode back into his house and slammed the door as he went.

Flame had managed to survive the night, but just

172

barely. The tide had reached her chin before it had begun to recede and she was shivering with the chill. Her wet dress offered no warmth and the rocks at her back were like ice. It had to be daylight and Joaquin would be out searching for her, combing the hills for her, but would he think to come down to the sea? He'd never mentioned the cave—was there more than one? She had one hope and one hope only: that Joaquin would find her and soon.

Miguel did not dare light a fire to cook but he had plenty to eat for breakfast. Might as well take the little bitch something, he thought, and grabbed an apple as he started back down the cliff to the cave. She was too thin as it was, he'd have to feed her to make her worth more. It would be fun to make her eat, he laughed as he thought what he'd really like to force down her throat! Miguel stopped to light the lantern he left at the cave's entrance, and holding it aloft, made his way over the slippery rocks.

Flame saw the light and strained to see who was coming. She could make out the man's form as he crawled along. Of one thing she was instantly certain—he was not Joaquin. She was terrified.

Miguel placed the lantern at Flame's feet and swore in disgust, "What a mess you are, señorita, even worse than last night. Why are you so wet?"

Flame recognized his voice immediately. "Miguel, is that you? Did you do this to me?"

His evil chuckle frightened her all the more. "Yes, little one, I took you yesterday as you walked near the grape vines. I had waited many days for a chance to get you, but you made it so easy. But why are you all wet, I left you on dry sand last night."

"The tide, did you forget the tide comes in twice each day? How could you have been such a fool? I nearly drowned!"

173

Miguel doubled up his fist and struck her, the force of his blow sending her head crashing back into the rocks. "Shut up, bitch! You will not call me a fool. Villarreal is the fool for thinking he could get rid of me so easily." Miguel dropped to his knees and reached for the collar of Flame's dress. He had not bothered to rebutton the garment and she could not stop his wandering fingers with her hands tied behind her back. Miguel traced a line down her throat to her breast then began to make circles around her pink nipple as he giggled, "How does Villarreal do this, is he gentle with women the way he is with his horses, or is he as mean as I am?"

Flame began to gag. She couldn't stand him touching her so intimately. He pulled her dress off her shoulders and continued to touch her lightly, watching her face closely as he did so. "Don't you like this, bitch? I am being so nice to you today." Miguel's hands closed over her breasts and he began to exert increasing pressure until Flame cried out in pain. When he released her she continued to sob, her tears rolling down her cheeks in great waves of despair.

"You are far more fun today. I like a woman who screams in passion. Beg me to kiss you, little one, beg me to do it."

Flame spat out her answer, "Never!" Instantly Miguel's fist crashed into her cheek again as he swore in disgust.

"Oh yes you will beg me, you will." He leaned down to kiss her, his rough beard scratching the soft skin of her face cruelly.

Flame was terrified. What if Joaquin couldn't find her in time? She could stand Miguel's fists, if he only beat her she could stand it, but the knowledge of what else he could do frightened her far more. She was tied up so she could hardly move, couldn't resist his awful hands and bruising mouth. She watched with horror as Miguel lowered his head to her bare breast and raked his stubble covered chin against her tender flesh before taking her nipple in his teeth. This time she fainted with the pain and mercifully when she awoke he was gone. He'd left the lantern and in its dim light she could see the marks his teeth had left on her breasts. Oh God, where was Joaquin, why hadn't he come? She cried pitifully, she was so cold and ached dreadfully, Miguel might kill her the next time he came back, he might kill her or do something even worse and she could never go back to Joaquin then. She cried until she was hoarse but still Joaquin did not come.

Joaquin had no appetite for lunch. Shoving his plate aside he began to get angry. How long was Flame going to hold out before she came home? He really had meant to apologize to her, to talk to her reasonably to see if there weren't some way they could learn to live together in peace, but he couldn't speak to her in any tone when she ran away like this! He was thoroughly disgusted with her as he got to his feet and went back to his desk. He forced Flame from his mind and returned to his ledgers, trying to sort out his accounts. He didn't give the bothersome girl another thought until she again failed to appear for dinner.

When Miguel returned to the cave he was angry, livid, and yanked Flame's hair to awaken her. "Your fine Señor Villarreal did not even leave his house today! I was sure you were the bait to lure him away, but no, he has so many women he cares nothing for you!"

Flame's courage deserted her completely then. It couldn't be true—Joaquin had to be searching for her, he wouldn't leave her like this, he had to come save her and soon!

Miguel pulled a small bottle of whiskey from his back

pocket and took a long swallow. "You are worthless except to sell, the first whorehouse we reach when we cross the border into Mexico I am selling you!"

"You are taking me to Mexico?" Flame asked wearily, not believing he wouldn't simply kill her there.

"As soon as I kill Villarreal we will go. Tomorrow maybe he will come looking for you. Oh, I waited too long, the sand is getting wet again, I hate this stinking cave!" He picked up the lantern and began to make his way across the rocks as he left the cave, swearing all the while.

Flame called after him, her voice a pathetic cry: "Miguel, please don't leave me in here, please!"

Miguel's cruel laughter was his only response and Flame was left alone in the dark getting wetter by the minute as the tide rose again. She pulled on the ropes which bound her wrists but could not loosen them, there was no way she could get free and she sagged back against the rocks unmindful of their sharp edges. A whorehouse in Mexico, what would they do to her there? She would fight them as long as she could, but she knew she could never win. They would probably beat her until she no longer cared, until she would submit to any humiliation as long as the man had the price. Joaquin was the only man who'd ever touched her with love, and now she would never see him again. She sobbed on as her thoughts grew more desperate, she would kill herself before she let another man take her, kill herself or kill him, but she'd not suffer the fate Miguel had planned for her without a fight and a fierce one.

By nightfall Flame was dizzy from hunger. Miguel had given her nothing to eat all day but the apple which he'd tossed beyond her reach. As the tide soaked her clothes she began to shake. If Joaquin weren't coming, she had no hope. She'd have to escape by herself, on

176

her own—but how? Her legs ached, her arms were numb, she could scarcely breathe . . . how could she escape?

The next morning Miguel found Flame unconscious. He struck her repeatedly but that failed to bring her around and he could not understand what was the matter with her. Maybe she was just cold, dazed by the chill of the water which had filled the cave as he'd slept. He went back to his horse and brought his blanket and some food. It would not help him if she died, he needed money too badly to throw away the one thing he could sell. Unless Villarreal had money on him when he killed him he'd get nothing for his troubles but satisfaction. It took him only a moment to cut the bindings on Flame's ankles and wrists. He wrapped her in his blanket and began to rub her hands and feet until at last she opened her eyes.

Flame shrank away from Miguel, tried to pull free, but he laughed at her feeble gestures. "Here, I have brought you some food. It is not hot but it is food." He offered his canteen and she drank the water in thirsty gulps, spilling most of it down the front of her dress before she reached for the bean-filled tortilla he offered. She had taken only three bites when she began to gag, then turned away to retch.

"No te gusta mi comida, señorita? Qué lastima, it is all you will get today!" He rebound her wrists and ankles before he left, muttering all the while about how he would kill Joaquin. "Maybe I will bring you his scalp. Would you like that, puta?"

"Dear God, you wouldn't!" Flame screamed at him, horrified by his gory threat.

"Yes, I would, it would be a pleasure to take that bastard's black hair and hang it from my belt! I wish he could see you now, he would spit on you. You thought you were too fine for me, didn't you? Well, you will soon be good enough for any man!'' Miguel hurried off, intent on his efforts to carry out his murder plans without delay.

Flame leaned her head back against the rocks and cried when he'd gone. She'd never get free, if Joaquin were dead she didn't want to be alive either. No whorehouse in Mexico could ever be as horrid as this awful cave, she thought bitterly. Surely no whore ever had to suffer so cruelly as this. Her mind created endless fantasies for her that day as she rested too weak to struggle against her bonds. Slowly an idea began to form in her mind. The cave was filled with rocks, jagged, rough boulders and small smooth stones, rounded by endless bouts with the tide. Could she find one which she could hide and hold to strike Miguel when he returned?

Maria went to the back door and looked out. It had been too long; something dreadful must have happened to the pretty little señorita. Joaquin was wrong to treat her disappearance so casually—young women were foolish, but not so silly as this. She walked out to the corral and waited for him to complete his conversation with José before she spoke. ''Joaquin, it has been two days, she would have come home if she could. She may have fallen, be lying injured and you will not even saddle your horse to look for her?''

''You know Flame, she has the grace of a fawn. She would not fall. No, Maria, she is merely doing this to spite me, I will not go look for her. That's exactly what she wants and I'll not do it!'' His expression left no room for argument as he walked past her toward the house.

Maria hurried after him, pleading again. ''But, Joaquin, what if one of the vaqueros has her?''

Joaquin spun to face her. ''What? One of my men?''

''Is it not a possibility? She is so young and pretty,

perhaps some man has her hidden away. Did that thought not occur to you?"

"No, it didn't, but wait here a moment and I'll speak to José about it." Joaquin returned shortly, a relieved look on his face. "José says no one has been missing from meals or the bunkhouse the last two nights. All the men are accounted for, Maria. You are wrong, she is just hiding to get even with me and she can hide until she rots for all I care!" Joaquin strode past the woman and slammed the door, but he hadn't fooled her. She knew he was worried about the young woman but was too proud to admit it. Maria returned to her own work with a heavy heart. Joaquin had made a terrible mistake this time, she just knew it.

Flame sat huddled in the blanket as she thought of a plan. If she could trick Miguel somehow, fool him into untying her again, she might have a chance. Otherwise she would be at his mercy again. Her mind returned to Joaquin again and again: why had he sent no one to look for her? He cared so little that she could be gone for days and he'd not worry about her? Her anger gave her the strength to endure the day, to keep plotting, to be ready when Miguel returned. She kept the jagged rock in her hand; she'd have to drop it when Miguel untied her but she could find it easily if he didn't make her move for a moment or two. She would hit him as hard as she could, stun him at least to give her the time to flee. Surely Joaquin would not refuse to help her if she went to him and told him what Miguel had done to her. He couldn't be that heartless.

Miguel was very drunk when he scurried over the rocks at the entrance to the cave. His plan had not worked at all. Joaquin would never search for the little bitch apparently and each day he remained on the ranch it became more dangerous for him. His presence could not go on undetected for much longer. He would have to leave at dawn. At least there was the night to look forward to; he'd have his pleasure with the woman . . . that he would have Villarreal's woman would have to be enough for the time being.

Flame heard him approaching, his steps sloshing through the water as he missed his footing time and again. She could smell the liquor. That would work to her advantage . . . the more he had drunk the better. "Well, have you killed Villarreal as you promised?"

"Ah, you are awake, that is good, No, the bastard refuses to look for you, he has not left his house and barns all day. I have decided to leave for Mexico at dawn, but first I think I will have some fun with you, señorita." He scratched her face again with his rough beard, he held her face to his, crushing her lips beneath his own.

Flame relaxed completely, made no effort to fight him and Miguel leaned back, surprised. "You have no strength left to fight me? Good, that will save me the time of beating you." He put his hand under her skirt and began to run it along her thigh and still she did not flinch.

"Miguel, untie me. I will not fight you. You know I always liked you, I asked José to let you ride with me but he never would. That's why Joaquin beat you so badly that day . . . he knew how much I liked you, that I would give myself to you when we went out riding. You were too rough with me that day, that was all. Had you been more tender I would have given myself to you eagerly." Flame made her voice as sweet as honey dripping from a spoon while she shut her mind to the repulsive touch of his hand which had now strayed between her legs. Miguel was rubbing her gently, arousing her against her will. She hated what he was doing, but the warmth from his intimate caress spread down her legs and she could scarcely catch her breath.

Miguel sat back on his heels but he did not lower his hand. "I knew it, I knew you were no better than a whore, mi puta. One man was not enough for you, eh?"

Flame licked her lips and continued to spin more elaborate lies. She could not move away from his touch yet she could no longer pretend to ignore it and a moan escaped her lips as she spoke. "Villarreal is no man at all compared to you, Miguel. He can barely satisfy himself, he never pleases me. I have heard the women gossiping in the kitchen, they said you know how to please a woman, that you are a real man, not a braggart like Villarreal who is all talk and no action. Untie me, Miguel, let me feel your body against mine. If I were untied I could do things for you. I know many ways to give a man pleasure, but I can do none of them unless you untie me. Hurry, I cannot wait to feel your strength."

Miguel reached for his knife and slit the bindings on Flames ankles. Then he stopped. He could easily rip off her underclothes and rape her now, there was no reason to untie her arms.

Flame saw his hesitation but wouldn't give up now. "Hurry, free my hands so I may touch you. Show me you are a better man than Villarreal, show me!"

Miguel could not resist her silken voice. He pulled her arms roughly as he cut the ropes which bound her hands. "There, you are free, now show me what you promised, señorita. Remove your dress, it is only in the way." Miguel held his knife to her throat as he gave his command.

"Let me rub my wrists a moment—you had me tied too tightly. Lay out your blanket, we can not make love on the sand as the crabs do!"

Miguel swore but followed her suggestion. He

spread the blanket out, then doubled it over to provide a softer bed. When he turned Flame was nude, standing beside him with a small smile playing across her lips. "Come to me, Miguel. Kiss me first, but gently, there is no rush." She stepped closer and Miguel tossed his knife aside as he wrapped his arms around her tiny waist. He had never seen a more beautiful woman and was so dazzled he never saw the rock she slammed into the side of his head with a strength born of terror. She thought for a moment she had failed to stun him but then he swayed away from her, tottering slightly before he collapsed in a heap at her feet.

Flame peered down at him. He was so still, she heard no breath escape his lips but dared not touch him to make certain her blow had been a fatal one. She grabbed up her wet clothes and with frantic haste ran past Miguel's still form to the mouth of the cave. It was nearly dark and she paused only seconds to pull on her soggy dress before scrambling up the face of the cliff to find Miguel's horse tethered in a clump of bushes. Her hands shook violently as she untied the reins but she did it and swung herself up into the saddle with her last bit of strength and prayed she could reach the safety of home without fainting.

The ride to the ranch house had taken all of Flame's energy and she slid from the horse's back, barely able to stand. She stumbled across the yard and through the back door. She didn't pause as she passed by the kitchen, but Maria saw her and screamed, "Madre de dios, señorita!"

Flame wanted only one thing, to find Joaquin and tell him what she thought of him for leaving her at Miguel's mercy while he lifted not one finger to save her. She ignored Maria's frantic call and went straight to the study where she found her guardian seated at his desk, calmly working on his ledgers just as she had known he would be.

When Joaquin heard Flame come in the door he glanced up at her briefly, then went back to his work. "It's about time you came home, Maria has been very worried about you. I know I shouldn't have yelled at you about the library but hiding for more than two days was more stupid and—"

"Joaquin!" Flame's voice was a vicious snarl. "Just look at me!" She put her hands on the edge of the large walnut desk and leaned against it to keep from falling.

Joaquin threw down his pen, too relieved to see her to pretend he was angry any longer. But as soon as he looked up his eyes widened in horror. Flame was drenched from head to toe, her beautiful hair stringy and matted, her dress torn and stained. Her arms were covered with long ugly scratches and her right cheek was badly bruised and swollen where she had been struck.

"Dear God, Flame, where have you been!" He leapt to his feet and rushed to her side.

Flame screamed at him, hysterical now, the terror of the past two days and nights overwhelming her. "Where the hell have you been? Miguel Torres caught me and took to me to some hellish cave down by the point and—"

"What?" Joaquin grabbed her shoulders but slackened his hold instantly when he saw her wince in pain at his touch.

"I was walking just before dinner Tuesday night, by the vineyard. Miguel had been watching the house, waiting for just such an opportunity to find me alone. He hit me, knocked me unconscious, when I awoke I was tied up in that wretched cave. He forgot about the tide and I nearly drowned before he returned the next morning."

Joaquin was horrified by her tale. How could he have

been so callous not even to have considered the possibility something was wrong, that she had met with some accident. "Oh Flame, I am so sorry, I thought you were just trying to get even with me for yelling at you."

Flame shook her head sadly. "Miguel expected you to search for me, Joaquin, he was waiting to kill you. But you didn't come looking for me, nobody did." She began to sob then and couldn't stop. She knew how dreadful she must look, but she felt worse.

Joaquin pulled her into his arms and held her tightly as he tried to smooth her tangled hair. "I'll get the bastard, Flame, I swear I will, I'll kill him for doing this to you."

Flame pulled away and looked up at him, her long lashes spiked with tears. "You don't understand. When you didn't come, when he told me nobody was searching for me, I knew I would have to kill him myself. He was drinking all the time, he beat me, he did other things to hurt me."

Joaquin was sick with shame. How could he have thought she'd do such a childish thing as hide from him just to get even. How she must have suffered, and he hadn't even gone out to look for her, not even for five minutes had he searched.

"When you still hadn't come to look for me today he said we were going to Mexico after he, after he—"

"After what, Flame, what did he want to do?" Joaquin held her tenderly in his arms, trying to calm her, but she was trembling as she spoke and nothing he did seemed to help. "Tell me exactly what happened."

"He was going to rape me, so I killed him." Flame's eyes searched his face waiting for the look of revulsion she was sure would come. She saw only amazement in Joaquin's eyes however.

"You killed him, Flame? Are you positive? How did you do it?"

184

"With a rock, a jagged one. I hit him on the temple. He just crumpled up—I know he was dead—he was too still to be alive."

Joaquin leaned back against his desk and pulled Flame into his arms. He could no longer deny his emotions, he was furious with himself for having let her suffer so. How could he have been such a fool? She could have been killed and he hadn't even known she was in danger. When she looked up at him her gaze was so trusting, so filled with love he could not bear to think he had come so close to losing her.

Flame reached up to kiss him, her lips touching his ever so lightly, but his response was far more loving than she had dared hope. His arms enfolded her, wrapped her in his warmth as his mouth devoured hers. He had missed her terribly, wanted her, loved her so dearly and all his feelings were in his deep kiss. Finally he lifted his head and his face was filled with remorse as he gazed down at her. "Flame, if only I had known, I would have torn this ranch apart looking for you. I'm so sorry I failed you when you needed me. You are such a brave girl in spite of your size, but how were you able to strike Miguel, I thought you said he had you tied up."

Flame looked away, unable to answer. It made her sick to remember what she'd done . . . she could still feel the sickening touch of Miguel's fingers moving up her thigh. She shuddered.

"Flame, please tell me, you can tell me everything."

His eyes were so warm, so filled with love Flame made an effort to go on with her story. "I told him the same thing I told you, that if he'd let me go I wouldn't fight him. He made the mistake of believing me. I had the rock ready and when he cut the ropes I—"

The look on Joaquin's face stopped her abruptly. He was obviously disgusted beyond words with her treachery. He dropped his hands from her waist and stood up, moving away from her swiftly. "You're tired and cold; I shouldn't keep you here just to satisfy my curiosity. Go to your room and I'll send Maria in to help you with your bath."

Flame's spirits were plunged to the depths of despair by Joaquin's rejection. "Don't hate me, Joaquin, I only killed him to get away. There was no one to save me but myself—I was so afraid he was going to kill you."

"Hate you?" Joaquin pushed his hair back from his eyes and turned to face her. "I don't hate you, Flame. I'm only sorry you had to learn that trick you used to get away from me. I'm ashamed of that, not of you. Now go to your room, I'll take care of Miguel's body in the morning."

"Will you tell the sheriff, will there be a trial?"

"God no! No one else need ever know of this, there's no point in making you repeat the story. Miguel will never be missed. Now just go and get out of those wet clothes, I don't want you to get pneumonia after everything else you've been through."

Flame hesitated a moment. She'd thought when he'd kissed her that he had felt something for her, it had been so real, his love so plain on his lips. But that moment was gone, he'd shut her out again and she turned to go, hiding her tears as she went. She disgusted him now, she knew she did, she'd killed a man and he would never forget.

Joaquin slumped down at his desk and laid his head across his arms. He'd barely slept for two nights and was exhausted himself. He could remember the morning he'd pulled Flame from her horse as if it had been yesterday, her voice soft as she'd pleaded to be set free: "Turn me loose, I won't fight you." Dear God he had meant to have her, he was no better than Miguel and he was dead for his mistake of trusting her. She was exactly like a mermaid after all, just as he had imagined, she had lured a man to his death with her silken voice and loving words. It was always madness to trust a woman, but Miguel Torres had learned that lesson too late.

Maria stood back as Flame stepped into the tub. The girl had turned away quickly but not before the older woman had seen the marks on her breasts, teeth marks plainly visible on her smooth white skin. The housekeeper gasped. "Señorita, he was wrong, wasn't he? Joaquin was very wrong, you were not hiding from him."

"No, I would never hide from Joaquin."

Maria moved closer to get a better view. The girl had been abused, and badly, but by whom? "It was one of the vaqueros, I know it was. I have seen the way they all look at you. Joaquin will surely kill the man who has done this to you."

Flame relaxed in the warm soapy water, feeling the lather sting the scratches on her arms but too content to be home again to care. "It is already done, Maria. The man is dead."

"But how can that be, when?"

"Joaquin knows everything, I will speak of it no more. Now help me with my hair and stop staring."

Maria grew increasingly alarmed. Most assuredly the girl had been raped: something had to be done to see there was no child. She knelt down beside Flame and whispered, "I know of certain herbs, medicines which can be made . . . I could get them for you."

"I am only dirty, Maria, and very tired, but I'm not ill."

"But, señorita, the man, he did not rape you?"

Flame's expression froze for the briefest of seconds as the scene in the cave came back to her all too vividly.

187

"No, I was not raped. Now go, I will see to my bath alone, just go." As soon as the woman left Flame began to cry. She took the soap and wash cloth and scrubbed herself all over but still didn't feel clean. Why had Maria reminded her of what had almost happened? Would she never be able to forget the horrid sensation of Miguel's touch? Her shame at what he'd made her feel? Was that what men did when they wanted to make love to women—they could just touch them, caress them and make women want to make love too? Flame shoved the cloth into her mouth and screamed, drowning out all sound. She would never have given into Miguel, no matter what he made her feel she would have fought him forever.

Maria did as she was told, but she was worried. Would the girl hide the truth? She went straight to Joaquin with her doubts.

"Yes, Maria, what is it? Is Flame all right?" His worried expression gave her all the encouragement she needed to continue.

"You have spoken with her?"

"Yes, she told me everything."

"And the man?"

"She believes he is dead. It is too late for me to make certain tonight but if he is not dead now he soon will be."

"But if someone should discover this crime, what will we do?"

"No one ever will. You must say nothing to the others. No one must ever know of this: I will not have any scandal attached to her name. No one must ever know what has happened to her in the last few days."

Maria frowned, still concerned. "She told me she was not raped, but I do not believe her."

"What?" Joaquin was shocked. "She wouldn't lie about such a thing."

"If you had seen her just now you would know. She has been beaten, there are even teeth marks."

"Oh God." Joaquin sank down into his chair, too sick too stand, "Why would she lie to me, to both of us?"

"Which of your friends would wed a woman raped by a vaquero, Joaquin? Would you accept such a bride yourself? I think you know why she lied. There must be no child. I could give her something, but it is dangerous, I would have to be certain it is worth the risk. She must give her consent. You must ask her again, be positive, it is possible it did not happen, although what sort of man would keep her for two whole days and nights and not rape her? How could that have happened?"

Joaquin's heart sank. What man indeed would not have taken every advantage? Miguel had made no secret of his desire for Flame, he'd tried to rape her once, that's why he'd been beaten and fired. "I will ask her again, Maria."

"Joaquin, what will happen to the señorita? She is too pretty to remain here. You got rid of Torres, now another man has gone further. You say he is dead, where will it end? Half of your men are not truly vaqueros, you know that, they are bandits, cholos, murders who cannot return to Mexico. They serve you well, but you have seen how they look at her. Find her a husband and soon. Let another man worry about her unless you plan to take her for yourself." Maria held her breath and waited for Joaquin to respond. She had seen how he watched Flame—he was no different from his men. His lust was every bit as plain, and it disgusted her.

Joaquin spoke with deliberate slowness to emphasize his point as he rose to his feet. "I can hardly find her a husband if she's covered with teeth marks now, can I? Just leave me in peace, I will talk to Flame again and insist she reveal the truth of what happened."

"It must be tonight."

"Yes, I will do it." Joaquin waited until Flame had rested and had something to eat before he went to her room. He knocked softly and was surprised by how quickly she came to her door. Her long hair was nearly dry and her soft curls contrasted sharply with her bruised face and tear-filled eyes. She tried to smile at him but he could tell she had been crying.

"Yes, Joaquin?"

In her white lace-trimmed nightgown she looked so very much like an angel, a small sweet angel, and Joaquin had no wish to remind her of the horror of her ordeal. "I must speak with you for a moment. May I please come in?"

Flame stepped aside to let him enter. "Of course, this is your house."

Her words stung him, but he was uncertain that had been her intention for there was no malice in her gaze. "Flame, I am very sorry I said that to you, this is your home now too. Thank you for working on the library, it is a great improvement. You were right, and I never should have gotten mad and yelled at you the way I did."

Flame was amazed. "Why Joaquin, are you apologizing to me?"

"Have I been so hard on you that you do not even recognize an apology when I offer one?"

Flame shook her head. "I know you don't really mean to be so cruel to me, I know that."

"Cruel? Have I been that mean?"

Flame looked at him but didn't answer. He was so handsome that whenever she had been away from him, even for only an hour or two, she was always surprised when she saw him again by how truly handsome he was. Even in the dim light of her bedroom his black hair shined and his dark eyes gleamed as he looked

190

down at her. His features were without the slightest flaw, but she knew she was staring rudely and glanced away . . . he could read everything in her adoring gaze and it embarrassed her to be so transparent in her emotions. "Cruel is too harsh a word perhaps, but you have not been kind to me, you know that."

Joaquin longed to reach out and touch her, to draw her into his arms again but he forced that thought from his mind. He could hardly ask his question as it was, he could never do it with her in his arms. "Flame, Miguel obviously beat you, I know you told me he did not rape you, but if in fact he did, I really must know. There is something Maria can give you to be certain you will not have a child."

Flame's cheeks burned with embarrassment and she turned away from his perceptive glance. "Is that what you're afraid of, that I'll leave bastards on your doorsteps? How can you ask such a question? Have you no regard for my feelings, no sensitivity at all to what I've suffered?"

Joaquin gestured helplessly. "I know I am probably doing this badly, and for that I am truly sorry, but Maria says there is no time to waste if she is to help you."

When she turned back to face him he was shocked by her anger. "Is that another apology, two in one day? I must arrange to be kidnapped more often!"

"Damn it all, Flame, just tell me: did he rape you or didn't he?" Joaquin put his hands on his hips, his anger now apparent too. "And you're not counting correctly, that makes three apologies I've given you tonight!"

Flame took a deep breath and stepped closer. "I told you the truth, Joaquin. I tricked him into thinking I was willing and then I killed him. I had hours to plan it while he was away from the cave lying in wait for you. It was not a spontaneous thing, I planned it and I killed him, a cold-blooded murder is all you could ever call it.''

Joaquin moved back. She was so lovely in her sheer nightdress he could think of little other than how badly he wanted to hold her in his arms once more. He made a desperate effort to gather his thoughts. ''You had no choice, Flame, he doubtless would have killed you when he had finished with you, it was clearly self-defense.''

''No, he planned to sell me to a whorehouse in Mexico.''

''Good lord, he told you that?'' But as he looked down at her he realized she was quite serious.

''Yes, beautiful white women are apparently in scarce supply there, although I probably would not have been considered beautiful for very long.'' Flame could no longer hold back her anger. ''How long would I have had to have been gone before you came to find me, Joaquin? A week, a month, several years? Would you have ever bothered to search for me? Would you have gone so far as Mexico? Oh, Joaquin, why do I mean so little to you that you do not even care if I am gone?''

''Flame, I misunderstood, didn't realize you were in any danger.''

''Can't you just tell me the truth? You didn't care! I don't want your apologies, what difference does it make now, I killed Miguel or you would have. Just go, he didn't rape me. I'm not stupid, Joaquin, I knew better than to think I could ever come home had he done it.''

Joaquin was appalled by her bitter words. ''What do you mean?''

''You know exactly what I mean. The disgrace would have been more than a man as proud as you could ever bear. I knew you wouldn't want me then, that's why I killed him. So, I am a murderess, I suppose, but perhaps that means less to you than had I been raped in the bargain.''

''Flame.'' When he reached out to touch her she moved away. What should he say to her now? Would he have wanted her to return had Miguel had his way with her? He looked at the proud tilt of her chin and the answer was so easy. He stepped up behind her and put his hands around her tiny waist to turn her around to face him again. ''You are no murderess, do you understand? No one will ever know what happened. I did not tell Maria it was Miguel, he will never be missed and his body will never be found. And as for me, Flame, you must never be afraid to come home to me, not ever. I am not the ogre you have made me out to be . . . I will always want you here with me, always.'' He lowered his head to kiss her, to lightly brush her lips to say good night, but when she came into his arms so easily he could not draw away. His tongue parted her lips gently and he wrapped his arms around her more tightly, hugging her to him as he lengthened his sweet kiss to a far more passionate one. He moved his hand over her breast in a tender caress, but she gasped in pain. When he pulled away, her eyes were filled with tears.

''I am sorry, that was stupid of me after what you've been through. Good night, Flame. I will take care of everything in the morning, and we need never speak of this tragedy again.'' Joaquin closed the bedroom door and was gone before Flame could reply, but suddenly she was afraid he might have misunderstood, misinterpreted her reaction. She ran to her door and called after him. ''Joaquin, come back!''

He returned to her doorway, a puzzled smile lifting the corner of his mouth. ''Yes?''

Flame reached up and kissed him lightly on the

193

cheek, then whispered, "It wasn't your touch that upset me, Joaquin, but I'm just so terribly bruised. I'm sorry."

"I know, Flame." He leaned down and kissed her lips lightly. "That was very sweet of you to think of my feelings. Thank you. Now I must leave you, good night."

Flame closed her door and leaned back against it. How could Joaquin know? Then she remembered Maria's watchful eye and blushed deeply with shame. That Joaquin knew what Miguel had done to her embarrassed her terribly, and yet he didn't seem to despise her for what had befallen her. She smiled to herself as she climbed into bed. Joaquin had been nicer than he had ever been to her—was it possible he might someday come to love her after all?

She shuddered again as she recalled her captivity in the sea-filled cave, but all that really mattered was that Miguel had failed to kill Joaquin. Any sacrifice would have been worth the price to save the life of the man she loved. She hugged her pillow tightly as she fell asleep, pretending she was once again in Joaquin's warm embrace.

Eleven

In less than two weeks' time all traces of Flame's encounter with Miguel Torres had healed or faded completely, leaving no reminders of that gruesome ordeal. She resumed her earlier schedule, riding each morning and spending the warm afternoons indoors. But if she were the same again to her immense delight, Joaquin was not. He had ceased to yell, shout, or ever be angry with her. He was now friendly, if somewhat reserved, and he'd begun to treat her so sweetly, as if he really wished to see her happy.

Joaquin had been most charming all evening, smiling frequently as he related an amusing tale of one of his trips to Mexico which had been more than a little dangerous at the time but somehow in retrospect seemed merely an entertaining interlude. Flame was always fascinated by his stories; she was so involved in his adventure that she hardly tasted her dinner. His life had been so exciting, but he never talked down to her or treated her as a child . . . but then he believed her to be eighteen, a woman grown and ready to assume a life of her own.

Flame smiled and nodded as she listened, but the realization that he would never have entertained her so formally or charmingly had he known her true age saddened her. Had he known she was only sixteen she would be in a convent school that very night, dressed in some plain drab uniform rather than in the red silk dress she loved so much. Joaquin liked it too, that was obvious in his appreciative glance when she'd come into the parlor before dinner. His eyes had lingered over her bare shoulders a moment too long and when he'd looked away she'd seen all she'd hoped to find in his glance. Yes, he thought her a grown woman, had not for a moment doubted her story and she would never tell him the truth now. The prospect of being instantly banished to a convent was all too real a threat. Joaquin would do it too, he'd send her away and not let her come home until she was really eighteen. By that time anything could have happened—why, he might even have married Maria Elena by then! But Flame had no intention of letting Joaquin know she'd lied about her age to stay with him. She also had no intention of letting that awful shrew, Maria Elena, get Joaquin either. Oh no, Joaquin was hers, and she hoped he would soon realize that too.

Joaquin paused to take a sip of his wine and thought again how incredibly lovely Flame was. He marveled at her fair beauty, so different from that of the raven-haired women of his family. He could not help but smile to himself, she had more fire and spirit than any of his cousins. Why were Spanish women always described as being so passionate when Flame outshone them all? He knew it then, he'd become positively adolescent in his praise of her. He loved her, adored her, and was helpless to hide the strength of his emotions any longer. "Are you finished, Flame? It's a beautiful night . . . let's go outside and sit on the patio."

Flame smiled up at him as he helped her from her chair. He had been in such good spirits of late, hardly himself at all. In spite of her fears, he'd never mentioned Miguel again and acted as though the entire episode had never occurred. Well, she'd certainly not complain, she liked him so much better when he smiled at her as he was tonight.

Once outside Joaquin strolled around the patio for a few minutes, then pointed out the constellation Orion to her. "That bright group of stars there, can you see the three that make up his belt? Do you see them?"

Flame followed his arm but couldn't find the right series in the myriad of stars. "I'm sorry, I can never make out the figures, nothing ever looks as it should to me. I see the stars but not the pattern. Show me again, please."

Joaquin looked down at Flame's upturned face. She was peering so intently at the night-time sky that she didn't see him move until his lips covered hers. He gathered her into an embrace, crushing her slender body against his chest as he kissed her. Flame lifted her arms to encircle his neck; she had to stand on her tiptoes to reach him but the effort was most worthwhile. His mouth was warm upon hers with the faint taste of brandy making his kisses even more delicious. He kissed her eyes, her throat and then swept her up into his arms and carried her over to the wooden bench under the bougainvillea vine in the corner of the patio. He sat down, placing her gently across his lap, then lowered his head and kissed the length of her throat again before he began to loosen the hooks which secured her bodice so his lips might caress her warm, full breasts.

Flame stroked his soft shiny hair, gently separating the strands with her slender fingers as she relaxed completely in his arms. She had longed so to feel his touch again, she loved him so dearly and his kiss was like magic, drawing her further and further into desire. She felt the same longing she had felt before, she wanted more of him, all he could give, she wanted him so desperately . . . she held him tightly, clinging to him as he kissed her again and again until she was lost in the perfection of his love.

Joaquin looked down at Flame's sweet expression and knew she'd never ask him to stop, would not even be able to speak the words, yet he dared go no further. He had only meant to kiss her, to hold her—how had he nearly taken her like this, like wild creatures whose passion for each other knew no limits except the depths of their own desire? He pulled her close to his heart and held her tenderly until her breathing was even and steady once more.

"Joaquin, why did you stop?" Flame sat with her head leaning against his shoulder, very relaxed, quite content just to rest in his strong arms, but too curious to remain quiet.

Joaquin sighed and gave her an affectionate squeeze. "I am your guardian, Flame. I am supposed to protect you from reckless young men, but I fear your greatest danger lies in my arms."

Flame tried to understand his words but could not. What danger did he mean? What possible danger could there be in his love? Then she realized he hadn't said anything about love, hadn't even mentioned marriage, only warned her of danger. Perhaps she understood him after all. "Put me down, Joaquin." She took her arm from around his neck and got to her feet, none too steadily she found. "You needn't worry, Joaquin, I would never have stopped you, but it would have been impossible for me to stay here with you had we made love. Please understand that. I won't stay here and be your whore." Flame turned to walk away but Joaquin leapt to his feet, caught her wrist in his hand and spun her back to face him.

"My God, Flame, is that what you think I want?"

"I have no idea what you want. Suppose you tell me." She stood looking up at him, loving him so dearly and believing he felt nothing but lust for her. "Who's

198

supposed to protect me from you, Joaquin?''

Joaquin began to swear, losing his temper with her completely as he hadn't done in many days. "What did I do wrong, Flame? What have I ever done to make you think such a thing? How could you believe I'd use you so badly?''

Flame tapped her foot impatiently. "You've had many women, haven't you, Joaquin?''

He was ready to explode with frustration, her question pushed him beyond his endurance. "I'm thirty-one years old and no monk. I won't deny that I've known my share of women.'' More than my share, he admitted to himself.

"Would you care to tell me again that you don't want a wife?''

Joaquin shrugged. "Yes, I've said that, I'll admit it.''

"Now do you see what I mean? You do like women, you've said so many times, you just did again, but you don't want a wife. What then, could I assume I'd be to you? Nothing but your—''

Joaquin reached for her then, pulling her back into his arms, kissing her with a passion that left her weak and clinging in his embrace. His voice was hoarse with desire as he whispered, "Now do you see, do you understand? You are everything to me.''

Flame waited, she held her breath and waited for him to continue but when he did not, her heart fell. He didn't love her enough to offer marriage, he didn't want her as his wife and she'd settle for nothing less. All he wanted was her love, but no matter what name he used she'd not be his whore. She pushed herself away from his arms. "I meant it, Joaquin, I love you too much to be nothing more than your mistress. Good night.'' She started toward her room but Joaquin called after her.

"Be certain to lock your door tonight!"

"But, Joaquin, I always have." Flame did lock her door as soon as she reached her room but even the thick wooden door couldn't block the sound of her tears.

Joaquin stopped by her room on the way to his, then forced himself to go on. If he held her in his arms again that night he'd never be able to stop with kisses and he knew she had meant what she'd said. She wouldn't stay in his house if they became lovers, she couldn't stay. He was her guardian, how could she ever have thought he'd use her so casually? Didn't she feel how much he loved her? Why didn't she understand how he felt?

Flame heard Joaquin's footsteps as he walked down the hall but she made no effort to stem the flow of her tears. She had never been so miserable. What was to become of her? Maybe she shouldn't stay another night in his house. She couldn't tell him no if he wanted her; if he came after her again she couldn't say no. She wanted him so desperately, she loved him so much and wanted him, needed his love, she couldn't live without it. Yet she refused to be his mistress, to be little more than a diversion for him at his ranch. She knew he'd never be faithful to her: a man didn't have to be faithful to a mistress, only to a wife, and Joaquin had never wanted a wife. It was a hopeless situation, one from which there could be no escape. When finally she fell asleep her dreams were troubled, dark, menacing, filled with images of the horrid cave which had almost been her tomb, and when she awoke the next morning she felt far from refreshed.

Flame had ridden only a short distance from the ranch house when Joaquin came after her. Lady was swift, but no match for Diablo so Flame reined in her mount and waited for her guardian to overtake her.

"How many times must I remind you not to go out

alone!'' Joaquin was cross, his expression stern. He was never pleased with her willfulness, but especially not that day.

Flame flicked the the ends of her reins against her thigh and kept her gaze averted. ''I meant to go only a short distance, hardly out of sight of the house.''

Joaquin drew along beside her and continued to scowl. ''Oh really? Why? You're usually gone for hours.''

''I didn't realize you took any notice of my habits, Joaquin.'' Flame's eyes were a wide, innocent green when she finally dared to look up at him.

''Well I always have. Now what's the matter? I feel like riding with you today and you don't want to go far, why not?''

''I'm afraid I'm rather tired. I didn't sleep well last night.'' Flame was embarrassed that she had to remind him of their scene on the patio and looked away quickly to hide her blush.

''Come with me anyway. Tell me when you're tired and we can go back.'' He moved ahead of her without waiting for an answer, sending Diablo toward the mountains at an easy canter.

Lady followed Diablo as they rode. Joaquin led her up a hillside, up a steep trail Flame had never before followed. It wound from the floor of the valley to the crest of a hill. There he dismounted then helped her down from Lady's back, but he left his hands on her waist and pulled her close to give her a kiss. It was light, affectionate, and over long before Flame was ready to let him go. Joaquin chuckled at her puzzled expression and moved to the side of the crest.

''The view from here is magnificent, don't you agree? The sea's sparkle is so bright against the cool green of the grasses which blanket the valley. This is one of my favorite places on earth. Come here—sit beside me, Flame. Tell me what bothers you so about me.''

Flame hesitated briefly, then dropped down beside him. He was leaning back on his elbows, stretched out on the grass as if he had not a care in the world. Why had he forgotten last night's conversation so quickly? ''What bothers me? Everything about you disturbs me, Joaquin. Your looks, your smile, your words . . . most of all the fact that you are my guardian.''

''Other than the fact I am much too young to be a responsible guardian, what bothers you about our relationship?'' Joaquin was trying his best to understand her—his expression was both serious and reassuring; but his eyes were teasing, the sparkle plain in their deep brown depths.

''Don't you understand, Joaquin? I have no one. The woman who raised me is dead, the father I had hoped to know is dead. I have no one left who cares for me, who cares whether or not I live or die. If I have to leave you I have nowhere to go, unless I sleep in the ruins of my father's house.'' Flame gazed out at the endless expanse of sea.

''That's why I brought you up here today, Flame. We never have discussed your future as we should. We really must now.''

''Must?'' Flame wasn't interested in any discussion of her future unless it would include him, and she was sadly afraid it didn't.

''Yes, must. Is there something you'd like to do, someplace you'd like to visit, a trip perhaps?''

Flame shook her head. ''No, my ambition was always simply to come home to California to be with my father. Oh Joaquin, if only he hadn't died when he did! I wanted so much to see him again.''

Joaquin was too saddened by her words to respond for a moment. He hadn't even heard André mention

Flame, not once that he could recall, except their brief conversation when he'd agreed to become the girl's guardian. Yet Flame had obviously adored her father, hadn't understood how he had neglected her. "I miss him too, Flame. He was one of my best friends, remember?"

"I'm sorry, Joaquin, I didn't mean to sound ungrateful to you. It's only that I know I'm an awful nuisance to you, a dreadful bother, I know I am. If only I'd been born a boy things would have been so much easier for both of us. I'd be free to come and go as I wished, to rebuild my house, I would be no burden at all for you then."

"Well you most certainly are not a boy, Flame! God what a horrible idea—you are much too lovely to be anything other than what you are and you are hardly a nuisance. There are things we must discuss, however. Do you remember Don Diego Alvarado's son, Gabriel?"

"Wasn't he the one with the green eyes like mine?"

"Yes, that's Gabriel. Good, you do remember him. He was quite taken with you and his family would like to invite you to Los Angeles to their home for a visit."

Flame was surprised, but very pleased. "How nice of them, that's really so sweet of them to invite me. Do you think I should go?" Flame pulled up a long blade of grass and drew it through her fingers, giving it the concentration she dared not give her to distracting companion.

"That depends on you."

"Why, what do you mean?"

"I think Gabriel was more than a little impressed with you, Flame. He might propose marriage."

"What!" Flame could scarcely believe his words. "But, Joaquin, we don't know each other at all!"

"Still, you remembered him. There were plenty of

young men here that weekend and you remembered Gabriel, didn't you? Besides, the purpose of the visit would be to allow you two to become better acquainted.''

''Gabriel was very nice, but—''

''Well, do you want to go or not?'' Joaquin only wanted her to refuse so he could tell Don Diego quite honestly that she had declined the invitation with regret. He held his breath and hoped she would say no.

''Would Gabriel, or any of your other friends, Rafael for instance, want me for his wife? I have no Spanish blood at all. I got the impression you hated all of us from the East for the way you'd been treated when California became a state, the way property was lost, the way—''

''I know the list of grievances, Flame, you needn't recite them. Yes, we don't trust Anglos all that much and with good reason, but our prejudice doesn't extend to beautiful women.'' Joaquin tried to remain calm but he vowed to himself the next time she mentioned Rafael he was going to strangle her.

''I see. Well perhaps you could help me write to them and thank them for the invitation, but I can't accept it. If I went they'd think I was interested in marrying Gabriel, wouldn't they? I'm no more interested in getting married now than you are, Joaquin.''

''To tell the truth, I've been thinking quite seriously of marriage, Flame.'' Joaquin watched her expression closely from the corner of his eye while he pretended to be enjoying the view of the landscape which stretched before them. A sly smile played across his lips, he was able to keep from laughing out loud by the barest of margins.

''I see.'' Flame understood then, if he were to marry her presence in his home would be very awkward. Surely no bride would want her to remain in his home.

"You do?"

"Yes, your wife won't want me around. I can't blame her. Do you think I could find someone to rebuild my father's house so I'd have somewhere to go? The country is so pretty here and the Lannier ranch is still mine, isn't it?"

Joaquin was stunned. He'd been teasing her—he'd never expected her to calmly accept the news he'd decided to marry and not even inquire as to who his intended bride might be. "Flame, just whom do you think I've decided to marry?"

"One of your cousins? They are all very pretty, and you'd want a girl whose family came from Spain wouldn't you?"

"Spain? Why do you think that?" Joaquin was becoming more confused by the second.

"You seem like such a close group, so proud of your heritage . . . I only thought it would be natural for you to pick one of your own kind to be your wife."

"Don't you think I'd be wiser to go to Spain, back to Castile for a wife? After all if I'd insist upon a Spanish bride I might as well have an authentic one!"

Flame was puzzled. Why was he getting angry? "Yes, you could do that I suppose."

"Christ! I never thought about breeding children the way I breed horses!"

Flame's expression filled with alarm. "Joaquin, whatever is the matter with you?" She was trying so hard to be calm, not to scream, to yell and beg him not to marry someone else. It was so difficult for her to appear to be an adult all the time, and he was making it impossible for her now.

Joaquin sat up straight and glared at her. "I thought you meant what you said to me last night."

"I said far too much last night. Our argument was my fault. Will you please forgive me?" She looked down at the blade of grass in her hands. She couldn't believe she had refused to be his mistress when he had never even suggested such a thing!

Joaquin reached over and gently lifted her chin with his fingertips. His voice was almost a whisper, all the anger gone. ''Then you don't love me, Flame, not even in the smallest amount?''

His use of her own words made her smile. ''No, that was true. I do love you, Joaquin, so very, very much.''

Joaquin leaned over until their lips met. He kissed her—softly at first, then gathered her into his arms and began to kiss her with almost an animal abandon, as if he couldn't get enough of her. His passion would have frightened her witless had she not loved him so much. He held her close to his heart and kissed her hungrily until she clung to him, pressing her soft slender body along the length of his.

Joaquin's lips traveled slowly down Flame's smooth throat as he unbuttoned her blouse. He ran his fingertips over her softly rounded breasts as his kiss strayed lower until his tongue could caress her firm pink flesh, teasing her flushed skin until she could bear no more of his intoxicating touch and moaned softly.

''Flame, I love you so, I love you so much.'' He had never said those words to another woman but he meant them now. He could not say them often enough to her, and he told her again and again how much he loved her as his kisses became more demanding. His hands moved over her slender body, caressing her more boldy, then slid under her belt, gently awakening within her a desire which matched his own.

Flame was lost in her passion for Joaquin. Her small hands reached up to touch his face, to caress his strong body which cried out for hers. She was swept along by the need for him his kisses always created; his easy touch brought such ecstasy she wanted only to give herself to him, to give her very soul into his keeping. But as he began to remove the last of her clothing, the final barrier which separated them, something warned her—a voice, a shadow, a memory of what she'd been carefully taught all her life—and she was suddenly terrified of him. She pushed him away, crying as she pulled her clothes back into place. "No, Joaquin, no. Please stop . . . don't make me do it now . . . please don't." Flame got to her feet and ran to Lady, grabbing the startled mare's bridle and leading her back down the steep path.

Joaquin watched Flame go without saying a word. He couldn't have called out to her if he'd tried. He rolled over on his back and groaned in frustration. He had never wanted a woman as much as he wanted Flame. It was so right, so beautiful—why had she run away just when he'd thought she'd wanted him to make love to her, to finally complete what they'd begun the first morning he'd seen her. He sat up and slammed his fist into the ground, hardly wincing at the pain that gesture brought. Damn, she was riding alone again too! He struggled to his feet and walked over to Diablo. The horse was watching him and shook his finely shaped head, sending his gleaming mane flying.

"That never happens to you, does it, boy? No mare was ever so fickle as that woman!" But Joaquin was smiling: he loved Flame far too much to do anything more than smile. He would let her go . . . they'd have a lifetime to make love now.

Flame put her foot in the stirrup and swung her leg over Lady's back as soon as she reached the level ground of the valley. She dug her heels into the mare's sides and headed back toward the house without turning to see if Joaquin were following her. She was shaking so violently she could scarcely hold the reins in her hands and tears streamed down her face as she rode home. What would Joaquin think of her now? She'd run away from him like a frightened child. He'd said he loved her, over and over again he'd said it as he'd kissed her, and if he hadn't asked her to marry him he had at least mentioned marriage. Why had she run from him like some stupid girl who'd been too afraid to finish what she'd begun? He'd have no respect for her now that she'd left him like that, run away when she knew he loved her and wanted her as much as she wanted him. Her whole body ached, demanding the love she'd refused to accept, and she cried all the harder.

Once she'd reached the barn she pulled the saddle from Lady's back, removed her bridle and sent the mare out to the corral without brushing her shiny coat as she always did. She didn't want to be anywhere near the barn when Joaquin returned, so when she'd returned her saddle to the tack room she ran into the house and called Maria to ready her bath. She couldn't get out of her clothes fast enough; she pulled off her boots and flung them to the floor. She was still shaking when Maria came into her room and the older woman sensed something was amiss instantly.

"Señorita, are you ill?" The kindly housekeeper reached out to touch Flame's forehead but found it cool. "What is wrong little one? It wasn't one of the vaqueros again, not one of the men?"

"No, it is nothing, I'm fine." Flame stepped into the steaming tub and the warmth of the water helped to soothe away her tension, but she was far from calm and Maria hesitated to leave.

"Señorita, if one of the vaqueros has been too forward, has followed you, please tell Joaquin. He will fire the man, send him away."

Flame shook her head. "You don't understand, Maria, I can't tell Joaquin about this. It's no concern of his, now please go."

"As you wish, señorita." The woman left quietly, only the swish of her long skirt as she moved across the wooden floor broke the stillness of the room. She'd speak to Joaquin as soon as he returned. Then she began to wonder: she'd seen Flame leave and return alone—Joaquin didn't permit that. She'd have to speak to him to remind the girl again before another vaquero took a liking to her the way Miguel Torres had. Would there be no end to the problems Joaquin had because of the beautiful little woman?

Joaquin didn't return to the ranch house for hours. As long as he was out riding he had stock to check and colts he wanted to see, and it was late afternoon before he came home. When he came over the rise nearest his house he saw Rafael riding up and spurred Diablo so he might meet his friend on the road.

"Rafael, I didn't expect to see you again so soon after your last visit. What brings you back? I promised to come to San Francisco soon." The two young men embraced and José came to take their mounts to the barn.

"Captain Rodriguez has fallen ill. I hesitate to hire another man to replace him but his ship will sail in two weeks and cannot go without someone in command."

"Blast the luck! I swear I hate those ships, Rafael, let's sell them all. They are too much trouble to keep afloat. I know my father loved them, but I do not."

"They have made you rich many times over, Joaquin. You'd have to pay to transport your hides to New York if you didn't own your ships. You'd lose the revenue from the cargo they bring back to San Francisco too. It would be financial suicide to sell those ships."

"As always you are a practical man, and right." Joaquin led his friend into his study and poured him a glass of wine. "So Rodgriguez is ill. How ill? Will he not recover in two weeks' time?"

Rafael shook his head. "No, he may never recover. The doctor believes it is his heart."

"I'd sail the damn *Reina* myself, Rafael, but for—" Joaquin caught himself abruptly before he said Flame's name, remembering that at their last parting Rafael had made his feelings for the young woman very clear.

"You've done it before, Joaquin. You are a fine captain in spite of your dislike for the sea."

"I will come back with you to San Francisco and we will find a man to replace Rodriguez. It may take the full two weeks before the *Reina* sails to find a good one."

"Unfortunately that's probably true. Honest and hardworking men are never in generous supply." Rafael sipped his wine slowly, then sat forward in his chair, his real interest now apparent. "Where is Flame? Is she well?"

Joaquin's smile was immediate as he thought of his love. "Yes, she is fine. I don't know where she is at this moment since I've been out all day, but she'll join us for dinner. She'll be happy to see you again, for she mentions your name frequently." Too damn frequently, he thought to himself.

"Joaquin, I think it was a mistake for me to leave here without speaking to her myself. She is too independent a woman not to be consulted on a matter so important as her marriage. Even if Rodriguez had not fallen ill, I would have come to see her."

Joaquin sighed slowly. His last excuse had been feeble, and now he had none. He shifted uncomfortably in his chair, got up to refill their glasses with the deep red wine, then sat back down, and still had thought of nothing to tell his frind.

"Joaquin, what is the matter with you? Can't you give me some sort of an answer this time? I know you feel Flame is too young, but at eighteen she is certainly

210

old enough to marry. Many women are married by that age and I can provide for her well.''

Joaquin waved away Rafael's comments with one sweeping gesture. "It is not that you are not a fine man, my friend. I could wish no better husband for her than you, but the truth is I have fallen in love with her myself and—"

"What!" Rafael leapt to his feet. "But you knew that I loved her, had spoken for her!"

"Yes, I know, but when I refused you before it was because I loved her. I didn't admit it then, not even to myself, but I have loved her for a long time, perhaps since the day we met." He knew the truth of his words as he spoke them. He had always loved Flame, since she had been no more than an exquisite child he had adored her.

Rafael was outraged by his friend's confession. "What does she say? Has she accepted your proposal?"

"No, I haven't asked her to marry me as yet, but she knows how much I love her."

Rafael's eyes narrowed to vicious slits. "But you have kept her here in your house? Joaquin, if you have been—"

"No, Rafael, do not worry." Joaquin rose to his full height, he had a slight advantage over Rafael in stature and drew some comfort in that fact now. How could he deny anything, he wondered, he'd nearly made love to Flame only hours before, would have gladly had she not run away. Would he have been able to face his friend so coolly then?

Rafael was furious, as mad at Joaquin as he had ever been. He knew the man too well, knew how easily he seduced women and in spite of his denial he did not believe him. He could have killed Joaquin, slit his throat, shot him dead, strangled him with his bare hands, each

211

thought occurring to him in rapid succession. He loved Flame too dearly to leave her at Joaquin's mercy another instant. "Go find her, Joaquin, right now. I wish to speak with her. There is no reason for me to believe she would prefer you to me. Let us ask her. Go find her now—send Maria for her immediately."

"I will go myself. Wait here, Rafael, I will be only a moment." Joaquin was only too glad to leave his friend alone for a few minutes. Perhaps he would calm down enough to see reason. He had recognized the murderous gleam in Rafael's eye and had no wish to provoke him any further. He glanced in the library as he walked past, looked in the patio and when he didn't see Flame went on to her room. He knocked lightly at her door and heard her reply.

Flame had fallen asleep after her bath; she lay stretched across her bed, still wrapped in her towel. Joaquin's call had awakened her, but slightly, and thinking it was Maria she answered, "Yes, come in."

Joaquin entered swiftly, then stopped to stare. "Flame!"

Flame rubbed her eyes as she sat up, she tucked the towel more securely over her breasts and pushed her long golden curls away from her face. "I'm sorry, Joaquin, I thought you were Maria. What is it?"

Joaquin's eyes swept over her slender figure before lingering on her face. She was so lovely he could scarcely speak. "Flame, it is so difficult for me to remember why I came in here when you are so lovely."

Flame smiled sweetly. His expression was so dear she could not resist him. "Leave me and I'll get dressed, I will only be a minute."

"No, listen to me first. Rafael just arrived and he wants to see you right away. I didn't tell you when he first asked my permission to marry you and now—"

Flame leapt from her bed in one agile motion, her

212

green eyes flashing wickedly as she crossed the short distance between them. "What? When was this? Why didn't you tell me?"

Joaquin was surprised by her anger—everyone seemed to be mad at him at once. "Why do you *think* I didn't tell you?"

"I can't imagine why, Joaquin. After all it is my life we are discussing, isn't it? Am I to have no say as to whom my husband will be after all? Is this what you mean to do to me, promise me to Rafael and not even bother to mention it?"

Joaquin leaned back against the door and closed his eyes. "It was the last time he was here, Flame, after the party. I gave him every excuse I could think of because I couldn't bear the thought of your leaving me. I didn't know what you'd say and I couldn't run the risk of losing you."

"Oh Joaquin, had he asked me then I would have said yes. I thought you hated me then and I didn't think I could go on living here when I loved you so." Flame stepped closer, put her arms around his neck and drew his mouth down to hers. "And you didn't know how I felt about you? I have always loved you, since the moment I first saw you I have loved you." She reached up to kiss him, her lips cool and sweet upon his.

Joaquin pulled her into his arms, holding her scantily clad body close to his. He kissed her eyelids, her cheeks, the elegant line of her slender throat before his lips found hers again and he was lost in the love he felt for her, it overwhelmed him with longing. He pulled away her towel and began to caress her sweet, young body, he meant to take her right then as he could wait no longer when he suddenly remembered his friend was waiting to see her. "Oh Christ, I forgot all about Rafael. I have never seen him so angry, Flame. Get dressed and come talk with him." Joaquin drapped the towel around her nude form and secured it quickly before he stepped back.

"What shall I say to him?" Flame looked up at Joaquin, her bright eyes alight with mischief. That she had been standing naked in his arms did not embarrass her, she loved him far too much to even notice that breach of propriety.

"I don't care how you put it as long as you tell him no."

"Perhaps I can find a tactful way to refuse him, Joaquin. He has been a good friend to me and I know this will hurt him no matter how I say it."

Joaquin turned to open the door and found Rafael waiting on the other side. His friend needed only a fraction of a second to observe Flame's flushed cheeks and scant attire before he drew back his fist and hit Joaquin as hard as he could, the blow glancing off the taller man's cheek as he dodged away.

Terrified, Flame screamed, "Rafael, no wait, you don't understand!"

"I've already waited too long, Flame, that is obvious to me now!" He grabbed the front of Joaquin's shirt in his left hand as he brought his right hand back to strike him again.

Joaquin blocked Rafael's punch and shoved him away. "You want to fight me? All right, but I'll not fight here in Flame's bedroom, come outside."

Flame grabbed Rafael's arm in a vain attempt to stay his anger. "No, you needn't fight with him, wait!"

"Let me go, I'll kill the bastard if I can!" Rafael pushed Flame's hands away and followed Joaquin, yanking off his coat and tie and he walked briskly down the hall, eager for the fight to begin.

Flame was frantic. Could Rafael actually hurt Joaquin? Dear God, she couldn't let them fight each other. She ran to her wardrobe and pulled out the first dress she found, buttoning it as she ran barefooted out to the yard. Several men had already gathered, laughing and joking as if the fight were being staged simply for their amusement.

Flame saw José among the gathering crowd and ran to his side. "Stop them, José, you must stop them!" She grabbed the foreman's arm, dragging him along with her in a desperate plea for help.

"Señorita, I could not stop them no matter how badly you wished me to. They have fought each other before this, do not worry, they will not hurt each other too badly."

"Not hurt each other? My God, Rafael means to kill Joaquin! Don't you understand, he means to kill him!" Flame shrieked, her hysteria overtaking her reason. She couldn't bear to watch the two men, they were too vicious, their punches brutal. Rafael was indeed out for blood and although slightly smaller in stature, his anger gave him the additional strength he needed to provide Joaquin with an opponent both fierce and tough.

Flame covered her eyes. She couldn't stand it—the vaqueros' rude calls, the crushing sounds of the blows when they found their mark, the dust flying in all directions . . . it was all horrible, and she fled back to the safety of her room and cried pathetically until all her tears were spent. How could they fight like that over her? Did they think she had no choice, no say in the matter of whom she would marry? She couldn't hear the noise of the fight from her room and her worst fears filled her mind. What if one man severely injured the other? It was possible to beat a man to death—she'd seen Joaquin come close to that with Miguel. Was he more angry now? No nightmare was ever so terrifying as the minutes she passed that afternoon while the two men fought. She was mad at them, horribly angry, and so afraid one would be hurt in an argument that had no

215

purpose whatsoever. The choice was hers to make, not theirs!

Flame sat up as she heard footsteps pass by in the hall, but they did not stop at her door. She heard nothing else though she waited as long as she could before opening her door. The yard was quiet when she reached the back door, not a soul was in sight. Tormented by fear Flame turned toward the kitchen where Maria and several other women were preparing dinner. They seemed not to notice her presence as they worked.

"Maria! Where's Joaquin? What happened?"

"You did not stay to watch, señorita? It was a pity—they fought so hard all to impress you and you did not want to watch."

"Impress me? They made me sick! Where are they now?" At least neither appeared to be dead, she thought with relief, for Maria would not be working so nonchalantly had a tragedy occurred.

"Dressing for dinner I believe."

"They are going to eat dinner together, here, after that awful fight?"

"Yes, of course, the question was settled to their satisfaction. They will be friends again as before."

Flame's heart leapt to her throat, "Settled? Then who won?"

"You will have to ask them, I'll not speak for them. Do you wish me to come help you dress for dinner now too?"

"No, no!" Flame shook her head then ran back to her room and threw herself across her bed. Dinner was the last thing she wanted. She'd be fortunate if she weren't violently ill. She began to sob again as she tried to think what she could do. Would the winner just come for her as if she were the prize? At least they were going to change their clothes, wash off the blood. She was

216

going to be sick, she knew it. She lay back across her bed and closed her eyes.

Maria came in to get Flame later and found her still dazed, standing at the window staring out at the gathering dusk. "Señorita, they are waiting for you, you must dress. I will help you."

Flame turned to answer but couldn't, her eyes were still bright with tears. The two men she loved most dearly had fought over her as if she were nothing to them, a woman with no right to choose her own husband, and she could not forgive them for that insult.

"Come, sit down here, I will select your dress." Maria led Flame over to the chair in front of the dresser and began to brush her long curls. "You have so many pretty gowns. I will pick one they will like."

Flame felt numb, too angry to face either Joaquin or Rafael that night or ever again. Maria kept on talking, chattering on and on, but Flame scarcely listened to what the woman said.

"They have fought each other many times, little one, since they were no more than children. It is mere sport to them, do not worry so."

But Flame was worried, worried sick: what if Rafael had won? Would Joaquin just give her away? When she was finally ready Maria had to lead her to the door.

"Señorita, come, they have waited too long for you already." Maria could not understand Flame's despair: men always fought over women, everyone knew that, it could not be helped. So why was the señorita so distraught?

Flame walked into the parlor where Joaquin and Rafael were standing on opposite sides of the room. Both turned to face her, each looking embarrassed, sheepish about his actions that afternoon. Joaquin's cheek was bruised where Rafael's first punch had caught him off-guard and there was a cut over his left eye but other than that he didn't seem any worse for the altercation until he began to walk toward her and it was obvious to her there was something wrong with the way he moved. It would not have been noticed by a stranger, but it was by her. He might try and hide it but he had been hurt, if not badly then somewhat and it showed in his gait. He noticed her concern and shook his head. "It is nothing, now come and let's eat. I am famished."

Rafael also walked with a limp, and his right eye was nearly swollen shut. It would be quite black by morning. He took his chair across from Flame with a distinct hesitation, as if the effort to be seated were not worth the cost of pain.

When their dinner had been served Joaquin mumbled something which seemed to pass for grace and then began to eat with hardy enthusiasm. After a few bites he looked over at Rafael. "Is there any chance we might be able to find that Norwegian captain we met last year? Pedersen was his name, wasn't it?"

"We can try. I have no idea if he's in San Francisco or not, but it is possible that he is."

Flame had not taken a single bite. She sat and stared at the two young men. They looked awful, they could hardly move, and now they were going to calmly discuss some business matter? She interrupted them abruptly: "Would one of you care to tell me about the outcome of that disgraceful fight? Did you pick a winner or was it by some chance a draw? It certainly isn't apparent from looking at you two which was the victor."

The tone of her voice was a clear warning to Joaquin. He put down his fork and spoke in the calmest manner he could summon. "I won. You'll marry me, Flame."

"Oh really? And would you mind telling me why you thought I would ever agree to marry the winner of that ghastly brawl?"

218

Joaquin knew she was angry, yet he could see no way to avoid the scene he knew was coming. "Look, I'm very sorry that we frightened you, but—"

"Frightened me? My God, you scared me to death! Look at you men—you two could have killed each other! Did you think that would please me for some reason? Do you think I enjoy seeing men I love hurt? I am no mare who can be impressed by the strength of a stallion! I am a woman and what I understand is love, tenderness, feeling—not the brute force you animals turned on one another! Why in heaven's name did you think what you did was worth your effort when whom I'll marry is my decision and not yours!" Flame's eyes were as deep a green as her stunning gown. She looked sweet and innocent but her words stung with the sheer viciousness of truth.

Joaquin looked over at Rafael, hoping for assistance, but he provided no aid at all, just shook his head and frowned. He'd not interfere now.

"I thought I was your choice, Flame." Joaquin's tone was pleasant, but her response was not.

"Is this how you'd ask me to be your wife? It did not occur to you that perhaps I'd appreciate being asked? I didn't expect compliments, nor gifts, certainly not poetry, but I did hope to be asked with all the courtesy you possess, Joaquin. I'm sorry to see you didn't think of my feelings at all this afternoon. Is that what I am to expect from you? I can not bear to sit here and look at you two, it breaks my heart to see the way you've

fight a

I am

change the way I feel! I could

lady know which man I love!

happy to become his bride if

the manners to ask me as if he really were

gentleman everyone thinks he is!" Flame threw

219

down her napkin, and leaving her dinner untouched fled from the room so quickly her tiny feet barely brushed the floor.

Joaquin began to swear in his usual stream of foul epithets, but Rafael only laughed, he threw back his head and howled with laughter. "Joaquin, I think Flame has just beaten us both!"

Twelve

Joaquin stretched out his long legs, blocking the aisle next to their table, disregarding the angry stares of the sailors who had to make their way around him to reach the bar. He and Rafael had been in San Francisco for a week and as yet had found no man they'd trust to captain the *Reina del Mar*. Joaquin slammed his empty tankard down on the scarred table top and commented bitterly, "If we don't find a man by tomorrow night I'll have to take her myself, that's the only choice I'll have left."

"Yes, I know, but it will take you three months to make the voyage to New York and as long to return, to say nothing of your time in port. Do you want to give more than half a year to this, Joaquin?"

"Hell no, the five worst years of my life were those I spent on board the *Reina*. My father was the one who should have gone to sea and left me at home to run the ranch. Why is it fathers force their sons into the occupation they wish they had chosen for themselves?"

Rafael shrugged. After several tankards of ale he too was feeling quite philosophical. "Who knows, but it is a pattern repeated far too frequently. Remember that, Joaquin, and do not make the same mistake with your own sons."

Joaquin's reply could not have been more obscene—the rough-looking seamen at the adjoining table turned to stare in surprise for even they were not used to such foul language. They continued to stare in wonder at the two elegantly dressed Spaniards, obviously fine gentlemen, and shook their heads in disbelief.

Rafael chuckled at his friend's temperamental outburst. "Joaquin, you and Flame will undoubtedly have many sons, regardless of what you may think tonight." He had resigned himself to losing the lovely girl—it still hurt and he was afraid it always would, but he had accepted his loss as fact now.

"Didn't you understand what she said to me? She as good as refused me. We will have no sons." Joaquin's scowl deepened as he recalled her words.

"She disliked our fighting over her, you can't blame her for that. We behaved like two wild dogs fighting over a bitch and she was insulted, as well she should have been. She is a fine lady, Joaquin, innocent and so very sweet—I was very wrong to believe what I did when I saw you coming from her room. This whole unpleasant matter was my fault, and now, unfortunately, you are the one who must pay for it. I am sorry for that, my friend."

Joaquin opened his mouth to disagree, then thought better of it. There was no point in admitting to Rafael that his suspicions were indeed correct, that his relationship with Flame was by no means so chaste as he led him to believe. Instead he sought the safer course and changed the subject again. "I think perhaps I should captain the *Reina* myself, that will give Flame six months' time in which to grow up."

"She did not behave in a childish manner, Joaquin, we did. Will you become any more adult in half a year's time? I doubt it, for you are too set in your ways now to change." Rafael continued to stare at his foul-tempered companion. They had been up late each night gambling for increasingly higher stakes with Joaquin winning more each successive game. Rafael had never seen Joaquin on so self-destructive a binge. Frequently he gambled, but now he was pushing his bets to the limit, as if daring fortune to cross him. He was angry through and through, but Rafael understood the cause readily. Before this trip their evenings had always ended in the same way, in the arms of some expensive and exotic woman, but not this time. Now Joaquin would ignore his companions' invitations to visit houses where he had once found pleasure; he would take his winnings and depart to sleep alone, returning the next night to the gaming tables to gamble for even larger stakes. Rafael shook his head, it was no use. Joaquin would never find the peace he sought in the thrill of the cards, he'd already rejected the women, the answer was obvious, he simply wanted Flame. No other woman could ever make him happy, no game of chance could equal the excitement of her love. Rafael looked at his friend's drawn face and was surprised again by Joaquin's sorrowful expression. He had never thought the day would come when that man would fall in love, actually learn to care for a woman. The realization that he truly did love Flame had not been difficult for Rafael to accept, for Joaquin was absolutely miserable without the woman and it was plain in his every gesture and expression.

He knew they would have a difficult time signing a crew if Joaquin captained the *Reina*. He detested the sea and ran a ship with so strict a hand few men would serve him. Yet he had always earned his crews' respect, for no captain ever worked harder. The caliber of the captain made all the difference in a ship so sensitive as the China clipper and Joaquin was superb. He had learned so easily, understood how far the magnificent craft could be pushed and had absolutely none of the fear which handicapped lesser men. He could sail with the greatest of skill yet preferred life on his ranch so much more that he'd come to hate the ships which took him away from his home.

"Joaquin, I have seen you buy gifts, and expensive ones too, for women you scarcely knew. Have you given no thought to buying something to please Flame? You have never given her any present, have you?" Rafael was trying his best to lift his best friend's spirits with conversation in a lighter vein.

"I gave her the mare, Lady. I at least gave her a horse." Joaquin spoke without glancing up, his voice bitterly sarcastic.

Rafael laughed, then signaled the bar maid for another round: "A useful gift at least, perhaps better than jewelry after all."

"I have never seen Flame wear jewels of any kind, never. Have you ever noticed that she doesn't?"

"Yes, but you don't know her reason?"

Now Joaquin was intrigued. "No, what is it? Does she dislike jewelry for some reason? It would be just my luck to give her some if she does."

"No, but she sold all she owned to pay for her trip to come west, Joaquin. Her grandmother's estate undoubtedly includes some but she did not wish to wait for the reading of the will to bring it with her."

Joaquin winced with real pain. "I didn't know, poor child. You should hear her speak of her father, as if he were the finest man who ever lived."

"André was a good man, you've got to admit that."

"Yes, in many ways he was, but he never thought of Flame, never knew her. I wonder now how he ever thought to ask me to become her guardian should the need arise when he cared so little about her happiness."

"I suggested it." Rafael made no effort to hide his grin.

"You!" Joaquin sat up abruptly, at last leaving the

224

narrow aisle clear of his feet. "What possessed you to do that?"

"I had been helping him arrange his papers, deeds, documents of various types, whatever. I insisted he make some provision for his daughter when he wrote his new will. But had I known Flame, I would have named myself as her guardian."

Joaquin chuckled at last, his usual good humor restored. "You are every bit as irresponsible as I am, Rafael. We make a fine pair of guardians for a beautiful young woman."

"But very loving ones, no?" Rafael inquired slyly.

"Yes, very loving indeed. Do you really think if I return home and propose to Flame in a more gentlemanly fashion she will accept?"

"I have no doubt of it, much to my despair. I never had a chance with her once she'd laid eyes on you. She is like all women, they all prefer you." Rafael was not jealous, merely commenting on what he'd observed over the years to be true.

Joaquin hastened to disagree. "That is not true. We are enough alike to be taken for brothers; in fact, we have been mistaken for such on more than one occasion. I see very little difference between us and while I may be able to beat you senseless with my fists, I think you are far the better man. You have the ability to reason carefully where I have only my temper to guide me. It has cost me too much—I hope it has not cost me Flame."

"Perhaps you are growing up at last, Joaquin, if you have finally realized your temper is your greatest enemy. But when it comes to women, it is your charm which leads them to prefer you. I fear that while I am almost as handsome as you are, I am not nearly so charming."

"You could be though, if you but tried. Now what

should I purchase for Flame, emeralds do you think? Although she really doesn't need jewels with those incredible eyes of hers."

"No, but they would please her. That you thought of her and took the time to bring her a present would please her enormously."

"Now look who is being charming." But as Joaquin laughed he realized the real difference between himself and his friend. Rafael really cared for women, liked them, treated them with tender respect, where he himself had always only used them. Suddenly he was ashamed. "No, Rafael, in many ways you are a far better man than I will ever be."

Rafael looked past Joaquin then and to his amazement he saw Olaf Pederson coming in the tavern door. "Joaquin, I think we have found our captain and you will be able to return to Flame quickly after all!"

Unfortunately, it took Joaquin and Rafael the better part of three days to draw up a contract which satisfied Captain Pederson and in that time an earnest young man from the East arrived in San Francisco. For years afterward Joaquin would ponder the remarkable stroke of chance which brought them together, one full of love and hope, the other filled with hate and lust for revenge which would hasten his own demise. For on the night Captain Pederson at last agreed to take command of the *Reina del Mar,* Alex Richmond of Philadelphia took a seat opposite Joaquin in a game of chance where no one was to be the winner.

Alex Richmond ran his fingers around the inside of his stiff white collar, then tried to relax. He had become more nervous with each successive hand. Never had he played cards with such a serious group of gamblers and he knew he was in way over his head. The Spaniard was the very devil to beat, he won nearly every hand—and far too easily, as if poker bored him totally. Alex could

226

detect no pattern to the man's play, it was impossible to predict with certainty if he were merely bluffing or held a hand none could beat. Alex disliked the dark-eyed man more each minute. He'd not spoken when they'd been introduced, hardly looked at his companions except with a chilling stare that made Alex's blood run cold. He was obviously very rich, his well tailored suit very fine, and his companion at the next table was nearly his mirror image. Devils, both of them, and they were two men Alex hoped never to meet again. Finally he could take no more and threw down his cards. "That's it for me tonight. With luck like I've had I'll have to return to Philadelphia long before I'd planned to depart."

Joaquin raised an eyebrow quizzically. "You are from Philadelphia?"

"Why yes." Alex was surprised by the Spaniard's sudden interest in him. "Have you ever been there?"

"No, but my ward is from your city."

"You have a child from Pennsylvania in your care?" Alex was amazed by that news. "How did you come to be responsible for a child from the East?"

Joaquin got to his feet, scooping up his winnings as the others also decided to call it a night. "I did not say my ward was a child."

"Well, no, but I assumed—"

"That is your problem, Mister—I'm sorry, what was your name?" Joaquin seemed to have little interest in the reply to his inquiry.

"Richmond, Alex Richmond."

"Well, Mr. Richmond, you'd do well to give up poker, you assume too much. My ward is eighteen, hardly a child anymore."

"An eighteen-year-old boy?" Alex was still perplexed.

Joaquin shook his head. "You're wrong again, as

227

usual. My ward is female.''

"What is her family name? Perhaps I knew her."

"Perhaps. Her last name is Lannier."

"Flame!" Alex leapt to his feet so quickly he nearly upset the table.

Joaquin looked the astonished young man up and down slowly, his dark gaze piercing in its intensity. "I see that you did indeed know her."

"Know her! We were engaged to be married!"

Now Joaquin was the more astounded of the two. He looked closely at the fair-haired young man, but could not believe his ears. How could Flame have been engaged to this dandy, and when? He gestured toward a small room off the side of the gaming tables, "Would you care to speak to me for a few minutes in private, Mr. Richmond?"

Alex needed no more than a second to reply. "Of course." He followed Joaquin into the smaller room and licked his lips as he took a chair. So Flame was in California and the ward of this man who looked more like a pirate than a guardian? The silver-handled knife at the man's belt had shone with a menacing gleam all evening and he could imagine how the villain would deal with someone he caught cheating him at cards. His anger with Flame's treachery made him bold, however, and he knew if he thought quickly enough he could cause her as much embarrassment as she had caused him. He'd teach the bitch a lesson she'd not soon forget. "I beg your pardon, did you say eighteen? Flame is only sixteen years old."

Joaquin leaned back against the door and crossed his arms over his chest. "Only sixteen, you say? Are you certain?"

"Positive of the fact. I've known Flame for twelve years, ever since she came to live with her grandmother in Philadelphia when she was four."

"When were you engaged to her, Mr. Richmond?"

"This past spring, in April, it was all arranged, but when Flame's grandmother died suddenly she just disappeared. I had no idea where she'd gone. My only hope was to come to California and try to contact her father." That was of course a complete fabrication—he'd never even considered looking for her after what she'd done to him—but he hoped the lie would make his story more convincing.

"Did you really expect to find her in this establishment?"

"No, of course not. I've just arrived in California, it is a large state and I had no idea where to look except that I thought she'd be with her father. How did you come to be her guardian?"

"André Lannier is deceased." Joaquin had not altered his original opinion: he didn't like Alex Richmond in the least.

"Oh, we didn't know that. Mrs. Bellefontaine's lawyer had never kept up a regular correspondence with Mr. Lannier and after her death we couldn't find his address in her things, probably because Flame took it herself to foil just such a search."

"Mrs. Bellefontaine was Flame's grandmother? If I have ever heard her name before this I had forgotten it."

"Yes, she was the one who contacted my parents about our marriage."

"Wasn't that a bit unusual?"

Alex looked up at Joaquin and judged him correctly: the man was obviously a gentleman in spite of his threatening demeanor. If he were Flame's guardian his behavior was undoubtedly extremely proper, therefore, he would be unable to dispute any tale Alex wished to concoct. He tried his best to appear flustered, "Mister, ah—"

"Villarreal."

"Yes, thank you. Mr. Villarreal, may I trust that what I say will be kept in the strictest of confidence?"

Joaquin agreed impatiently, anxious to hear the end of the young man's story. "Yes, of course, say whatever you wish, it will go no further than this room."

"It has been over four months, her condition is not obvious?"

"What are you saying?" Joaquin straightened up to his full height, but his horrified expression gave Alex all the encouragement he needed to continue.

Alex got up from his chair and began to pace the floor. "I was never sure she really was pregnant, she was not a virgin when I first had her but—"

Joaquin sprang at Alex, grabbing the young man's coat lapels in his two hands and lifting him clear off the floor. "How dare you!"

Alex struggled to get free as he continued to lie, "If she is your ward you must know what she's like. I've never had another woman like her, don't you agree? She's better than any of the women I've had here in San Francisco, they are pretty but lack her skill."

Joaquin could not hide his shock as Alex went on to compare Flame to Celeste and another of the city's better known prostitutes, women Joaquin knew all too well.

Alex grew bolder by the minute—this was almost worth losing so heavily to the dark-eyed bastard. "Flame is very sweet, so affectionate, but the things she knows how to do. . . ." He went on to describe several particularly enticing perversions he'd only read about, adding all the details he could remember to give credence to his tale. "Do you by any chance own a small whip?"

Joaquin fell back against the door, too sick with shame to respond. It couldn't be true, none of it could possibly be true!

"But if you say she's not pregnant, and it would be obvious by now if she were, perhaps that is why she came to California. She was undoubtedly too embarrassed to tell me her suspicions proved false after I'd agreed to marry her when she wasn't even certain the child was mine. I felt it was the least I could offer since the babe might have been mine. But apparently she was mistaken, or perhaps she took something to cause a miscarriage. Is she seeing any of her friends from the Presidio?"

"What, she knows men from the Presidio of Monterey?" Good God, what else? Joaquin could stand very little more.

"Yes, she had several friends, lieutenants who came out to California about the same time she did. I was going there next, I was sure if she'd arrived here she would have contacted them immediately. Frankly, I'd always thought Bradley was the baby's father, but since you say she isn't pregnant I will worry no more about seeing her again, it was the child I was concerned about most."

"Mr. Richmond, do you really expect me to believe this ridiculous tale of yours?" Joaquin asked skeptically.

Alex appeared very offended. "Why of course, it is no tale, but the truth. I can't believe you haven't held her in your arms, at least kissed her. She never could keep her hands off me. She is simply the most affectionate woman ever born."

Joaquin tried to swallow the painful lump which filled his throat as he turned away. Yes, Flame was affectionate all right, and no matter how he tried to fight Alex's words they rang true. She had nearly given herself to him on more than one occasion, before she even knew his name for Christ's sake. He'd been the one who'd stopped short of making love—it was only the last time they'd been together that Flame had been the one to say no. Only after he'd mentioned marriage had she said no. Dear God, was that why she'd gotten so frightened? Was she terrified that he wouldn't marry her if he made love to her first and found her not a virgin? He was sickened by Alex's story, filled with shame and the awful dread that it was all true. "Are you positive of her age, Mr. Richmond?"

"Yes, she turned sixteen in March. I attended the party at her home in fact."

"So she was barely sixteen years old when she arrived here?"

"Yes, that's correct." Alex was enjoying himself immensely. Apparently he'd caught Flame in a lie about her age and that only added to his fun.

"Could you describe her to me, Mr. Richmond?" Joaquin's gaze grew stern as he turned back to face the young man. He had only this one last hope that Alex had the wrong girl in mind when he'd told his story.

"Yes, easily. She is slight, very slender and so graceful, moves like a dancer. She has golden red hair and eyes of the most incredible green. She's probably the most beautiful young woman I've ever seen. If I were you, Mr. Villarreal, I'd sleep with her every chance I got, she is incomparable in bed. Just keep her away from Bradley and the others, I'm afraid she has an insatiable appetite where sex is concerned. She's more than one man can handle and two or three don't seem to faze her in the least, why I remember one party where we—"

Joaquin stopped listening. He couldn't take any more: it was too disgusting to hear and obviously true. "Where are you staying while you're here in San Francisco?"

"At the Palace, why?"

"No reason. You'll forgive me if I do not invite you to visit Flame at my ranch?"

"Yes, of course, it would be awkward. Perhaps Flame has reformed, wants to lead a moral life for a change, and I'd hate to upset her if that's what she's trying to do. Well, at least I can return to Philadelphia with peace of mind knowing she's in your obviously capable hands."

"Good-bye, Mr. Richmond." Joaquin cashed in his chips and left without speaking to Rafael. He'd leave for home in the morning. He prayed Flame would deny everything—perhaps she didn't even know an Alex Richmond. But Joaquin's heart sank: Alex had known Flame's name immediately and his description of her was perfect. There could be no mistake, he knew Flame all right. But dear God, how could any of that filth have been true? He found sleep impossible that night and left at first light to begin the long ride home, but now he dreaded each step that took him closer to the woman he loved. How could she be only sixteen? That was preposterous, he was nearly thirty-two, he would be exactly twice her age then, she couldn't possibly be only sixteen, no more than a child. No, none of it was true. That was the only plausible explanation: Alex Richmond was a damned liar and not one word he'd said had been true.

Flame strolled listlessly around the patio. It had been a miserable two weeks for her with Joaquin gone. Tears came to her eyes each time she thought of how he'd left her. He and Rafael had ridden away before dawn with not so much as a message left for her. She'd not seen them after her angry words at dinner and she was so ashamed of the way she'd spoken to Joaquin. Their fighting had upset her so, she couldn't help it, she couldn't bear to see them hurt, not like that, not fighting over her. She'd not be the cause of any more arguments if she could help it. The fact Joaquin had left without seeing her, without at least leaving her a note saddened her greatly. What if he had lost interest in her now, didn't want to marry her after all? What if he had misunderstood her words and thought she didn't want to marry him? She sank down upon the wooden bench and blinked back the tears which again stung her eyes. What was taking Joaquin so long in San Francisco? José had told her Joaquin had sailed his own ships himself in years past—what if he were so angry with her he'd decided to return to sea? He'd be gone for months then, possibly even years! Oh it was terrible to be left behind like this with no word of what he was doing. How awful to be a woman, to always be left behind! Had he not thought she'd enjoy going to San Francisco too? Then a truly horrible thought occurred to her: what if he had a woman waiting for him in that city, maybe more than one! It would be difficult for him to keep a woman on the ranch, but in a large city like San Francisco it would be a simple matter to accomplish discreetly. He visited the city often, perhaps too often . . . how could he have so much business to which to attend? Why didn't he come home?

The next afternoon Flame sat in the kitchen practicing her Spanish with Maria for want of anything better to do when José rushed in the back door. "Joaquin is home, señorita, he has just taken Diablo around to the barn!"

Flame dropped the fruit she had been sorting and dashed past José, out the door and across the yard where she met Joaquin walking wearily toward the house. She was thrilled to see him home at last and ran up to him throwing her arms around his neck. "Joaquin, I thought you'd never come home, I've missed you so and I'm very sorry about the way I spoke to you, I love you so!" She was so overjoyed to see him, to feel his arms around her again, that she didn't notice his hostile expression.

Joaquin pulled Flame's arms from around his neck quite gently, then pushed her away. "Would you at least allow me to walk into my house, Flame? I'm tired and I'll talk with you later after I've had time to bathe and change my clothes." He continued on past her into the house but Flame didn't follow, she was too stunned by his rude rebuff to move. He'd treated her as if she were some hideous insect to be brushed off his coat, not at all the way she'd hoped or expected to be greeted. He certainly hadn't spoken to her the way a man speaks to the woman he loves and Flame was devastated. Did he really think that she cared his clothes were dirty, or that he smelled of his horse's sweat rather than of the spicy soap and brandy as he did in the evenings when they dined together? She turned away from the house to the corral and called to Lady. The mare came up to the fence and Flame began to pat her soft velvet smooth nose as she cried, "He doesn't love me anymore, Lady, he doesn't love me at all and whatever shall I do?"

Joaquin found Flame later, still standing with her horse. As he approached he thought how small she looked, how thin, how impossibly young. That she had been crying upset him, he hadn't meant to be so rude. "Flame, forgive me, I was just tired, come here to me." He pulled her into his arms and kissed her forehead then brushed away her tears with his fingertips. Then he remembered he'd not bought her anything. He had left San Francisco so hurriedly, and in no mood to buy presents, but now he was sorry for that oversight. He had hurt her and no apology would help erase the pain he just given her, and then the questions he wanted to ask would seem so harsh too. Why was everything going so badly for them?

"Will you come inside with me now? I want to talk to

you. I've missed you too, Flame, really I have.''

Flame tried to smile as she looked up at him but the sorrow still showed in her eyes. "Yes, I'll be happy to come inside with you.'' But as they walked in she moved ahead of him, didn't take his hand as he had expected her to do. She was afraid now, really frightened. Was he going to say he didn't love her anymore, didn't want to marry her after all?

Joaquin closed the library door and turned to face her. "Flame, it's very important to me that you tell me the truth. Will you promise to do that now please?''

Although she didn't understand his question she agreed readily. "Yes, of course, what is it, Joaquin?''

"I want to know exactly how old you are.''

Flame moved away from him, turned away as her fear overwhelmed her. He knew she had lied to him, he knew!

"Flame, you will answer me this instant! How old are you?'' Joaquin's voice held more than a threat of anger. He was positively livid, certain she had lied: it was all too obvious in the way she was avoiding his eyes.

Flame replied in a voice so low he couldn't understand her words. "I'm sorry, Flame, I didn't hear you, tell me again.''

Flame turned back to face him. She felt utterly defeated, he'd send her away now, she had no hope he loved her still. "I am sixteen, Joaquin.''

"I see. Well, would you please tell me why you thought it necessary to lie to me about your age. I'd really like to know why you did it.''

"Oh Joaquin, you know why! You were going to send me away to school and I didn't want to leave you!''

Joaquin frowned as her words caught him by surprise. He remembered that morning all too well and the desire which had tormented him then returned with a painful clarity. "We'd only just met, Flame. I don't see how you could have been so upset at the thought of leaving me. Was it the convent that you objected to most?"

"Yes, that terrified me, but most of all I simply didn't want to leave you. Will you make me go there now? Do I have to go away now, Joaquin?" Flame wrung her hands anxiously, she was ready to beg, to promise anything if only he wouldn't send her away.

Joaquin ran his fingers through his still-damp hair and sighed. "Somehow I don't think a convent is an appropriate place for you, Flame. Sit down a minute, let's see if we can't talk this over." He waited for her to take a seat, then tried to think calmly for once in his life. So Alex had been correct about her age. Was everything else he'd said true then also? He took a deep breath and forced down his fiery temper. "I am sorry you lied to me, Flame. It complicates things for me considerably now to find out you are only sixteen. I am almost thirty-two."

Flame relaxed somewhat. He hadn't banished her yet and she hoped to make him see that how she felt about him was the only thing which really mattered. She smiled as she replied, "Does two years matter so much to you? I never thought of your age, not once, and I don't believe you ever thought of me as anything other than a woman, Joaquin. I can't believe whether I'm sixteen or eighteen matters to you. It shouldn't if you really love me as much as you said you did."

"Flame, be reasonable, sixteen is so very young!"

"Are you embarrassed your friends will find out my age and tease you, is that it? Oh Joaquin, if I hadn't come to California when I did, I would have had to marry a man I didn't love, it was all arranged. My grandmother wanted to see me married, that was her only ambition, and she thought sixteen old enough for the responsibilities of a wife. She raised me to be a rich man's bride and that was always her only dream. The moment I turned sixteen she began to plan my wedding.''

Joaquin bit his lip to keep from exploding in a complete rage. The effort was only partially successful. ''Your grandmother wished you to marry so young? Why have you never told me such an important thing, Flame? Why have you never mentioned that fact to me?''

Flame was surprised by his anger, for Alex mattered so little. ''My grandmother wanted me to marry a man named Alex Richmond, mainly because his family was wealthy and respected. But I didn't love him, and I had planned to run away long before the wedding. I tried to change my grandmother's mind, to make her understand he wasn't my choice, but she cared nothing for my feelings. She cared only for Alex's money.''

''When was this wedding to have taken place?'' Joaquin swallowed to keep from choking on the bitter anger which filled his throat. Every time she spoke she confirmed Alex's story.

''In April.''

''I see, well, did you have a long engagement?''

''No, I never considered myself to really be engaged to him since I never meant to go through with the wedding regardless of my grandmother's plans. I had just learned what she'd agreed upon with Alex's parents the day before she died and I left right after her funeral. I guess it was about a week he thought we were engaged, certainly no more.''

''Did this Alex Richmond know you didn't plan to honor your grandmother's promise? That you had no intention of marrying him?''

Flame shook her head. ''No, I let him think I meant

238

to marry him—I needed the time to get away. But I wish you wouldn't make it sound as if I'd disgraced my family name: there was no possible way I could honor a promise my grandmother had made knowing full well how much I despised Alex Richmond!''

"I see."

When Flame looked up at Joaquin his expression frightened her. His eyes were like ice, so cold and hard, not in the least bit trusting. "I never told you about Alex because he simply wasn't important to me. I would never have married him, never. They couldn't have gotten me in the door of the church, I mean that, Joaquin, and even if they had managed to drag me inside I would never have repeated the vows." Flame's pretty lips were set in a determined line as she recalled Alex's hateful touch. No, she would never have married that fiend.

"I imagine he was quite disappointed by your sudden and apparently unexpected departure."

"I doubt it. He wanted me, I know that, but he didn't love me. It would have been no marriage at all when we had no love for each other."

Joaquin turned away from Flame and walked to the window to gaze out at the vineyard. He had never faced such an impossible dilemma. Flame not only knew Alex but his story about being engaged was true. He didn't even want to look at the lovely golden-haired girl, not ever again. He took another deep breath and held it . . . he had no idea what to do with her now, none.

"Joaquin, who told you about my age? I know so few people here in California I can't imagine who it could have been . . . unless, say—did you meet Lt. Bradley or Lt. Martin at the Presidio? Was it one of them who told you?"

"How do you happen to know two Army officers, Flame?" Joaquin spoke without turning back to face

239

her.

"I was a friend of Richard Martin's sister, he introduced me to John Bradley, they were in the same class at West Point."

"Your grandmother approved of your seeing those men?"

"No, not at all. She felt military men had no prospects for the future, not nearly enough money for her to think them worthy of me. She didn't want me to see them."

"But you continued to do so, against her will?"

"Well, they came to parties, I—"

Joaquin interrupted quickly: "When was this, Flame? When did you meet Lt. Bradley?"

"In March I believe it was. He was on leave before coming out to the Presidio."

"So you were seeing him about the same time you were becoming engaged to Alex Richmond?" Joaquin turned to face her again but his expression hadn't softened.

"Yes, that's true, but—"

"Flame, I want you to leave this room. Just get up and leave right now." Joaquin spit out his words through clenched teeth.

"Joaquin, but why?"

"Just go!" Joaquin strode over to the door, threw it open, then returned to his place at the window, leaning against the sill so he wouldn't have to face her.

"Joaquin, you're not making any sense! Alex meant nothing to me! I would have told you all about him if I'd thought he was important, but he wasn't!"

Joaquin was too furious to respond. It was all true, every damn word of Richmond's outrageous story was true. He rested his head across his arms and tried to think what in God's name he could do with her.

Flame stood rooted to the floor, her feet planted

firmly. She'd not leave him in such a mood. "Joaquin, I'm sorry that I lied to you about my age, truly I am. I will do anything you ask, just tell me what I have to do to please you again."

Joaquin snarled angrily without turning. "If you left this room I would be pleased!"

Flame shook her head sending her bright curls flying. "No, I won't leave you until you tell me what's going to happen to me. What do you want from me, Joaquin?"

When he turned to look at her he knew she had been right: he thought of her only as a woman. Surely no child would ever have the courage to stand up to him as she always did. He could command the full crew on his ships, a hundred men on the ranch, but this one particular woman was more trouble than countless numbers of men. When she was as mad as she was now her green eyes glowed with a brilliance that was nearly hypnotic, her cheeks were flushed giving her sweet face the same glow which passion brought. He stepped closer as he spoke: "Only one thing would please me now, Flame. I want you to be my mistress."

"Not your wife?" Flame's defiance wavered under that insult but did not end.

"No, not my wife. I said mistress. You know exactly what I want from you and I think you know very well why."

"Because I lied to you about my age? Because of Alex? You no longer want me to be your wife?" Flame was astonished, she had seldom seen Joaquin so angry, and she had seen him more often furious than not, but this was different. He was barely able to control the fiery temper which raged within him and she was at a loss as to understand why. His eyes glared into hers with the blackest of hates, with not a trace of the love which had filled his gaze before he'd gone to San Francisco. The muscles along his jaw were tensed, tight from the strain of his anger and yet she stood firm, calm in the face of his temperamental outbursts. He has his way too often, she thought suddenly; he is more of a spoiled brat than I ever was.

Joaquin's eyes lingered on her face, then swept down to her breasts which were so tantalizingly outlined by her sheer cotton dress. He wanted her, God how he wanted her, ached to hold her again and this time there would be no need to stop before he had satisfied his passion for her completely. Her game was over. His expression was one of unconcealed lust. "You refused to be my wife, Flame. I have now withdrawn that proposal. I want you for my mistress. Don't worry, you'll be well paid, I'll provide you with every luxury and I think we'll both be far happier with that arrangement than we would have been as husband and wife."

That he would insult her so brazenly appalled Flame, but she was never at a loss for a ready retort. Her voice was low but her meaning clear: "You must ask my guardian's permission, but let me warn you now: he is a fine gentleman who loves me most dearly, truly loves me with all his heart, and will no doubt refuse your disgusting request. You see, sir, I am but sixteen years old and much too young to take up the life which you suggest!" She left the library at a run and sprinted to her bedroom where she slammed the door with a force that nearly tore the old wood from its hinges.

Joaquin stared after her, his consternation growing. How had she managed to pronounce the word gentleman as if it were the vilest obscenity? He went out to the liquor cabinet for a bottle of brandy and a glass and began to drink, one glass followed quickly by another. He lost count and did not leave his room to go to dinner, but neither did Flame.

Flame sat on her bed, too angry to cry. Why would

242

Joaquin treat her so meanly, why? What was the matter with the man? He'd fought his best friend for the privilege of marrying her and then he'd turn around and insult her like this? It was an outrage, she'd not go looking for him, he would have to come to her with an apology or she'd never speak to him ever again. She most certainly would not remain in his house unless he begged her forgiveness for his insult. She would have to go visit Gabriel Alvarado, or write to Rafael—he would come back and take her to his house in San Francisco if she but asked him to, she knew that. Her mind made up, Flame continued to sit in her room, her hands clasped tightly in a ball. No, she'd not remain in Joaquin's house unless he apologized—and soon!

Thirteen

It had been three days since Joaquin had last spoken to Flame, three wretched days in which he had not once been sober. He had drunk the fine French brandy he loved so well until he'd tired of it and then he'd switched to the rich red wine from his own vineyards. Drinking didn't help, however, nothing did. The pain only worsened, grew by the hour rather than diminishing and he was no longer able to bear the agony which tore his heart in two. For a few moments he'd held his pistol in his hands and thought how sweet the oblivion it could bring would be, but he had swiftly rejected that cowardly option. He had to get away from the torment Flame had caused him, there had to be some escape. He'd considered returning to San Francisco to the arms of the women he knew so well—beautiful women, highly skilled in the art of giving men pleasure—but the idea had revolted him completely. He'd never be able to forget Flame in another woman's arms, he'd only want her all the more. Having at last tasted the wonder of true emotion, real love after so many years of the pursuit of the gratification of his masculine drives alone, Joaquin was overcome by the loss he had suffered. To lose love after having come so late to recognize it was the worst torture he could imagine and far more than he could endure.

He crossed the room to the window and looked out

across the vineyards. Row after row the grape vines grew in such perfect order—gnarled old vines, but their fruit was so sweet, their wine like no other. He couldn't bear his loneliness any longer and grabbing his hat as he ran out the door went swiftly to saddle Diablo. The horse was eager to run and Joaquin gave him his head, sending the stallion on and on toward the mountains. He had no purpose for the trip, none other than flight, flight from the pain that tore at this soul. He turned back and looked toward the sea but all the pleasure was gone from the spectacular view. Without Flame it meant nothing, it was dust.

Her name escaped his lips as a hoarse sob. All her beauty, her sweetness, how could it all have been a sham? How could her innocence have been no more than pretense, how could it? Joaquin wiped away the bitter tears which filled his eyes—he'd not weep for her, he'd never be so weak. She was a liar, a tease who'd taunted him with her pretended virtue all the while knowing he'd eventually give in, give her whatever she wanted, even make her his wife all for the sake of possessing her as his own. He would have given her any treasure to have known the joy of holding her in his arms, to have had the pleasure of filling her soft, slender body with his love, his life.

He recalled the day he'd plucked her from the back of her horse, nearly made love to her under the trees. Why had he stopped? If only he'd made love to her then, he would have known there had been others, he would have known months ago she wasn't at all the sweet, innocent creature he'd thought her to be. He would never have fallen in love with her then: they would have enjoyed countless pleasures, but never would he have said he loved her, nor suffered the agony which his love for her had brought him now. He rode Diablo across the fields; few cattle lifted their heads from their grazing as he sped by, gone before he could be noticed. It was afternoon when he realized he was near the church. The cool interior beckoned to him, the promise of peace lured him inside and he entered, found a seat in the last pew and leaned his arms on the next. Despite his promise he wept, wept bitter tears for the dear woman he'd loved and now knew had been only a dream.

Father León entered the dimly lit building and scanned the pews. He's seen Diablo tethered outside but where was Joaquin? Joaquin never came to his church—they had been friends, confidants for many years but to find Joaquin in the small sanctuary was unheard of. Finally seeing his friend way in the back, he approached the still form of the young man and he called out softly, "Joaquín, what has happened?"

Joaquin lifted his head and leaned back, unable to respond. His face was wet from his tears but he made no move to hide that fact from the priest. The gentle cleric slipped into the pew beside him and stared, dumbfounded. Never had he expected to see Joaquin Villarreal in such a sorry state. "Joaquin, tell me what has happened. I will try my best to help you . . . we will pray together. Now what has happened?" The stillness of the adobe chapel was unbroken as he fingered the rosary which hung suspended from the white cord at his waist. What terrible catastrophe had befallen Joaquin?

Finally Joaquin began to speak. He told the priest everything: how he'd loved Flame, truly loved her for so very long, his whole life, it seemed—and how when he'd at last expressed that love to her she had welcomed his affection so sweetly, returned his devotion readily. But he could not continue, the rest of the story stuck in his throat.

The priest touched Joaquin's shoulder. "You are not ashamed to have fallen in love, are you? Flame is delightful, such a dear girl and she loves you too, that has been obvious to everyone.''

''No, it was all a lie. She's no better than a whore, a lying, cheating whore!''

Father León gasped at Joaquin's foul words. ''How could you say such a terrible thing about Flame, she is as pure as a virgin could be!'' He grabbed hold of the back of the pew to steady himself. ''No Joaquin, that's impossible, what are you saying?''

Joaquin sighed slowly then related the encounter he'd had with Alex Richmond. He left out nothing in that man's wretched narrative, certain it had all been true. ''Another thing, Padre, she told me she was eighteen, when in fact she'd just turned sixteen when she arrived. I would have sent her to Santa Teresa Convent had I known she was so young. What a travesty that would have been! Can you imagine a whore like that in a convent? No wonder she cried so pathetically when I suggested it.'' Joaquin thought of Miguel Torres then . . . why had she killed him? Perhaps because he had abused her so badly—she'd certainly not been fighting for her honor as she had claimed. She had no honor to lose. And Rafael, what had really taken place between them? Somehow that hurt most of all, that she'd undoubtedly been with Rafael. He hadn't bothered to ask her about that disgrace, he couldn't.

Father León was beside himself. ''Joaquin, surely the girl denies this man's tale!''

Joaquin shook his head. This was the hardest part of all to tell. ''No, she admitted that she had lied about her age, and she admits to having been engaged to Richmond, even though she had no intention of marrying him. She even admits to knowing the Army officers.''

''Madre de dios!'' The priest crossed himself quickly, aghast at having heard such a story in his church. He slumped down in the pew, as dejected as

247

Joaquin. He racked his brain for a solution to his friend's torment and the same answer came to him again and again. "Joaquin, you must forgive her."

"What?" Joaquin's response was an incredulous snarl.

"Don't you see, don't you see the power which brought you here today is the only answer? You must think only of the love you have for her. You must forgive her and marry her as you wished to do when you thought her a virgin."

Joaquin was astonished. "Forgive her, my God, where would I begin? How can you expect me to forgive her and pretend there were no other men before me?"

"No, you will not have to pretend. When you forgive her, Joaquin, the other men in her life will cease to exist, and the love she will bring to you will be as pure as you had wished it to be."

"But I could never forgive her, never!" Joaquin shook his head sadly as he stared down at her clenched fists.

The priest drew in a sharp breath and let it out slowly. "Can you swear to her that you have known no other women?"

A rude laugh preceded his answer. "I am a man, Padre."

The cleric continued with the same line of reasoning in a soft low voice: "Why is that different? I have never been able to understand that myself. That a man may have many women, hundreds, without damaging his good name, but a woman is permitted to know only one man, her husband. It does not seem fair to me. Why are men so eager to call women vile names when all the delightful creatures have done is satisfy men's desires? You call Flame a whore, yet I know for a fact there is at least one woman you visit each time you are in San

Francisco who could be called by no other name. But you tell me you are a man and therefore subject to different standards. I cannot comprehend why, but then I am only a simple village priest and not given to contemplating these questions as apparently you are.''

The cleric's words struck Joaquin with the force of a blow. No, condemning Flame for being easy was ridiculous when he considered the way he'd led his life. He had always taken whatever he could get from women, whether he'd paid in money, in jewels, or in only his sexual performance which had pleased his partner greatly. He'd gotten everything he could with no thought of the consequences, or of lasting love. He sighed and wiped his damp cheeks on his sleeve. What had he tried to do the first time that he'd seen Flame? He had kissed her, held her in his arms, nearly made love to her. He knew what she was like only too well. She was so soft and yielding, so gentle, so incredibly loving, the tears welled up in his eyes again, choking his words as he spoke. ''Padre, come back to the ranch with me now. I want you to marry us today, as soon as we return home, this very afternoon.''

''But Joaquin, we must publish the bans, plan the wedding. Don't you want to invite all your friends, not even Rafael?''

''God no, especially not Rafael. Come back with me now, I beg you to come. I will forgive her gladly, I would forgive her anything.''

The priest hesitated for only a moment. Joaquin Villarreal never held to tradition, or the conventions of the church, but whenever anyone needed help, money, medicine in time of illness, a job, he had only to ask Joaquin and the contribution was always generous. He could repay that generosity in only one way. ''Yes, of course I will come with you now if that is your wish. I will saddle my horse and come now.''

As they rode toward home Joaquin felt his heart lighten. How had he forgotten that forgiveness could be so sweet? He could scarcely wait to reach home and see Flame, to hold her in his arms again. He had no doubt that she would agree to his insistence that they marry immediately. Once home he leapt from Diablo's back and ran into the house calling her name excitedly.

Flame put down her book and looked up. What had she done now? She hadn't even seen Joaquin in days, not since that ridiculous scene he'd made over her engagement to Alex. She hadn't understood his questions then, and the more she'd thought of that afternoon the more confused she had become. What had he been trying to say, and why had he gotten so angry with her? Who could have told him her age? She stood up slowly, and answered his call, but her heart was heavy. She was far from eager to face another bitter argument with Joaquin.

Joaquin nearly collided with Flame as he ran into her room. He grabbed her around her tiny waist and breathlessly tried to explain. "Flame, I have brought Father León home with me. I want you to marry me, now, this very afternoon. Come, let us hurry." He took her hand in his and started to lead her out of the door but she pulled back.

Flame was astonished by Joaquin's suggestion, so surprised she could only stare up into his dark eyes too shocked to speak. Then the questions began to flood her mind. "Joaquin, please wait a minute. I am not Catholic so I do not know your customs, but don't people here like to be married in church? Don't the brides wear lace dresses, aren't there parties with music and dancing like the one you had here? What is all the rush? I have no gown and—"

Her words stunned him for a moment. She expected to be married in a large church ceremony in a long flowing gown? The inappropriateness of her desire appalled him. He swallowed his anger as best he could and swept her along at his side. "I want to marry you, Flame, right now. We don't need to be in church, our chapel here will be adequate. The dress you are wearing is quite beautiful as it is, surely dresses aren't that important and my friends don't matter to me either. We have more than enough food to eat, we don't need to have a banquet, nor music and dancing tonight either. Flame, I love you so much I can't wait another hour, let alone another day to make you my wife, please say you'll marry me now."

Flame gazed up at his intense expression with rapt attention and smiled, she loved him so dearly and knew he was right. What did anything matter if he wanted to marry her? Nothing was more important than their feelings for each other, and they were all that was necessary for the marriage to take place. "Yes, I want more than anything to be your wife. I want so much to marry you, Joaquin."

Joaquin summoned José and Maria to serve as witnesses then raced into his room to clean up and change into a suit. He searched through his dresser for his mother's wedding ring; her plain gold band would have to do until he could buy Flame one of her own.

Flame sat chatting with Father León as they waited for Joaquin. She sensed something new in the priest's manner—the way he looked at her was so odd—but she was too happy to inquire as to the cause of his curious attitude. She could not understand Joaquin's haste, nor why he had decided to marry her on that day of all days, she only knew she was thrilled by his proposal and delighted about becoming his wife. As the priest read the ceremony she repeated her vows in a quiet, firm tone. Why did brides cry at weddings? She wanted only to shout for joy, to tell the world that Joaquin loved her at last, loved her as she loved him, with a devotion that would last a lifetime. But when he took her into his arms to kiss her she sensed his tension, and she drew back. His kiss had been so cold, barely brushing her lips, not at all like his kisses had always been, so full of life and love. "Joaquin, what is it, what's wrong?"

The priest had been wrong, he realized. He couldn't forget the men. Alex Richmond's smirking face danced before his eyes and his anger returned, swelling up in his throat until he nearly choked on its evil force. Perhaps if he told her everything, since she had admitted the truth to him before, then all he need do was forgive her aloud and then they could be happy. Joaquin knew his thinking was far from logical, he had done more drinking than eating or sleeping for the past three days and his emotions were still in turmoil. As he stared down into his bride's cool green eyes the visions in his mind were not of her loveliness, not of her at all, but of the men, all the men she'd known before she'd met him, and he felt only revulsion rather than the sweetness of her love.

"Come with me, Flame." Joaquin paused to invite the priest to stay for dinner then took Flame's hand and led her into the library. "Sit down, I want to talk to you." He turned away from her to gather his thoughts into the proper sequence.

Talk? Flame settled herself into her chair, folded her hands in her lap and gave him her full attention. Then she began to giggle. "I'm sorry, Joaquin, but I didn't think that bridegrooms wanted to chat."

Her teasing comment, rather than amusing Joaquin, sent him into the blackest of rages. He spun around to face her and cried out, "Stop it! I know damn well you know what every bridegroom wants, you needn't remind me!"

Flame's eyes widened in horror, her long lashes

nearly sweeping her brows. What had happened to Joaquin? Her chin started to tremble and her eyes filled with tears but that seemed to make him angrier still.

"Forget the tears, damn it, don't try that act on me ever again. Can't you at least be honest with me now that I am your husband?"

Flame brushed away her tears on the back of her hand. "I'm sorry, Joaquin, I didn't mean to upset you. What is it you wish to discuss with me?" That he had been drinking heavily now seemed so obvious to her . . . why hadn't she noticed that before? Did he have to get drunk to have the courage to marry her? Why would a man who would step fearlessly into a ring with a bull be frightened of her? Suddenly all her happiness evaporated, dissolved under his menacing stare.

Joaquin took a step closer, his posture still threatening. "You realize I know all about Alex Richmond, all about the other men you knew in Philadelphia."

Flame stiffened, not up to going over this same misunderstanding again. "Joaquin, I'm sorry but I don't understand. Why would you care at all about Alex? I never loved him."

Her question disgusted him. She didn't seem in the least bit ashamed of her past—were there so many men she'd lost count? She'd not even offer the excuse that she'd loved Alex when she'd given herself to him? "Flame, what I'm trying to say is that I am willing to forgive you. I don't care about all the other men you've had. We'll begin our marriage as if none of it had ever happened, just promise me you'll be faithful to me from now on."

Instantly the implication of his request was clear and for a dreadful moment she was certain her heart had ceased to beat. She was devastated by his insulting suspicion. "Joaquin, you don't mean it, why you can't thank that I—"

253

He interrupted her quickly. "Don't lie to me, Flame, not another word that isn't true. I want you to understand I know everything and I've forgiven you for all of it, your past doesn't matter to me. Just don't lie to me ever again."

Flame leapt to her feet. "You've forgiven me? For what? For some hateful fabrication, some outrageous lie which some horribly evil person has told you?"

Joaquin took a deep breath and tried to control the absolute rage which threatened to explode within him: "Must we go over the whole tale from the beginning? How old are you, Flame?"

Her cheeks burned with humiliation, he knew she had lied to him about her age. Was that why he'd believe any awful story he heard? She had no one to help her, there wasn't a soul to stand up for her innocence, and if he wouldn't believe her, wouldn't accept her word, then how could she possibly be his wife?

"Well, are you ever going to answer me? Are you even capable of telling the truth?"

His taunt broke her heart, and her words escaped her lips in an anguished cry. "Oh? Joaquin, don't you believe me? Don't you trust me? I thought you loved me as deeply as I love you." She stepped forward, resting her hands lightly on his arm, but he pushed her away.

"Don't paw me, your fondling won't work, not this time, Flame. Just keep your hands off me."

Flame burst into tears. She could stand no more. "But Joaquin, I love you and there has never been anyone else, it's all lies, whatever you've heard, it's all lies. I've always loved you."

Joaquin was so furious he could barely control himself. "Stop lying to me! Even when I try and forgive you, to make everything as it should be between us, you'll lie. Go ahead and deny everything, have it your way, but I'm warning you now if I ever catch you with

254

another man I'll kill you both! God, how I hate you for what you've done to me!''

Flame felt faint—only the strength of her will kept her upright. Her whole world was gone, the man she adored despised her, her happiness of only moments before was shattered for all time and she had no further wish to live. She straightened her shoulders proudly as she looked into his eyes. ''Then kill me now, Joaquin, I'd rather die than live with you when you'd believe such horrid lies. There has never been anyone else.''

Joaquin looked down at her defiant expression and frowned. Why would she persist? He swore softly as he opened the library door. ''This argument is pointless. I'll have proof enough later, won't I?''

Flame's blush was as scarlet as her hair as she walked from the room ahead of her husband. Her back was straight, her head held high. He'd have his proof all right, if she didn't die in the trial.

The next few hours passed by with Flame seeing and hearing little of the conversations which took place around her. Her mind was a merciful blank as she sat at the dining room table looking neither left nor right. She ate nothing and took not a sip of her wine. She felt dead, she longed to be dead—that was her only desire, to die and be free forever of Joaquin and his anger. Father León touched her shoulder but she didn't respond until she realized he was leaving and told him good night. She saw him whisper something to Joaquin, but she didn't hear his words, only the younger man's angry retort.

In truth, she had no idea what more to expect from Joaquin that night. When the priest had departed they remained seated at the table, each lost in the depths of his own despair. Flame turned the gold band on her finger—his mother's ring, he had told her. Was it so? The ring was only slightly worn, not thin, she had died so young. Flame felt akin to her, to this woman whose ring she wore, so young to have died, just like her own dear mother. Flame shuddered. How long would she herself survive in this house married to a man who despised her, hated her with every ounce of passion in his soul? She was terrified of him now. Would he beat her into the submission she would have so joyfully given him out of love only hours before? She still felt faint, and feared she would be sick at any second. "Joaquin, may I please be excused? I'd like to go to my room now, I don't feel well."

His black eyes stared clear through her as he looked up, noticing her presence at his table for the first time in many minutes. "No, go to my room and wait for me there. I won't be long. I'm sure you know what to do."

"Do? Why no, what is it you wish me to do?" She had no idea what he meant her to do but was too frightened to risk his anger should she fail to accomplish the unnamed task not to ask.

Joaquin rose slowly to his feet, as if her question were too tiresome to merit a quick response. He walked around the table till he stood behind her chair. "Remove your dress and undergarments, then get into my bed. This is nothing new to you—stop pretending. Your lies make me sick!" He helped her from her chair with the same gentlemanly grace he used each evening, then returned to his own place at the head of the table and sat down.

Flame was blinded by her tears as she fled the dining room. She'd never obey him, never. He would have to kill her first. She ran straight to her own room and bolted the door. She went to her wash-stand and splashed cold water on her face in hopes that the chill would help to clear her mind. She sat down on the edge of her bed and folded her hands tightly in her lap. She didn't care how politely Joaquin spoke when he came to her door, she'd not open it.

Joaquin kicked open Flame's door with one blow from his boot. He couldn't believe her act: her pretensions of innocence revolted him. How could she expect him to believe her after what he'd heard, after what she'd admitted to him herself? What she was was obvious to him, but he decided to let her play her game until she admitted the truth. He scooped her up into his arms and carried her down the hall to his room. He then kicked that door shut behind them and dumped her in the middle of his large bed.

"Were you lost? I said for you to wait for me in my bed. You've been in it before so I can't believe you couldn't find it tonight."

Flame scrambled off the bed, stumbling as she got to her feet. "Joaquin, wait, please." Seeing that her hoarse sobs only enraged him again she tried her best to regain her composure, to force herself to reason with him while she still could. "Joaquin, I—"

Joaquin's eyes were like ice, glinting menacingly as they swept over her trembling figure. "Hush, your pathetic act doesn't change a thing, so just be quiet for once, if you can." He sat down on his bed and pulled off his boots, hurling them against the wall. He unbuttoned his shirt, never once glancing over his shoulder in Flame's direction until he had removed the white cotton garment and tossed it over a chair. He stood then to remove his belt, drawing it slowly through his hand as he turned to face her.

Flame gasped in terror—he was going to beat her, she knew he was. He'd threatened to do it once and he was ever so much more angry with her now than he had been then. He'd probably kill her too, or leave her body so badly scarred she'd only be pitied, never to be loved or kissed by another man ever again. She backed away from him but to her immense relief he merely threw his

257

tooled leather belt upon the chair where his shirt lay.

"Joaquin, I know you loved me once, please don't hurt me, please don't." Flame's luminous eyes pleaded with him for mercy.

"Believe me, Flame, hurting you is the farthest thing from my mind. Now take off your dress, you're just wasting time and I'm not in the mood to be patient." He stepped closer, clad only in his tight-fitting black pants, his bronze chest bare, the muscles firm and hard across his flat stomach.

He was strong, but Flame already knew that and the sight of his half clothed body only terrified her all the more. She reached for the tiny buttons at her throat but could not unfasten them, her knees grew weak and she sagged back against the cool adobe wall, her hands pressed at her sides in desperation.

Joaquin's voice was a teasing whisper. "Why are you so shy tonight, my dear, when there have been so many others? Why would one more man, and your husband at that, cause you to be so nervous? Surely you've undressed more swiftly than this." He drew near then began to unfasten her buttons himself. They were small and took all of his concentration to manage but he carefully undid them all. When her dress slipped to the floor he reached for the lace tie at her waist yanking the bow which held her petticoats and sending them falling in a heap at her feet. The ribbons which held her white silk camisole and pantaloons in place were no problem at all to him. In a matter of seconds he had her free of all apparel and lifting her slender body into his arms carried her back to his bed.

"Your beauty always amazes me, Flame, your figure is perfection, your creamy skin like silk to the touch. You must be the loveliest woman ever born." He moved his fingertips gently down her slender throat to her breasts, cupping them tenderly in his hands as he bent down to kiss their pink-tinged tips. The puzzled look in her eyes only amused him and he chuckled, "I meant what I said, Flame, I don't care about your past, only your future and you'll spend that with me, only with me."

"You must teach me what to do, Joaquin, I don't know what it is I must do to please you." Flame had never felt more helpless. She slipped under the crisp, clean sheet in order to cover herself and wished with all her heart he understood why she had every reason to be shy that night. But as usual, his sarcastic response was a cruel disappointment.

"Teach you?" Joaquin scoffed impatiently, "from what I've heard it will take considerable imagination to find something you don't already know how to do extremely well!"

"My word means nothing to you, does it, Joaquin? Am I no better than a whore in your view?" Flame's clear green gaze swept her husband's expression closely, searching for some glimmer of trust but sadly, found none.

"No one is ever going to call my wife a whore," Joaquin responded with fierce pride. "Enough of this senseless debate, let's just get this over with swiftly so that we may be honest with each other from now on.".

Flame's fingertips wrinkled the sheet nervously as she watched Joaquin cast off the last of his clothing. She had never before seen a man naked but found herself only curious, not in the least bit revolted by the sight of his powerful body now that it was fully exposed to her view. His physique was too splendid to inspire any reaction save awe, for his build was muscular and lean, while the deep bronze of his skin glowed with vibrant health. Surely no more handsome man had ever lived and when she lifted her gaze to his face his dark eyes shone with unmistakable desire, but their deep sheen was loving, no longer filled with the fury he'd turned upon her that afternoon. As he sat down on the edge of the bed beside her she tried one last time to make him understand the truth. "I have been honest with you, Joaquin, I always have."

"My dear, I realize you're only sixteen but I fear you do not even know the meaning of that word. Now come here to me."

Flame held her breath, not knowing what to expect as Joaquin leaned across her, forcing her down gently among his pillows. "I won't fight you, I'm now your wife and no matter how little you think of me, I am now yours." She reached up to caress his deeply tanned cheek as she'd always loved to do. His skin was warm, smooth to her touch and she tried to relax, to let him have his proof without any struggle or attempt to resist his forceful affection.

Joaquin drew back, her suddenly subdued mood far more perplexing that her fright had been. "You are mistaken, Flame, for I think a great deal of you. I find it impossible to be angry with you when your beauty is so exquisite, far too distracting for me to concentrate on any thought but your loveliness." He drew the sheet back slowly to reveal her lissome figure to his view then bent down and brushed her shoulder softly with his lips. "It is your skin, I think, it has the same warm blush of pink which gives the finest pearls their glow of life." He looked up then, as if he expected some reply to his compliment.

Flame swallowed the painful lump which filled her throat and whispered, "Thank you." She recalled the afternoon she'd stood nude in his arms, so eager for his loving kisses she'd not felt the slightest bit of embarrassment as he'd drawn away her towel . . . but now everything had changed and the joyous confidence she'd known that day had deserted her completely. It was all she could do not to tremble uncontrollably, yet she forced herself not to display such weakness. The down of the pillows was soft at her back and Joaquin's touch so light, yet nothing was as she'd expected it to be when he'd insisted she marry him that afternoon.

"Put your hands on my shoulders, Flame." Joaquin whispered as he pulled her into an easy embrace. "You needn't be so terrified of me, I don't care if you've been with a thousand men, you belong to me now and you'll be mine forever."

Flame could no longer speak, but lifted her arms to encircle his neck, drawing him close so she might kiss him, her lips trembling slightly at first then responding eagerly to his deep kiss. His mouth continued to caress hers with an enticing slowness, soft and sure as he lay down beside her, bringing the whole length of her youthful body into contact with his. Gradually the warmth of his strong, lean frame melted the tension in her supple limbs, restoring the calm to her spirit. She moved her fingertips across his broad shoulders then down the rippling muscles of his back, slowly savoring the delicious sensation of his smooth sleek body against her own. She held him tenderly in her arms as his lips traveled down the silken skin of her throat, playfully nibbling her earlobe before his mouth returned to hers with renewed delight. She cared little whether his exotic taste was his alone or that of his fine brandy as its luscious flavor assailed her senses again. She was lost in him then, her fear dissolved by his slow tantalizing caress and lazy warmth. She moved closer still, drawing him near as her fingertips counted his ribs with an enchanting touch then slid over his narrow hips before her hands returned to encircle his waist with a loving embrace. She hugged him tightly as his hand moved gently over the soft swell of her breasts, teasing the rosy crests to firm, flushed peaks before straying across her flat stomach then down between her thighs.

Flame shivered as he touched her. His caress was light at first, sensuous, then grew more possessive, drawing forth the most exquisite of sensations until she moaned softly, thinking she could stand no more, but she could not find her voice to beg him to stop. She had surrendered herself to him completely now, too filled with pleasure to remember why she'd been so afraid. His mouth left hers then, his tongue hot, burning with desire as he teased the tender softness of her breasts before returning once again to enjoy the sweetness of her delectable kiss. Flame grew dizzy for he gave her so little time to draw a breath, his mouth now devouring hers with an unrelenting passion, and as he held her more tightly she felt herself being drawn into him, until his ragged breathing was her own, the very air in his lungs sustaining her life as well as his. She could see through his dark, flashing eyes, take in the dim light which surrounded them with a shimmering warmth until the pounding of his heart filled her ears with a deafening roar which drowned out all awareness except the overpowering sensation of his nearness and strength. She wanted him desperately now, the passion which surged through her slender body bringing an aching hunger from deep within; she called to him softly, her words an enticing invitation. She whispered his name with her last conscious thought as his first thrust seared deep within her with a blinding heat. Yet the sharp cry of anguish which filled her ears was his, not hers, as if the pain their union had brought had been far greater to him than to her. She wound her fingers in his thick, black hair to pull his mouth back to hers, to make him finish what he had begun. She could not bear his sorrow when their love had always been meant to be, she had been born to be his, she was certain she had been created only for him. Captivating, entrancing, she lured him past all reason, her tongue teasing his as she drew him deeper into her spell. He had such grace, such easy strength, she welcomed him joyfully, slid against him to heighten his pleasure as he began to move within her with a slow, forceful rhythm to dominate her delicate body with a cadence as old as time. The warmth he gave grew within her, swelling until she was swept away on the tide of his passion, their spirits soaring higher and higher as their souls as well as their bodies fused into one joyful being. Flame had not even imagined making love to be so splendid as Joaquin had made it, violent yet tender, the ecstasy so intense it was nearly pain, and she wept with the joy of knowing her husband's love and at last being totally his woman. His body had conquered hers with such masterful ease, she lay in his arms, exhausted by pleasure and too content to whisper more than his name as she fell into a deep, dreamless sleep, her heart overflowing with love for the fascinating man she had married.

When Flame awakened it was long past midnight. Her consciousness returned slowly but it was the silence which brought her fully alert, for the room was much too still. She reached out for her husband but found herself alone in his oversized bed. She sat up hesitantly, then lifted her hands to push her tangled hair from her eyes and saw instantly that Joaquin's clothes were gone from the nearby chair. What had she done wrong? She adored him, loved him more than life itself, had given herself to him with such abandon, and he had left her to spend her wedding night alone? Was he so disgusted with her as that? Nothing she ever did pleased him, not even her obedience or her innocence had pleased him that night or he would never have left her so alone. She was overcome with sadness, filled with a sorrow deeper than tears. Maybe he would rather have found her to be the whore he imagined, then she would have at least known how to please him and he would not have had to bear the humiliation of being proved wrong. She knew Joaquin was far too proud a man to accept what he'd done with grace—no indeed, he would only blame her for everything, be furious with her all over again for proving his outrageous lies wrong with the one proof he couldn't ignore. She felt so cheated. He had taught her life's ultimate mystery, then disappeared as if the beauty they'd shared had meant nothing to him. How could she remain in his bed, or for that matter in his house when he had taken the only gift she had to offer and then left her with no good-bye? Did he think she had no pride, no self-respect? Did he think she would not understand his neglect for the clear rejection that it was?

She got up quickly, slipped her dress over her head then picked up her lace lingerie and carried it back to her own room. There was no sound coming from anywhere in the house as she crept back down the hall, but she opened her door cautiously then peered inside. It had been ridiculous to think Joaquin might have gone there. She quickly found the pants she wore for riding, a clean blouse and an old serape José had loaned her to ward off the chill of the early morning air. She searched through her wardrobe, the satin and silks rustled as she moved them aside to find her cotton dresses. She rolled three up into a ball and pushed them into her small tapestry traveling bag along with her hairbrush and slippers. She pulled on her boots and thought no more about leaving her pretty clothes behind—what did clothes matter to her when her whole world had been destroyed? She turned to look at the room she'd grown to love and tears filled her eyes again but she brushed them away. She had no time to weep, she had to leave now, to escape Joaquin and his irrational anger forever.

As she tiptoed to the back door she peered into the dining room and to her surprise saw Joaquin seated at the table. He was slumped over, his head lying across his arms and an empty bottle of brandy by his side. Flame felt herself being drawn into him, repelled and yet attracted the way she had felt watching the long-legged spiders which had lived in her grandmother's garden. She was fascinated by him: he was so still, so relaxed, his chest rising and falling in an easy rhythm as he slept. His silver-handled knife lay next to his right boot where it had slipped from his grasp and she stared down at the weapon in horror. It would be a simple matter to kill him as he slept, to plunge the knife into his back clear to the hilt. She picked it up stealthily, quietly wrapping her fingers around the handle, careful not to let it fall to the floor and wake him.

As Flame gazed down at the man who was now her husband she saw in his handsome face only the Joaquin she had always loved. His long dark lashes made shadows on his cheeks: they were so thick they blocked the light which fell across his face. He was so handsome, and that very afternoon his proposal of marriage had offered the paradise she'd longed for. But he'd destroyed that dream swiftly with his dreadful accusations. Flame stifled the cry which filled her throat and thrust his knife into her bag. He'd know she had taken it as he'd slept defenseless, but would he ever understand why she had not turned it upon him? She closed her eyes and blinked away the last of her tears. She would remember the warmth of his kisses, the light of his smile, but how could love have been so cruel, fate so unkind? Had he truly loved her as he claimed he did he would have believed in her word with no proof at all. He would simply have believed in her out of love. What good was his promise of love when he had so little faith in her? She was finished with him, she'd had more than enough, for if his devotion meant only the doubt and anguish he'd given her that day then she wanted no more of it ever again.

She slipped out the back door and ran through the darkness to the corral. Lady answered her quiet call and came quickly, nuzzling her mistress's hand with her velvet-smooth nose. Flame led the mare from the corral and walked along beside her until they were some distance from the house. Then she leapt upon Lady's back and dug her heels into the horse's sides. The mare responded with a burst of speed that carried Flame far away into the night, far from the man she loved, the man who had failed to be her husband from the moment their marriage had begun. As she rode swiftly down the path she waited for a bullet from one of Joaquin's vaquero's rifles to rip through her back but no shot came. The only sound was the soft rhythmic thud of Lady's flying hooves as she carried Flame farther and farther from the home she'd hoped never to have to leave.

Fourteen

Flame pulled the warm woolen blanket more snugly around her shoulders. The August weather in San Francisco was not nearly so warm as the weather had been on . . . she silenced that thought abruptly, pushing the memory of Joaquin and the ranch with the lazy sun-drenched days they'd shared to the back of her mind. But tonight for some reason Joaquin's image would not be put away, his handsome, smiling face hovered in her thoughts making sleep impossible again. When the memories flooded over her, came back to her so vividly she gave in to them, going over each detail of her wedding night again as if perhaps that effort would put the ghosts of her past to rest.

Suzanna Lewis had cried and her father, forgetting his vocation, had sworn a bitter oath when she had told them her story in a halting, tear-choked voice. She had begged for help, assistance in hiding anywhere, she didn't care where she had to go to escape the man who was now her husband but who had rejected her love so coldly.

The Reverend Lewis had paced nervously up and down the worn rug which covered the even more worn floor of his parlor. He knew in his heart what he wanted to do, but he was as much afraid of Joaquin Villarreal as Flame was. "My dear child, you may not stay here with us, it is too close. Your husband will probably

267

come here when he discovers you gone, he may be on his way here at this very minute.''

Flame had cried all the harder then, fearing no one would help her to leave Joaquin if the Lewis family did not. "Please, oh please, you must help me. I have no other friends here, none at all.''

The minister had to glance at his daughter's pleading expression only once before he realized he could not refuse Flame's request, but he tried one last time. "He is your husband now, you will grow used to a man's affection in time, all wives do.''

Flame became hysterical then, no longer able to maintain the tenuous hold she had on her emotions. "No, no, you don't understand, it is not Joaquin's love that terrifies me but his suspicions! He asked me to marry him today because he said he loved me too much to wait any longer but the moment we were married he accused me of the most dreadful things. I won't be his wife now, not when he'd believe lies rather than the truth of my words.'' Flame choked on her tears: how could she stay with him when she would never again be able to offer her own body as the proof her husband demanded? Demanded and then rejected, she remembered bitterly.

Suzanna Lewis could no longer bear her friend's tears and knelt by her side to hug her. "Please don't cry, Flame, we'll help you, won't we, Daddy?''

Reverend Lewis had momentarily ceased to pace and suggested what seemed to him to be the most sensible alternative. "Do you wish to return to Philadelphia, Flame, is that what you want to do, to go home? It will be difficult but we can find the money for your train fare somehow.''

"No, my grandmother is dead, I have no one there, I can't go back now.'' Alex was there, she thought with a shudder. She could never return home when he would be waiting, no, that was impossible, she'd not go there.

"The only other choice then is to leave here and go north to San Francisco. My uncle is also a minister, he has a large congregation in that city, perhaps some family among them would be willing to take you into their home."

"San Francisco? Joaquin goes there frequently, I'm afraid he'd find me too easily there." Flame was confused. What would he do with her, she wondered—which would have made him more angry, running away or staying where her presence would be a daily reminder of his folly?

The preacher was fast losing his patience, he'd been awakened in the middle of the night by a hysterical woman with an impossible demand and he was tired of her objections to his every word. "Flame, he is usually down at the port, isn't he? His business is shipping, he would hardly spend his time combing all the respectable homes in the city searching for you. He'll never find you but you'll have to work, you won't be able to live as you have here."

Encouraged by the hope he offered, Flame quickly agreed. "I would be willing to perform any task, I'll be a kitchen maid, anything, just help me to get away from Joaquin!"

"But, Daddy, Flame is a wealthy girl, why should she have to work, all her clothes are so pretty and—"

"Look at me, Suzanna, I have nothing but the clothes on my back and the few things I could grab as I ran from that accursed house. I'll work at any job, all I want is to be free."

"Then you must leave now, Flame. Go and wake your brother, Suzanna. Jimmy will not be missed for a few days as I would. He will take you to my uncle's home, I'll write him a letter explaining your situation. Hurry, Suzanna, wake Jimmy at once and tell him to saddle two horses. It's probably a good thing you are dressed as a boy, it will attract less attention on the road. There will be no problems with travelers finding you too attractive to ignore either. I'll turn your horse loose after you've gone, she should return to the Villarreal ranch by morning and with luck Joaquin will think you were thrown. It will take him days to search his own property thoroughly before he has time to look elsewhere."

"Leave Lady behind! But she is all I have!" Flame's anguish filled her plea.

"Yes, and she's so unusual a horse that anyone seeing her would remember and tell Joaquin the minute he'd asked if you'd happened by. You know I'm right."

"Yes, but I hate to lose her." Flame tried to be brave, but her life had taken too many dreadful turns that night for her to have much stamina left to endure any more disappointments.

"Jimmy knows how to reach San Francisco without using the main roads, that way you'll have less chance of being seen or molested. Wear one of his hats, I don't want anything to happen to you. Two men will attract no notice, but a beautiful young woman is not safe on any road."

Flame gasped at the horror of his prediction. She wanted no attention at all from passing strangers—from any man, ever again. She ached all over and there was no time to rest before she was gone again, riding beside Jimmy who turned a bright crimson when he heard what had happened. He seldom spoke during their journey but his glance was sympathetic and Flame felt safe in his company. They kept off the well traveled path and camped in secluded spots each night and although it took longer to reach San Francisco that way, Flame was not seen by anyone along the way.

Robert Lewis read over his nephew's letter several times, the story it told was a complete fabrication, but Flame had insisted no one else was to know who she was or what had happened to her to cause her sudden flight to San Francisco. "My dear, this is the saddest story I have heard in many a year, your dear husband dead and all your possessions lost in the fire which took his life. How ghastly for you, of course I understand your need to get away from such unpleasant memories." The minister had been shocked by the disheveled creature Jimmy had brought to his doorstep, her tale was tragic and her eyes so filled with sorrow he never doubted a word in the letter. She'd used her real name, her maiden name, Linda Lannier, and had called her mythical husband John, that was the first name which entered her mind, she was afraid to select any more unusual first name for her newly deceased mate for fear she would be unable to remember it herself.

"Was there no one to help you that night?"

Flame had gone over her story so many times in her mind she could repeat the tale flawlessly now. "We had only a small farm, no regular help, the fire started in the barn, then spread rapidly to the roof of our home. John was leading the horses from the burning barn when the roof caved in on him. He died instantly. At least I have the comfort of knowing he did not suffer." She covered her eyes with her hand and held her breath, praying he would believe her. She relaxed considerably when it became obvious to her that he did.

"Such a terrible tragedy, my dear, but now we must find you a home." Robert Lewis could scarcely keep his mind on his task when he looked at Flame. She had bathed and changed into one of her dresses and was so stunningly beautiful he had gasped in dismay as she had entered his study. She was far too lovely to remain a widow for long, a fact which gave him an idea immediately. "There is a widower in my congregation who recently had to dismiss his governess, she was quite young and unfortunately very irresponsible. He complained to me only yesterday of his desperate need for a woman to care for his two children."

"A man with children? There are no ladies, perhaps elderly ones who'd need a companion?" Flame wanted only to hide forever, she'd never come out if at all possible. She was terrified Joaquin would find her, somehow locate her hiding place. The minister's question interrupted her chain of unhappy thoughts as he replied.

"An elderly woman? I hardly think a girl of your age would prefer the company of a dowager to that of Seth Randall and his family. He is a wealthy man, there are several servants employed in the household so you would have no housekeeping duties. His two small children would be your sole concern. Let me send him a message right now, it might be possible for him to stop by this evening to meet you."

Flame had nodded her assent. She couldn't insist on anything now, she could only pray that Seth Randall would like her enough to take her into his home. She had had a governess herself until her education had been taken over by tutors, surely she could convince the man she could do an adequate job.

Seth had also been touched by Flame's sad story. There were actually tears in his eyes as he listened to her recount the details of her husband's death. When he had received the message to come for the interview he had almost refused, but now he was captivated by the young woman who sat before him. She was obviously young, extremely young to have borne such a tragic loss, but would she be able to raise his children competently? "Mrs. Lannier, forgive me, I do want to help you, but I must consider the welfare of my family first. I have two children, Molly is three and Matthew five, they were so fond of their last governess but she spent more time meeting her boyfriends in the park than caring for my babies. I don't want any more such problems.''

Flame had risen from her chair, her green eyes glowing defiantly in the reflected light from the fire on the hearth. "God in heaven, do you think with my beloved husband not in his grave even one week I would be likely to make assignations with strangers in the park? Good night, Mr. Randall, I am not interested in working for you!" Flame had started for the door but Seth had leapt to his feet, blocking her way.

"Forgive me, Mrs. Lannier, I never meant to insult you so rudely, but I am concerned that my children receive the best of care.''

Flame swallowed her pride and tried to compose herself as best she could. She needed the job too badly to do otherwise. "I need work, Mr. Randall, desperately. I would be a most devoted governess—of that you may be certain—and I assure you I am finished with love. My dear husband meant the world to me and with him dead everything I loved is gone. I will give your little girl and boy my undivided attention, they will never be neglected while they are in my care.''

Seth reached out to touch Flame's cheek, then caught himself. She was so lovely he was very sorry he'd been so rude. "I would give you days off, time to go places with your friends.''

Flame shook her head. "No, I'll need no days off, I am a stranger here and have no friends to visit.'' To risk being seen in the city was a danger she planned to avoid.

Seth found her determination to avoid friendship extraordinary since she was so incredibly attractive men would undoubtedly want to come to call. She would soon have friends of that he was sure. "Will you come

273

home with me now? I'm certain the uniforms Mary-belle had will fit you until we can have some new ones made for you."

Flame stiffened for only a second. She'd never worn second hand clothes, never, but what did that matter now? She was no longer the wealthy girl who had no cares, she was dirt-poor and in desperate need. "If her uniforms fit me new ones will be unnecessary. My needs are very few, Mr. Randall."

Seth frowned as he followed her from the study. A beauty who cared so little for friends or fashions? He could hardly believe what he heard, but as soon as he saw Flame with his children he knew she would be a perfect governess. She was kind yet firm and so affectionate they adored her immediately. Seth counted her coming to his home as a great blessing, a godsend, she was the answer to his prayers.

Her memories at last complete Flame drifted off to sleep, but Joaquin gave her no peace then either. His dark eyes shone in her dreams, his mocking smile taunting her cruelly and she awoke with a start, her face drenched in perspiration, her heart racing wildly. She'd been foolish to think she could ever escape Joaquin, how could she when his presence filled her soul so completely? She lay back down on her pillow and closed her eyes tightly. Why hadn't she killed herself with his knife as he'd slept, so when he'd finally awakened from his drunken stupor he would have found her lifeless body at his feet. If only she had known how his memory would continue to torment her she would have done it, and gladly.

Seth Randall paced nervously as he explained his request to Flame. He'd come to like her so much, to enjoy her sweet company in his home so well, but he knew her husband's death was much too recent for him to speak of his feelings for her as yet. "You would be doing me such a favor, Linda, if you would accompany me to the Williams's dinner party. They have introduced me to every unmarried woman in the city and I cannot face another evening of their solicitous attentions. Please come with me."

"Seth, you must know what you suggest is impossible. I am employed here in your home, it wouldn't look proper for you to escort me."

Seth frowned, surprised by her refusal. "I hadn't thought of that. You mean there might be gossip?"

Flame blushed as she looked down at her palms. The scars from her fall were faint now. When had she ever cared about gossip? Never in her life had she cared what others would think of her actions, but she did now. No one must ever learn of her presence in San Francisco: she dreaded leaving the house to take the children across the street to the park, a dinner party was out of the question. "There is also the fact that I am a widow, still in mourning, Seth. It has been only three months since I lost John." She hated to lie to him, he had been so thoughtful, but it could not be avoided. She'd remain in mourning for the rest of her life if she could. It was a socially acceptable excuse for avoiding men's attentions, and shun them she would, forever.

"Would you consider helping me to entertain here then? Act as my hostess, Linda? I have so many friends who have been so kind as to entertain me since Jane's death. I must begin to repay their hospitality."

"Don't ask me to take your wife's place, Seth, I would not want to attempt to do that."

Seth crossed the room quickly and sat down beside Flame, his face filled with sympathetic concern. "Linda, I don't mean that. I know how much you miss your husband, believe me I do. I'll always miss Jane, I love her still but you wouldn't be taking her place. You

275

would only be helping me as a sister would if I had one.''

Flame sighed unhappily. ''I will help select the menus, prepare the table settings, flower arrangements, whatever you wish, but I could not help you entertain your friends, I simply could not.''

''You are too charming a young woman to spend all your time brooding. It would help you to meet more people. The ones I'll invite would be the same you've met at church on Sunday, they wouldn't be strangers to you.''

''Your friends from church?'' Flame was reassured by his words, all the people she'd met there had been most kind to her. They were prosperous business men like Seth, and their wives and children were sweet. Still, was it possible one of them might know Joaquin? She should have thought to have dyed her hair the night she left him, how could she have failed to realize a red-haired woman would be so easy to find?

Seth stared at Flame's changing expressions. She was so lovely, but her sadness permeated her whole being with despair and he wanted so badly to see her smile. ''Linda, please say you'll help me here at home.''

''I have no clothes for entertaining, Seth, only my uniforms and a few other dresses but nothing nice enough to wear for your friends.''

''That's easily arranged. I'll have my wife's seamstress come by tomorrow afternoon. She can make whatever you'd like, but I hate to think of your wearing black, please don't ask her for gowns in that color.''

''I am a widow, Seth, what would people expect?'' Truly she felt like one, the man she had loved had vanished, to be replaced by a villain who despised her, she really was a widow for the Joaquin she had adored was dead. It was then, that very afternoon, that she began

276

to split her memories into two parts. She could bear to remember the man who had loved her, kissed her so tenderly, but the man who had believed such vicious lies and then abandoned her on her wedding night she suppressed from her thoughts entirely.

"Why don't you suggest subdued colors then, dove-grey or dark blue? Brown would be pretty with your hair, anything but black."

As Flame looked into his sparkling blue eyes she realized suddenly how much he'd come to care for her. She had never considered him to be anything more than her employer but he was a handsome man. He was blonde, with eyes which were as clear a blue as the summer sky and he was young still, in his late thirties she thought. "I'll ask for grey then, if that is all right with you."

"Yes, that's fine, then the matter is settled. Thank you, Linda, you are doing such a wonderful job with Molly and Matthew, they love you already."

"And I love them too." Flame watched as Seth walked from the room then put her head in her hands and wept. This was all she needed—if Seth were to fall in love with her she'd have to leave his home. But as always her dilemma was the same. Where could she go?

Mrs. Ligget, the seamstress, was a plump woman in her fifties who'd been sewing for forty years and loved her work. She chattered constantly as she measured Flame, exclaiming happily over her delicate figure and petite size. Flame found herself smiling in the good-natured woman's company: she was infectiously pleasant and Flame had had so few chances to relax and laugh since she'd been in the Randall home.

While Seth and his children had loved her almost immediately, Flame knew the rest of his household had not. She was not used to being a servant and did not feel comfortable joining in the employees' gossip. They therefore considered her aloof and given to putting on airs above her station when she had only been too full of sorrow to be friendly. She soon learned to avoid the rest of the staff entirely, she ate her meals with the children in the nursery and preferred their company to any other. If she were disliked it concerned her not at all, she felt safe and that was her foremost concern.

Mrs. Ligget drew her tape measure through her nimble fingers. "There, that is the last measurement, your waist is exactly twenty-three inches."

"Are you sure?" Flame looked at the woman in surprise, "It's always been twenty-one."

"Really? Hold out your arms again then, sweetheart. There, you can see for yourself: twenty-three inches and not a fraction less."

"I don't understand what could have happened. I'm not any heavier but I've noticed my uniforms are getting snug."

Mrs. Ligget sat down and after pursing her lips thoughtfully offered what seemed to her to be the only reasonable explanation. "It sounds to me as though you are pregnant, dear. The waist is the first place it starts to show."

Flame gasped for breath as a wave of faintness passed through her; she grabbed the back of a nearby chair to steady herself and tried to think. She had been ill a few times in the morning but she slept so poorly it hadn't occurred to her it was anything but exhaustion. How could she have been so stupid? She'd not even counted the days . . . could it have been three months?

Mrs. Ligget grew alarmed as Flame's pallor increased. "Linda, dear child, Seth said you were a widow, and a recent one. Is it possible you are pregnant? I'm not just being a nosey old woman, I'll adjust the seam allowances to give us plenty of material to let out when I make the gowns if you are carrying your late husband's child."

Flame sank down into the chair as her vision blurred, her hands were trembling and she still couldn't seem to catch her breath. The whole room appeared to be spinning about her and she couldn't see Mrs. Ligget's face clearly. Only her firm grip on her chair kept her upright—she was stunned, terrified of the possibility she felt must be true.

"Put your head down for a second and rest, love, I didn't mean to give you such a scare. Are you feeling better now? How long have you been a widow?"

"Almost three months." Flame admitted hoarsely.

"And you never suspected, didn't realize what had happened?"

"No, I've just had so much on my mind I forgot the possibility even existed. I never imagined this could happen too."

"I'll give you the name of my physician, check with him to be sure. Maybe you're not pregnant, honey, the shock of losing your husband must have been a dreadful one for you."

"Yes, it most certainly was. I'll never get over it." Flame pushed a stray curl back into place. If she were pregnant what would Seth say? What man would want a pregnant governess? A governess was never even married, let alone had a baby on the way!

"Linda, what shall we do with your dresses, have you decided which ones you'd like? We can decide that much today at least."

"You make the choices, Mrs. Ligget, I like all your designs. It doesn't matter which ones you make—I'm sure they'll be lovely."

As Mrs. Ligget gathered up her implements she offered another suggestion: "Since the children will be sleeping for another hour or so why don't you get dressed and I'll take you to my doctor's office now.

Flame nodded absently and got dressed. She did want to be certain, maybe it wasn't too late to take something to get rid of the child. What had Maria wanted to give her when they'd feared she'd been raped? Why hadn't she asked the names of the herbs?

The grey-haired doctor confirmed Flame's fears: she was indeed pregnant and as healthy a young woman as he'd seen in years. He assured her she'd have no trouble giving birth to a healthy child.

Flame chose her words carefully, afraid to do more than hint at what she wanted. "I have heard there are things a woman might take, certain medicines, if she doesn't want to bear a child."

The doctor's reaction was swift and hostile: "Medicines is hardly the word, Mrs. Lannier, they are poisons, and very dangerous ones. At three months you are too far along to do anything other than kill yourself with such potions, they won't induce a miscarriage now. If that was your intention in coming here to see me you've wasted your time for I never permit a patient of mine to take such desperate measures."

"Oh no, I was just curious, I didn't mean that I'd considered taking them myself." Flame blushed, certain the man saw through her ruse, and turned away in embarrassment.

"You are a widow, are you not? You must want this child then. Your husband would have wanted to leave a child, a son perhaps—any man would."

"Yes, I'm certain he would want a son—would have wanted one, I mean." Flame slipped on her shoes and picked up her woolen cape, a gift from Seth. "The baby will be born in April then?"

"Yes, just take good care of yourself, get plenty of rest and you'll have a fine baby."

Flame tried to smile. "Thank you, doctor." She returned to the Randall home and managed to sit calmly

280

through dinner then put Molly and Matthew to bed, but the minute she was alone she became hysterical. She wept bitterly over her unexpected fate. Why, after all the other sorrow she'd suffered, had Joaquin done this to her too? Children were supposed to be born out of love but Joaquin had never truly loved her and his child would be an all-too-graphic reminder of the marriage she'd never really known. Yet as the days stretched into weeks the child grew within her until she could feel the tiny elbows and knees struggling for room as she lay quietly in her bed at night. She began then to think of the baby as her child, hers alone and she wished with all her heart for a baby girl, a daughter she could love and hold, for she couldn't face the prospect of trying to raise Joaquin's son to manhood alone.

Mrs. Ligget kept her secret and the gowns she fashioned were so cleverly made that Flame's condition was not apparent for several months. She altered her uniforms herself, raising the waistline slightly, and tied her apron less tightly. She was careful to remain seated whenever Seth were around or to stand quickly behind one of his children, and he never suspected a thing until Flame realized the time was rapidly approaching when her secret could no longer be kept. She tried to explain her situation to him, to tell him the truth—so many times she tried to let him know about the baby, but the words simply stuck in her throat. He was such a kind man, she hoped he would allow her to stay in his home until after her baby was born; but then she had no idea what would happen to her all alone in the world with a small baby to care for when she'd be barely seventeen years old herself.

Finally Flame withdrew completely into the children's world and avoided seeing Seth for several days while she attempted to summon the courage to tell him her news. Finally she had no choice, for he had invited several couples for dinner and asked her to wear her prettiest dress, the one which was his favorite. Flame had to glance in the mirror above her dresser only once to recognize it was too late: she was too far along and not even Mrs. Ligget's wizardry with a needle could hide her condition now. She could offer some excuse to avoid joining his guests that evening, but what good would that do when the following day would bring no possible way to escape what had to be faced? She'd have to tell him and right then, that very moment before the guests began to arrive and he sent someone to find her. She called his name softly as she entered the parlor. "Seth, may I speak to you for a moment?"

"There you are—come and sit down beside me, Linda. We have a while to talk before everyone arrives." He stood quickly and indicated the place next to his on the small sofa.

Flame took a few steps forward and then hesitated. "Seth, would you please just look at me? There's something I must tell you."

"What's wrong, is something troubling you?" His eyes swept over her slender figure, then strayed back again to survey her waistline. Was he imagining things?

Flame saw Seth's confused stare and nodded her head. "I'm pregnant, Seth, I can't hide it any longer. Mrs. Ligget made my dresses to disguise my condition but the baby's due in April and—"

"April!" Seth moved across the short distance which separated them and put his hands upon her shoulders. "April is only two months away! You've been pregnant all this time and not told me? Why? This is your husband's child, is it not?"

"Yes, this is my husband's baby." That she would not deny.

"Then why didn't you tell me? I had no idea, simply

282

none, and you've been working much too hard. I never would have allowed that had I known.''

Flame lowered her eyes as her tears began to fall. He was going to fire her now . . . she blinked several times but could not stem the flow of huge tears which streamed down her flushed cheeks.

''Linda, look at me. Why didn't you tell me?''

Flame wiped away her tears on the back of her hand. ''Because I knew you wouldn't let me stay here if you knew, you just said so yourself, the work is too difficult for me now.''

Seth looked down into her beautiful green eyes, shimmering brightly now under their veil of tears. ''Linda, I would never ask you to leave. You are a part of our family now. My children love you and so do I. I know this may seem like an inappropriate time for a proposal, but I would be so honored if you would become my wife.''

Flame stepped back, shocked by his question. ''Marry you? Oh no, I can never get married again, never.''

Seth smiled at the determined tilt of her pretty chin. ''You are still very young, Linda, you'll recover from the shock of your husband's death in time. I know you will and I can wait for you. You need never leave our home, not ever.'' Seth pulled her close, drawing her head down tenderly upon his shoulder as he spoke.

Flame continued to weep as he talked to her in a soft, low tone, trying his best to reassure her of his love. He was very gentle and it felt so good to be held in his arms until Flame realized she could never marry him, not since her husband was alive and well as far as she knew. There had to be a long jail term for bigamy and she knew Joaquin would see she served it should he ever find out she'd married Seth. In spite of his tender touch she grew chilled, and stepped away from him. ''No,

Seth, I won't give you hope where none exists. I can never marry you. My memories of my husband simply won't permit me to encourage you.''

Seth's heart fell but he still smiled bravely. ''Well, perhaps it is too soon, I shouldn't have spoken of marriage as I did, forgive me.''

''No, it is I who should beg for your forgiveness for ever doubting your kindness and affection. I will always want to stay here in your home.''

If Seth Randall's guests found the fact that his pregnant governess acted as his hostess odd they kept their opinions to themselves that evening. The young woman was so beautiful and if Seth called her a widow then perhaps she really was. There was a sadness about her which everyone noticed—something in her eyes, an expression which told of such sorrow that none ever inquired as to the details of her past for fear of upsetting her. She was so young to have been widowed, and now expecting a child, the poor dear had obviously been through a terrible ordeal and deserved only sympathetic compassion.

The after-dinner conversation with the ladies which had always bored Flame to distraction in the past took on a new excitement that evening as the women shared the stories of their babies with her. Not all the stories were happy ones, but Flame found a kindred spirit in every mother where she'd never known such a sisterhood existed and was greatly encouraged by that show of love.

Mrs. Ligget appeared as if by magic as soon as Flame's labor pains began. The young woman had begun to think the day would never arrive when her child would be born but in spite of all the wives' tales she'd heard she really had no idea what to expect until she felt the first pain strike.

''There's no reason to fret so, love. The pain isn't so

bad if you accept it. Think only of the lovely baby you'll have. It won't be long, the doctor will come to help us when it's time. Seth insisted that he be here although I don't really think we'll need him. What will your family think, won't they be proud?" The kindly woman wiped Flame's perspiring forehead with a soft cloth as she kept up a steady stream of what she hoped would be distracting chatter.

Flame shook her head. "I have no family living, all are dead. I am the only one left."

"Even your dear mother, lass?"

Flame had not thought of her mother, not at all until that instant and the scene in the churchyard flashed before her eyes with a blinding light. Her mother had died giving birth, died in pain as she was suffering now. Surely the doctor had lied, she was too young, her figure too slender, she would die just as her mother had and her dear little baby would die too!

Mrs. Ligget became alarmed when she saw Flame's anxiety increasing rapidly. Second by second the girl's terror grew and she hurried to reassure her: "Dear, you must try and relax between the pains, they have only just begun and you mustn't fight them, you must save your strength for later when you will really need it."

Flame's mind refused to let her body relax and the pains worsened with each contraction, never giving her any rest as they sliced through her body in endless waves of agony. When the doctor arrived Flame was delirious, the fear and pain having robbed her of all reason. She knew she was dying the worst death possible. Joaquin had succeeded in killing her at last, his child's assault upon her body would bring her death and she would welcome it for in death she would finally be free. She felt her soul drifting away from her body, floating pleasantly until she was above all her pain. Her

285

voice was no more than a whisper as she reached for Mrs. Ligget's hand: "Tell Joaquin I am dead." She could say no more as she saw her mother's face—she saw her clearly as she had never been able to see her before. Her mother was smiling, waving as she ran toward her. "Mama, have you come back for me at last?"

Mrs. Ligget looked up at the doctor, a worried frown creasing her forehead. She'd delivered many a babe herself but feared something was dreadfully wrong now. "What did she say? I couldn't understand her, did you?"

"No, she's just fainted. I have never seen any woman so frightened as this, you should have called me at once and not left her to get into such a state. Now please help me—I want her to be proud of her son when she awakens. He's a beautiful boy—look at his eyes. They're such a deep shade of brown they're almost black and he has a full head of hair. I was expecting a blonde child, a fair baby like his mother. You bathe him while I attend to her. She will be fine with some rest."

"Yes he is a fine boy, isn't he, doctor? Linda will be so pleased." Mrs. Ligget cuddled the tiny infant in her arms. He peered up at her closely but did not cry and she squeezed him more tightly to her ample breast, delighted to see her fears had been groundless after all.

Flame slept until late afternoon. Her labor had been mercifully brief but she was too numb to realize or appreciate that fact now. She heard voices then drifted off to sleep again, not sure if she were alive or dead and not even caring. Night had fallen before she awakened once more and Seth was seated by her side.

"Linda, do you want to see him? You have a son and a very handsome one." He took her hand and held it tightly as he smiled down at her. His eyes filled with the

286

love he couldn't hide.

Flame sighed softly. Of course the baby was a boy, how had she ever been so foolish as to hope for a girl, a daughter she could love instead of Joaquin's son? When Seth returned with the baby she knew him instantly—with his black eyes and bronze skin he could be no other man's son. She thought only of the handsome, affectionate Joaquin she had adored . . . she could love that man's child and did immediately.

"What is his name, Linda? Have you chosen one?" Seth put the baby into her arms and smiled warmly at the little family. He had been as shocked as the doctor had been by the dark-eyed child. Why had he assumed Linda's husband had been fair like himself?

Flame smiled down at the bright-eyed boy. She took his tiny hand in hers and then brought it to her lips. It was not a Spanish custom to name a child for his father, but since her son would have none of the Villarreal wealth or power, he should at least carry his father's name. "His name is Joaquin."

"Joaquin? Where did you ever find such a name? Is it Indian?" Seth was clearly astonished by her choice.

"No, it is a Spanish name. I want to name him for a man I know, a friend once."

"Your husband's friend too?"

"Yes, you could say he was my husband's closest friend." Flame held her son and touched his nose lightly . . . he was a precious baby, very cute and sweet. She prayed with all her heart he would grow up to be as handsome and strong as his father, but nothing at all like him. The baby would be her son, hers to raise and he would be good and fine and he would love his mother as his father had never loved her.

Seth watched Linda as she fondled her baby, she hadn't seemed shocked by the boy's looks. "Linda, your husband was dark, like this child?"

Flame smiled as she nodded. "Yes, he looks exactly like my husband, from his golden skin to his black eyes he is my husband's child. I can see nothing of myself in him."

Seth continued to sit at her bedside, but he was puzzled . . . had she ever really been married? He knew nothing of her past except what she'd told him when they'd first met. He knew nothing about the husband who had left her so tragically alone. Was any of that story true? He shrugged then and bent down to kiss Flame's cheek, he didn't care at all about her past, only her future mattered to him and he would make certain her future included him. Now that her child had been born perhaps she would be more at peace within herself, more able to accept the love he meant to offer so willingly. He would be patient. Time would heal her broken heart, dissolve her sorrow, and then he would be there, waiting to make her his wife.

Fifteen

Rafael waited patiently until after they had finished eating their dinner before giving his news to Joaquin. He watched him refilling their glasses from the bottle of brandy which seldom left his side. It didn't seem possible that Joaquin could have changed so drastically in the year Flame had been gone. He'd been so sure of himself, so damn proud, always in command of his empire, his ships, his ranch, himself. He had conquered all of life's challenges save one, and Rafael marvelled again that one tiny girl had managed to break a man like Joaquin Villarreal. Yet he readily understood his best friend's anguish, for he had loved her too. He swallowed with difficulty as he thought of the pain the news he bore would bring Joaquin.

"I'd like for you to stay sober tonight for a little while longer, Joaquin." Rafael sipped the last of his brandy but refused his host's offer of more.

"Why? There is no point in my ever being sober again." Joaquin's once handsome face was haggard by lack of sleep, dark circles marred the skin beneath his bloodshot eyes and his hair, which had been such a shiny black, was now flecked with grey and sorely in need of a trim.

Rafael spoke in a whisper, afraid to say the words out loud. "I have found her, Joaquin, I have found your Flame."

His brandy snifter crashed to the floor as Joaquin leapt to his feet. "My God, why didn't you tell me at once? Where is she?"

"San Francisco." Rafael sat calmly in his chair. He felt far from relaxed but as usual he didn't allow his emotions to show.

"But that's impossible! We've been all over that town, we've been in every home she'd ever visit—the Opera, the theatres, so damn many restaurants, endless parties . . . where could she have been that we didn't find her?"

"I know we have covered San Francisco most thoroughly. I still have not recovered from our last trip." Rafael sighed with regret. Well known in California, Joaquin Villarreal had been flooded with invitations once he'd let it be known he would accept them. He had gone everywhere, but sought only one face, that of his exquisite young bride. Wealthy mothers of marriageable daughters had flocked to invite him to partiés and Joaquin had gone to them all. He was always polite, always a gentleman, he had charmed everyone but called at no young ladies' homes. He had broken more than one heart but he cared only for his own, he wanted Flame, longed for her to return to his home, and that mission consumed all his energy. No other young woman held his attention, a fact which drove many a young lady nearly mad with desire. No one was informed of his marriage, but he remained faithful to his wife, he wanted only to be her husband and to make up for the terrible wrong he had done her.

"Joaquin, everywhere we went we asked for Flame, described her beauty but no one had ever heard of her because we were simply looking in the wrong places. She has always been wealthy, pampered, spoiled, and we expected to find her among her own kind . . . that is where we made a fatal mistake."

As Joaquin dragged his heavy chair across the wooden floor to sit down opposite his friend his eyes filled with dread. "Rafael, she's not dead—"

"No, I saw her myself only a few days ago."

"How did she appear? Is she well?"

"Far more well than you, I'd say. You would never have recognized her though. We could have passed her by in the street and not known her, in fact we may have done so."

"Why would that have happened? How could I not have known Flame? Did you speak with her? What did she say?" Joaquin bombarded Rafael with questions, giving him no opportunity to respond.

Rafael reached out and touched Joaquin's shoulder with a comforting pat. "Sit back and I will tell you the whole story."

"No! I can't bear this, Rafael! Tell me where I may find her and I will leave tonight!"

"We have searched for her for a year—a few more minutes' delay will not matter. Last week as I was crossing the park on my way to an appointment, I should say first the day was quite windy and—"

"Damn the wind, where is Flame!" Joaquin screamed in frustration, no longer able to bear his friend's composure.

"Please, just let me continue. As I said, it was windy. A young governess with two small children and an infant in a carriage came by me. I gave no particular notice, I wouldn't have noticed her except that at that instant the wind whipped her white cap from her head and I recognized that golden hair immediately. One of the children, the little boy I believe, ran after her cap and they continued across the park into their home."

"Flame didn't see you though?" Joaquin's eyes narrowed. He did not want her warned that her whereabouts had been discovered.

"No, I followed them, wrote down the address of the house, a Mr. Seth Randall lives there, a widower. It took me some hours to find a mutual friend but by the next evening we had been introduced and I invited Mr. Randall to dine at my home."

Joaquin sat back in his chair, his gaze still suspicious. "How old a man is Randall?"

Rafael smiled. He knew what Joaquin was thinking: a lovely young woman employed in the home of a lonely widower was bound to receive considerable attention, but he allowed his mind to wander no farther. "Slightly older than you, thirty-five perhaps, a devout Christian gentleman by the way. He attends St. Mark's Episcopal church where the priest is a Reverend Lewis, an uncle, believe it or not, of the Reverend Lewis here."

Joaquin swore bitterly. "I knew it, I knew he had to have been the one to help her leave me. How many times have I begged that man to give me some idea of where I might find her?"

"Well, his motives were doubtless noble. Flame was a member of his flock as you will recall, you are not. Please remember also, that she and Lewis' daughter were good friends—she may have confided all sorts of secrets to Suzanna, including the reason she left you. She must have given her some story of your wedding night."

"Still, he could have given her a letter, some word from me so that she would understand how sorry I am for making her suffer so needlessly. She wanted to be married in church, Rafael, to have a new gown made, to invite all our friends and have the celebration she deserved, and look what I gave her." Joaquin shrugged helplessly, "I gave her none of the joy that was so rightfully hers."

"I quite agree, your actions were despicable in the

extreme, but let us not dwell upon them now." Rafael forced back the anger which flooded his heart each time he recalled how Flame had been treated. That Joaquin had ever had the courage to come to him with the tale still amazed him and that he had not killed his friend on the spot did too. "As I was saying, I had dinner with Seth Randall and in the course of the evening I inquired about his children. He began to tell me a most amazing story about his good fortune at finding a devoted governess, a woman he desperately needed after his wife's untimely death."

"When was this?"

"His wife died a little over two years ago, I believe, caught pneumonia and died within a few days."

"God, no! When did he hire Flame as his governess? You are not trying a case here, Rafael, can't you just tell me this story straight out without all these annoying details?"

"Joaquin, get hold of yourself! Flame left here on July 22, 1870 and she entered Mr. Randall's employ a week later, on July 29."

"The man recalls the exact date?"

"You know when she left here, don't you?" Rafael considered his point obvious.

"Yes, of course but—"

Rafael waved away Joaquin's response with an impatient gesture. "I know, at any rate he remembers the date, something to do with someone's birthday actually. She came with the Reverend Lewis' recommendation, said her name was Linda Lannier, which of course it is. She said she had been recently widowed, her dear husband, John, having been killed in the fire which destroyed their farmhouse and all their belongings."

"I see, convenient story if too familiar, thinking again of her father, wasn't she?"

"Probably. At any rate it explained her lack of

worldly goods and desperate need for work. She was beautiful, penniless and alone; Randall could not resist taking her into his home.''

''So she is his governess still?''

''Yes, she never leaves his home except to take the children on outings or to attend church services each Sunday. Seth told me she refuses all inquiries by young men who wish to call, she claims she loves her dead husband still and can't bear the thought of another man's attentions. That is a great frustration to Seth, by the way: she has refused his proposal of marriage on numerous occasions.''

''The man told you all this when you had just met?'' Joaquin asked skeptically.

''Yes, I am ashamed to admit I got the good man quite drunk, but he told me everything I wished to know.''

Suddenly Joaquin leaned forward in his chair. ''Rafael, you said there were three children, two older and one in a carriage? If Randall's wife died over two years ago—''

Rafael tried to suppress his smile as he nodded. ''I wondered when you'd think of that. The babe *is* Flame's child, Joaquin. Your son.''

The pain that announcement brought spread rapidly over Joaquin's drawn face. He opened his mouth to speak but no voice came, he was simply stunned, too shocked by that revelation to respond.

''She named the boy Joaquin, told Seth that was the name of her late husband's best friend. The lad was born in April of 1871, almost nine months to the day, or should I say night, that she left here. I would not ever suggest that the boy is any but your very own.'' Rafael's voice was stern, but perhaps he'd misread Joaquin's disbelieving expression.

''No, I didn't think otherwise, the babe is mine, I

know there were no others. But dear God, Rafael, how could this have happened?''

"You know all there is to know, Joaquin. A man need sleep with a woman no more than once to make a child. She was not one of your whores who possess the skills to avoid such predicaments, but an innocent child. You said yourself that you did not stop when—''

"Damn you! I know what happened all too well, you needn't recount it. I simply never considered a child could result from that damned night.'' Joaquin got to his feet and began to pace slowly near the fire.

"What do you plan to do now? It has been a year since she left you, your son is three months old. Now that we have found her, what action do you wish to take?''

Joaquin was silent for a long while. "All this time I thought we'd just find her, walk into the Opera, or some elegant party and see her across the room. She was so lovely, so full of life . . . do you remember how much she loved to dance?'' He turned then to face Rafael. "You say she seldom leaves Randall's home?''

"It is exactly as I told you, she has little contact with the outside world, speaks to the governesses from the neighboring homes when she takes the children to the park, people from their church, but that's it. She takes her meals with the children and sleeps in the room next to their nursery. She leads a life so exemplary even a man with morals so strict as yours would accept her for his wife.'' Rafael's last sentence was meant to wound, and it did.

Joaquin's expression grew bitter. "I have paid, Rafael, God knows how I've paid for what I mistakenly believed about Flame. You needn't remind me of my stupidity, I've lived with it each wretched hour since she left me. She was the most beautiful creature I've ever seen, and no more than sixteen.'' His voice trailed off to a whisper, then he could not go on.

Rafael was a practical man, he'd heard enough of his friend's self-pity. "Joaquin, you can't face her as you look now. You'll have to stop drinking, get some sun. I haven't seen you ride Diablo in weeks. Flame loved you but you were very handsome then and she thought you so fine and strong. She would not be pleased to have you come begging for her to return, beaten and sick as you look tonight."

Joaquin dropped back down into his chair, slung one leg over the arm and pushed his long hair back from his eyes. "I no longer care how I look."

"That is more than obvious, but Flame will care. You must pull yourself together, if not for yourself then to please your wife and son."

Joaquin looked up, a cunning gleam lighting his dark eyes. "I will not beg her to come back. She is my wife and I can force her to return to me."

"My God man, have you learned nothing from this past year? Only love will bring that woman back to you and Flame is more than worth the effort it will take to make her come willingly."

"Love? I thought I loved her before, Rafael, and look what I believed about her. How can she ever forgive me for the things I said to her, for believing such dreadful lies about her? I was so crazed with jealousy I saw none of her goodness and now you tell me there's a child . . . how will I ever be able to look at him without remembering our wedding night? She didn't scream at me, didn't yell at me for being such a fool. Instead she showed me a love more beautiful than any I had imagined existed. Then she vanished as if her presence had been no more than a magnificent dream. So how could there have been a child?"

Rafael rose slowly to his feet. "I can stand no more of your anguish tonight. I've found her, now you must go to her yourself and ask her to return home and be your wife.''

Joaquin reached out to stay his friend's departure. "If you would but speak with her first—"

"No! Don't ask that of me, Joaquin. I will never send Flame back to you after the inhuman way you treated her. You must win back her love and trust all by yourself." Rafael was thoroughly disgusted with Joaquin's request.

Joaquin realized instantly what he'd asked, how had he forgotten his friend loved her still and he would never have doubted her word, never. "She married the wrong man, my friend. She should have married you."

Rafael sighed sadly. He was tired of Joaquin's sorrow. "No, she married the man she loved, it was always you she loved and I'm certain she loves you still."

"How can you believe that?" Joaquin had no hope such a prediction could possibly be correct.

"She named her son for you, didn't she? She also kept your knife, Joaquin . . . you still fail to see what she meant by that gesture? It is late, I can discuss this no more tonight, I'm going to bed."

Joaquin sat quietly thinking long after his friend had left him. Why hadn't she killed him when she'd had the chance? He would have to ask her that question himself, and soon. But to have a son, that was the most remarkable news of all. He stared into the glowing coals of the fire for hours, but he drank not another drop of brandy.

The late morning sunshine filtered through the trees as Joaquin waited for Flame and Seth Randall to emerge from the crowd leaving the service at St. Mark's church. He had never attended a Protestant church service before that morning but had found it not uninteresting and surprisingly like his own. He'd come in late and sat in the last pew. He wanted only to be certain Flame was there, and she had been. He had taken Rafael's advice: in the month since he'd learned of Flame's whereabouts he'd stopped drinking entirely, actually slept at night after putting in fourteen-hour days on his ranch. His vaqueros weren't pleased to have his renewed presence but they had worked as hard as he with his leadership. Fences had been repaired, corrals rebuilt, the barn painted, the house thoroughly cleaned, and when Joaquin left for San Francisco he had never been more fit, nor looked more handsome.

Rafael had neglected to mention that Seth Randall was also a handsome man, a fact which gave Joaquin a moment's pause. He was tall, with greying blonde hair and a pleasant smile which he used frequently as he greeted his friends. But Joaquin couldn't take his eyes from Flame. Seth's two children stood by her side and she held her own son in her arms. The child's golden skin and black hair seemed out of place with what appeared to be a husband and wife who were both fair. Joaquin circled the crowd, walked up behind Flame and gently scooped his son from her arms. The boy giggled in delighted surprise as if he recognized the dark-eyed stranger immediately while Flame and Seth were too surprised to speak.

Joaquin smiled broadly at his wife. "Mrs. Lannier, I'm so happy to see you again. I meant to come call but you left town so soon after John's funeral I had simply no opportunity to do so." Joaquin turned from the startled young woman to Seth. "Mr. Randall, I am Joaquin Villarreal, a close friend of Linda's, and you and I also have a mutual acquaintance, my attorney, Rafael Ramirez." He juggled his son to extend his hand and Seth gripped it warmly.

"Mr. Villarreal, my pleasure. Are you visiting here in San Francisco?" Seth searched his mind frantically for what he'd heard of the man. He'd no idea Linda and her husband had been acquainted with so influential a person, but he knew Villarreal had millions and the power in the state that went with such a fortune and he hoped to impress him favorably.

Joaquin responded politely to Seth's attempts at conversation but his eyes never left Flame's pretty face. She had grown thinner which made her features all the more delicate and sweet but the expression in her wide green eyes was one of such terror it sickened him. When she reached up to take her son away from him he turned back toward Seth, effectively blocking her reach. "Tell me, Mr. Randall, were you also a friend of John Lannier's?" From the corner of his eye he watched Flame blush. That he knew of her ruse seemed to confuse her, she was embarrassed and it showed plainly in her high color.

"Unfortunately no. I'm sorry to say I never had the opportunity to meet him. He must have been a fine man."

Joaquin continued to cuddle his son, who was now hugging his father's neck and pulling his shiny dark hair. "No finer man ever walked the earth. He was my closest friend for many years and I will always miss him. His death was such a tragedy." When he glanced back down at Flame her expression had changed: she no longer seemed so frightened, merely puzzled.

"Why Linda, then Mr. Villarreal is the friend for whom you named your son!" Seth appeared to be very pleased with his deduction.

Flame bit her lip nervously to hold back the tears of anger which were fast filling her eyes. She was furious: how dare Joaquin just walk up like this, as if he were truly her friend! Still, she could not deny the child bore his name. "Yes, my boy is named for him."

Seth continued in an expansive tone, seemingly unaware of the import of his remarks. "You know, the boy even resembles you to a great degree, Mr. Villarreal. His coloring and eyes are almost identical to yours.''

Joaquin laughed and held the boy at arm's length. ''You think so? Frankly I'd say he is the image of your husband, Linda.''

Flame was nearly beside herself with his teasing now. Was there no limit to the man's outrageous nerve? ''Yes, he is indeed his father in miniature.'' Then for some reason she could not resist adding a taunt of her own to the ghastly scene they were playing: ''Of course, you remember there were people who never could tell you and John apart. You looked enough alike to have been brothers.'' Flame smiled up at Joaquin, showing him proudly she could play his game as well as he . . . but what was he after?

Joaquin was surprised but delighted by Flame's remark—she had her old spirit after all—and he grinned happily. ''That's true, but you never had that problem, did you, Linda?''

''No, I never did.'' Flame searched her mind frantically—how had he found her? He had mentioned Rafael. Had Seth told him about her? Suddenly Seth's insistent voice brought her back to reality.

''Linda? I'm sure Mr. Villarreal would like to come home with us for dinner. Why don't you invite him?''

Joaquin interrupted before Flame could reply: ''Some other time, perhaps. I'm really quite busy this afternoon.'' He carefully returned his still-smiling baby to Flame's arms and stepped back as he prepared to take his leave.

''Are you really, Mr. Villarreal? It's not something you couldn't postpone? We would all love to have you spend the afternoon with us.'' Seth had no intention of allowing Joaquin Villareal to slip away before he'd had an opportunity to further his own business interests by making friends with the wealthy man.

"Well, I—" Joaquin looked down at Flame, waiting for her to issue the invitation herself.

"Yes, please join us, Joaquin." Flame could not believe she had said that, but Joaquin's eyes sparkled as he grinned back at her. He was even more handsome than she had remembered but it hurt so to look at him. . . . She turned away to place her baby in the beautiful wicker carriage Seth had bought for him.

It was a short walk to the Randall home. Seth's two children were entranced by Joaquin. Matthew was especially curious about the Villarreal ranch and proceeded to pester Joaquin with questions to which the tall man replied quite seriously, as if the small boy were as expert a horseman as he was himself. Flame found herself listening to their conversation with growing admiration for her husband,—she hadn't remembered him as being so patient, she'd remembered only his temper, not his charm. She shuddered suddenly and Seth took her elbow, a gesture which wasn't lost on Joaquin.

Once in the Randall home Flame excused herself quickly to see to the children's lunch and naps. Seth had hoped for an opportunity to discuss several important issues of state politics as they related to his business, but found Joaquin unresponsive to his inquiries. The man wanted to discuss only one topic, Flame.

"Frankly, Mr. Randall, I was very surprised when Rafael told me Linda was employed here in your home as your governess."

"Surprised? In what way?" Seth frowned, not comprehending Joaquin's confusion.

"That she is no governess should be obvious to all." Joaquin sat forward in his chair, his expression serious and determined.

Seth coughed nervously, then gestured in response. "I'm sorry, I don't follow you, Mr. Villarreal."

301

"Linda is a wealthy woman in her own right. Her ranch borders mine. She was quite naturally distraught over her husband's sudden death, and then having the child after his passing must have been very difficult for her too."

Seth nodded sympathetically. "Yes, you know she hid her pregnancy from me until it became impossible for her to disguise her condition any longer. I don't know how to explain it, but I was never certain she had really been married at all. I thought she might have had an affair with someone who'd not offered marriage for some reason . . . the child is so dark, I imagined the man might have been an Indian."

"You have a very vivid imagination, Mr. Randall." Joaquin frowned impatiently. "Let me assure you Linda is indeed a married woman. I attended the wedding ceremony myself."

"You mean she was married, don't you?"

"Yes, what did I say?" Joaquin paused anxiously— had he given away something he'd meant to hide?

"You just said she is a married woman, but she is a widow."

"Of course, forgive me. I speak Spanish almost exclusively on my ranch, sometimes my English suffers from lack of practice."

"Nonsense, Mr. Villarreal, your English is perfect. But I am getting off the subject. If Linda is wealthy, why would she remain in my employ?"

Instantly Joaquin realized his mistake had been a serious one, but there was no way out of the situation he'd created for himself except to forge ahead. "She was beside herself with grief at John's death. Naturally she didn't want to remain on the ranch where they'd been so happy together. I must talk with her about her property, though. Perhaps you would permit her to speak with me privately for a few minutes after we have dinner?''

"Why yes, I've never considered Linda as an employee here. This is her home as well as mine."

Joaquin held his breath in an attempt to hold his temper, but then had to ask his question: "Mr. Randall, John Lannier was my friend, and so is Linda. What are your intentions toward her?"

"Well, frankly, I hardly know what to say. I have asked her to marry me on more than one occasion, but she has no wish to remarry. But she told me all her possessions were lost when her husband died; I had no idea she had property. Is her ranch of considerable size?"

Joaquin was disgusted by Seth's interest, which he considered much too keen. "No, but I have been overseeing the running of her ranch for the last year and have no wish to continue to do so."

Seth was startled by that announcement. "But what would happen to her holdings if you did not supervise them?"

"I mean to purchase the land outright, at a fair price."

"Oh, I see. Well, talk to her yourself then, she never referred to her home as a ranch, I had assumed there had only been a small farm."

Joaquin had no idea what Flame might have told Seth but he was saved from any further embarrassment at having to explain his comments when she returned to the room. She looked at him quickly but he shook his head—he'd not told Seth the truth nor would he, and he wanted to assure her of that. He had no idea what had been served for dinner even as he ate it. Making small talk was agony for him, he wanted only to take Flame into his arms and make love to her as tenderly as he had on the night they'd been married. He was thankful when Seth at last excused himself but he had no wish to remain in that man's home. "Come with me, Flame, it is a beautiful summer day, let's not waste it. I cannot bear this house another instant, please let's go." Joaquin swept Flame along beside him as he moved out the front door. The day was a warm one and many people were strolling in the nearby park.

Flame had been no more comfortable during Sunday dinner than Joaquin. A thousand questions had filled her mind but as soon as they were alone she blurted out her main concern: "Why did you come here today, Joaquin? What do you want from me now?"

Joaquin stopped walking abruptly and turned to face her. "I want you, Flame. You are my wife and I've come to take you and our son home."

"But why? In God's name, why?" Flame stood glued to the spot where she'd stopped, her fists clenched tightly at her sides.

Joaquin stepped closer, and smiled shyly as he reached out to touch her soft cheek. "I love you, Flame. I want you to come back home with me because I love you."

His answer shocked her, and she replied angrily, "Yes, you said that once, you also said you hated me too. You tricked me into marrying you and then you—" The tears began to roll down her cheeks and Joaquin pulled her into his arms, holding her gently in his embrace as he stroked her hair, removing her hairpins and releasing her golden curls to send them cascading down her back.

"I know what I said to you, Flame. I believed a man who wanted you for himself; his lies very nearly drove me mad. But I'll make it all up to you now, my love, I swear I will, I'll spend the rest of my life trying to make you happy." Joaquin tilted her face up to his. Her long lashes were spiked with tears and he bent down to kiss them away. "Will you come home with me, Flame?"

Her answer chilled him to the bone. "Never." She

put her hands upon his chest and pushed herself away from his embrace.

"Oh Flame, why? Is it because of Seth? I know he wants to marry you—do you want a divorce so you can marry him?"

"I'll never marry again! Never!" Flame shuddered with the horror of that thought. She'd never trust another man to honor his wedding vows when Joaquin had not meant them.

Joaquin grasped her arms forcefully. "Flame, what is it? Was this too much of a shock for you to see me today? I've searched up and down this whole state for you, every damn day since you left me. I wanted to send Rafael to speak to you first, I was so afraid you'd be frightened of me and you have no reason to be."

"Frightened? I'm terrified of you and why shouldn't I be? I'm afraid I'm going to be sick." Flame turned away from him and covered her mouth with the back of her hand, then as almost an afterthought she turned back to confront him. "You'd ask Rafael to come see me? How could you send your friend, my friend, to me on such an errand?"

Joaquin shrugged. "I have no pride left, Flame, none at all. I'd do anything to get you back. I want you so badly it's all I can do not to take you in my arms and kiss you right here, I don't care who sees."

Flame looked around them and realized at last that they were standing in the middle of the park, the subject of stares from many pairs of curious eyes. "Come over here so we may sit down." Flame walked to a nearby bench, partially secluded by a large pepper tree, which afforded at least a modicum of privacy in the public park. Once seated she turned to Joaquin and tried to explain her feelings in a rational manner. "I never told you this—perhaps I should have that first day we met but I remembered you, Joaquin. All the

305

years I spent in Philadelphia your face haunted my dreams.'' As it still does, she admitted to herself, if not to him. "I'd forgotten your name, but not you. That's why I quit fighting you the day you pulled me off my horse. As soon as I'd seen your face I knew you were the man I'd always loved.''

"You were just a child when you left, Flame—about the size of Molly. How could you have remembered me?'' Joaquin leaned back against the bench and stretched out his legs to get more comfortable. His pose was relaxed but he most certainly was not.

"Children are capable of love, Joaquin, perhaps the most selfless kind. When I found out you were my guardian and wanted me to stay with you until I married I was ecstatic with happiness but I knew I'd never want to marry any man but you I loved you so.''

Joaquin's expression grew sad. She'd been a child still when they'd married—she'd been so beautiful, with a woman's body but a child's heart and mind. He tried to treat her gently now. "I never would have let you marry anyone else either, Flame. You were always mine.'' His gaze darkened as he remembered Alex's evil lies. When Flame's hand touched his arm he jumped in surprise.

"I never understood what happened, Joaquin. I didn't understand why you were so mad about my engagement to Alex or that I knew John Bradley. Had I realized the import of your questions when you first came back from San Francisco I would have left your house that very night. But I didn't even understand what you were asking me until after we were married and then I had no way to escape your anger. I still can't comprehend why you wanted to marry me when you thought so little of me.''

Joaquin had to force himself to explain, to bring back the horror of that day. "I was simply too proud a man,

Flame, too arrogant to admit how much I needed you, loved you, until I could no longer hide it. I loved you desperately then, but when I was told you were a—oh, I'll never repeat those lies—the damage was done a year ago and the revenge taken then too.''

Flame was puzzled by his admission. ''Revenge? Do you mean you married me only to gain revenge?''

''No!'' Joaquin pulled himself up straight as he continued his bitter tale. ''Are you afraid of me, Flame? Let me tell you something, when I realized I had destroyed our hopes for happiness by believing his lies I found Alex Richmond. Rafael stopped me before I tore that son of a bitch apart with my bare hands but I'm responsible for his death all the same.''

Flame's eyes widened in horror. ''You killed Alex?'' She slumped back against the park bench, stunned by his confession. Of course, it was all so simple now, no one but Alex would have wanted to see her hurt, no one else would have known enough of the truth to do such a devastating job of betraying her.

''Yes, listen carefully and I'll tell you all about it. If you report me to the authorities I'll be hanged for certain.'' Joaquin could relate that night with perfect recall. ''Rafael and I waited for Alex to return to the Palace Hotel. My friend called to him, luring him into the alley where I was waiting. I gave him no time to plead for mercy or offer any excuses for what he'd done by slandering your name. Rafael stood guard while I beat Alex into unconsciousness. It was a simple matter then to carry him aboard the *Reina*.'' Joaquin paused to reach for Flame's trembling hand. ''I meant only for him to have to work for his passage home. He'd lost considerable money gambling so I was certain that when he disappeared it would be generally assumed he'd left town to avoid paying off his debts. Apparently he got into some kind of argument with another seaman

307

and later was found lying on deck dead of knife wounds. I have always felt responsible for his death because I put him on board the *Reina* as punishment. I wanted him to suffer through enough back-breaking work to pay for what he'd done to us, but he didn't live nearly long enough for that."

Flame was appalled. "I can't believe Alex is dead."

"He deserved to die one hundred times for what his lies did to you and me." Joaquin brought her hand to his lips. He knew instinctively that Flame would never report his part in the man's death—she would never seek revenge as he had.

"Don't tell me anything else about it, Joaquin, I don't want to know and I'll never speak of what you did to anyone." That Alex was dead sickened her, but it hadn't been his lies which had destroyed her marriage, it was the fact Joaquin had believed them. Why couldn't he see that?

"What can I do now, Flame? Please say you'll come home with me, I want more than anything to have the chance to be a father to my son and to be your husband again."

Flame's determination was clear in her sparkling green eyes. "No, Joaquin, that would be a mistake for both of us. I could never live with your anger, your suspicions—we would both be miserable."

Joaquin brushed her objections aside. "Flame, I would never treat you so badly ever again. How I could have believed such scandalous lies I'll never know, but I've lived with that nightmare for twelve long months and I want so much to give you happiness now." He raised her hand to his lips, kissing her palm, tenderly hoping his affection would convince her even if his words did not.

As Flame stared into her husband's dark eyes the feelings his kiss aroused were indescribable. The same warmth she had always felt at his touch flooded through her, the very same sweet longing that was almost pain came back to her in an instant. Yet how could she trust him—he had promised to cherish her forever, but clearly had not. "Joaquin, I find it so difficult to believe what you say is true."

Her comment amazed him, yet he understood her fears. He had made a mockery of their marriage vows within minutes of the ceremony, offered vile accusations on a night he should have filled with love. "Flame, I know why you left me, why you would not want to be the wife of a man who had ridiculed your innocence. But I want so much to be your husband, and this time I will give you no more sorrow, only love—all that any man can give to a woman will be yours." Joaquin took a deep breath as he looked into her lovely eyes. "Flame, if you won't come home with me I will surely die of loneliness." He cupped her face tenderly in his hands and kissed her lips, very softly so as not to frighten her again, but when she didn't draw away his mouth became far more demanding. He parted her lips easily with his tongue and she wrapped her arms around his neck, eagerly accepting his love as she always had.

"Flame?" Joaquin smiled down at her. She seemed to have difficulty catching her breath and gasped as she looked up at him. She straightened her dress modestly and folded her hands demurely in her lap, but she couldn't hide the blush which colored her cheeks with a delicate hint of pink.

Joaquin knew instinctively that if he asked her to return with him to his hotel room as he longed to do she would never agree, so he rose quickly and drew her up beside him. "I told Seth we were going to discuss your property. Tell him I made you an offer and that you're considering it. I'll come back tomorrow afternoon

309

when the children are napping and we can talk again.''
He escorted her back to her doorstep and with a courtly
bow wished her good day, then turned and walked off
down the sunlit sidewalk.

Flame stood in the doorway and watched Joaquin
until he'd vanished from sight. He was as charming as
ever, even more handsome, but were any of his promises true? She fought back her tears as she closed and
locked the front door. Why had everyone warned her to
be careful of Rafael when it had been Joaquin's love
which had nearly destroyed her?

The next afternoon Flame closed the nursery door
softly so as not to wake the sleeping children, then
wiped her perspiring palms on her apron. If only she'd
thought about it she would have changed out of her uniform, but the prospect of facing Joaquin again had
made her so nervous her costume had escaped her notice entirely. At least she'd worn her hair the way he
liked it, caught up in curls at the crown which then
trailed down across her shoulders . . . it was really
much too long but she'd not thought of trimming it and
had no time now.

She had just started down the stairs when she heard
the doorbell and stopped where she was, but she paused
only a moment to gather her courage before descending
the staircase and crossing the hall to open the door. It
would be far better to just get it over with quickly, to see
him and say what must be said without postponing it.

''I hope that I'm not too early. I wasn't certain what
time to come.'' Joaquin smiled as he came through the
door. Her choice of garb surprised him—the grey dress
with its long white apron was attractive, but he had difficulty accepting the fact she was another man's governess and not simply his own stunning wife. ''I must
compliment you on your uniform, it is very becoming.'' He grinned at her, hoping his charm would

brighten her mood, but was disappointed by her reaction.

"My dress? I'm sorry, I know I should have changed my clothes but I hope you don't want to go out. The children might wake and cook is too busy to watch them this afternoon."

Joaquin was concerned: he'd never made her so nervous before, he hadn't meant to now. "Flame, I like your dress, you look lovely and I prefer to stay here so I might see my son again." He took her elbow and led her into the parlor where he insisted she sit down beside him on the sofa.

Flame twisted her apron ties nervously. She couldn't look at him, she just couldn't. He was too handsome, his gaze too loving—but she couldn't forget his temper and the arguments which had constantly raged between them. Just sitting next to him was torture, her skin tingled all over and she could scarcely breathe. She didn't understand how her body could be so weak as to still crave his touch and the tension she felt was nearly unbearable. She said the first thing which came into her head. "How did you find me?"

"Actually it was Rafael. He recognized you one day when you were in the park with the children."

"I see. I didn't realize he knew Seth. He's never been here to our home."

That she would refer to Randall's home as her own angered Joaquin but he swallowed the fiery burst of temper before it reached his lips. "No, he made it a point to get to know him after he'd seen you. He knows nearly everyone in the city and it wasn't difficult for him to win an introduction to Seth."

"So that's how you learned what I'd told Seth about my husband?" She glanced up at him shyly, forgetting her dread for a moment in the warmth of his smile.

"Yes, it's a very good story too, covers all the details

311

of your past very neatly, even if it's not the truth." The minute he'd spoken Joaquin regretted his words but that was too late.

"The truth? I had no further need for the truth, Joaquin. It did not serve me well with you so I felt no reason to continue using it."

"I'm sorry, Flame, I didn't mean to remind you of—"

"Remind me?" Flame's eyes flashed angrily as she abandoned all caution and stared up at him. "Do you think I could have forgotten what happened for even one second? You told me you loved me, loved me so dearly you could not live another day without making me your wife. I have never been so happy as the afternoon I married you, but you know how long that happiness lasted, don't you? We weren't married even half an hour before you began to swear at me and accuse me of all sorts of lewd behavior. That was your idea of undying devotion? Now you think you can walk up to me one Sunday afternoon and say, 'I love you, Flame, please come home and everything will be different.' Well I will never go home to you, Joaquin, never. Your promises to me, even to God mean nothing. Maybe I loved you too much, I was only sixteen and knew so little of men. I thought you were wonderful yet you believed the vilest of lies about me. That I proved them wrong did not even satisfy you. When you left me alone on our wedding night I knew my only choice was to leave you, and for good." She turned away from him and stared out the window. She wasn't going to cry in front of him, she'd been on her own too long now to let him see how very weak she was still.

She had expected some response from him, an argument perhaps, more apologies, additional sweet promises, whatever, but she had expected at least some response. She sat waiting patiently but the time

312

stretched on and when Joaquin still said nothing Flame turned back to look at him again.

Flame's angry rejection had dashed all of Joaquin's hopes completely. He felt so miserable he did truly want to die. She'd never come home willingly—all her lively spirit, her beauty, her sweet love would never be his again. He'd never see his son grow to manhood, never teach him to ride or to love the land of his ancestors. No, he'd have nothing now but the rest of his life to live in the most wretched of loneliness, remembering his ridiculous suspicions and how he'd killed Flame's love.

Flame stared at Joaquin in disbelief. The tears streamed down his face but he made no move to hide them from her. She looked at him more closely then and saw the subtle changes she'd missed the day before. He was far too thin, and even his deep tan failed to hide the new lines around his eyes. That his glossy hair was now turning grey at the temples only made him that much more handsome, more distinguished. But that a man so proud as Joaquin Villarreal would weep over what she had said to him convinced her of his love as his words never could have. He had suffered as much as she, every bit as much, because he knew he had failed her. She didn't need to rebuke him for it. He knew her pain, he had lived with it as clearly as she had. She reached up to touch his cheek, wiping away his tears tenderly with her fingertips. ''Oh, Joaquin, what have we done to each other, my love?'' She put her arms around his neck and pulled his head down upon her shoulder to comfort him as if he were a small child. She felt only love for him then, the love she had always known. He hadn't destroyed that tender feeling at all: it grew within her heart as she held him close. ''I'm so sorry, Joaquin. I didn't mean to hurt you.''

Joaquin was thoroughly humiliated to realize Flame

had seen him cry. It was so unmanly—he was totally ashamed—but when she began to speak in her low, sweet voice he forgot all of his masculine pride in the hope her words offered now.

"Everything will be all right, somehow it will, Joaquin, I know it will. We've found each other again and we can be happy together, I know we can." She smoothed his hair lightly then leaned forward to kiss his lips softly before she released him.

Joaquin's eyes swept her face, his confidence growing when he saw the happiness which lit her eyes. "Is it possible you can forgive me for not trusting you, for not knowing immediately that Alex's lies couldn't possibly have been true?"

Flame smiled as she took his hand in hers. "Yes, I think I could forgive you anything, I love you so."

Joaquin pulled her into his arms, kissing her with all the hunger and desire he'd felt so long, and she returned his passion, shyly at first but with a growing warmth. She slipped her hand inside his shirt to caress his warm skin, her fingertips playfully counting his ribs as she teased him. She wanted him desperately and cared little where they were until the front door slammed shut and Seth Randall strode into the room, shattering their loving closeness with an angry shout.

Joaquin stood up, then stepped away from Flame, turning his back toward Seth. Perhaps it was permissible after all to weep in front of one's wife, but never would he let another man see his tears. Flame understood Joaquin's mood and smiled sweetly at Seth, who was staring at her with his mouth agape. He could not believe his eyes: here was the woman who repeatedly told him she wanted nothing to do with men very nearly making love in the middle of the afternoon—in his parlor, for God's sake!

Flame was too happy to care about Seth's obvious

bewilderment. "Good afternoon, Seth."

"Good afternoon. Señor Villarreal, don't bother to tell me you were discussing Linda's ranch because I won't believe you!" He was livid, and growing more so by the second. The man had the gall to inquire as to his intentions and then had returned the next day bent on seducing Linda himself.

Joaquin had regained his usual composure and turned back to answer, "I won't insult you, Mr. Randall. I realize your eyesight is probably excellent and what we were doing unmistakable."

"As long as Linda resides in my home I am responsible for her well-being. Suppose you tell me just what your intentions are!" Seth took a step closer as he shouted angrily at Joaquin.

Flame leapt to her feet and darted between the two men. She'd never seen Seth so angry but she knew all too well what Joaquin was like when he lost his temper. But Joaquin surprised her this time: he slipped his arms around her waist and stepped back, pulling her along with him. The shock of his strength startled her and she tensed rather than relaxing against him as he had expected she would. He dropped his arms and moved away—he'd assumed too much, obviously way too much, and his touch had frightened her again.

"Tell him whatever you'd like, Flame, it is all up to you now." Joaquin frowned as he turned away, unable to hide his disappointment.

Seth looked between them, his consternation growing. "Flame? Linda, what is going on here?"

Flame saw Joaquin's disgusted expression and sighed unhappily. What had she done wrong, why was he so upset? "Flame is a name my father called me, and Joaquin has always called me that too. I've only recently used Linda which is my real name. You needn't ask Joaquin to state his intentions toward me, Seth,

315

there's really no need for that."

"I disagree, Linda. I don't care how good a friend you might have been to her late husband, Villarreal, you owe me some kind of an explanation for your conduct just now."

Joaquin straightened up to his full height, several inches above Seth's and answered calmly, "And if I refuse?"

Seth frowned as he realized he was very close to starting a fistfight with a man well known for being a more than formidable adversary. It would have been suicide to provoke him and Seth knew it.

"Seth, this is all my fault. Joaquin need explain nothing to you. He is my husband."

"Your what? Linda, how can that possibly be? When did you have time to marry him?" Seth was astonished—he'd always hoped to win Flame eventually, to marry her himself someday. Her announcement came as a devastating shock to him.

"I married Joaquin in July of 1870, a few days before I came to work here for you." Flame felt as though she had cast off a heavy burden. Having finally told Seth the truth was a great relief to her conscience, but his pained expression touched her with a deep stab of remorse.

Seth was still stunned, perhaps even more. "Why would you have come to work for me when you should have still been on your honeymoon? Why in heaven's name did you tell me you were a widow?"

Joaquin walked over to the windows and pulled back the lace curtains to look out at the park across the way. He'd let Flame explain in whatever way she wished, but he held his breath, dreading what she would say. Would she tell Seth the truth?

"I'd rather not explain any of our problems to you, Seth, it is too long a story and not really one that concerns you in any way. Let's just say we had an argument and I ran away. It's as simple as that. I hadn't seen Joaquin since that night until yesterday.''

"And your child, the boy?''

"He is Joaquin's son.''

Seth shook his head as he slumped down in his favorite chair. Its comforting contours did little to ease his pain. "I don't believe any of this, Linda, it's just too fantastic. What do you want to do now? I assume you want to go home with him, is that right?''

Flame looked over at Joaquin, whose back was still turned. "I don't know what to do, Seth, truly I don't. I had thought I'd always stay here with you. I never expected Joaquin to find me, nor wanted him to.''

"You mean you aren't leaving us then?'' Seth's face lit with the hope of possibility her words offered.

Flame shook her head. "This has all been such a shock, so sudden, I don't know what I want right this minute. I don't want to hurt you, Seth. You've been wonderful to me. But do you understand now why there never could have been anything between us? I am a married woman, I always have been or I would not have refused your love. Had I truly been a widow, I would have married you the first time you proposed to me, before my baby was born.''

Joaquin walked back to stand beside his wife but made no move to touch her again as he spoke. "You know that I want you to come home, Flame. If you need more time to decide you have it. Take all the time you need, I want you to be sure, to have no doubts that I can make you happy.''

Seth glared up at Joaquin and gestured impatiently toward a chair. "If you'd stop strutting around her like a blasted peacock and sit down, Villarreal, maybe we could discuss this more calmly.''

Joaquin laughed, then smiled down at Flame.

317

"Would you say that I strut? Is that what I do?"

Flame shook her head impishly. "Somehow the word swagger seems more appropriate. I've always thought of you as being more like a pirate than a peacock, but there is definitely something unique about the way you move."

"Do you find it objectionable?" A playful smile crossed Joaquin's lips as he inquired politely.

"No, not in the least."

"Well, I have never noticed myself. Now, Seth, do you mind if I cease calling you Mr. Randall? It seems a trifle too formal here. Do you want me to sit down and calmly debate this issue with you, is that your suggestion?"

"I thought we could discuss it . . . after all we both love Linda and want her as a wife."

"Yes, that may be true, but she is already my wife, isn't she? If she isn't in love with you after spending all these months in your home I'd say you've already lost this debate. Regardless of what she said, had Flame loved you she would have married you anyway whether or not I happened to still be her legal husband. Anyway, I know for a fact it makes Flame livid to see me fight over her affections so while I will sit down, I won't argue with you. Flame can make up her own mind as to which of us she wants. She knows us both and the choice is hers, entirely hers. I have learned not to try and impose my will upon her. If she wants to marry you then I will give her a divorce as quietly and quickly as Rafael can arrange it. I won't stand in the way of her happiness."

Flame fought back her anger. He was right of course—she didn't like him fighting over her; but his damn superior attitude didn't please her either. He was giving her the choice, at least, and she couldn't help but love him for that. He was letting her go and graciously too if she so desired.

Seth was curious. "You mean you've actually fought other men for Linda before today?"

Joaquin nodded, "Yes, I'm afraid so, on numerous occasions in fact." He could see Seth's alarm growing and continued, "She absolutely forbids me to duel over her, or I could have settled several scores with much less effort than it took to do the job with my fists."

Flame saw the terror mount in Seth's eyes and understood immediately what Joaquin was doing. His tale wasn't exactly a lie, but it wasn't strictly the truth either. Seth was a dear, sweet man, so gentle and kind. He would make some woman a wonderful husband, but not her. He'd been one of the best friends she'd ever had and she loved his children as dearly as her own and would miss them so, but she knew without any doubt in her heart that she loved only Joaquin. He still frightened her a little, but he enchanted her completely and she prayed they would be happy together this time. She just wanted to go home with him and said so. "Seth, would you bring the children to come and visit us next summer? I'll miss you all so much, but I want to go home, I just want so very much to go home with my husband."

Joaquin stared up at Flame, so lost in the sight of her it did not immediately dawn on him that she had chosen him. When it finally did he leapt to his feet and swept her into his arms. He turned toward Seth only briefly. "Will you please excuse us? I'd like to take up where I left off before you came home and interrupted us." He lowered his head and kissed Flame with a kiss which left Seth Randall only too certain who had won her heart. He got to his feet slowly and closed the front door softly on his way out.

Sixteen

Flame lay her son gently in his cradle. Then, rather than getting into bed herself, she returned to the comfortable rocking chair to rest while she contemplated the changes the coming day would bring in her life. This was to be her last night in the Randall home and she'd known real contentment there . . . she loved Seth's children dearly and knew she would miss them when she returned home. Home. She turned the word over slowly in her mind. She was going home with Joaquin in the morning. To have discovered she loved him still had been a great shock, one from which it would take some time to recover, and yet she had no such luxury.

She thought back to the afternoon they'd spent together . . . he'd seemed so happy, played with the children, amused them for hours before he'd left, and she knew he'd really enjoyed himself with them, truly liked them. She'd never thought of Joaquin as being so gentle, such good fun. Still, as she rocked slowly in her darkened room her anxiety continued to mount.

It had been a mistake for her to agree to go with him so quickly. She really needed more time to adjust to being with him once again—after all, they'd not seen each other in months and he could scarcely expect her to begin their marriage as if she were an ecstatic young bride just beginning her honeymoon rather than a wife who had been on her own for a year. She had matured in so many ways, had had only her own resources upon which to depend and she knew she was no longer the willful girl Joaquin had loved. She'd been forced to grow up quite suddenly and although Seth was a kind friend she had not loved him. She had shut out all thought of love as being an impossibility for her once she'd left Joaquin: how could she again be as affectionate as she had once been after a year of denying the strength of the emotions which existed within her?

How indeed was she to now please her husband when she had failed so miserably in that task before? No matter how she tried, she could not forget the way he'd left her to spend her wedding night alone. He'd not offered an explanation or an apology for that cruelty, so what other reason could she believe other than the obvious one? If only her grandmother had taught her how she might give her husband pleasure she would not have been such a terrible disappointment to Joaquin. She'd asked him to teach her how to make love but he'd been in no mood that night and had only laughed at her request, and she'd not risk the humiliation of being laughed at for asking him that same question again.

It was nearly dawn when Flame finally climbed into her bed and went to sleep. When the children awoke that morning she was far too tired to get up and care for them. She was also far too sick with worry to face Joaquin, and so remained in bed, hoping her husband would believe her too ill to leave for the ranch that day and go away.

Molly Randall went into her father's room and tugged at his hand. "Come help us, Daddy, Linda's sick and she can't get up!"

"What?" Seth dashed down the hall to her room. "Linda, are you truly ill?" He put his hand to her cheek but found her smooth skin cool. "You have no

321

fever. What's wrong?'' Seth was perplexed and said so: "You've never been ill, never, not a day. Even before the baby was born your health was fine.''

Flame covered her mouth as she yawned. "I'm so tired, Seth. I couldn't get to sleep until quite late last night. Will you please send Joaquin away? Tell him I can't leave for home with him today after all.'' Flame shut her eyes again and tried to go back to sleep.

Seth knew there was no way he was going to be able to tell Joaquin Villarreal to go away. The man would probably just shove him aside and come upstairs for Linda whether she were feeling well or not. He turned toward his children and saw they had changed the baby's diaper by themselves and nearly had him dressed. "Matthew, Molly, please leave Joaquin in his cradle. Linda will see to him in a minute. I want you two to go on downstairs and have your breakfast. Now run along, I'm sure cook has it ready.'' As soon as the children were out of the room Seth took the chair from in front of the dresser and moved it beside Flame's bed so he might sit beside her while they talked. "Linda, look at me. I have no intention of even attempting to send your husband away, not unless you tell me what is really troubling you this morning.''

When Flame opened her eyes she could barely focus them on the blonde man's face. "Oh, Seth, I'm so sorry. I don't want Joaquin to be angry with you. I'll get up, but I just can't leave for the ranch today.''

Seth weighed his words carefully. "Do you really want to go home with him? If you can't face leaving to-day, will you be able to go tomorrow?''

As Flame sat up her long golden curls spilled over her shoulders, making her look no more than twelve, as sweet and innocent as she still truly was. "I do want to go home, Seth, but I—''

"Are you afraid of him, Linda, is that the problem?

You were married less than a week before you left him—it doesn't take any great leap of logical thought to surmise what happened. Did he mistreat you, beat you perhaps? Are his sexual appetites perverted? Did he ask you to do unnatural things?''

Flame's eyes widened in horror at those questions. ''No, Seth, nothing like that. Joaquin is not like that at all.''

''Well whatever it was he must have been a great failure as your husband or you would never have left him as you did. Would you like to tell me about it? Maybe I could help, I at least made my wife happy. What went wrong for you?''

Flame shook her head. She couldn't tell Seth the truth—she'd never admit to anyone how little her husband had thought of her character—but maybe he could answer some of her questions. ''Seth, I know men are expected to be experienced, but how is a woman to learn how to make love?''

Seth sat back in his chair, his mouth agape, hardly knowing how to respond. ''Linda, didn't your mother ever tell you what to expect from marriage, about being a man's wife and pleasing him?''

''My mother died when I was four, Seth. My grandmother told me things, but they were so vague—mostly about how men want only one thing from their wives—but she never explained to me what I should do.''

Seth had never been so embarrassed. He knew he had been too blunt with her, asked her questions which had quite naturally led into their present discussion, but he hadn't expected the subject to take such a surprising turn. Here was the woman he loved dearly, asking him for advice she needed to be another man's wife, and he couldn't bear that. ''Linda, isn't there some woman you could ask, some friend?''

Flame brushed away the tears that were again filling

her eyes. "There isn't time now, Seth. I thought that *you* were my friend."

Her obvious state of panic alarmed Seth all the more. "Linda, I'm sorry. I'll try my best to answer you, but remember, I'm a man, and I don't have any clue to a lot of things a woman could tell you. I think making love is something a man and his wife learn how to do together. Unfortunately, some men don't care at all for a woman's emotions—they think only of satisfying themselves, when each should want to give the other pleasure."

"But if a man enjoyed being with his wife, wouldn't he tell her so? Wouldn't he want to hold her in his arms, to just be with her?"

Dear God, Seth prayed, what had Villarreal done to her? He got to his feet and moved the chair away. "I love you, Linda, but Joaquin was your choice and you should save your questions for him. It's plain only he has the answers." Seth walked from the room, slamming the door angrily behind him.

As the baby began to cry Flame collapsed across her pillows, sobbing uncontrollably. What was she going to do? She loved Joaquin so, but she was terrified. She'd not made him happy before, he'd always been furious with her over one thing or another—what hope did she have she could fill his home with happiness now? She got up slowly and went to pick up her son. He was too hungry to care that his mother's tears were falling on his face while she fed him his breakfast.

Seth was still so angry he could scarcely see as he answered Joaquin's knock at his front door. God in heaven, what had the man done to Linda?

Joaquin brushed past Seth, hardly aware of the man's ill-humor. "Is Flame ready? I'll help her to pack if she isn't."

"No, she's not ready. In fact she's still in bed and

may never be ready to leave for all I know!''

Joaquin had no time for the man's temper tantrums. ''Look, I know you wanted Flame—Linda if you prefer—to stay here with you, but she is my wife and—''

''And nothing, Villarreal, nothing! Come in here with me.'' Seth walked into the parlor and motioned impatiently for Joaquin to take the chair opposite his. ''Linda has never been ill, not once in the time she's been with me, and suddenly she is too tired to get out of her bed. I don't think she's tired. I think she's just plain scared to death of you!''

Joaquin was stunned. Flame had been so happy the previous afternoon: she'd not seemed afraid of him then, not at all. But if she'd told Seth what had really happened between them then there was no hope, she'd changed her mind about returning home with him. ''What did she say?''

''Say? Why nothing really, she just asked a few questions that made it obvious she knows absolutely nothing about married life. How did she happen to have your child when she has no idea what to expect from marital relations? What in God's name did you do to frighten her so? From the looks of you, Villarreal, I'd say you could talk a woman into anything. What happened with your wife?'' Seth was so outraged he'd forgotten his caution of the previous afternoon.

Joaquin fought back his anger as best he could. His first impulse was to throttle Seth and step over him as he carried Flame out, but he knew that brutality would hardly gain her respect. ''It's really none of your business, Randall. I was incredibly stupid and broke Flame's heart, and I've spent the last year trying to find her so I can make it up to her. Now if you don't mind, I'd like to go upstairs and speak with her. You can stand beside me if you wish, if she truly doesn't want to come home with me then I'll leave and you'll never see me here again."

Seth shook his head emphatically. "No."

"What?" Joaquin was astounded by Seth's new-found courage.

"I said no. If Linda is too sick with fright to get out of bed I'll not permit you to go up to her room."

Joaquin sighed at this unexpected obstacle, then rose slowly to his full height. "Do you really think you can stop me?"

"Probably not, but I'll try." Seth stood up quickly and braced himself for a fight he knew he couldn't possibly win, but the men were interrupted by squeals of delight as the two Randall children found Joaquin with their father. They came running into the parlor and danced around their new friend.

"Your children seem to be excellent judges of character, Seth. Come, children, let's go upstairs and see Linda." Joaquin took Molly's and Matthew's hands and started up the stairs.

Seth Randall groaned in frustration, following the small parade up to the second floor. He could hardly fight a man surrounded by small children, especially when the children were his own.

Joaquin knelt beside Flame and stroked her long golden hair as he called her name softly. Finally she turned her head to look at him, but the deep green of her eyes held only fear, the same look he'd seen in the eyes of wild animals caught in traps. That sight disgusted him and filled him with revulsion: it had never been his purpose to frighten her into accompanying him home. "Are you really ill, Flame? If so I'll summon a physician immediately." He continued to pat her head lightly, to reassure her, to be loving as he wished to be.

Flame shook her head, then closed her eyes. The

matter settled in her mind, she was asleep again in seconds.

Joaquin shook her shoulder—forcefully this time, no longer sympathetic. "Flame, wake up! I'm taking you home, right now, do you understand? If you want to get dressed then get up and dress. Otherwise I'm taking you home in your nightgown!"

Molly and Matthew began to giggle and bounce on her bed, making it impossible for Flame to rest. She pushed herself up into a sitting position and Joaquin moved to sit down beside her upon the edge of her bed.

"Must we go today, Joaquin? Must we?"

"Yes. I don't want to spend another night alone in that hotel, I'm taking you home today and that's final." Joaquin felt her tension and tried again to reassure her. "Flame, do you remember what I told you about Lady? You told me I was wrong, that love could heal any hurt. You were right. You brought her spirit back just with your love, your gentle care. If love will restore an animal's heart surely it can do the same for us. Let me at least try to be your husband. Please let me try."

Flame looked into the radiant light which shone in his warm brown eyes and began to smile herself. She'd be a fool not to try, since she knew she loved him still, and dearly. "I'll get dressed, Joaquin. It won't take me a minute to pack."

"Would you like my help?"

Flame's panic was instanteous. "Oh no, I can get dressed by myself!"

Joaquin chuckled as he got to his feet. "I meant that I would be happy to help you pack your things."

Flame's blush was as attractive as ever. "No thank you, I got Joaquin's things ready last night and it won't take me long to gather my belongings."

"I'll wait downstairs then. Come on, children,

Seth." With a satisfied smile Joaquin ushered the two laughing children and their despondent father out the door.

Flame was astonished by the magnificent carriage which stood waiting in front of the Randall home. It was brand new, very elegant, drawn by four of Joaquin's thoroughbreds, matched bays with dark glossy coats and silky manes and tails. But more surprising still were the men who stood near it. As the driver called to him, one man carrying a shotgun climbed up to sit beside him while the other three men mounted their horses. She remembered them all from the ranch, tough-looking vaqueros, all heavily armed, and she turned to her husband to inquire as to the reason for their presence. "Is all this show of force necessary?"

"Did you expect me to carry you home on Diablo's back? I know you and I could have ridden comfortably enough, but I thought the boy might be a problem. There was also the question of your luggage. I didn't realize you'd have so little." Joaquin smiled easily as he answered her question.

"But the carriage is one thing, these armed men quite another. They are what worry me, Joaquin."

Joaquin grew more serious then. "I know it's a bit much for the city but we've a long way to go, Flame. I never travel alone anymore, it's simply too dangerous. I've tried dressing these men in livery but they still look like the cutthroats they are—which is of course why I employ them. And they're much more comfortable in their own clothing."

Flame had not considered the matter of their safety. Could they be robbed, murdered on the journey home? She hesitated, but Joaquin took her arm and helped her up into the carriage, then handed their baby into her arms once she was seated.

Joaquin turned to shake hands with Seth. While certainly not friends, they each had earned the other's respect. "We do want you to come visit us next summer, Seth. Bring Molly and Matthew with you and we'll be happy to entertain you for as long as you can stay."

Matthew grabbed his father's arm and squealed in delight. "May we go, may we?"

Seth laughed as he hugged his son. "You can see my children will not allow me to refuse your invitation, Joaquin." He was far too tactful a man to add that his own love for Flame would not allow him to ignore it either. Standing and waving as they drove away, he hoped with all his heart his dear Linda would be happy at last.

The slow rocking motion of the carriage soon began to lull Flame to sleep. She yawned and sat up, trying to appear alert, but Joaquin only grinned and reached out to take his son.

"Go to sleep if you like, I'll watch the boy."

"You don't mind? He isn't too much for you?" Flame was surprised at how loving a father Joaquin had turned out to be.

"No, not at all. I've missed so much by not knowing the baby even existed, I want very much to take care of him now."

"He is more fun each day, Joaquin. You have not missed so very much—he is barely four months old."

Joaquin frowned for an instant, the concern plain on his handsome features. "Flame, if I hadn't found you, would you have ever let me know that I had fathered a son?"

Sitting across from her husband, watching him cuddle their child, it seemed impossible she could have lived in such terror of being found. Tears filled her eyes and she blinked them away hurriedly. "I'm sorry, Joaquin. I meant to tell the boy. When he was older I would have told him who his father was."

Joaquin shifted the child on his lap, his voice soft and low as he asked, "What did you think I'd do, Flame, take him away from you?"

"No, I never thought you'd do that, but I never expected you to come for me as you have. I always knew you'd come for me if you discovered my whereabouts, but my worst fear was that you'd simply arrive with your men and take me back at gunpoint. It never occurred to me that you could be so kind as you have been these last few days, or that you would be so gracious as to give me a choice." But even as Flame spoke those words of praise she saw the light change in Joaquin's eyes and she knew she had never really had a choice when he had such power. That she had had any say in her return home had been an illusion. "I did choose to come home, Joaquin, I am not your prisoner, but what if my answer had been no? Would you really have given me a divorce if I'd wanted to marry Seth?"

Joaquin looked away quickly, avoiding his wife's all too perceptive gaze. "That's what I said, wasn't it?"

"You didn't mean it though, did you!" His reluctance to reply had given her all the answer she needed. He hadn't meant for her to have any choice at all unless her choice was also his.

"I won't lie to you, Flame. I could have had my men pick you up in the park and bring you home any time in the last month, that's how long I've known where you were. You know I had every right to do that too, to bring my wife back home. I knew that would infuriate you, however, so I tried what I considered to be a more gentlemanly approach first."

"First! Then what, you'd have kidnapped me!" Flame was infuriated all right. She'd known on the night she'd fled his home he'd never let her go willingly—how could she have forgotten his pride for even one minute!

330

Joaquin sighed impatiently. "Flame, you told me yourself you wanted to come home with me and I'm overjoyed to have you back. Let's not argue about this anymore."

"No, I no longer enjoy arguing as I used to, Joaquin. Perhaps you will find me so changed you will no longer wish to have me as your wife."

"That would be impossible, my dear." Clearly Joaquin thought that idea absurd.

"Would it? I've had to endure a year of loneliness, of heartbreak I didn't think I could survive. I could not have been more wretchedly unhappy had I truly been a widow."

"That you were not is a fact for which I am most grateful." Joaquin could not help but laugh at his own joke but he had noticed the change in her himself—she was, if possible, even more lovely, but her manner was completely different. She was shy now, hesitant rather than quick-tempered and defiant as before. Had he done that to her, changed the lively, bewitching girl he had loved into this fearful woman?

Flame chewed her lower lip nervously. "Please don't laugh at me, Joaquin, please don't. I can't bear it." She looked down at her hands. His mother's ring had not left her hand, she'd not removed it once since he'd slipped it on her finger.

Joaquin followed her glance. "I meant to buy you your own ring, I should have had it for you now."

"A ring doesn't matter to me, Joaquin." Flame didn't look up at him again. She'd never really felt married in spite of the ring on her hand or the child on his lap. She'd never been his wife, never belonged to him, nor he to her for that matter. They were little more than strangers now—strangers who loved each other, but strangers nonetheless.

"Would you tell me one thing, Flame, answer one

question for me?''

Her smile delighted him, it was immediate and teasing. ''That depends upon the nature of your question. I'll make no promises before I hear it.''

Now that she was smiling happily he hesitated to ask, yet he was too curious not to. ''I have often wondered why you took my knife that night, when you could have killed me so easily. Why didn't you do it? You must have wanted to do it.''

Flame's eyes took on a somber light as she replied. ''The thought did occur to me, I won't deny it, but only for an instant. I never could have done it though, I could not have killed you.''

Her level stare surprised him. He had never thought of Flame as being hard or cold but that she could calmly dismiss his question confused him. ''Why not? You had a good reason, your description was quite accurate. I did trick you into marrying me, I did it to end my own torment when instead I should have been thinking of what would have been best for you. Had you killed me it would have been deserved. You had good reason.''

''Yes, that's true, but not the desire. You'd said you despised me, Joaquin, hated me for what I'd done to you although I had no idea what you were talking about. I'd never said that to you, I had only loved you with all my heart. But had I known then how your memory would haunt me I think I would have killed myself. When I did consider suicide it was too late— you wouldn't have known I'd done it. Then when I learned I was carrying a child I no longer wanted to die.''

Joaquin felt his throat tighten with the pain of her words. She had given him only love and that she had considered destroying herself to escape the sorrow he'd given her appalled him, sickened him totally. He knew he would have killed himself too then. He tried to think

332

of some way to reassure her. Now that they were alone he wanted to say something to let her know he understood her fear of him. It would take time, he knew that, but he prayed it wouldn't be long before she'd be willing to share his bed again. He didn't want her to worry anymore the way she had obviously nearly made herself ill with worry the night before. He knew if he asked her she would submit to his desires and that thought repelled him. He wanted her to want him as she had before he'd ruined everything with his unfounded suspicions. She might have forgiven him for what he'd done but he would never forgive himself, not as long as the fear was so clear in her eyes. He wanted to see only trust in her expression when he made love to her, the trust and love which used to shine in her gaze. Now even when she said she loved him, her eyes held only dread.

"Flame—" Joaquin looked up at his wife, hoping to make her understand that he'd be patient. But her eyes were closed; she was sound asleep, her head resting lightly against the side of the carriage.

It was early afternoon when they reached his uncle's home. Joaquin leaned over to touch Flame's knee gently. "Flame, we're here, wake up." He'd always hated riding inside a carriage—he'd brought an extra horse, in fact, just so he could ride, but the day had passed by so quickly as he'd played with his son and held him while he'd napped. All the while he'd watched Flame as she'd slept. He'd been so afraid he would never see her again. Now he had his whole world within his reach and he couldn't stop smiling. "Flame, wake up."

Flame covered her yawn as she sat up straight. "Are we stopping now?" She reached out to take the little boy onto her lap. He was chewing his fingers noisily, anxious to eat, but she'd wait to feed him until they

333

were shown to their room. "I'm sorry I slept so long, I hope the baby wasn't too much trouble for you."

"He is no trouble, Flame, he is a delight. Now we're spending the night with my Uncle, Tío Carlos, do you remember him? I think you may have met him once, he often stops by my house on his way to Los Angeles."

"I'm sure I'll remember him when I see him. What did you tell him about me, Joaquin?" Flame hugged her son, kissed his rosy cheeks and combed his fine dark hair with her fingertips. He was as handsome as his father, his eyes bright, his smile charming.

"Only Rafael knows the truth, no one else does. I told my family only last week that I had married. I don't know what to say, frankly. Can you think of any possible reason to give for our separation other than the truth which I certainly will never tell."

Flame yawned again as she shook her pretty head. "Let's just refuse to discuss it then, surely no one would be so rude as to ask us would they?"

"Let's hope not."

Uncle Carlos was delighted to see Flame again and she remembered him instantly. He joked with Joaquin about his fine son and escorted them all into this house where he made them feel at home at once. If he were curious about Joaquin's startling announcement of the week before he was too fine a gentleman to let his curiosity show in front of Flame.

While the lazy afternoon was relaxing, Flame and Joaquin had been given only one room and her thought the whole time was of what Joaquin would expect of her when they had to share a bed. She scarcely touched her dinner, the food was delicious but simply refused to go down her throat. When Joaquin helped her from her chair and they said their good nights she walked to their room beside him, but when he took her hand she knew he could not fail to notice how badly she was trembling.

Joaquin glanced down at Flame and cursed his own folly but he could find no way to tell the woman he wanted so desperately that he'd be patient. It was all he could do to keep his hands off her as they walked down the hall, but when they reached their room suddenly an idea seized him. "Flame, feed the baby and go on to sleep. I need to check on the horses, it might take me hours. I'll see you in the morning." He bent down to kiss her forehead lightly then left the room at a pace just short of a dead run.

Flame stared after her husband. "The horses?" Hadn't the men had time to feed and water the animals by now? They were beauties—perhaps they were more delicate than they appeared and did require special care of some sort—but still she was puzzled by Joaquin's hasty departure. She put on her nightgown and brushed out her long hair before taking her son from the cradle Tío Carlos had provided. Then she remembered Joaquin had disappeared that afternoon when she'd been ready to feed the baby. Perhaps he thought his presence might embarrass her and wished only to give her some time to nurse the baby in private. Yes, that was undoubtedly it. He was being so considerate of her feelings she was genuinely touched. He had been so sweet to her all day, so polite, so attentive to her conversation at dinner; they had managed to spend a most pleasant day together . . . now all that remained was the night.

Joaquin sat in the barn for two hours playing poker with his men. He often played cards with them when they traveled but if his attention to the game was erratic they pretended not to notice. He was so nervous he could hardly sit still and finally threw down his cards and went out to walk around his uncle's fields until he was exhausted. When he reached their room, Flame was sound asleep, curled into a snug ball on the far side of the bed.

Joaquin undressed and got into bed beside her. He had thought he was too tired to want her that night but he was overcome with longing as soon as he saw her again. If only he could just hold her in his arms without waking her, he thought. He moved closer to her and tried to slip his arm under her shoulders but she awakened instantly.

"Joaquin, what is it?" She sat up, startled, reacting by swiftly avoiding his touch.

"I'm sorry to have bothered you, Flame. I didn't mean to wake you. Go back to sleep." He moved away from her, stretched out on his own side of the bed and closed his eyes. He hadn't meant to frighten her, but her reaction had told him he had. At least she hadn't jumped out of the bed, he mused—that was something, if not much. He fell asleep quickly, longing for the woman who lay inches from his side but seemingly miles from his grasp.

Flame lay still until she realized Joaquin had gone to sleep. What had he wanted, she wondered. She'd expected him to at least want to kiss her, if not much more. Now she was puzzled. Why had she worried so about how to please him if he didn't even want to kiss her?

Joaquin was up and dressed when Flame awoke the next morning. She looked over at his side of the bed, moved her hand over the sheets but they were cold, no longer holding a trace of the fiery warmth she'd remembered. Well, if that was their first night together it was not at all what she had expected it to be—and, she realized with a start, not what she wanted either. Joaquin had once been so affectionate, what was wrong now?

That day passed more slowly than the first. They stopped along the way to get out and rest, to let the baby rest in the sunshine, but arrived at the hotel where Joaquin always stayed in Santa Cruz by nightfall. There was no need for explanations there, a fact for which they were both relieved. Once their son was asleep Joaquin began to pace nervously around their room. He wasn't at all tired and Flame appeared to be wide awake also. He searched his mind for some excuse to leave her again but none came to his mind. Finally when he could stand being near her and wanting her so badly no longer he had to leave. "I'm going out for a walk, Flame. I guess being cooped up in that carriage all day is too much for me. Don't wait up."

Flame looked up, a worried expression darkening her brow. "You won't go out alone, you'll take one of your men with you so you'll be safe?"

"Yes, of course." That she was concerned for him made him feel that much worse about lying to her.

"You have an extra horse . . . why don't you ride tomorrow if you'd rather? I'll be fine alone."

Now Joaquin was perplexed. He had thought she was growing more comfortable in his company, but perhaps not. "It makes no difference to you then?"

"Why no. I'm sure you'd prefer to ride, go ahead. Don't be concerned about me." Flame picked up the book she'd brought along to read and pretended to concentrate on the open page but the minute he left the room she began to cry. It did matter to her, a great deal. She wanted to try and be his wife and he didn't even seem interested in her. He'd not touched her all day except to help her in and out of the carriage. She got ready for bed and got under the covers alone again, buried her face in her pillow and cried herself to sleep, crying for the man she was afraid to approach.

Joaquin found his men downstairs in the hotel saloon and sat with them again although he didn't order a drink. They talked about horses, races they'd won, men they'd fought, women they'd loved while Joaquin sat and nodded, his thoughts on the lovely creature he'd left alone upstairs. When he went back to their room she was asleep again but he knew better than to try and hold her now. He undressed in the dark and got into bed beside her, carefully trying to avoid waking her. He lay still and listened to the soft rhythm of her breathing and finally it lulled him to sleep, but nothing helped the gnawing hunger for her love which tore away at his insides. His dreams were strangely disturbing and he awoke shortly before dawn far from refreshed. He looked over at Flame. Her golden hair lay fanned out across her pillow and her expression was so sweet it took all his self-control to leave her to get up and dress. Nothing was going as he'd wanted it to. He swore as he put on his riding clothes and left the room to summon his men to prepare for their journey.

Flame was horribly tired by the time they stopped that evening in Monterey. To make matters worse, they would be staying with more of Joaquin's relatives—Maria Elena's family, she learned as he helped her down from the carriage.

"Does she know we are married?" Flame's eyes searched her husband's face apprehensively. She did not remember his cousin with any fondness and dreaded seeing her at such a difficult time.

"Yes, her whole family knows, I told them when I stopped by on my way to get you."

"What did you say about me?" Flame had missed him, she was sorry she hadn't insisted he ride in the carriage with her again. His charming company had made the other days go by so quickly.

"I said I would bring you and my son by on our way home," Joaquin grinned at her, one of his most charming smiles. He had missed her dreadfully too.

"Were you so confident I'd come home with you?"

338

Flame returned his smile. She had been tempted to reach out and touch him, to put her hand on his chest, but drew it back at the last minute, uncertain of his response. "Though of course I would have been with you whether I'd agreed to come willingly or not, wouldn't I?"

"Don't you dare start that again, Flame!" Joaquin cautioned angrily, but was interrupted as the entire Alvarez family and most of their household staff came rushing out to surround them with excited cries of greeting. Flame tried to recall, then was certain she remembered Joaquin mentioning that his aunt had been his mother's sister. She wondered if his mother had resembled his Aunt Teresa, so pretty and petite . . . she'd make it a point to ask him later. The friendly smiling group was chattering rapidly in Spanish, enveloping Joaquin and admiring the son he held proudly in his arms, but none seemed to notice her. She stepped back out of the way and waited for Joaquin to introduce her to his aunt and uncle, but he seemed to be lost in the conversations about him. She shifted her small travel bag nervously between her hands and waited, becoming more ill at ease each second. Finally Joaquin looked up and saw her predicament and frowned. She looked so lost and alone; he was furious with himself for not realizing she hadn't been able to understand any of the joyous words of welcome all uttered in his native language, the one still foreign to her. He pushed through the crowd just as the tears began to fill her eyes.

"Flame, I'm so sorry. Stay right beside me, my love. They didn't mean to ignore you so rudely."

Flame glanced past him to Maria Elena who'd turned their way with an expression that glowed with hate, not welcome. Flame tried to smile up at her husband but he felt her trembling hand and cursed to himself. She was still afraid, not at all like the high-spirited girl who'd put Maria Elena in her place so easily the year before. That was the vibrant young woman he'd adored, but he knew only too well what had happened to that sweet innocent girl, and he gripped his wife's hand more tightly.

By the end of dinner Flame's head ached dreadfully. She'd managed to sit through another meal without eating a bite, but no one had noticed. Joaquin had tried to include her in the conversation but the Alvarezes constantly reverted to Spanish, all laughing and talking at once about good times they had shared. Flame longed only to be excused so she might go to bed, but as they left the dining room Joaquin's Uncle Arturo took him aside and she found herself being escorted into the parlor by Maria Elena.

"I am very surprised to see you here with Joaquin. I thought you had learned your lesson and would not return, Flame." The haughty young woman's words were uttered so softly that neither her mother nor sisters overheard.

Flame turned to face the dark-eyed beauty and smiled sweetly. "Joaquin is my husband, why shouldn't I be with him?"

Maria Elena moved closer still, whispering her insults viciously: "Everyone knows what happened. In spite of your beauty you weren't woman enough for Joaquin. He needs a woman whose passion is a match for his own. He only brought you back because he wants his son!"

Flame gasped, devastated by Maria Elena's words. "What do you mean everyone knows?" Tears flooded her eyes. How could anyone know what had happened?

"Oh yes, we all know about you, Flame. He told everyone what a failure you were in his bed."

Flame ran from the parlor, dashed away as swiftly as her tiny feet would carry her back to their room. She slammed the door, desperate for some security in a house where all were laughing at her. Her sobs woke the baby who also began to wail, frightened by his mother's tears. Flame threw herself across the bed, heartbroken that Joaquin would have betrayed her trust so cruelly again. Dear God, would he do it again and again, endlessly? How could he have told his relatives she was a failure as a woman, how could he have ridiculed her like that after the way he'd treated her? Flame cried all the harder then—maybe it was true. She had been carefully taught to smile and flirt, to dance and converse in the most enchanting manner, but no one had taught her how to please her husband, and now she knew that was something that couldn't be learned.

Joaquin had seen Flame bolt from the room and stopped only long enough to excuse himself to his uncle before following her. When he found both his wife and small son crying pathetically he hardly knew what to do. He scooped up the baby in his arms and knelt down beside Flame. "What happened? Did Maria Elena say something which upset you?" That was an understatement, he realized: she was hysterical, crying so hard he was greatly alarmed. He laid the boy down among the pillows and pulled her into his arms. "Flame, you must tell me what she said. I'll wring her neck for hurting you so badly, but you must tell me what she said!"

Flame could scarcely catch her breath. If Joaquin didn't love her nothing mattered anymore. She couldn't bear that terrifying thought: after living so long alone with no hope of ever finding love again, to discover his words had been lies had broken what was left of her heart.

Joaquin didn't want to strike her, he would never do that, but somehow he had to get her to calm down. He held her more tightly and spoke softly, calling her name

341

over and over again. "Flame, please tell me what she said."

Flame looked up at him, her vision so blurred by her tears she couldn't see his face clearly. "She told me everyone knows—that you told them."

Joaquin frowned: he still didn't understand what she meant. "Told them what?"

"That I wasn't woman enough for you, that I ran away because I was frightened of being with you, that I'm worthless as a wife, that you only wanted your son, not me." Flame sobbed as she spoke but Joaquin understood each awful word.

"My God, you believed her? You actually believed I'd say such things about you?" Joaquin was furious—that Maria Elena would tell such lies to hurt Flame and that she would believe such trash appalled him. He released her as he stood up abruptly, then gathered up his son and left his wife to cry alone. When he reached the parlor he dropped his boy in Maria Elena's lap.

"There, see if you can get him back to sleep! Since my wife is too upset by your lies to care for him then you must!"

"But Joaquin!" Maria Elena had no idea what to do with the sobbing youngster. She held him tightly and simply stared as his little face grew red as he screamed.

"No, you listen to me! My wife is a saint, do you understand? You are not woman enough to wipe her shoes, Maria Elena!"

The hostile young woman flinched as she realized Flame had repeated her taunt to him. "But Joaquin, I didn't mean anything. I was just teasing her."

"Trying to destroy our marriage is your idea of fun?"

Teresa Alvarez now became alarmed. "Joaquin, the girl is shy, perhaps she misunderstood what my daughter meant."

342

"That woman was the most loving and carefree creature to ever grace this earth until she married me. I drove her out of my house with behavior I'm too ashamed to admit to anyone. That she's willingly come back to me took more courage than all five of you possess. I'm sorry, Arturo, we will have to leave now, this instant. I will not remain in a house where my wife has been so maliciously insulted."

"Joaquin, you exaggerate, you can't leave now, it is too dangerous to travel at night." Arturo Alvarez tried to reason with his volatile nephew.

That his uncle's statement was true didn't matter to Joaquin. "The stage travels at night without mishap and we can also. Besides, there can be no villains abroad tonight who could hurt us any more than we've already been hurt here in your house. Send someone for my men, we are leaving as soon as they can ready the carriage." Joaquin turned back to glare at Maria Elena. "If you so much as speak one word to my wife ever again I'll tear your wicked tongue out by the roots!"

When Joaquin returned to Flame she was no better. Her sobs still racked her slender body and he was beside himself. He picked her up and cradled her in his arms, kissing her face as he spoke. "We're leaving, Flame, I won't stay here. It's not true, not a word of it. Maria Elena was lying. You are a wonderful wife and I adore you." He held her tenderly and rocked her as if she'd been his son, but nothing he said or did seemed to help. When they left his uncle's home Flame was still crying and she wept until she fell into an exhausted sleep, still cradled in her husband's arms.

Joaquin had never been so angry. What had possessed his cousin to be so mean? At one time he'd thought he might marry her someday, was that it? Was she so jealous of Flame she'd say any nasty thing that

343

came into her head just to hurt her? Rafael, Maria Elena and he had grown up together; she was several years younger but had always tagged along after them. Was that it—she was so envious of Flame she'd do anything to cause her grief? Why hadn't he realized that and avoided staying with his aunt and uncle? Now the damage was done: Flame had been so crushed she might never regain her confidence. Worst of all, Joaquin knew she had believed his cousin's spiteful lies, actually believed she was a failure as a woman and that his interest lay only in his son. Nothing was going right. He was trying his best to please Flame, to earn her respect once again, and now his hopes were shattered.

They reached the Villarreal ranch shortly before dawn. It had been a treacherous journey: Joaquin knew full well they never should have risked traveling at night with horses worn out from a long day's trip, but he had wanted so desperately to reach home. Flame would be safe there with him, but as he carried her into the house he hesitated . . . where should he take her? It was clear to him she needed more time before she would be ready to live as his wife, and with that thought in mind he carried her into the bedroom that had been hers. It was a large room, there would be plenty of space for the baby's cradle, and he hoped she would be reassured to find herself in familiar surroundings when she awoke. He placed her carefully on her bed, covered her tenderly with a light quilt, then bent down to kiss her cheek sweetly before he went into his room to sleep alone.

It was late afternoon when Flame awoke. She felt drained, so tired she could scarcely see the view from the large windows, but she soon realized where she was and knew then that Maria Elena's words had been true. Her husband didn't want her: not only would he not make love to her, he wouldn't even let her sleep in the same room with him now that they were home and he had a choice. She began to weep again and couldn't stop. Her marriage was over before it had ever begun, and the pain of returning home with Joaquin was proving to be even worse than that which had driven her away. There would never be an end to her tears.

Seventeen

Joaquin and Rafael sat in silence after Flame left them. Neither seemed to have the desire to speak. When Rafael finally spoke it was in a voice filled with rage.

"What in God's name have you done to her?"

Joaquin's eyes were sad as he looked up and shrugged. "I've not touched her. Yet you see how she is, so nervous she's nearly hysterical, she neither eats nor sleeps, but I have done her no harm. When I brought her home from San Francisco I had only the highest hopes for our future together, but now, I know my dreams will never become reality."

"Was she this way in Randall's house? I could barely hide my shock when I first saw her this afternoon. She has grown far too thin, Joaquin, pale, so distracted she did not seem to be able to follow along with any of our pitiful attempts at conversation tonight. I watched her sit without eating all through dinner and you say she does this constantly? Has she been this way since the very day you brought her home?"

"She was slender, but not so thin as she is today, and yes she seemed nervous but I thought that was only her surprise at having been found. I told you what Maria Elena said to her—those vicious lies simply destroyed her. I've tried, God knows how I have tried in every way I know how, but I can't make her happy. She's

346

never gotten over those awful insults of my cousin's, never recovered from that hurt. Fortunately one of the women here has an infant and cares for Joaquin too, as Flame can no longer nurse him. She cried and cried over that disappointment too, as if she were no longer able to be the boy's mother.''

Rafael hesitated, then decided there was no need for embarrassment between them. ''Does she respond when you make love to her?''

Joaquin's face filled with despair as he shook his head. ''I have not made love to her yet.''

''But why not? I know how dearly you love her . . . what agony you went through without her.'' Rafael was simply astonished.

''Have you ever tried to make love to a woman who is paralyzed with fright? It is not an easy task, one which I do not even know how to begin. She won't come near me, Rafael, she shies away from me, cowers, as if she were a hound I had beaten.''

''But why? She shouldn't be so frightened of your touch. Have you not promised her, shown her, reassured her that she need have no fear of you, nor of love?''

Joaquin sighed. He could hardly bring himself to explain. ''In every way I could think of. But it's no use—she grows more tense and distant each day.''

Rafael sat forward, a sudden idea lighting his expression. ''Could she fear having another child? What did she tell you about the birth of your son? Did she have a difficult labor, much pain?''

''I don't know, we've never discussed Joaquin's birth.''

''Never? You did not once inquire?''

''No.'' Joaquin did not see his friend's point.

''Joaquin, do you know how her mother died?'' Rafael rested his arms on the edge of the dining table,

347

ready for a long session with his friend.

"I remember when she died, but no, I don't recall the cause. What was it?"

"She died in childbirth, Joaquin. Her infant son was buried in her arms. Flame didn't know, not until the day I took her to see her father's grave and she read her mother's tombstone. She was heartbroken to learn how her mother had died."

"Dear God." Joaquin closed his eyes as he slumped back in his chair, his friend's words too sad to bear.

"And you never inquired as to her labor? She must have been terrified, perhaps hysterical with fear, yet the topic has never come up in your conversation?"

Joaquin felt sick with shame. "I had no idea, none. She must think I'm the most unfeeling of husbands."

"Probably." Rafael found the situation appalling. "She was the most beautiful woman I had ever seen that afternoon I met her at the train station. She looked like a princess, not like the ghastly apparition she resembles now. She's been here a month and you've not made love to her once? I can't believe that, Joaquin. I am positive you know how to make love to a woman, to give her such great pleasure she would not deny you your own. Have you spent so much of your time with whores that you have no idea how to treat a lady, your wife, a young woman who really loves you? What do you do with her in your bed each night, just hold her in your arms without speaking?"

Joaquin frowned sullenly, not pleased to take Rafael's abuse even though he felt somehow it was deserved. "She has her own room. I thought it would help her to adjust to being back here with me more readily."

"What did she say about that? Did she ask for her own room—she wants it still?"

"I've never asked her," Joaquin admitted slowly.

For once Rafael swore as bitterly as Joaquin usually

did but he was furious with the man's insensitivity. "Just exactly what did you tell her when you brought her home?"

"She was sleeping when we arrived home. I carried her into the room that had been hers. She knows where mine is, where she might find me."

Rafael lost all control then: "Joaquin, your stupidity continually amazes me! I know you love Flame, and yet you constantly treat her most cruelly. When you know Maria Elena destroyed all her confidence in herself how could you ever expect her to have the courage to approach you?"

"I did not want to be too demanding. I thought I'd just wait, try and be patient until she was ready to come to me."

"I see—how thoughtful. She knows that then, you at least told her that in those exact words?"

"No, I never put it in words but I assumed—"

Rafael's chair toppled over behind him as he leapt to his feet, his fury too great to contain. "Are you blind, Joaquin, do you see nothing? How could you have ignored her like this? What must she think? It must be obvious to her that you care nothing for her, don't love her in the slightest. You have been no husband at all to Flame, none at all. A fool could see she's dying of loneliness. Yes, that woman is dying right before your eyes and you don't even reach out to take her into your arms! I am leaving here tonight, Joaquin, and I am taking Flame with me."

Joaquin sat for a moment, then got to his feet and kicked his own chair out of their way. He was taller than Rafael, stronger if not quicker, but he hoped Rafael would not choose to fight him again, for there could be only one result this time and he dreaded the thought of killing his best friend. "No, I'll never let her go. She's mine. I'll kill you before I'll let you have her."

Rafael pulled his knife from its sheath at his belt. The long slender blade glowed with a wicked gleam as he turned it in his hand. "Then try your best, Joaquin, because I mean to take her. She deserves a man who will at least try to please her, who will see she does not starve herself to death at his table!"

Joaquin drew his own knife then, the one Flame had returned to him, and moved to Rafael's left. Both men knew the other's faults, but respected each other's strengths more. They circled each other stealthily, kicking the chairs out of their way as they went.

Flame heard the loud clatter made by the careening chairs, then Joaquin's angry shout. He always spoke Spanish to Rafael, but he was swearing now from the tone of his voice and she couldn't imagine what was wrong with him. He couldn't possibly be fighting with Rafael again, could he? She ran from her room down the hall. She could hear both men arguing now although she couldn't understand their words. When she rounded the corner of the dining room the sight of their drawn knives terrified her. "Joaquin, no! Stop, you'll kill him!" She ran into the room, throwing herself between her husband and Rafael, clinging to her friend heedless of his knife which slashed through the folds of her skirt as she wrapped her arms around his waist.

Rafael's left arm closed around her waist immediately, drawing her close. "Do you have your answer now, Joaquin? Flame's choice is clear and it is not you!"

Flame spun to face Joaquin, her face filled with rage. "Is that what you're fighting over? Is it me again?"

Joaquin looked into his bride's terror-filled eyes and threw down his knife in disgust. "Take her and get out, Rafael, but my son stays here with me. Now go on, get out of here before I change my mind."

Flame began to scream at her husband, furious with

his generosity where she was concerned. "Am I to have no say in where I go and with whom? Am I to be given away as if I were nothing to you? How dare you treat me so badly!" Flame grabbed up Joaquin's knife from where it lay and dashed from the room with tears streaming down her anguished face.

Joaquin was too stunned to speak. What had he done? She thought he had given her away as casually as he gave thoroughbreds to his friends? He brushed his hair back from his eyes and looked over at Rafael only to find him staring wide-eyed at the knife in his hand. The blade glistened with blood—bright, red blood which dripped to the floor—and splotches of the gruesome liquid marred the old wood in the direction Flame had run.

"Dear God, I have killed her. I didn't know, Joaquin. She threw herself against me so suddenly, I didn't realize she'd been stabbed."

Joaquin ran from the room but the trail of blood led out the open back door and as he raced outside he saw Flame. She was riding Lady as a fleeing Indian might, with neither saddle nor bridle. Her hair flew out behind her as the mare streaked from his view, disappearing under the trees at the end of the pasture. He looked down at the bloodstained dirt . . . she'd bleed to death if he didn't catch her, and swiftly! He dashed across the yard and whistled for Diablo, grateful the stallion was near the barn. He swung himself up on the horse's back, grabbed hold of his long, thick mane with both hands and dug the sharp heels of his boots into the horse's ebony flanks.

Diablo reared back on his hind legs, nearly throwing Joaquin before he took off with a great burst of speed after the Appaloosa mare. Diablo was far more swift than Lady and they soon had the mare in sight. Joaquin screamed in terror when he saw where Flame was

351

heading: straight for the Cypress trees at the edge of the cliffs. Instantly he knew what she'd do—she'd ride Lady off the precipice, killing them both on the jagged rocks below. He watched the gap narrow between them; Diablo was straining to cover the distance, but Joaquin gouged the horse's sides with his heels urging him to even greater speed. As Joaquin drew near Flame turned to look back and ducked away to elude his grasp. In one final gamble to stop Lady Joaquin turned Diablo to her opposite side, placing the stallion and himself between Flame and the sea. As Lady veered in fright from the danger of the cliff Joaquin grabbed Flame around her waist, pulling her off her mare. Diablo moved parallel to the cliffs and continued to run at a full gallop. Far from subdued, Flame raised Joaquin's knife, but he saw to his horror that she meant to use it on herself, not against him. He had no way to halt his mount but held his seat by the pressure of his knees alone as he took Flame's hand by the wrist and hurled the knife far from her grasp.

At last Diablo slowed his fearsome pace, but Joaquin held Flame even more tightly as he slipped from the stallion's back. The hysterical girl began to kick him; she socked his chest and screamed the second her feet touched the ground.

"Why didn't you let me go! Why? You should have let me go!"

"Flame, you nearly killed yourself!" Joaquin began to shake her soundly but she became even more enraged.

"Damn you, let me go! I don't want to live if you don't love me! You're killing me now, I can't bear any more!"

"Flame!" Joaquin wrapped his arms around her but she still continued to fight him wildly.

"How could you give me away? That I am the

mother of your son is not reason enough to keep me?''
Flame struggled so violently Joaquin lost his hold on
her and she sprinted away from him, back toward the
gleaming sea which beckoned at the cliff's rocky edge.
Joaquin leapt after her, making a flying tackle, tearing
her skirt and tripping her as he lunged for her legs in a
valiant effort to stop her flight. Flame fell to the ground
breaking her fall with her hands and Joaquin scrambled
to his knees and held her fast.

The young woman's cries became even more wild
now that she was trapped. ''Let me go! I can't live if
you don't love me!''

Joaquin threw his body over hers in a last effort to
hold her still. He locked his fingers around her wrists
and turned her on her back. Her green eyes glowed up
at him, reflecting the moonlight, their expression wild,
fierce, blazing, all sign of sanity gone.

''What in God's name must I do to prove I love you,
Flame? Isn't it enough to know I'll burn in hell for all
eternity for what I've done to you already? Must I have
your death on my conscience too!''

Somehow the pain and despair of his words cut
through her hysteria and Flame ceased to struggle, but
her words shocked Joaquin all the more. ''I'd fight the
devil himself for your soul, Joaquin. You'll never see
hell because of me.''

Joaquin leaned back, relaxing the pressure on her
wrists, but she made no renewed effort to fight him.

''Don't ask me to live without your love. I know you
love your son, he's yours, but let me go. If you'd give
me away to Rafael I can't believe you'd grieve when
I'm dead.''

Joaquin was astounded. ''Flame, don't you know
how desperately I love you? But I had no hope that you
still loved me, that you wanted my love.''

''Always, Joaquin. I have always wanted you.''

353

Flame began to cry with a choking sound from deep within her throat. "You would not even let me in your room."

Joaquin pulled Flame into his arms and kissed her face, her throat, her tear-filled lashes. "I love you so much, Flame, I never meant to hurt you as I have, never." His mouth covered hers, stilling her sobs with a kiss which demanded a response. Her hysteria had become his and he couldn't get close enough to her as his hands tore away her clothing so he might touch every part of her lovely body. He lowered his lips to her soft full breasts, his tongue a flame as it flicked across her cool flesh then down across her smooth flat stomach.

Flame wound her fingers in his hair, drawing him close as his kiss set her whole being on fire with the desire she'd tried so unsuccessfully to suppress. The ecstasy poured though her in waves more powerful than the sea which pounded the cliffs nearby. When Joaquin's lips at last returned to hers she wrapped her arms around his neck and arched her back to meet his thrusts as he moved to possess her fully. Their lovemaking was violent, but their emotions flowed in such perfect harmony they felt the heights of rapture in each other's arms, as if their fiery passion had been shared with the greatest tenderness rather than the wildness of their long-denied love.

Joaquin buried his face in Flame's silken hair as his final thrust went deep within her. He felt her slender body tremble beneath his own, then relax completely with the warm rush of calm he'd longed to give her, and he knew she had again found contentment in his arms. He cradled her tenderly now in his loving embrace, kissing the length of her soft smooth throat, when suddenly he remembered the blood. What had she done— had she simply seduced him deliberately to let her life's

354

blood drain from her body as he took her for his own? Had she done that to him, succeeded in killing herself while she lay in his arms? He spoke calmly so as not to frighten her, his voice low and still husky with passion. "Flame, where did Rafael's knife strike you? You are hurt and I must take you back home. Where are you hurt?" She had fought him so fiercely he prayed the wound had been only a slight one, yet his mind was filled with visions of blood.

Flame smiled up at him and answered in a voice which was surprisingly strong. "My left thigh, but do not worry, I cannot even feel it so it cannot be serious." But she was wrong. When Joaquin pushed himself to his knees he found what was left of her dress soaked with blood, the dark stain spreading clear to the hem. Her blood was all over him too, it covered him like a second skin and he recoiled in horror. He tore off his shirt and wound it tightly around her leg, trying desperately to stem the flow of blood which still oozed from the deep, jagged wound.

He lied as he lifted her into his arms, wrapping her in the shreds of her dress: "It is a slight wound, Flame, when we reach home I'll send for a doctor. Your leg will be fine." He kissed her lips once more and whistled for Diablo, who appeared instantly from the shadows with Lady following close behind. Joaquin held Flame across his lap as they rode slowly toward his home; he stroked her hair and whispered softly, but in his heart he prayed they weren't too late. How could he have forgotten she had been so badly hurt? Had she done it deliberately? He had to know, but how could he ask such a question? It implied treachery of the worst sort imaginable.

"Flame, had you forgotten the wound? It didn't hurt when I first kissed you?"

When she looked up at him her face was as pale as the

355

moon. "Please let me die in your bed, Joaquin. Let me pretend for tonight that I really was your wife."

Joaquin cried out then, his anguish too great to bear. He had killed her, he had! He dug his heels into Diablo's sides, urging him to run fast and then faster toward the ranch. But when he laid Flame tenderly upon his bed she was already unconscious.

Eighteen

Joseph Wainwright shifted his medical bag from hand to hand as Rafael escorted him to the front door of the Villarreal home. He knew Villarreal only by sight and by what was left to treat of the men who'd suffered beatings at the rancher's hands. He tried to recall the last time he'd seen the man—one of the last of the Californios, the Spanish aristocracy in the new world, a dying breed, the doctor mused. He sucked in his protruding stomach but knew the gesture was a futile one: even in his youth he couldn't have matched Joaquin's powerful physique. His first impulse had been to refuse Rafael Ramirez's frantic request for help but he'd soon realized one did not refuse Joaquin Villarreal anything and prosper. He knew the man to be both harsh and cruel, certainly one who would not take kindly to a poor outcome of his wife's injury. Wainwright prayed her wound was not a serious one despite Rafael's sense of urgency. He'd be paid well if he brought the woman back to good health but he shuddered to think of the consequences should his efforts fail.

Nothing in the portly doctor's memory or imagination had prepared him for his meeting with Joaquin that night. There was not the slightest trace of arrogance in the man who welcomed him at the door, only pain and deep despair.

357

"Thank you for coming here tonight, Dr. Wainwright, your promptness is greatly appreciated. Come with me please, my wife is in our bedroom." Joaquin strode off with the doctor and Rafael following close behind.

"I did not even know you had married, Señor Villarreal." The doctor struggled to catch up with Joaquin but he couldn't match the taller man's long stride. Who had he married, Joseph wondered. Some fiery Spanish beauty no doubt, a woman who'd match her husband's temperament flame for flame.

"Yes, we married in July of last year." Joaquin held the door open as the doctor proceeded him into the room.

Joseph Wainwright approached the large bed slowly, dreading what he might find, then turned back to stare wide-eyed at Joaquin. He'd recognized his patient immediately and could not have been more shocked. "Isn't she André Lannier's little girl?"

"Yes, she is his daughter, but certainly no child. She is my wife." Joaquin and Maria had dressed Flame's leg as best they could before bathing her carefully and slipping a clean white nightgown over her slender body. Rafael had already left to summon the physician before Joaquin had returned with Flame but the wait for the man to arrive had been interminable for Joaquin.

The doctor was puzzled. "How was she injured? Señor Ramirez did not explain."

"See to her first, Doctor, I will answer your questions another time." Joaquin took Rafael by the arm and both men left the room leaving the doctor alone with his patient.

When Joseph Wainwright had finished his examination he sighed sadly and wiped his perspiring brow with his handkerchief. The knife wound was far more serious than he'd anticipated. There was no hope, none. He swallowed with difficulty as he thought of how his report would be received by Joaquin. The man would soon be a widower, of that he had no doubt. There was no way to soften the news he would have to give, nor was there any kindness in delaying the truth. He found the rancher and his friend seated in the dining room, staring at the coals which were all that remained of the raging blaze which had been burning in the fireplace when Rafael had first drawn his knife.

The doctor searched his mind frantically for compassionate words. "Señor Villarreal, I am so very sorry."

Joaquin sprang to his feet and came forward. "Yes, what do you think?"

Joseph reached out to touch the distraught man's arm, a gesture he would not have considered before that night. "I am sorry, but there is nothing I can do, she has lost too much blood. Whoever bandaged her leg did a fine job, but it was simply too late. Why wasn't she attended immediately? I saw her dress thrown over the chair, it looks like she bled for hours."

Joaquin struggled against the formless terror which threatened to overwhelm him—he would not give in to such panic, not now, not yet. "There must be something you can do for her!"

"No more than summon Father León to perform the last rites." The doctor's voice was kind, sympathetic.

"No! No, there must be some way to save her!" Joaquin gripped the doctor's shoulders in his hands and nearly shook him, as if that would change the man's mind.

The doctor shook his head. "When I return to town I will send the priest. I fear your wife will not live out the night. This is a sad night for me also; I was with her mother when she died. I will send the priest . . . it is all I can do."

359

"The priest is not needed, my wife is not of my faith." Joaquin sank back down in his chair and put his head in his hands while he tried to think what else he could do.

"The Reverend Lewis then?"

"Never!" Joaquin screamed at the doctor, his anguish far outweighing his self-control. He would never send for that bastard—he'd known all along where Flame had gone, all those months he'd searched so frantically for his wife that fiend had known where she was and hadn't told him.

Rafael could not bear Joaquin's grief too: his own was already crushing him beneath an unbearable weight. "Doctor, she is alive still, if she survives the night, if she is alive at sunrise, can we not save her?"

The doctor sighed. Rafael Ramirez was another of the damn Spanish gentry: thought their wealth and power could work miracles but this time they'd be sadly disappointed. "I'm sorry, but you can't fight the angels. They will take her before dawn."

Joaquin lifted his head. "What did you say?"

Joseph repeated his words but to his surprise Joaquin's face lit up with hope. What was the matter with the man, had he gone mad?

"Rafael, send José for the padre, then come and pray with me. Flame told me tonight she would fight the devil himself to save my soul. I can do no less than fight the angels for hers!"

The doctor was left staring after the two young men. He had no desire to make the long trip home on horseback at night but he had no choice. The prospect of being in the Villarreal house when Flame died was too terrible to risk. He grabbed his bag and left as José did, but he still had no answers to his questions and knew when he returned he'd have to bring the sheriff along with him to get them.

Rafael knelt beside Joaquin at Flame's bedside all through the night, their voices blending in an ancient harmony as they intoned their prayers in an endless chant. When Father León joined them he was amazed by their faith, then recognized their devotion as a love too strong to accept the triumph of death. At dawn the chubby cleric struggled to his feet and opened the shutters to let in the sunlight but he didn't disturb his pious companions. The padre stepped near the bed and peered down at Flame. Her cheeks were touched with the palest tinge of pink, her breathing steady and even, the sweetest of smiles curving her lips as she slept. She was very much alive and he turned to Joaquin, shaking his shoulder soundly. "Son, come and look at her!"

Joaquin turned his head, almost afraid to follow the priest's command. He reached for Flame's hand and tenderly kissed her palm but as he replaced her hand on the bed her fingers gripped his in a steady clasp before they relaxed again. Her gesture was a slight one but he understood and turned to drag Rafael to his feet as he got to his own.

"She is alive, we have done it!"

Rafael laughed as he embraced his dear friend warmly. "God has done it, Joaquin! Surely it was God who answered our prayers!"

Joaquin was too happy to argue. "Yes, of course, it was God who has heard our prayers, but Rafael, why didn't we think to ask the doctor what we should do for her now? Do you know, padre, what must we do?"

The older man shrugged. "Keep her warm, have Maria prepare some nourishing soups, but I would not try and wake her while she is sleeping so peacefully. You two should get some rest now yourselves, then we can continue our prayers for her recovery this afternoon."

Hours later when Flame awoke she was more tired

than she had ever been but the bed was so warm and comforting she had no desire to leave it. She glanced about her slowly, wondering where she might be, since the room was obviously not her own. She shifted slightly but the searing pain which shot through her leg stopped that effort immediately. She heard voices coming from a long way off. They grew louder as she strained to listen . . . then she recognized them. It was Rafael and Joaquin, but what were they saying? She closed her eyes and listened to the two friends. Their voices were soft and low as they spoke with a rhythm she found very soothing, but why were they talking here when she was trying to sleep?

Flame opened her eyes again and followed the sounds of the deep voices. Joaquin was close enough to touch and she reached out, stroking his shiny dark hair. "Joaquin, what are you doing?"

Joaquin leapt to his feet, then bent down over his wife and brought her fingertips to his lips. "We are praying, my love, Rafael and I are praying."

"Really? Can't you pray in the chapel, I'm trying to sleep." Flame smiled happily as she looked up at her husband's adoring face.

"No, I wanted to pray right here, beside you. Nowhere else will do. Please bring some soup, Rafael—are you hungry, Flame? Can you eat something?" He could scarcely contain his joy, her green eyes were so beautiful and he'd been so afraid he would never see their happy light ever again.

"No, I don't want to eat." The mere thought of food was exhausting to her.

"You must try, you must, Flame. You've got to eat to grow strong again. Please try and eat something, try for me."

"I'll try to eat if you want me to." Flame made an effort to sit up but the pain was too great and she collapsed against her pillow as her eyes filled with tears.

"Here, I will hold you." Joaquin sat down on the edge of his bed and held Flame's head in his arms as he did his best to feed her some of the steaming soup Rafael had brought. He'd had little experience feeding his son, he realized. Now he could appreciate Flame's problems in teaching their baby to eat. He began to laugh. "I'm sorry, Flame, I'm too clumsy, I'll have to practice with my son."

"Yes, that would be nice, he would like that." Flame pushed his next spoonful away and closed her eyes. She'd fallen asleep again, blissfully unaware of the anguish she'd caused him all through the long night and into the day.

For the next three days Joaquin never left Flame's side. He brought her tea and broth, bathed her face, combed her golden hair and sat for hours just holding her hand in his as she slept. He allowed no one else to tend her until he could stay awake no longer and lay down beside her in an exhausted daze, afraid to leave her side while he rested.

Flame snuggled against Joaquin's warm body and smiled to herself. She'd never awakened to find him by her side, and it was so very pleasant. His hair was still damp, he must have come from his bath, and his skin smelled of the spicey soap he used. Some unusual spice with such an enchanting aroma—not cinnamon, but just as enticing. She blinked back her tears as she thought how dearly she loved him, but she was still too weak to hold him in her arms as she longed to do and simply lay by his side enjoying the presence of his strong, lean body next to hers. Why was he always so warm when she was so chilled, cold clear through? Sleep overtook her again but when Joaquin awoke he found her still curled in his arms, dreaming peacefully with an expression so sweet he could not resist giving her lips a soft kiss.

He pushed her hair away from her cheek and began to kiss her throat. He had meant only to kiss her but when his lips brushed her creamy skin his longing for her was more than he could endure. He placed his hand under her shoulders and turned her gently to face him. "Flame, Flame." His voice was soft, low and mellow as he coaxed her awake.

Flame smiled shyly as she opened her eyes and stretched out, pressing her body against the length of his. His desire was obvious but she did not draw away. She turned her lips up to meet his and relaxed against his broad chest.

"Let me make love to you, Flame. I won't hurt you. Please."

As Flame looked into her husband's eyes his loving gaze was so overwhelming she felt as if she were drowning in his affection, pulled into a desire so strong she had no strength to resist had she even wanted to do so. "Joaquin, I will always want you but I can do little now to bring you pleasure."

A sunny smile lit Joaquin's face, an expression she had seldom seen but had remembered in her dreams for so many years. "My love, your pleasure will be mine." His lips met hers but he was very gentle, so careful, exploring her mouth slowly as if he'd never get enough of her sweet taste. He drew her nightgown up and began to caress her whole body, his fingertips moving over her breasts, tracing circles around the tips until he took her firm pink nipples between his lips, his tongue savoring her smooth young flesh.

Flame lifted her arms to encircle his neck: her fingers separated his thick, glossy hair into silken strands. She loved him more deeply each hour, wanted him so very much, yet she could barely move, could do no more than hold him in the lightest of embraces. Their last night together was no more than a blur, the pain and passion mixed in her memory until she could not untangle one exquisite sensation from the other. But she understood at last that Joaquin loved her, was pleased with her—she knew at last that he loved her as much as she loved him, and she was overjoyed to feel his warm touch upon her tender skin. As his hands strayed lower her breath caught in her throat. His touch was gentle yet knowing as he pressed his fingertips against her. His hand moved away to caress the smooth inside of her thigh but then returned to tempt her again and her voice escaped her lips in a hoarse whisper: "I love you, Joaquin, I love you so." Her whole body was infused with his warmth, she felt weak, unable to do more than moan as his mouth strayed down her body to linger in a kiss she could not resist.

Flame lay back upon her pillows, floating in the delicious sensation Joaquin brought to her. She had not even known it was possible for a man to give a woman such rapture in this way. She wanted him so badly, wanted so much more of his strong body than this exquisite touch, and she called to him again to take her as he had upon the cliffs. She tried to pull away from him but could not—he pulled her back, his hands firm upon her hips and he did not release her until he knew he could give her no greater joy. As he gazed down at her she lay with her eyes closed, breathing so deeply she appeared to have been drugged by his love, but when he kissed her lips lightly her small hands clung to his shoulders, her voice a breathless plea.

"Do not stop now, Joaquin. I want you."

"No, my love, I would only hurt you." He buried his face in her long curls and kissed her flushed cheeks but she would not be still.

Flame moved against him, her tantalizing touch giving him no peace. "No, you mustn't stop, please."

Tears filled her eyes and Joaquin drew away from her: her cheeks were too deeply flushed, her eyes too bright; he was draining away all her strength, and he grew frightened.

"No, I wanted only to please you, Flame, that is enough for me."

"But not for me." Her voice was a seductive whisper. "Do not make me beg for your love, not ever again." As she began to kiss his face softly he knew she had won, she was love itself and he had never felt such deep pleasure as she gave to him. Her skin was cool against his, silken, with the sweet scent of the perfumed soap he himself had used to bathe her. He knew all her dear body now, every inch of it, but he wanted her very soul, he wanted her to be his wife forever. He pulled her against his hips as he began ever so gently to take her. He moved with an easy, slow rhythm, afraid to surrender to his own passion, but she pulled his head down to hers, her tongue flicking across his lips then plunging deeper, claiming his mouth for her own. She called his name softly and moved her hands down his lean stomach until he shuddered, all rational thought gone as she captured his spirit once again. He took her hungrily then, his aching need for her which he'd held in check far too long unleashed. He wanted more and more of her sweetness until their bodies fused into one, bound for eternity by the depth of their love, an endless, bright, dazzling haze of love.

Flame lay nestled in Joaquin's arms. He had hurt her, the weight of his body had hurt her terribly, but she hadn't let him see her pain. She wanted only to love him, to give back the joy he so easily gave to her. Had she died in his arms it would have been worth the cost to her and she smiled, her deep contentment spreading over her lovely face with a delighted smile.

"Why are you grinning like a vixen, my pet?" Joaquin's smile was no less wide than hers. He had never been so happy, so at peace with himself.

"You see, I told you that was what I wanted, for us to share that beauty together."

Joaquin kissed her again, a long loving kiss, his mouth still not finished with hers. He was learning to know her mouth as well as his own, her small perfect teeth, teasing tongue, the light touch of her playful lips as she kissed him in return. She was absolute perfection, a woman made simply for love, and he adored her. When he glanced down at her again the light in her eyes had changed somehow . . . some thought had crossed her mind, and he grew curious as to what it might be. "What is it, my love? Your expression is so serious. Why?"

"I was thinking how pleasant it would be to die in your arms."

"What?" Joaquin's gaze darkened instantly as the horror of her words pierced his heart with fear. "Are you in pain, have I hurt you?"

His panic startled her and she rested her hands against his face to reassure him. "Joaquin, I am fine. I feel better now, right here with you at this very moment than I have ever felt in my entire life. I'll never have enough of you and your delicious loving. And no, you haven't hurt me at all."

Joaquin kissed the slender curve of her throat with a desperate longing filling his words: "I can't bear the thought of your death, Flame, I can't bear it! Don't ever speak of it again."

"But I will die someday, Joaquin, one of us will die first and the other will be left so terribly alone."

"Flame, stop that this instant!" Joaquin's eyes filled with tears and he turned away, ashamed to have let her see his tears again.

"Oh Joaquin, my love, my dearest, I will not leave

you, not ever again. If only I hadn't left you before, I'm so sorry that I did but truly I did think you didn't want me."

"Not want you?" Joaquin closed his eyes and rested his forehead against hers. "How could you for even one second have thought that I didn't want you."

Flame reached up to smooth back his hair, lightly patting his cheek as she drew her hand away. "You left me all alone, Joaquin. What was I to believe but that I hadn't pleased you?"

Joaquin gathered her up into his arms and hugged her so tightly he was afraid her ribs might crack and released her quickly. "I was too ashamed to stay, Flame, that was all. I had never really known love before that night and I was so ashamed of the things I had believed, the awful things I'd said to you. I didn't think you'd ever forgive me and when I awoke the next morning you were gone."

"If only I had stayed, Joaquin, we would have had the last year together like this, instead of the loneliness and fear. When I think of the love we've missed it breaks my heart."

"It was my fault, Flame, never yours, but we're together now and that's all that need matter to us." He cupped her pretty face tenderly in his hands and kissed her with a loving sweetness, but even as she clung to him they heard the sounds of hoofbeats approaching the house with a driving urgency and their intimate mood was shattered. Joaquin swore bitterly as he got up from his bed and reached for his clothes.

Flame drank in the sight of her husband's powerful body. He was such a handsome man, with perfect proportions, his shoulders broad, his hips narrow, his limbs muscular and strong. His skin was a golden bronze which still glowed from his recent passion and she could not help but smile when he turned back toward her.

"You'll not even pretend to cover your eyes?" Joaquin grinned at her as he fastened his belt.

"Should I pretend to be shy when you know so well that I am not? If the sight of my body is attractive to you, why do you think I would not be just as happy to look at you? I am only sorry that we were not together like this before Joaquin was born, I know I was so much prettier then."

Joaquin came back to sit down beside his wife. "Why do you think that, my love? You are so beautiful now."

"Having children leaves marks, you can see that it does and I am not as perfect as before." Flame's eyes were sad. She hated the stretch marks no matter how faint they were upon the creamy skin of her breasts.

Joaquin traced a line with his fingertips. "You mean these marks, Flame? They are nearly invisible, and hardly a flaw. That you have borne my child only makes you that much more dear to me, that much more precious in my sight. It is my child who has left his mark upon you, Flame, my son, and I think only of love when I see them. Do you understand now? To me you are all the more beautiful for having had my child and I am pleased to find you think me reasonably attractive too." He leaned down to brush her lips lightly with his before he stood up to go. "I'll see who is here and be right back."

"Joaquin?"

"Yes, my love?"

"You know damn well you are a lot more than just 'reasonably attractive'!"

Joaquin laughed, delighted she was feeling well enough to be teasing him once again. "Yes, I do, but I still like to hear you say it. Now I'll be back as soon as I can."

Flame yawned and stretched slowly so as not to strain her leg. She had not even dreamed love could be so nice, so exquisitely beautiful as it was with Joaquin. Why hadn't her grandmother told her the truth instead of her tales about the demands men make upon women which they had only to endure? Did women try and keep their pleasure a secret? She would certainly not tell any daughter of hers, should she ever have one, such rubbish. Men were too nice, too loving to frighten young girls so needlessly. She sighed sleepily and wished again that she'd never left Joaquin. Had she waited only one day he would have made it all up to her, he would have known the truth and wanted to beg her forgiveness. But as Flame lay remembering Joaquin's bitter accusations on their wedding day she was filled with a sense of dread. What if he ever doubted her word again? Could that horror ever happen again? The fear which filled her heart was too painful and she forced it away with a shudder.

After an absence of only a few minutes Joaquin entered their bedroom. "It's Dr. Wainwright. He was here the night you were stabbed—he's brought the sheriff and Reverend Lewis with him. Are you up to seeing them? I would like for you to see the doctor at least."

Flame saw the tension in Joaquin's stance and grew frightened. "Why would the sheriff want to come here?"

"Rafael and I didn't tell Wainwright how you'd been injured, we couldn't tell him the truth. Apparently he's talked with Lewis and used his imagination to come up with an explanation of what happened." Joaquin sank down upon the bed beside her and took her hand in his.

"Reverend Lewis? Oh dear, Joaquin, what can we tell them, how can we ever explain what happened?"

"I don't know, none of it makes any sense now does it?"

"Let me see the doctor, but first get me a clean nightgown and some soap and water, I'm afraid what we've been doing will be far too obvious to the man if I don't do something to clean up first."

Joaquin chuckled, but he had to agree, he had no wish to deny the joy of their love but her embarrassment was understandable. His scent was unmistakable upon her delicate skin. "Flame, I will help you. You can't take care of yourself yet, you're as weak as a kitten."

Flame's voice was a caress against his ear: "No, send Maria to me, if you start to bathe me I will never want to speak to the doctor."

"I see what you mean, you're right. I'll get Maria, but just this once. I want to take care of you, Flame. I'll always want to take care of you."

"Yes, my love, now hurry. Tell them I was asleep and am too vain to see them without my maid's attentions."

"They'll believe that easily enough, I only hope they'll believe everything else you tell them." He turned toward the door but hesitated when she called his name.

"Joaquin, what could the sheriff do?"

"Arrest me I suppose, for attempted murder."

Flame's face paled with fright. "Oh dear God no!"

"Flame, I'm sorry, I didn't mean to alarm you. It won't come to that, he can't take me off my ranch and he knows that. Now don't worry."

But Flame was worried sick, she was terrified; as Maria helped her bathe and dress her mind raced for some plausible explanation to offer. She couldn't even stand up yet she had to defend her husband and Rafael somehow, they could come to no harm for the crime of

371

loving her.

Dr. Wainwright came into the room alone at first. He placed his medical bag on the end of the bed and gazed down at the young woman whose imminent death he had so incorrectly predicted. He had seldom seen anyone in more vibrant good health. "Señora Villarreal, I'm Joseph Wainwright. I'm sure you don't remember me but I knew your parents and I recall your being a delightful child. Would it be all right if I examined your leg, please?"

"As you wish, Doctor, but my husband has changed the bandages each day and I am feeling quite well."

"Yes, that I can see." The physician unwrapped the dressing and inspected the wound carefully. It was healing more rapidly than he'd thought possible. "Señora, you are doing very well indeed, beyond my wildest hopes."

"I understand you had no hopes, Dr. Wainwright. Fortunately for me my husband chose to believe otherwise."

"Well, yes, Señora, but I wonder if you would answer a few questions for us. The other night I could get no response from either your husband or Rafael Ramirez."

"Quite understandable, don't you think? They were extremely upset over my accident."

"Would you wait a moment before you say any more, Señora. Let me call the sheriff and your friend, Reverend Lewis."

"Why are they here, Doctor?" Flame held her breath: if the minister repeated the story she'd told him on her wedding night Joaquin would be in no end of trouble.

"As I said, we have a few questions." The stocky man left the room but returned promptly with the minister and a tall, balding man who wore a sheriff's badge

372

on his leather vest. "Señora, may I introduce Sheriff Thompson, and you know the Reverend Lewis."

Flame nodded at the two men and turned to take Joaquin's hand. He'd followed the others into the room and came to her bedside while Rafael took a place at his side. She hadn't seen Rafael since the dreadful night of the knife fight and was shocked by his disheveled appearance. Where Joaquin was bursting with vitality, Rafael's face was drawn and haggard, his expensive suit wrinkled as though he'd slept in it, indeed his whole manner was one of the most wretched exhaustion. She longed to reach out to him, to take his hand too, to reassure him, but she knew that would have to wait until the sheriff had gone.

Sheriff Thompson cleared his throat nervously and shuffed his feet. He was obviously ill at ease and couldn't seem to decide where to begin.

"What is it you wish to know, Sheriff?" Flame gripped her husband's hand so tightly he moved to sit down on the edge of the bed and placed his arm around her shoulders in an effort to give her moral support.

"Well, now, Mrs. Villarreal," the man began uncomfortably. "The doctor told me you received a knife wound. Would you please tell me how that happened?"

"It was an accident," Flame replied calmly.

When Flame volunteered no more information the man tried again. "How did this accident occur?"

"My husband and Mr. Ramirez were using their knives. I happened to stray too close and was struck. It was an accident, as I told you."

The balding man felt the minister nudge him in the back but the defiant tilt of Flame's chin had already convinced him she'd never tell the truth. He tried speaking to her husband instead. "Señor Villarreal, would you care to explain what you and your friend were doing with your knives when your wife happened to stray too close?''

"No, I would not." Joaquin stared back at the sheriff without the slightest trace of fear in his gaze.

"Señor Ramirez, perhaps then you will be able to explain things more clearly?''

"No, I have nothing to add."

The sheriff turned back to the Reverend Lewis, the frustration apparent in his tone: "Well, would you like to say something at least?''

Flame interrupted immediately: "No! You may not! What I told you was spoken in confidence and you may not repeat it!''

Reverend Lewis was almost too surprised for words but quickly recovered. "My dear, it is not too late, come with us now. You needn't remain here in a house where you are not wanted."

Flame felt Joaquin stiffen but moved her hand to cover his. "I talked with you over a year ago, Reverend Lewis, my husband and I have resolved our misunderstanding completely and are very happy together. You were most kind to help me, and I will always be grateful for that, but I regret with all my heart that I ever left Joaquin. I am more than content to be his wife and will remain here with him always.''

Reverend Lewis stepped closer to her bed. "Can you swear that this so called 'accident' was not an attempt upon your life?''

Flame scoffed at the ridiculousness of that question; "Don't be absurd, my husband would hardly have stabbed me in the leg had he wished to kill me. He would merely have slit my throat."

The sheriff gasped in horror and grabbed the minister's arm. "Come on, let's go, this has been pointless. I'm sorry to have disturbed you, Señora."

The minister shook him off.

"No, wait. Where have you been for the past

month? Since you returned home you have not come to my church nor, has anyone seen you in town, not even once.''

Flame smiled sadly. "I'm sorry you have expected me to come. I would love to see Suzanna if you would permit her to visit me, but I have taken my husband's religion and will visit your church no more. I appreciate your concern, but really it is unnecessary for you to worry about me any further. I am very busy here and have had no time nor any interest in visiting in town.''

The Reverend couldn't believe his ears. He remembered her fright when she had fled Villarreal too well—she had been terrified of the man then, perhaps she still was. Could he have threatened her child? Was that how he brought her back home? Knowing she'd not speak when her husband could overhear he turned to the lawman and insisted, "Sheriff, I wish to see charges brought against Villarreal and Ramirez for conduct so careless as to endanger Mrs. Villarreal's life.''

The sheriff frowned anxiously then cleared his throat again. "If Mrs. Villarreal herself has no complaint you'd never make that accusation stick.''

"Perhaps not, but I wish to see the charges made anyway. That these two men could behave in such an irresponsible fashion as to have narrowly missed taking this young woman's life is an affront to the entire community. It's well known that Joaquin Villarreal has no respect for any law other than his own out here—that he is loose in our midst is an outrage!''

Joseph Wainwright spoke up quickly: "I'm inclined to agree with him, Sheriff. Señora Villarreal was not treated for at least an hour after her injury. It was that lack of care, not the stab wound itself, although it was very serious, which endangered her life.''

Flame looked up at Joaquin but his dark expression was impossible to read. He glanced down at her and

375

frowned, warning her not to respond.

His companions' words had finally convinced the sheriff something was amiss. "Is that true, señora? You were not given any medical attention after you were stabbed?"

Flame swallowed with difficulty. She was feeling worse by the minute, she was very tired and beginning to become nauseous too. "It is true but it was due to my own foolishness, not to my husband's or Rafael's lack of interest in my welfare." Even to her own ears her excuse sounded feeble. There was no way to explain she'd been trying to kill herself.

The sheriff hesitated no more than an instant before stepping forward. "I think you two better come with me. Judge Fielding will be down from Sacramento next week and he can decide if a crime has been committed or not. This is beyond me."

Flame cried out in anguish: "No! No! You'll not take them to jail because of me!"

The sheriff shook his head. "You could have died, Señora. This is not a matter I can drop."

"Had I died it would have been by my own hand and no other! Now get out of here all of you!" Flame turned toward Joaquin and began to sob pathetically, her tears soaking his white cotton shirt, and he pulled her into his arms, holding her tightly against his chest.

"As you were so kind to point out, Reverend, my wife was near death only a few days ago and your visit here today has obviously tired her. Should you ever repeat your vicious accusations or imply to anyone that Flame is suicidal you will regret it. Do you understand my meaning? Sheriff Thompson, get off my property before I summon my men to escort you off. Don't come back here unless you obtain a warrant for my arrest and then I'll warn you you'll have to take me by force. I will never go with you willingly to answer for so unfounded

376

a charge. Should you have the audacity to return I cannot predict the outcome nor guarantee your safety."

The sheriff knew he was beaten. He had never wanted to come to the Villarreal ranch in the first place and he swore under his breath as he left the room followed by the minister who continued to argue Flame's life was in jeopardy. Rafael left the room with them to make certain they went straight to their horses.

Joseph Wainwright hesitated as he picked up his medical bag. "Señor Villarreal, is your wife all right?"

Joaquin glanced down, then gasped in terror. Flame was limp in his arms and a bright red stain had begun to spread over the sheet which covered her. "Oh my God, she's bleeding again. Help me, Doctor!"

The doctor struggled to stem the flow of blood from Flame's leg while Joaquin watched helplessly by his side. When Rafael came back into the room he looked up for only a moment. "Are they gone?"

"Yes, and they will not return. I reminded them I am your attorney and that they have absolutely no grounds for an arrest. Coupled with your comments, that will make them extremely hesitant to return. But what has happened to Flame?" Rafael joined the two men at her bedside.

Joseph Wainwright looked between the two men's anxious faces and tried to reassure them. "I've stopped the bleeding. She was doing so well—I'm sorry, this setback is all my fault. It is obvious to me now that your wife adores you. I sincerely believed her life was in danger, but it is I who have caused her this pain today." He continued to apologize as he rebound Flame's thigh, all his concentration centered on her pale face and shallow breathing.

Joaquin sagged back against the wall and closed his eyes. "I can't lose her, doctor, I can't. Not now after we've finally found each other again."

The physician turned toward Joaquin and frowned. "Then her recovery will be doubly hard on you but I beg of you, if you truly love your wife take your pleasures elsewhere and give her time to heal and grow strong."

That advice hit Joaquin with the force of a savage blow. He straightened up as he inquired, "What are you saying?"

"I cannot forget her mother nor her father's terrible grief when he lost her. Your wife is very frail, Señor Villarreal, if the strain of pregnancy did not kill her then most assuredly childbirth would as it did her mother. I beg of you—you must know other women who would welcome your favors. Leave your wife alone until she has completely regained her health."

"I have always been faithful to my wife and I will continue to be." Joaquin reached out to take her hand in his. "How long will it be before she is strong?"

"A year possibly, perhaps a little longer."

Joaquin was overcome with sorrow. A year? Dear God how could he survive a year without touching Flame? Without holding her in his arms, loving her as he had that very day? Then he was seized with panic: "What if she is pregnant already?"

Rafael looked up quickly. "But how can that possibly be? You said only the other night that—" Then he knew, he knew by the look in Joaquin's eyes. He had made love to her since the accident. When, that very night? Was that why she'd received no attention, no care? Joaquin had been so busy making love to her he hadn't taken care of her at all? He would have let her bleed to death while he satisfied his own lust? Rafael felt sick. He recalled that Joaquin had changed his clothes before he'd returned with the doctor. Why? Had his clothes been drenched with Flame's blood? Rafael could take no more. He strode from the room and made

378

his preparations to return to San Francisco, too furious to stay and hear any more.

"Is your wife pregnant? You know that for a fact?"

Joaquin shook his head. "No, but it is possible." He cursed to himself—what had he been thinking of to have made love to her not once but twice since she'd been hurt? He'd thought only of love, never of the risk to her.

The doctor rinsed his hands in the basin on the washstand before turning back to face Joaquin. "If I were you I'd pray that she isn't. She is young and will be strong again, you'll have many children, I assure you."

Joaquin leaned down to kiss Flame's lips lightly. "I cannot leave her alone, doctor, I cannot, she is much too precious to me to ignore."

"My God man, don't you understand me? She almost bled to death! It will be months before she regains her health, her strength . . . the ordeal of childbirth would kill her if she's not strong! If you can't leave her alone then take a trip or send her somewhere, make up any excuse you have to, but leave her if you must. Don't risk getting her pregnant for at least a year—but if she is pregnant now, then not even God can help her. Your prayers will not save her a second time."

Nineteen

More than a week passed this time before Flame was lucid again. Her spirited defense of the men she loved during the sheriff's interrogation had left her drained of the little strength she had recovered. Joaquin kept her alive by his loving attentions alone, carefully spoon-feeding her broth, gently coaxing her to drink Maria's herb teas whenever she was conscious enough to try. She clung to life tenaciously but by such a thin strand, barely alive at all as she slept most of each day, her breathing so shallow it could not be heard.

She had broken all but two of her long oval nails fighting Joaquin on the cliffs, so he sat for an hour one afternoon carefully giving her a manicure as pretty as any lady's maid could have managed. He loved her so, any service no matter how slight was a joy to him, but he was deeply worried, terrified she might not survive. No matter how diligently he prayed, fear for her life still filled his heart.

Dr. Wainwright stopped by the ranch frequently. He had seldom seen a more devoted husband, a man so tender and loving that his wife's slightest comfort con-sumed all his attention. He had come to respect Joa-quin Villarreal as he never thought he would, but surely no man so devoted to a woman could possibly have the black heart he had imagined him to possess when he'd first been summoned to tend Flame.

380

"Joaquin, you will do her no favor if you become ill yourself. Go to bed. Maria can care for Flame when she awakens."

Joaquin had not moved from his wife's bedside in hours. He held her hand in his as he watched her sleep. "I keep thinking of how I lived before I met her. I do not want to return to being that arrogant bastard ever again. I will simply kill myself if I lose her."

"My God, man, how could you say such a thing? What of your son? You'd abandon him?" The physician was aghast at Joaquin's morbid promise.

"I have asked Rafael to be his guardian. He will raise the boy and oversee the ranch until my son is grown."

Joseph put his hand gently on Joaquin's shoulder. "You have actually discussed this with your friend?"

"Yes. He understands, for he loves her too. My life would not be worth living without her. I will cease to exist if she dies."

The doctor was greatly distressed by the younger man's words; he searched his mind frantically for some way to make him see the fallacy in his plan. "Don't you think Flame regrets never having known her mother or father? Would she wish the same fate for her own child?"

Joaquin's interest in the other man's comments was suddenly keen, for the doctor had hit upon the one statement he recognized instantly as the truth. "Flame wanted more than anything to know her father, I'm certain she's always missed her mother too. She has been so alone in the world, for far too long she has lived all alone with no one to love her, and I have failed her so miserably as her husband."

"You would wish the same life for your boy? Set him adrift with no parents to love and guide him as he grows? Rafael is a fine man from what you say, but

381

he'd never be the boy's true father. Your wife would never allow such a gesture, you must put it out of your thoughts entirely. Flame would not want your death on her conscience, nor would she want her son to exist as alone as she has been all her life.''

"No, I know it would be a cowardly thing to do, but to live without her now would be more than I could bear." Joaquin released Flame's hand and bent down to kiss her brow. "Does she seem any better to you, Doctor? I cannot tell, she is so pale and thin, such an ethereal creature now." In his mind he always saw her as she had been that first morning he'd pulled her from her horse's back, laughing, defiant, and so incredibly loving it broke his heart to think how she'd suffered because of him.

"She is growing stronger each day, Joaquin. Healing can be a slow process, but she will be well again before long. Now please go and rest, you are overtired yourself or you'd be able to see she is better and you'd never suggest such a foolhardy thing as taking your own life to honor her.''

"No, she would be furious with me I know. Thank you for making me see reason: I will not speak of suicide again. Wake me if she calls for me, don't hesitate to send for me.''

"I will call you when first she wakes, now please go and rest." Joseph Wainwright took Joaquin's chair and sat down slowly. He'd never understand what had happened, but he'd kept Flame alive as best he could, she'd survived this long so he was reasonably certain she would recover her health in time, but it would be a good long time.

Flame couldn't understand how she could have lost more than a week of her life, but Joaquin insisted that a week had passed since the sheriff's visit and she believed him. "Where is Rafael, won't he come in to see me?'' Her voice was breathless. She could scarcely speak she had so little energy; the effort was exhausting for her.

"He's gone, my love, he couldn't stay when there was so much for him to do in San Francisco." Joaquin wouldn't forget their last conversation before his friend had left. He'd seldom seen Rafael that livid, outraged to realize he'd made love to Flame when she was so ill. He had not even tried to explain, there was no excuse for his behavior, as usual. Rafael had no pressing business to which to attend, he was simply too angry to remain under Joaquin's roof.

"Joaquin, would you give me your permission—would you allow me to write to him?" Flame gripped his hand in hers, her eyes imploring his consent.

"Flame, you cannot even hold a spoon to feed yourself, how could you write a letter?" He hadn't answered her question, he realized. He could refuse her nothing but the last thing he wanted was for her to begin corresponding with his best friend, his constant rival for her affection. He was filled with anxiety but afraid to ask . . . was it possible she felt something for Rafael, love perhaps?

"You could write the letter for me, Joaquin."

"What do you wish me to say?" Joaquin tried to smile but his jealousy nearly choked him—what could he do if she'd fallen in love with Rafael?

Flame closed her eyes and tried to rest a moment before replying. Why was the simple chore of breathing in and out such a dreadful strain, she wondered. "I want him to know I don't blame him for what happened to me. I want him to know that I am getting well."

"I'm certain he knows you don't blame him, Flame. He's wise enough to realize that."

"No, you must let him know! Didn't you see how wretchedly unhappy he looked? Didn't you understand how he felt?''

Joaquin let go of her hand and stood up. ''Why is it you and he seem to be able to read each other's emotions so easily when they escape my notice entirely?'' He crossed to the window and gazed out over the green hills in the distance. ''Am I so lacking in sympathy, in simple concern for others I will never see another's need?''

''Oh Joaquin—'' Flame's words stuck in her throat: she was too tired, could no longer keep her eyes open nor her mind clear and drifted off to the dreams which filled her days. Soon she was once again riding Lady across the sun-drenched fields. She was well and free, and the light poured over her, warming her clear to her soul.

''Flame?'' Joaquin rushed to her side and called her name again but relaxed when he saw how comfortably she was sleeping. ''Can you see my pain too? Can you see how I hate myself for what I've done to you? For nearly destroying the most incredible young woman who ever lived?'' He left her room and went to find his son. The boy was so lively and smart, so like his mother in spite of his dark coloring. Joaquin could stand no more of the guilt which filled him as he looked down at the frail shadow of his wife. He loved her far too much to ever let her see his pain.

''Please, Joaquin, did you write to Rafael?'' Flame had just finished eating the little bit she could for dinner and tried to stay awake a few minutes longer to talk with her husband.

''No, but I have paper and ink here. Tell me again what you wish me to say and I will do it.''

''You are not happy about my request?'' Flame could tell something was wrong, the light in his eyes was not the happy one she loved.

Joaquin sighed. It was so unlike her to ask permission for anything—she had always done as she thought best without asking him first, and that she could no longer do so hurt him more than her defiance ever had. "If I can grant any request of yours, my Flame, I will do it most gladly, but your wound was my fault and not his and we both know that."

Flame's confusion was obvious as she looked up at him. She was so thin she seemed to be all eyes as she turned her gentle gaze to his face. "How was it your fault?"

"I do not want to think of that night, not any of it. Rafael pointed out with his usual piercing logic that I had been no husband at all to you. He wanted to take you away, to give you the happiness you so rightly deserve. I told him he'd have to kill me first and he drew his knife to try. I have never loved another woman, Flame, I had tried to show you patience and you felt only neglect. Rather than make love to you night and day as I longed so desperately to do I showed you such slight warmth you mistook my feelings for indifference. Everything that has happened to you has been my fault, never Rafael's, he merely showed me what a blind fool I'd been, I would never have let him have you but when you rushed to his side I thought—"

"That I loved him? Oh Joaquin, how can we be so blind to each other's love? I didn't want you to kill a man, any man, and especially not Rafael. He is like a brother to you."

"Yes, he is the brother I never had and I am his, but we are so different, Flame, such complete opposites in temperament I do not know how we ever grew so close."

"Would you please tell Rafael when you write the letter that I think you are the most wonderful husband who ever lived and he need have no further worries

385

about my happiness. Will you tell him that, please?''

Joaquin laughed at her choice of words. ''Flame, that's a lie, I'm a failure as your husband, and you know it.''

''When have you ever failed me, Joaquin? When you prayed all night for my life? When you spent hours at my bedside just holding my hand so I would have the comfort of your touch? When you have patiently fed me because I have not even the strength to eat? No, Joaquin, you have never failed me, you have saved my life, you alone and I will always adore you.''

Joaquin brought her pale hand to his lips and kissed her scarred palm tenderly. ''And you have saved mine, Flame, truly you have. Now go to sleep and I will write your letter for you.''

Flame's eyes glowed with love and she smiled. ''When will you come back to your bed, Joaquin? I do so want to be your wife again.''

Joaquin was seized with panic at her request. She was much too frail, far to delicate to bear the weight of his body or the consequences of his love. ''Flame, you are my wife and you always will be, now go to sleep and cease to worry. I will love you forever but I will not share your bed until you are strong again.'' He bent down to kiss her forehead before he left the room. Dear God, how was he to stay out of her bed? He had moved all of his belongings to one of the guest bedrooms and put her things in his room. But it was far easier to move clothes than emotions he had found. She considered herself to be in his room, in his bed and so did he. That he dared not sleep with her was torture of the worst kind, he wanted her more each day yet had no hope that she would be well any time in the near future.

The autumn days were so warm and sunny Joaquin carried Flame outside to the patio after their lunch. She weighed so little it frightened him to hold her in his arms, for she seemed too delicate to withstand even the slightest caress let alone being held. They sat in the sun while he read the last chapter of a book he had begun reading aloud that week to amuse her. She enjoyed hearing him read, he gave the story all the dramatic feeling it deserved and was so wonderfully entertaining. She laughed and thanked him graciously as he finished the last page.

"You should have been an actor, Joaquin. That was marvelous!"

"It is only that my audience is so appreciative, Flame." He frowned to himself as he thought of the many times he had put on an act for her. He did it still, afraid now to let her see how worried he was over her frail health. Yes, he was becoming a fine actor, but as he looked up then he leapt to his feet. "Don't you dare try to walk by yourself, Flame!" He caught her in his arms and lowered her back into her chair.

"Why not? I've got to start walking again, no matter how much it hurts. Why don't you help me instead of treating me like a porcelain doll? I won't break, now give me your arm and help me this time."

"Flame, if you fall—"

"How can I fall if you are with me? You will catch me won't you? Of course you will, now help me up!"

Joaquin swore but did as she requested, but the effort was too great for her and she collapsed against his chest. He swung her up into his arms and sat down with her upon his lap.

Flame put her arms around his neck and hugged him. "Sometimes I think I'll never be well again, Joaquin. It's taking far too long for my leg to heal, longer than I can bear."

"It has been little more than a month, and you very nearly died. Now don't be discouraged, you will be able to run before long, to ride Lady as much as you used to. You will be well soon, I'm sure of it." Joaquin spoke his lies with a smile.

Flame reached up to kiss his lips softly. "And what else will I be able to do?"

Joaquin's breathing quickened in spite of his best efforts to remain unmoved. "Flame, stop it!"

"Don't tell me I'm not strong enough to love you! I know what I feel and I'm more than well enough now to share your bed, and still you won't move back into your own room?"

"Flame, you can't even walk! Don't tell me how strong you are, I know only too well how slowly you are mending, now let's discuss something else. I have been meaning to ask you about something you told Reverend Lewis. You said you had adopted my religion. I was not aware that you had done that."

"I did tell him that didn't I?" Flame continued to hug Joaquin's neck making rational thought all but impossible for him. "It seemed to me if you could save my life by the power of your prayers then I was foolish not to learn them. My prayers have never been answered, but if yours are then—"

"Flame, you are still such a child at times. It's not the prayers that do anything, it is faith. You must simply believe, have faith that God will help you."

"But God never helps me, Joaquin. I believe, I really do. I went to church with Seth every Sunday and prayed, but God never answered my prayers."

"No, that's not true, he undoubtedly answered your prayers but you did not like his answer."

Flame was confused by his reply. She searched his face for some clue to his meaning and at last understood. "You mean the answer was no?"

"Apparently, but what was it you prayed for so diligently?"

Flame bit her lip nervously. How could she respond

truthfully to that question? She had prayed to escape him forever. Then her memory sped back in time to when she had prayed to be rescued from Miguel, or the night she'd begged God to make Joaquin love her enough to believe her word. Tears filled her eyes and she wiped them away quickly before he saw them. "It doesn't matter now. I only know God leaves me alone, totally alone whenever I need his strength."

"Oh Flame." Joaquin held her more tightly, hugging her gently against his broad chest. "You will never, ever be alone again my darling, I promise you that."

"You mean ever so much more to me than God ever has, Joaquin, he is not real to me as you are, he has never loved me as you do."

Her words shocked him. He had never heard anyone dismiss God so lightly, but he would not upset her by scolding her now. "If you wish to become a Catholic, I will ask Father León to come and give you instruction."

"No, not him, is there no other priest in town?"

Joaquin was surprised when he felt her shudder. "What is wrong, don't you like him for some reason? I thought the two of you had become friends when you first came to live here."

"No, I thought we were friends, but we were not." Flame tried to shut out the bitter memories of her wedding night but could not. León had believed all the lies too, he should have known better even if Joaquin had not. The priest should have believed in her innocence.

"We have become so close these last weeks, Flame . . . tell me what troubles you about the good man." Joaquin looked down at her frown, troubled that her mood had grown so dark.

"No, I will not. It should be enough for you to know

389

I am not comfortable with him. Why can't you teach me yourself?''

"Now that would be some catechism class! I've forgotten all I ever learned. I know what to do, what I believe, but I've forgotten all the history, all the reasons for my beliefs . . . those are the things you'd want to learn."

"No, I will pray here with you, Joaquin. I don't want to study with Father León."

"Because he performed our wedding ceremony? Do you blame him for that? You have forgiven me, Flame, why do you still blame him?'' Her silence gave him his answer, it cut him as deeply as the knife which had pierced her thigh and he pressed her for an answer: "Tell me, Flame."

Flame sat for a long moment and then tried to explain so as not to hurt her husband: "I still remember how he looked at me as we waited together before the wedding. You told him all of Alex's lies, didn't you? But rather than defending me, he believed them too. I can understand that you were jealous, but I thought that he was my friend and from what I had told him of my love for you, he should have known I was blameless.'' Flame could no longer hold back her tears, she lay her head on Joaquin's shoulder and sobbed, the heartbreak of that night still clear in her mind.

Joaquin could not find his voice to answer. He picked her up gently and carried her back to her bed where he put her down as tenderly as he could before leaving her all alone once again.

Their relationship changed that afternoon. Joaquin had said they had grown close but now he withdrew from Flame again. It had hurt him terribly to realize her memories of their wedding night were still so vivid and painful. He could make her forget her sorrow in only one way, and that way was forbidden to him now.

He longed so to make love to her, and could not, and that agony tore his heart in two. He became more distant each day: he was always polite, attentive, but his gaze was reserved and Flame could not help but notice a stiffness in his every gesture, as if any kindness to her were forced out of him against his will. He made up excuses to be away from the house all day as frequently as he could, but even that did not help ease his torment. He had only to see her again in the evening for her seductive presence to overwhelm him again, he simply loved her with all his heart and did not know how to deal with the emotion he had no choice but to deny.

Flame tried her best to get well, she ate as much as she could as he begged her to, she lay down to rest whenever she felt the slightest bit tired. She grew stronger each day until one evening Joaquin entered her room and found her standing by the window.

"Flame! Are you walking about with no one to help you?" He rushed to her side and when he put his hands around her waist his fingers touched easily.

"Joaquin, please, I will not break. I have been practicing each day and I will walk into dinner tonight. Just give me your arm."

That she was able to do it amazed Joaquin, but he could feel the pain jar through her with each step she took. She could not walk without limping badly and it pained him so to remember the grace with which she'd moved when first they'd met. She'd been as agile and swift as a fawn, but now she could not move without the pain of each step being etched on her determined brow.

The next afternoon Flame was seated on the sofa in the parlor. She held her son on her lap and sang to him, all the sweet songs she remembered from her own childhood, the songs she'd sung for a year with Molly and Matthew. As Joaquin stepped across the threshold he stopped to stare as the scene before him faded from sight, and he recalled an afternoon years before when his father had sent him to André Lannier's ranch to deliver some message. He'd found Deborah seated in the parlor with her daughter on her lap. That gorgeous child had been Flame; she'd run to him and he'd held her in his arms as he'd talked to her mother. He had never seen Deborah alive again, the next time he'd been at André's home the beautiful young woman had been buried and Flame taken back East. He rubbed his hand over his eyes and looked at his dear wife again. She looked so much like her mother, was his memory a warning he should heed without delay? Wainwright had told him to wait a year, but it had been barely two months and he was dying from his desperate need for her. His desire was choking him, crowding out all other thoughts so that whenever they were together he ached to possess her again. He'd had so little chance to love her, he could not bear to wait ten more months, yet the memory of her mother's death haunted him. No child of his would kill her, not Flame, not his precious Flame.

Joaquin paced up and down in front of the sofa with a purposeful stride. "I've decided to go to Mexico, Flame. I've thought more and more about finding a stallion for Lady. Appaloosas are unique, you were right, she should have one of her own kind to sire her foals and I could use another stallion. And I really must see my business contacts in Veracruz—my ships have had problems with the port authorities of late and I do not want that nonsense to continue."

Flame was ecstatic. "When do we leave, Joaquin? I have wanted so badly to visit Mexico, to see all the places you've been and to meet your family and friends there." Her eyes shown brightly as she gazed up at her husband, her delight in his forthcoming trip readily apparent.

"Oh, Flame, I'm so sorry, but not this trip, it would

392

be much too strenuous for you. I'll have to leave the ship in Acapulco and travel overland to the capital and then on to Veracruz. The journey would be exhausting for you, you might fall ill and I simply won't risk that. I'll be busy traveling to ranches looking for horses and I wouldn't want you to have to remain alone in Veracruz. The trip is simply impossible for you now, Flame."

"You'd leave me here all alone? Not take me with you?" Flame could scarcely hold back her tears, her happiness had turned so quickly to the most disappointing sorrow.

Joaquin knelt by her side and took her hand in his. "I won't be gone long, only a few months, Flame. Maria will be here, José can run the ranch. I'll have Rafael come to see you each month."

"Each month!" Flame cried out in alarm. "How long will you be gone?"

"I'm not certain—it is difficult to estimate how long everything will take. Six months, perhaps slightly longer."

"Oh, Joaquin, no, please don't leave me, please don't go away now!" Flame threw her arms around his neck but he carefully took her hands in his and pushed them away.

"I must go, Flame. I have put off this trip for far too long as it is. I must go now."

Flame's perceptive gaze swept his expression, her clear green eyes drinking in the subtle change in his glance and she recoiled instantly. All she saw was pity in his eyes. Why hadn't she noticed that look before? He couldn't love her and leave her like this. It was all too obvious to her: he felt nothing for her anymore but pity and wanted to be free of her for as long a period of time as he could manage. She watched him closely as he hugged their little boy, lifted his baby son into his arms.

393

She looked down at her hands and blinked back her tears. What was the point in begging him to stay? If he'd not remain with her out of love, she'd not force him to stay out of duty. "When will you leave?"

Joaquin looked down at her bowed head. She seemed so small, so afraid. Why did it have to be like this when he loved her so dearly? "One of my ships sails at the end of next week."

"So soon?" She brushed the tears from her eyes as she spoke. "Which one is it, the one you sailed, the *Rana del Mar*?"

Joaquin laughed at her unintentional humor and shook his head. *"La Reina del Mar,* Flame: *The Queen of the Sea* is the ship's name. Ranas are frogs."

"Frogs! Oh how will I ever learn Spanish, Joaquin, I try so hard and still I get all the words confused."

"I don't know, Flame, I rather like the name. *Frog of the Sea* would be a most intriguing name for a ship. The next vessel I buy will be immediately rechristened."

Flame could not help but laugh with her husband's gentle teasing. "Joaquin, you wouldn't, that would be a ridiculous name."

"So what? I can call my ships whatever I please. As it so happens, it's not the *Reina* I'll be on but the *Estrellita Pacifica* this time."

"I know that one. *Little Star of the Pacific,* right?"

"Yes, you have it, Flame." He leaned down and kissed her soft lips lightly, then got to his feet, carrying his son outside to play.

Flame remained seated in the parlor but the happy mood Joaquin's teasing had created did not last. She was plunged into the deepest despair by the prospect of his leaving. Six months! How could she bear it? She stood slowly and walked to her room where she studied her appearance critically in the mirror above the dresser. She had no figure at all now: her breasts were no more than slight swellings, she'd had more of a bustline at twelve than she did now, her dress hung loosely on her, unattractive in the extreme. No wonder Joaquin didn't want her, wouldn't sleep with her. Why would any man want her now? If only she hadn't grown so dreadfully thin!

Maria came in a short while later to bring linens for her bath and gestured helplessly at the clothing which littered the room. "What are you doing, Señora, you don't like your dresses any longer? If you are giving them away I know many who will love to have them."

Flame had strewn her clothes about the room as she'd tried on one dress after another finding none fit to her satisfaction. "Look at these, Maria, nothing fits, not one dress, how can I ever hope to please my husband when I look like a scarecrow dressed in someone else's clothes?"

Maria put out a hand to brush a curl from Flame's cheek. "You please him, Señora, do not ever doubt that. I have never known a man who loved his wife more than Joaquin loves you."

"You don't understand, Maria, I know he loves me, at least he did once and he still says that he does, but just look at me. I'm no longer pretty and he doesn't, he won't, oh, it's just not the same between us now. He treats me as if I were some fragile invalid when I want so desperately to be treated as a woman, as his wife." Flame's eyes again filled with tears of frustration.

Maria hugged the slender girl, trying her best to reassure her. "Señora, you nearly died, you must be more patient. You will regain the weight you lost, but you have lost none of your beauty."

"But he's leaving, Maria, going to Mexico for months! I have no time, I want him to want me now! I still want him and I can't bear it that he doesn't want me!" Tears poured down her cheeks, she couldn't stand the loneliness, the aching need for him which filled her heart.

Maria was greatly saddened to see Flame so distraught. "We can alter your gowns or make new ones. We have bolts and bolts of fine fabrics—I should have thought of it sooner. Do not cry, little one. Where would you like me to begin?"

"Could you make my red dress fit me? Joaquin always liked that one so well and it is my favorite dress too." Flame's expression lit with hope.

"Of course I can do it. Now put it on for me and I will bring my pins."

The red dress was ready for Flame to wear the night before Joaquin was to leave for San Francisco. She asked Maria to prepare his favorite dishes and she spent extra time arranging flowers from their garden to make the table festive. As for herself, she combed her hair into the most becoming style she could fashion, with curls hugging her cheeks to soften the angles of her thin face. Her eyes were beautiful still, she knew that, but nothing she did would hide the despair in their depths.

When Joaquin saw his wife he was touched by her beauty as always. "Are we having a party, Flame? You look so pretty tonight, as lovely as ever."

Flame smiled sweetly and waited for him to come close and kiss her but instead he merely took her arm and led her to her chair. She sat down and put her napkin in her lap but her eyes were filled with tears she made no attempt to hide.

Joaquin reached over and touched her hand. "Don't cry, my love, I will be home soon and then things will be different between us."

Flame looked up, a puzzled expression upon her sweet features. "How will they be any different? I am well now, Joaquin, quite well enough to—"

"Flame! Let us enjoy dinner together without arguing please. I have a lot left to do, things I still must pack, so let's not waste a minute of the time we have left to share.''

"I'll be happy to help you pack. Why didn't you tell me you needed my help?'' Flame offered enthusiastically.

"I can do it, Flame, I've just put off packing and it takes time. I shouldn't have waited until the last minute like this to do it but you needn't trouble yourself with it.'' Joaquin tried to keep Flame amused for the rest of the meal but he knew she was too depressed to appreciate any of the humor he tried so hard to affect. They lingered together at the table, neither wanting the evening to end, until finally Joaquin had no choice.

"It is late, Flame, let me walk you to your room. I must gather my things, but I'll see you in the morning before I go.''

After he had turned and left her at her door without even so much as a hug Flame could no longer hold back her bitter tears. She sat in her room sobbing. He didn't love her anymore, that was plain to her, he didn't love her at all.

Maria knocked lightly at Flame's door before entering but she had only to look at her mistress's small weeping figure to know the pretty girl's plan had not succeeded. "Don't cry so, Señora, he is just worried about you. You have been so ill. When he returns you will be well and he will—''

"Oh leave me alone! I don't want to hear any more of your excuses when the truth is so plain to me! Just leave me in peace.''

When Maria had left her Flame hung up her favorite dress and slipped her lace nightgown over her head. The fullness of it hid her lack of figure and its soft folds were feminine and, she hoped, alluring. She brushed out her hair until its golden curls shone, then opened her door and listened for the sounds from her husband's room. She waited until all was quiet then entered without knocking. Joaquin was just closing his suitcase and looked back over his shoulder, frowning as he saw her.

"What is it, Flame? I'm very busy." He kept his back to her but her sweet perfume filled the air, calling to him as possessively as her presence did. She was so lovely he could not bear to look at her. All dressed in white lace she resembled an angel and he knew that's exactly what she'd be if he couldn't keep away from her that night.

"I have waited so patiently, Joaquin. I have waited for you to come to me. Tomorrow you will be gone . . . don't you want to spend this last night with me?"

Joaquin answered without turning: "Go to bed, Flame, I am tired and I must leave early. Just leave me alone."

Flame leaned back against his door and tried to catch her breath. She couldn't move, her feet wouldn't take the first step to go. "Do I have to beg you again, Joaquin, will you leave me with no pride at all?"

Joaquin crossed the distance between them in two paces. He grabbed Flame's arm tightly, opened the door and shoved her through it. "When I want a woman, I'll do the asking, now go!" He slammed the door in her face and turned away. Dear God why did he have to hurt her so badly, he couldn't stand to leave her like this but there was nothing else he could do. He'd make it up to her later, he would . . . then he stopped still. How many times had he said that to himself, to her? Would they never have the happiness they both craved? Would he be endlessly begging her forgiveness for actions he couldn't explain?

Flame couldn't see for her tears as she fled from the house. She ran to the corral and Lady was there, as if waiting for her to come. Flame grabbed her mare's mane and buried her face in the long coarse hair. The gentle horse stood patiently, not moving as Flame wept on and on.

The man moved so quietly Flame was unaware of his presence until he spoke. "Señora, what are you doing out in the moonlight all alone?"

Flame turned at the man's call. She didn't recognize him, he was one of Joaquin's nameless vaqueros. There were so many of them and she knew only a few by name or sight. The man wasn't tall, but powerfully built; he carried a rifle in addition to the pistols in his gun belt.

"A beautiful woman should not be alone on a night like this." The man smiled, his even white teeth gleaming in the light of the full moon.

"You think I am beautiful?" Flame wiped her eyes on the sleeve of her gown and returned the friendly stranger's smile.

"But of course. You are a very beautiful woman. Señor Villarreal does not tell you that constantly? Is that why you are crying as if your heart were broken? Why are you not in your husband's bed where you belong?"

Flame leaned back against the corral and whispered shyly, "My husband does not want me in his bed."

"I had not taken him for such a fool, Señora." The man dropped his rifle silently to the ground as he reached for her shoulders. He held her back against the corral, pinned against the rough wood as he kissed hungrily, greedily, as if she were his woman and he would never have his fill of her. Finally he lifted his head and gazed down into her dazed eyes. "My name is Juan. You should at least know my name."

Flame swayed weakly in his arms. "Please, Juan, please let me go."

"You have changed your mind, Señora? You are no

longer lonely? That is a great pity since I have just begun.'' He kissed her again, more brutally this time, forcing her head back against the rails of the corral so she could not escape his passion.

Flame felt the man lifting her nightgown but had no strength to fight him. She was powerless to resist his rude caress. She gagged under his kisses as his tongue filled her throat, his hands were rough as he tried to hold her legs apart and she felt the cold metal of his belt buckle press against her bare stomach. Dear God, she was going to be raped, and most savagely, not twenty feet from her own house and she had no way to defend herself from the attack. She struck out against Juan's face but her blows were futile. She felt faint, only his hands held her up, her legs had ceased to support her slight weight. For an instant, Juan lifted his lips from hers and Flame screamed in terror, her shriek pathetically weak. Then the brutal man struck her, ending the piercing cry almost before it had begun. But Joaquin had heard her call and ran from the house in a frantic rage.

Juan had no chance to defend himself against Joaquin. He was no match for his boss's strength nor skill and Joaquin beat him without mercy until the vaquero's face was a bloody mask covered with the dirt where he'd fallen. But Joaquin wasn't satisfied yet, he grabbed a rope from a nearby post and lashed the hapless vaquero to the corral spread-eagled, bound so tightly he couldn't move. As Joaquin drew his knife Flame screamed again and again, bringing a score or more of the men from the bunk house out to see the cause of all the commotion. With a deft slash from his weapon Joaquin opened the front of Juan's pants, exposing the miserable man to everyone's stare. ''We all know how to castrate calfs, Juan, but is there one among you that has ever done this to a man?''

400

Juan begged, he pleaded in incoherent moans as he realized what Joaquin meant to do to him. Flame put her hands to her ears to shut out his pathetic cries. She didn't want to see this horror but she couldn't make herself move to run away; she was fascinated by the ghastly scene.

The vaqueros were silent. A few cigarettes glowed in the darkness, their bright tips the only sign the group was even alive. Not a man spoke up to stop Joaquin.

Joaquin drew his knife blade slowly across Juan's exposed flesh and laughed as the man's terror increased. "It is too dark to do a good job of this tonight, I will wait until morning." He turned away from the quaking man and spoke to his men; "If my wife wishes to walk my land naked at noon I do not want to see an eye upon her, do you all understand? I will make certain that she is the last woman any man touches should any of you be so foolhardy as to try this outrage ever again." He slid his knife into its sheath and lifted Flame into his arms and carried her back into the house. When he reached her bedroom he put her down gently but then turned and slammed her door shut with a vicious shove.

"Is this what I can expect from you while I am gone? You are so hungry for a man you'd accept any man's attentions, you don't even care who he might be?"

His anger frightened her, terrified her and she shrank back away from him. "No, it wasn't like that, I only went outside to see Lady and Juan—"

"Juan is it, you knew the man?"

"No, no I didn't know him at all, Joaquin." His face was set in a hard, cruel expression, one she had nearly forgotten but instantly remembered from their first months together when their fights had been almost daily occurrences. "Juan just walked up and then tried to rape me."

401

"Only tried to, you mean he hadn't already finished before you screamed?"

"No! No, he didn't do it, you don't really mean to—"

"I sure as hell do, as soon as it is light enough I will do it. If I must make an example of one man to keep you faithful to me then I'll do it, Flame."

"But I'd never be unfaithful to you, Joaquin, don't say that!" Flame was stunned by his threat, as well as his accusation.

"There are one hundred men on this ranch, Flame, and barely two dozen women, what did you expect to find outside at this late hour? When you hear Juan's screams in the morning you'll know what he's suffering and why. Then maybe you'll remember to stay in your room at night! Alone! I'll make certain neither José nor Maria leaves you alone for a minute while I'm gone if this is how little I can trust you." He grabbed the key from the lock and she heard it turn the bolt after he'd gone out into the hall and slammed the door. He'd locked her in her room!

Flame felt sick with fear and put her hand to her mouth but drew it away in pain. Her lips were cut and swollen from Juan's harsh kisses, the bruises would show by morning. She sank down on the bed, so filled with terror she couldn't move. Would Joaquin really do it? Mutilate a man for what he'd tried? She knew then that she had invited Juan's attentions by her remarks: he had only taken what he thought she'd offered. It was all her fault, not really his and she couldn't bear to think how horribly he would suffer for what she had tempted him to do. She got up and tried the door but it was securely locked; she looked around the room but wrought iron bars covered the windows blocking that means of escape.

She crossed to the windows and scanned the ornamental design of the iron railings. She was so thin now she was certain she could slip through and pulled a chair under one window to try. In a matter of seconds she was through the bars and dropped to the soft earth below. She looked hurriedly for guards then quickly walked back to the corral where a handful of vaqueros stood arguing while Juan pleaded in hoarse sobs to be set free. The men turned in surprise when she approached them.

"Cowards! You call yourselves men? You'd let Joaquin do this tomorrow and not one of you will try to help one of your own?" She began to untie Juan as rapidly as she could, the coarse strands of the rope cut her fingertips but she continued to struggle against Joaquin's firm knots. "Damn sea captain! How has he tied you, Juan, you have no knife?" Seeing one gleam at his belt she drew it and slashed the rope, releasing him from his cruel bonds. "Now go! Get your horse and flee before Joaquin finds out what I've done, go!" She turned to the vaqueros who still hadn't moved. "Sheep! Go inside the bunk house and find him another pair of pants at least, have you no pity? Help Juan to escape or it will be one of you the next time!" Her words finally had an effect and the group dispersed carrying the bloodied Juan with them. Flame threw down his knife in disgust and walked back to her window but when she tried to reach the bars she discovered they were too high up from the ground and she had no strength left to pull herself back up.

José walked up quietly behind Flame and put his hands around her waist. "Here, Señora, I will help you up."

"Oh, José, you frightened me. I thought it was one of the others." Flame relaxed against him as he tightened his hold upon her ready to pick her up.

"No, Señora, you need never worry about one of the

men bothering you ever again."

"Because of Joaquin's fiendish threats you mean?" Flame was still trembling with the fright of that horrid thought.

"No, because of your own courage. No man here wants to dishonor you now. If you will defy Joaquin Villarreal, when you are no more than a thin slip of a woman, then you have their respect as well as their hearts."

"I would do anything to keep my husband from killing for me again, José."

"Again, Señora?" José whispered curiously.

"I have said too much. Help me up before he finds out what I've done. Do you think Juan can get away?"

"Do not worry, I will see that he does but you needn't have worried so, by morning Joaquin would have seen the error in his threat and not carried it out. It would have been beneath him and by morning he will see that. When he lets his temper rule his actions as he did tonight there is no one more cruel, but he will again be a reasonable man by morning."

"Thank you, José, but I could not take that chance, what if this time he hadn't regained control of his temper?" Flame struggled back through the bars, carefully replaced the chair at Joaquin's desk and got into his bed. She still thought of it as his bed and his room even if he refused to share it with her. Her leg ached dreadfully, the pains shot all the way down from her hip to her toes but she didn't cry. It was a small enough price to pay for freeing Juan from Joaquin's terrible revenge. When at last she fell into an exhausted sleep she slept so deeply she did not awaken until late the next afternoon.

Maria had come into the room to check on her mistress several times but this time had remained sitting quietly at Joaquin's desk while she waited for Flame to awaken. As soon as she saw the young woman stir she approached her bed. "How did you do it? Joaquin was furious. Do you have another key, is that how you got out?"

"How could I possibly get out of here, Maria? I have no key, I am my husband's prisoner as you can see. But it must be late, when is Joaquin leaving?"

"He left at first light, Señora, he did not wish to disturb your sleep."

"He left without telling me good-bye? He left no message for me, no word at all?" Flame sat up and clutched the soft white sheet tightly in her hands—surely he could not have been so mean as to have left not even a letter for her.

"What was he to say after the way you behaved last night, Señora? The disgrace was more than he could face again." Maria's face was stern, her expression as difficult to read as her Indian forebearers.

"The way I behaved! You make it sound like I tried to rape Juan!"

"Perhaps. I was not there."

"Get out of my room, get out!" Flame screamed at the housekeeper then sank back down upon the bed and wept. Why hadn't God let her bleed to death in peace? Why had she been kept alive to face this wretched loneliness? "Dear God in heaven, will you never hear my prayers?"

Twenty

Flame drew her shawl up around her shoulders and nodded absently while Rafael spoke. She wasn't cold, only afraid her condition was becoming obvious. She was so thin the slight swelling of her abdomen seemed enormous to her. She shifted uncomfortably in her chair and tried to concentrate on her friend's words.

"I've brought you another letter from Joaquin, perhaps this one will be more to your liking." Rafael knew she hadn't been listening. He was worried about her: she seemed so withdrawn, not even as well as she had been on his last visit. She walked without limping when he was with her, but he'd seen her when she hadn't known she was being observed: she had moved much more slowly then, using her hand against the wall for support. That she would never move as she once had, with a dancer's fluid ease so that she almost floated as she walked, pained him to the very marrow. No matter how often he reminded himself her injury had been an accident he could not forgive himself for having hurt such a beautiful creature, leaving her damaged beyond repair.

Flame took the envelope from him and lay it across her lap. "Another itinerary? Has he changed his plans again?"

"No, not that I know of. Go ahead and read it now, I need to go outside and find José."

"You don't have to leave me, Rafael, it isn't a love letter that will make me weep with its sweet words and pretty phrases." Flame slit open the tan envelope with her well shaped nails and withdrew the two thin sheets of stationery. She scanned the neatly penned lines hurriedly. "Marvelous, this one's about horses." She read it though several times; the letter was polite and informative, but nowhere did Joaquin say that he loved her or missed her, although he did inquire about his son. She refolded the letter and replaced it in the envelope. She had been foolish to hope, to wait for some word from her husband that would let her know he was as grieved by their separation as she was. It was becoming more apparent with each letter that he cared nothing for her anymore.

"What happened between you, Flame? You two were so much in love the last time I saw you together." Rafael's dark gaze filled with a sorrow nearly as deep as her own.

"You have eyes, what do you see? I'm not pretty anymore, I'm still far from well, and Joaquin no longer loves me." Flame was too tired to cry at her desperate admission—she had cried endlessly since Joaquin had left, and she knew she would never cease. She was careful, however, to cry alone, never in front of the others on the ranch. She couldn't bear any more of the pity she saw in everyone's face when they looked at her now.

Rafael could not believe his ears. Flame was too slender, but her features were only that much more delicate and lovely because of it. Her skin was creamy and her hair glistened with golden highlights: truly she had never been more beautiful than she was that very afternoon. He leaned forward and touched her knee lightly, "Flame, you are the most beautiful woman who ever lived. How can you think otherwise?"

"Unfortunately, Joaquin does not see with your eyes, Rafael, and neither do I. I have a mirror; don't think you can fool me with polite lies, for I can see the truth." Flame closed her eyes and rested her head against the back of her chair. "Here, you read this letter, tell me if it's from a man who loves his wife."

Rafael read the letter slowly, trying to find something she had missed, but it was not there. "The Appaloosa stallion sounds like a beauty. You've got to admit that, Flame—he thought you would be pleased to have a mate for Lady."

"Yes, I am and I would recognize the horse anywhere, he has described his markings in such detail." She was just so tired that nothing mattered, certainly not a stallion so far away in Mexico.

"Do you ride Lady much now, Flame? Have you been out riding at all lately?"

"No, I don't want to ride anymore." Flame sighed sadly.

Rafael could take no more of her self-pity. She and Joaquin were a perfect match, they both knew how to get so depressed they made themselves ill; only Joaquin had always turned to brandy and apparently Flame had yet to discover liquor. God help her if she ever did! He got more angry by the second watching her as she sat so still. She was only seventeen years old and acting like she was at least one hundred! "Damn it, Flame, stop feeling sorry for yourself! I don't know what the hell is the matter with Joaquin, or with you for that matter, but I'm sick of this. Now stand up!"

"What?" Rafael's temperamental outburst jolted Flame out of her lethargy in an instant.

"Get up, let's go for a walk if you won't ride. Come on."

"Oh Rafael, no, I'm much too tired to go outside."

"You wouldn't be so damn tired if you'd go out and

408

get some fresh air! Now come on, let's go!'' He put his arm around her waist, helped her up, and led her outdoors. He soon realized, however, that he'd made a serious mistake, for she could hardly catch her breath.

''I'm sorry, Rafael, I can't keep up with you. Can you wait just a moment while I rest?''

''Oh Flame, it is I who am sorry. Come, let's sit down here.'' He pulled her down beside him on the soft winter grass. They hadn't gotten more than fifty feet from the house. ''Maybe it's a mistake for you to be here alone, Flame. Why don't I take you up to Joaquin's Aunt Teresa's home in Monterey? Her daughters would love to have you and the baby come for a visit.''

''You're not serious?'' Flame couldn't believe that he was.

''Of course I am. Won't you come with me? You can bring the boy and stay as long as you like. Teresa told me to invite you.''

''Did she really? And what did Maria Elena say? I can't believe she'd be so thrilled to see me or Joaquin's child either.''

''But Maria Elena is in Mexico, have you forgotten that? She sailed on the *Estrellita* with Joaquin.''

Flame stared at Rafael with eyes that really didn't see him at all. ''He took Maria Elena with him?'' She knew then her marriage was over: if Joaquin had taken another woman with him instead of her then it was finished. But why in God's name did it have to be that serpent, Maria Elena?

''Didn't Joaquin tell you their plans?'' Rafael grew alarmed: Flame had grown horribly pale and her hand which clutched his felt like ice. He grabbed for her shoulders but it was too late—she had fainted, and collapsed across his lap in a heap.

''Flame, Flame!'' Rafael bent over her, he rubbed

her hands and tried to wake her but she didn't stir. Finally in desperation he gathered her up in his arms and carried her back into the house. Maria ran after him as he took her into Joaquin's room.

"She has fainted again?"

Rafael lay Flame gently upon the bed and hurriedly covered her with a quilt so she'd not become chilled. "What do you mean again? Has this happened to her before?"

"Yes, but she won't let me send for the doctor." Maria wrung her hands anxiously as she looked down at the pale young woman.

"Send someone for him immediately! Just do it, woman, I will stay here with Flame, now go!" Rafael was furious—why hadn't Flame called for the doctor if she'd been ill? Women did not faint frequently for no reason. He took her hand in his and then, making sure no one was watching, brought her fingertips to his lips. Her wedding ring was so loose upon her hand he was surprised she'd not lost it. He sat by her bedside remembering the night not so many months before when he and Joaquin had prayed all night for her life. Perhaps they had stopped saying their prayers too soon.

Joseph Wainwright examined Flame thoroughly in private, then went to find Rafael. "Where has Villarreal gone?"

"Joaquin is in Mexico. He planned to be gone another three or four months at least but I will send for him tomorrow. He will return immediately if Flame is seriously ill. It was my fault she fainted, I mentioned something which upset her. It was unintentional, but the damage is done. But Maria told me Flame has fainted before—what is wrong with her, Doctor? Her husband thought she was getting well."

The physician gave Rafael a quizzical glance. "Then

410

she did not tell you about the child?''

''What child?'' Rafael was confused only a few seconds. ''Oh no—Flame is not pregnant, is she?''

''Yes, she most certainly is, four months actually but you'd never be able to tell by looking at her figure.''

''I had no idea. I was here last month to spend Christmas with her but she gave me no reason to suspect such a thing had happened to her. This is terrible, she's too frail, much too weak still.'' Rafael's anxiety continued to mount.

''Yes, you're absolutely correct. I told Villarreal to leave rather than risk getting her pregnant but I thought he'd at least inquire as to her condition before he left!''

''Flame has no idea why he left; as usual he told her nothing. He has often gone to Mexico in the past, this was just another business trip as far as she knows, but I didn't realize that was his motivation for travel either. We are not on the best of terms unfortunately. Well, what can you do to help Flame? She is so depressed and so lonely and if she is pregnant too—''

Dr. Wainwright nodded. ''Do you have the feeling we've done this all before? Her husband can't get here in time, Rafael, he's too far away to arrive in time to help her.''

Rafael could barely whisper his question, ''You don't mean—''

''Yes, I'm afraid she won't live much longer. Her physical condition is too poor and her mental state worse. She has lost all will to live. I can't keep her alive when she wishes so fervently to escape all her pain in death.''

Rafael needed no more than a split second to formulate a plan. ''I can make her want to live, I know exactly what to tell her. Would it be all right if I went in to speak with her now? Is she awake?''

The physician shook his head. "No, she is sleeping but if you know of anything which would give Flame even the slightest reason to grasp onto life tell her as soon as she awakens."

"So that I do not make the same mistake twice, when I convince Flame tonight that she wants to get well, and not only will get well but will have a healthy baby, what should I do to care for her?"

"You are not returning to San Francisco in a few days' time?"

"No, I will stay here to take care of Flame myself until Joaquin returns. She is much to precious to risk."

Dr. Wainwright wiped his brow on his handkerchief and sat down opposite Rafael. "I will tell you how best to treat her, but first will you tell me something, answer a question for me?"

Rafael shrugged, "You realize it is unethical to bargain for your services in such a fashion, Doctor?"

"Of course."

"As long as you acknowledge that, go ahead and ask. But I will make no promise to answer."

"You are a hard man, Rafael, but my curiosity gives me no rest. What really happened that night? How did Joaquin come to stab Flame?"

"He did not do it. I did." Rafael answered calmly, as if he were replying to a question about the time of day.

"You! But how could you have done such a thing?"

"It was exactly as Flame told the sheriff. It was an accident, a most unfortunate one, but an accident all the same."

The doctor leaned forward, his expression intense. "What were you and Joaquin trying to do?"

Rafael's level gaze did not waver as he replied. "Kill each other."

"But why? What could have brought friends as close

as you two to such a fight?''

"Flame, of course, only Flame."

The portly doctor slumped back in his chair. "I will never understand you Spaniards, never. Your pride, your cruelty, your damn romantic natures which would lead you to kill your best friend over a woman."

"First of all, we are not Spaniards but Californios, or citizens of the United States if you prefer, and Flame is not just any woman. She is like no other."

"She is not yet eighteen years old, Rafael, and you two are grown men. What is it about her that is so fascinating? She is a beauty, even now when she is barely alive she is still a great beauty, but there must be something more. Why do you love her so?"

Rafael stood up slowly and walked over to the liquor cabinet. "Would you like a drink? Joaquin had a generous supply here."

"No, thank you. Won't you answer my question?"

Rafael did not reply until he had filled a shot glass to the rim with whiskey and drained it in one fast gulp. "You expect me to analyze love for you, Doctor? I am an attorney, not a poet. If you had ever known Flame when she was well you would not have to ask such a question. She is simply the most enchanting of creatures. Her beauty is nothing compared to her spirit: she would defy a man with her dying breath all the while swearing she loved him, and she would be speaking the truth. The love of such a woman is worth any price, any risk, but she is Joaquin's wife and not mine, so I will make her well again for him."

"Yes, I'm sure you will, but do not try to fool yourself, Rafael. You want her to be well again for one reason alone, for yourself." The doctor realized he had said far too much as Rafael's expression changed, his gaze growing as black as his eyes, and Joseph understood how easily the man could kill for Flame. "Forgive me, I have said too much. Come back and sit down with me and I will tell you how to help Flame. If you can make her want to live then half the battle will be won.''

After returning to Flame's room Rafael sat down beside her bed to go over in his mind the tale he wanted to spin. He could be extremely persuasive when he wished to convince a judge and jury that justice was on his side. He lost few cases, in fact; he was so thorough, so logical in his approach, so difficult to distract from his purpose that he earned every opponent's fear and respect. As he sat with Flame's hand held lightly in his he sifted through the words he might use: the most abrasive of adjectives, revoltingly descriptive phrases. He would convince her most dramatically of the consequences of her death. He would make her want to live forever. It would be pure fiction, of course—well, almost. There had been a time when Joaquin would have killed himself for her; they had discussed it quite seriously one night when they were certain she'd live. They had gotten very drunk and discussed suicide at great length, but that was four months ago and Rafael was certain Joaquin no longer harbored such gruesome thoughts.

When Flame awoke she smiled sweetly at Rafael, embarrassed at having fainted and for the moment forgetting the cause. ''I'm sorry, I fainted again, didn't I?''

Rafael brought her hand to his lips as he leaned closer. ''Why didn't you tell me about the baby, Flame? You haven't told Joaquin the news either, have you?''

Flame closed her eyes and for a moment appeared to be sleeping again. ''I tried to convince him I was strong, but he knew better. I can't do it, Rafael. I thought I was well enough for love, to have another child, but I just can't do it. I am too weak, I have no

414

strength—although I rest continually I am never refreshed. It's no use." Flame placed his hand upon her stomach. "When I was four months along with Joaquin I could feel him move—the tiniest of sensations, but I knew he was there. This time the baby is too small, Rafael. I have never felt it stir. It is too tiny and will not survive and neither will I. I'm going to die just like Mama. Would you do something for me? Could you find someone to make me a tombstone like my mother's? I want Joaquin to know about the baby . . . if I don't live until he comes home, please tell him about our baby."

Rafael had never expected anything so sad as this. That she had thought so much of her mother's tragic death pained him terribly. He was overcome with longing for her and gathered her up into his arms, holding her tightly against his chest. He held her close to his heart while he fought back the tears which choked his throat with anguish. When he had been small his father had often beaten him but he'd never cried, not once. He forced even the remotest possibility of her death from his mind, distracting himself from the pain of his emotions as he had done as a boy. Were she to die he would grieve forever; but not tonight, he swore—while she still had one breath of life left in her body he'd not weep. He shifted her slight weight across his lap and tilted her face so she had to look up at him.

"I want you to listen, querida, listen with great care to what I have to say. I do not want to have to repeat this ghastly story. Do not faint either for I'll just wake you and make you listen to me again, do you understand?"

Flame's green eyes seemed enormous as she looked up, giving him her full attention. "What is it, Rafael, what's wrong?"

"Every word I'll tell you is God's own truth, Flame.

415

Do not make the mistake of doubting me.'' He paused a minute, mainly for dramatic effect, before he continued. ''When you were so ill, Joaquin had me draw up a legal document, an addition to his will, which names me as your son's guardian should both of you die. If you die, Flame, Joaquin means to take his own life. He will not go on living without you, he can't face that, it would be no life at all for him. He wants to join you in death, and he will do it.''

Flame gasped in terror and clutched frantically at his sleeve. ''No, Rafael, no, he wouldn't!''

''He will, Flame, yes he will. He told me to send for him should anything happen to you while he is away. He wants to die here, so he can be buried with you: he would come home but he will kill himself soon after he arrives. He told me where I could find him, he said you'd know the place where he'd do it. There are some oak trees at the edge of the valley about a mile south—it is a very lovely spot and he said you would remember it. Do you know where he means?''

Flame nodded her head, too numb to speak. The tears poured from her eyes but she made no move to brush them away. Dear God, she thought, he remembers that morning too, as well as I do. Does he wish he'd made love to me then? Our lives would have been so much different if only we had made love then.

Rafael continued in a calm steady tone: ''He means to ride Diablo and take Lady, Flame: he'll destroy both animals before he turns his pistol on himself. If by some chance Joaquin's first shot does not kill him instantly then I'll finish the job for him, I swear I will.'' Rafael knew Diablo would have to break at least three of his legs before Joaquin would even consider destroying the stallion of which he was so proud, but he thought that touch added an authentic quality to his story which would make it sound too true to question. ''I told him the only way he could be absolutely certain that his first shot would do it is to put the pistol in his mouth, but—'' Rafael had expected Flame to faint if anything; he barely got her over to the wash stand in the corner before she became violently ill. She retched repeatedly, frightening him far worse than her fainting spell had. Finally he carried her back to Joaquin's bed and lay her gently down upon the pillows.

It was several minutes later before Flame could speak but when she opened her eyes they blazed with a deep green fire. "You are a damned liar, Rafael Ramirez, now get the hell out of my room!"

"What?" Rafael could not believe Flame would doubt his tale. "It is the truth!"

"The man has left me, Rafael, don't you understand anything? He has left me and taken his very attractive cousin to Mexico! He will probably never come home and he'd be only too happy to find me dead if he did. He would never kill himself over me, never! He simply wouldn't do such a stupid thing and I would hate him forever if he did! How do you expect me to believe you'd help him do it? You would never allow Joaquin to kill himself, you'd tie him up, or keep him drunk, whatever you'd have to do but you'd never help him take his own life! Now get out of here and let me die in peace!"

Rafael could not help himself but he began to laugh and couldn't stop. She was so right, his story had been preposterous, and he'd been a fool not to realize how well she knew both him and Joaquin.

"You're going to sit there and laugh while I die!" Flame reached out to slap him but Rafael caught her hand easily in his.

"You are not going to die, Flame, not for a good many years. I'm sorry you've been so unhappy here by yourself. I should never have left you alone like this

417

when you were so depressed. Joaquin hasn't left you, I'm positive he hasn't. All the time you were gone, Flame, he was never unfaithful to you, not even once. We went all over this state searching for you, we met more beautiful young women than I could count and not once was he unfaithful to you, though the opportunities were many."

"And what about you, you had no such opportunities?" As soon as the words left her lips Flame realized the full import of her question. She had done it again, demanded something from him she was not ready to accept or return.

Rafael's grip tightened on her arm until she winced in pain. "I have no reason to be faithful to you, Flame, you are Joaquin's wife and not mine. You are nothing to me."

Flame's eyes stared defiantly into his, as if she could read all his hidden desires with the greatest of ease, which indeed she could. He could deny it as long and as loudly as he wanted to but she would never believe him. She leaned closer to him until their lips were nearly touching and whispered, "Liar."

Joseph Wainwright walked up to the bedroom door and, hearing no sound, looked in; but when he saw what appeared to be Flame kissing Rafael he stumbled, sending the door crashing into the wall as it flew open.

Flame only smiled at the poor man's embarrassed blush. "Come in, Doctor. Rafael is merely trying to convince me that life is far preferable to death, and he has been most persuasive in his approach. Aren't you men hungry? I haven't been so hungry in weeks. Now come, Rafael, take my arm and I will come into dinner with you."

Rafael grinned happily and helped her from the high bed, pulling her against his side as they left the room. "I think perhaps you were trying to teach me a lesson too, Flame.''

"Well, you have improved so greatly in the last hour, Flame, I can scarcely believe my eyes. Whatever methods Rafael uses they are far more effective than mine.'' The physician saw in an instant in the sparkle in Flame's eyes that she was indeed worth any fight no matter how great the cost. She was more than beautiful, she was joy of love itself, filled with the spark of life. Her skin gave off a radiant glow as she smiled up at Rafael, oblivious once again to the doctor's inquisitive stare.

With Rafael's tender attentions Flame began to grow stronger each day. He supervised every detail of her daily routine, even the preparation of her meals, to be certain she ate enough nutritious foods to give her body the energy it needed to nurture not only her, but the tiny life within her as well. One night he surprised her with a milk and egg conconction which he brought to her bedside himself, but his brief description of his recipe met with instant disapproval.

"Raw eggs? You expect me to drink raw eggs?'' Flame's expression filled with revulsion.

"Just try it, they are tasteless I assure you. I put other flavorings in the milk also. I'm sure you'll like it, now just take a sip and you'll see.''

Flame made a face but brought the glass to her lips. The drink was really quite good, creamy and smooth, warm, and she recognized the taste immediately. "Flavorings you'd call that? That's Joaquin's brandy, isn't it?''

Rafael chuckled at having been caught. "Yes, I didn't know he ever gave that to you.''

"He doesn't, but this is the way he tastes.'' Flame drank as much of the soothing liquid as she could before she looked up at her friend again. She could tell her comment had embarrassed him, and she apologized.

419

"I'm sorry, Rafael, that sounded rather crude, didn't it? But he is my husband, or at least he was."

"You needn't remind me that you are another man's wife. Now if you're finished I'll take the glass back to the kitchen." He did not enjoy being in her room at that late hour. Her lace nightgown did nothing to hide her slender charms and he shifted his feet nervously, anxious to be gone. He got along well with her during the day, it was only at night when he lay awake thinking of her that her beauty and sweetness tormented him almost beyond endurance. Would Joaquin never return home so he might leave and escape the misery her presence always brought?

"Sit down a minute. I will finish your drink—it is really delicious and I appreciate your taking the trouble to make it for me. Now, do you know what I'd like to do?" Flame's teasing smile was full of mischief.

"I'm afraid to guess. What is it?" Rafael pulled up a chair and sat down beside her. He tried to treat her as a younger sister whenever possible but he had no clue to her thoughts and her actions were always unpredictable.

"I want to rebuild my father's house. I can remember how it looked fairly well. Do you think it could be rebuilt?"

"Well of course it could, but why would you wish to undertake such a project? Aren't you happy in this house?"

Flame knew her sorrow was apparent in her every gesture and was surprised he dared ask that question. "No, I am not happy here. This is Joaquin's home and he doesn't want to share it with me. How will I ever be happy when I have to live here all alone? I want my own house, a house I can show my son and tell him about how I lived so close to his father when I was small. Would you help me to find someone to rebuild it,

420

Rafael?"

"I am certain that Joaquin would not approve, Flame."

"Why not? He doesn't care what happens to me anymore. Would it be so dreadfully expensive to build a house? Mine was not nearly so large a home as this one . . . would it really cost so very much?"

"It's not the cost that would upset him, Flame." Rafael scowled. She knew Joaquin well enough to know what his reaction would be—a most hostile one, of that he was certain. But Joaquin was not there, he was, and he knew she'd never be content with her life as long as her husband remained in Mexico. He had tried unsuccessfully to convince her otherwise but she still insisted Joaquin had left her for Maria Elena. He had been there at the ranch for more than two weeks and while her health was improving he knew that in her heart she was still as miserable as she had been on the day he'd arrived. Maybe building the house would provide just the diversion she needed. "I will speak with José about it tomorrow, he undoubtedly knows someone in town who could direct the work if we supply the labor and materials. Do you want to duplicate the original house?"

"Could it be done? I've made some drawings—" Flame reached for the drawer in the nightstand, then drew back, as a puzzled smile crossed her pretty face.

"Flame, is something wrong?" Rafael leaned forward as he inquired.

"Give me your hand, Rafael, quickly. There, do you feel it? That's the baby!"

Rafael could scarcely breathe as she held his hand to her body. Her lace gown was sheer and the blood rushed to his ears as she pressed his hand closer. "Flame, please." Then he felt the child move—the smallest of kicks, but he felt it plainly and began to laugh with her, his desire forgotten in the sheer joy of feeling the new life. They remained still as though frozen for several seconds before Flame released his hand and spoke excitedly.

"Oh Rafael, the baby is alive! I've been so afraid, oh I wish Joaquin were here with me." Flame bit her lip to hold back her tears. Joaquin didn't want to be with her, didn't love her at all.

Rafael got to his feet swiftly and replaced his chair near the wall. "Flame, you have no idea how much I wish Joaquin were here too. Now good night."

"Must you go? Can't you stay and talk with me for a while longer?" Flame still had a child's innocence at times: that Rafael loved her she knew full well, that his desire for her gave him no peace occurred to her not at all.

"I'm tired, Flame. Go to sleep and dream about your baby. I'll see you tomorrow." He bent down and brushed the top of her golden hair with his lips before he left her room to go to his where he knew sleep would elude him for hours. His palm burned where he'd touched her and he swore under his breath, "Damn it, Joaquin, this is your child! It is you who should be here with Flame and not I!"

Using Flame's drawings and men José located in town supplemented with workers from the Villarreal ranch construction was begun promptly on Flame's house. Rafael took her over frequently in the buggy to see how the work was progressing. He had been right in his hopes the project would lift her spirits—she was thrilled with the prospect of owning her own home and her whole mood improved dramatically as the work progressed swiftly toward completion. The Lannier home, unlike Joaquin's abode, had been a two-story frame structure; André had built the Colonial style house to make Deborah feel more at home in California. The house had been very lovingly built with great care to detail, all to please Deborah. Rafael made certain its replica would please Flame just as greatly.

"Everything is coming along according to schedule, Flame. You will need to choose the paint and decide on which furniture you wish to bring over until your things we have ordered from San Francisco have arrived."

"Is there any chance that it will be finished by my birthday, Rafael? Can we spend that day here together?"

"They will try their best to finish it for you by the middle of March, but perhaps Joaquin will be home by then and you'll want to celebrate your birthday together in his home."

Flame's expression changed as she glanced away, unable to let him see how swiftly her happiness faded at the mention of her husband's name. "Why is it not obvious to you as it is to me that he has left me? He left me to live as best I can while he tours Mexico with his cousin."

"Stop it! He has not left you, damn it! He has always gone to Mexico, he travels frequently, he'll be home before long, he has only been gone for four months!"

Flame blinked back her tears. "Four months has been unbearable to me, Rafael. Had you not come to stay with me when you did surely I would have died of loneliness, you know I would have. Joaquin doesn't care that I am lonely or he never would have left. I could have died I miss him so."

Rafael tried to hold his temper but failed. "Do not remind me, Flame, I remember all too well." He had been with her for more than four weeks now and each day had been a joy to him. He held no illusions that she loved him, but she was fond of him and so appreciative of his company that he wished in his heart that Joaquin would not return for years. She had refused to allow him to send for her husband when she was so ill and he had not pressed her: it was understandable that she wanted Joaquin to come home out of love, not out of a tiresome sense of responsibility. Perhaps it had been a mistake not to send for Joaquin immediately, for Rafael knew there would be the devil to pay when he did come home. But they'd have to face his friend's anger when the time came so there was no point he could see in worrying over it now.

The morning of March 16 was cold and the rain which had delayed the completion of Flame's house continued, ending her hopes of spending her birthday on her father's land. She and Rafael remained at the Villarreal ranch close to the fireplace in the parlor while they watched her son attempt to walk about the room. At eleven months of age his walk was becoming more proficient each day, and although he still took frequent falls he loved his new game and giggled happily as he walked about the room.

Flame had loved Rafael's present: small gold earrings which she'd immediately put on. They were as exquisite as she. He knew her thoughts as they sat together, he needn't ask—as always she would be thinking of her husband and he could tell her depression was deepening by the minute. "Why don't you open Joaquin's present, Flame? I am curious about what he sent, aren't you?"

"No, not a bit, but there's something I want to give to you. Excuse me a moment." Flame left the room slowly, yet if her pace was not smooth it lacked nothing in terms of grace. When she returned she held out a brightly wrapped package for Rafael. "I wanted to give you something, to thank you for all you do for me. This is not a very grand gift, not what you deserve, but I hope you will like it."

Smiling, Rafael unwrapped the present and was astonished to find a beautifully detailed sketch Flame had drawn herself. It was a landscape, the trees and flowers near the ranch so carefully drawn the location was unmistakable. He was delighted. "I had no idea you could draw so well. Your plans for the house were perfect, but somehow I didn't realize you could do this type of art work as well. Thank you, I will hang this in my office and always remember the time I've spent here with you."

Flame took her place at his side on the sofa. "We have been happy here together, haven't we? You are so kind to stay, to be the friend I need so desperately."

"I will always want to be with you, Flame." Rafael kept his eyes on her drawing—he had said too much, far more than he had any right to say. She had chosen to marry Joaquin and not him, he had no claim to her love, none at all.

Flame reached over and took his hand in hers. "What would you be doing with your time if you were at home in San Francisco? Do you have many friends there?"

"I have more acquaintances than true friends, as anyone does, and there are others I must see as a business obligation only."

"Are there lots of parties? There were in Philadelphia, I imagine there must be in San Francisco too."

"Yes, I am invited to many parties but I seldom go."

"But why not? You are very handsome, so charming, and surely you must like parties. I know you like to dance and—"

Rafael put up his hand to stop her enthusiastic praise. "Please, Flame, stop. I know I am handsome, but certainly not charming, but I'm no recluse, not by any stretch of the imagination. I go out quite often

425

when I am home, but I much prefer being here with you. Now open Joaquin's present, I insist.''

Flame sighed sadly as she picked up the gift. ''Oh Rafael, I've not written even one letter to him—I've tried, but there seems to be no way for me to put into writing what must be said. What must he think of me?'' Flame toyed with the ribbon on the large box and after Rafael again coaxed her to open the gift she finally did. Joaquin had sent her an exquisitely beautiful dress made of the finest lace, the skirt layered in tiers. It was a lovely, elegant gown and she held it up for Rafael to admire. The color was the palest of pinks, the shade of pearls. She loved it, but as she looked at the tiny waistline she shook her head. ''Somehow, I don't think this will fit me.'' In spite of herself she began to laugh: she laughed until the tears rolled down her cheeks at the irony of Joaquin's sending such a marvelous present which she couldn't wear.

''How was he to know you are pregnant when you refuse to tell him? The dress will fit you perfectly after the baby comes, you can wear it then.'' He touched the soft folds of the skirt lightly. ''It is a lovely dress.''

''Yes, it is beautiful isn't it? But he sent no card, no message for me with it?'' Flame looked through the wrapping paper again but found no note.

''What did you expect him to say, Flame? What should he have written?''

''I'd like to know that he misses me, for I have missed him so terribly.'' Flame looked down at her boy, who was now playing contentedly with the box which had contained the new dress. ''His son will not know him, Rafael. When Joaquin comes home he will be a stranger to us both.''

''You will all get to know each other again, Flame, it won't take long. Joaquin may be home soon—he said he'd most likely be gone about six months and it's been five already. He hadn't planned to stay away forever.''

"Every day is another day too many! Why couldn't he have been here today? It would have meant so much to me if he'd come home to be with me today. You are so sweet to keep me entertained, but I would have loved to spend my eighteenth birthday with my husband.''

"There will be next year, Flame, do not worry so.''

"Next year may never come. We might not live so long.''

"Flame, don't you dare talk like that again. You are well, do not even think of death now, I forbid it!''

Flame was quiet a moment and then nodded slowly in agreement. "I found that document you told me about, the one naming you as Joaquin's guardian. I was looking for some blank paper in Joaquin's desk and found it quite by accident. Was any of that fable you told me true?''

"Yes. I think had you died the night you were stabbed he would have done it gladly. We talked about it—that's how I knew about the oak trees. Didn't you wonder how I knew about that?''

Flame shuddered and closed her eyes tightly before looking at him again. "You wouldn't have stopped him?''

"I would have tried, I most certainly would have tried, but Joaquin can usually beat me.''

"Usually, not always?'' Flame's pretty gaze held a teasing sparkle again in spite of their grim topic.

"No, it may surprise you to learn that on more than one occasion I have managed to get the upper hand. If Joaquin gets too angry he can be beaten, but only if I am not as furious as he. If we are both blind with rage then he always wins.''

"I hope you never have any reason to fight him ever again.''

"So do I, Flame.'' Rafael knew if they ever fought

again it would be over her and one of them would surely die. He had been ready to kill Joaquin before and he would try again if his friend still failed to make his wife happy when he came home. His thoughts grew increasingly dark until Flame's question startled him back to reality.

"I wonder what he and Maria Elena are doing today. Do you think he might have a moment to remember me?" Flame tried to hide her tears but Rafael saw them clearly.

"Flame, you are wrong. Joaquin has never loved another woman. You are his life."

Flame only shook her head—she didn't argue, she couldn't. She wanted to believe Rafael with all her heart, but how could that be true? "He didn't even kiss me good-bye, Rafael, he left me without saying good-bye."

"Perhaps he couldn't, Flame. You mean so much to him . . . maybe he couldn't bear to tell you good-bye it hurt him so."

"No, it wasn't like that. He was too angry with me to bid me farewell—that was his reason. He's gone, Rafael, I know he is, that's why I wanted to rebuild my house. I want to have somewhere to go when Joaquin comes home and tells me to leave."

Rafael opened his mouth to protest, and then didn't. What if what she believed were true? Joaquin's and Maria Elena's names had been linked for years. What the hell was he doing with his cousin in Mexico all this time? Joaquin was not the type to invite a woman on a trip for any reason save one. Finally he took a deep breath and let it out slowly. "I have grown exceedingly weary of defending Joaquin, Flame. If what you believe is true, if when he comes home things are not as you have hoped they will be—"

Flame lifted her fingertips to his lips, stopping his

promise with a gentle caress. "You needn't speak of it now, Rafael, I know. I cannot look at you and fail to see the love in your eyes. But we must remain no more than friends until Joaquin returns; we could not face him otherwise. He doesn't trust me, but he does trust you. If he even suspected there were more than friendship between us he would kill you."

Rafael took her hand in his and kissed her palm softly. "No, he could only try, Flame. Do not kill me so easily in your mind—my death is not such a certain thing as all that. I would have a chance, it is possible I could be the winner."

"There would be no winner: should one of you kill the other I would never love the one who survived, I would mourn for the rest of my life for the man who had died. I cannot bear the violence you have turned on each other and I will not be the cause of it ever again. Do you believe me, Rafael? If you kill Joaquin I will never be yours, so do not run the risk of provoking him."

Rafael stared calmly into her eyes and indeed he did understand. She had never been more serious. "Then I would be happy to die, Flame, knowing you would always love me."

Flame felt her throat tighten with tears as she looked at him. Every detail of his face was so dear, his mouth so inviting, and the desire she thought she would never again feel flooded through her with a rush of warmth. She wanted him then—as a friend, lover, husband— she wanted everything from him, and her eyes told him what her lips could not.

Rafael's fingertip traced a line down her soft cheek. "I think, my Flame, you are beginning to feel the same exquisite torture I have felt these past months. I will be patient, and when Joaquin comes home your conscience will be clear, but you will know how I feel, and should Joaquin ever tell you to go or should you ever wish to leave him you will know where to come."

His brown eyes were so dark, as deep as the night, and Flame saw her reflection in their shiny depths. She was drawn to him and could not resist his enticing attraction. He had brought the gift of life but what he offered now was death—Joaquin's, his own, then hers. When she fainted this time, he caught her.

Twenty-One

March gave way to April but Flame received no more gifts or letters from Joaquin. Time dragged by slowly for her, the days progressing at such an unhurried pace that she lost all track of time. Rafael looked at her now and thought her loveliness more exquisite than ever. She had regained some if not all of the weight she had lost and he was certain it was due to his milk and egg potion which he still insisted she consume at bedtime. Her golden hair curled in ringlets which extended past her waistline and glowed with a rich bloom of health. He had succeeded in his desire to restore her to good health but the time they spent together was still agony for him. He counted the hours, the minutes even, but there was no way for him to slow the days which sped by toward the inevitable hour when Joaquin would arrive.

They never spoke of their talk on her birthday, but it hung on the air between them, creating a tension neither could ignore. Maria would enter the parlor and find Flame and Rafael together, silent, each lost in his own thoughts, but she knew they were both thinking of Joaquin and she dreaded his return even more than they did. The whole ranch seemed to exist in a state of tension. The vaqueros argued, José swore over problems he would have been able to handle easily at other times, the women in the kitchen found food burning no matter how closely it was watched. Everyone was tense and unhappy and countless times each day prayers for Joaquin's swift return crossed their lips. They all missed him, his was the vitality that gave the ranch its life, but all remembered the violence which had surrounded his departure and feared what might happen when he came home.

One crisp clear day near the first of May Rafael took Flame's son out for a walk as she rested. He enjoyed the boy's company, they were good friends; Rafael would carry the child on his shoulders as he talked to him about the ranch, teaching him the names of the animals, or whatever caught the inquisitive boy's interest that particular day. They never had any precise plan, they just walked until Joaquin grew bored and then Rafael would take him back to the house. It was a pleasant routine and if the boy were spoiled it was only natural. He would inherit an empire and had no reason to be confined at so early an age into the needless discipline others might have imposed upon a small child. He was a Villarreal, and that was as close to being a prince as one could be born in America, and the child had a full and happy life on his father's magnificent ranch.

They had just crossed the top of the ridge near the house when Rafael saw the dust rising along the road as the carriage approached and knew instantly Joaquin was home. He and the boy watched the steady progress of the carriage as it neared the house both filled with curiosity at what its owner would bring. Rafael knew it would take all the diplomacy he possessed to keep Joaquin from killing him the minute he saw Flame, and yet as he stood and watched the carriage stop in front of the house he felt strangely elated. The long wait was finally over; no action Joaquin could force would be worse than the waiting had been.

He carried the boy down to the house and set him

down with a hug. "It's your daddy, Joaquin, hurry and call him Daddy, now run to meet him!" The child did as he was told, delighting his father with his wet, sloppy kisses. He had grown from a baby to a boy while his father had been gone. Tall for his age, he was a handsome child with a vocabulary of more than a dozen words, and he had been carefully tutored to say "daddy."

Maria ran to wake Flame, too excited to greet Joaquin first. "He is here, Señora, your husband is home at last, come quickly!" She opened the shutters to let in the late afternoon sun as she chattered noisily.

Flame pushed her hair from her eyes as she struggled to sit up. "Come and help me, Maria, I can not get up all that quickly now." She was shaking as she got unsteadily to her feet—Joaquin was finally home and she had not even the time to comb her hair? "Maria, wait, he has been gone for six months so a moment more won't matter. Please help me to at least fix my hair."

"Señora, it is beautiful already!" Maria grabbed Flame's hairbrush and began to arrange the tangled curls in some sort of order. "Aren't you excited? Don't you want to come and see him? He looks wonderful, so handsome, there has never been a finer looking man but you know that, now come!" Maria took her hand but Flame held back, afraid to face Joaquin now that the time had finally arrived. Whatever could she say to him? What would he say about the baby? And what would he say about the fact she'd not written to him even once? She was nearly faint with anxiety when Maria propelled her through the front door.

Joaquin did not see Flame at first, he was still holding his son and talking with Rafael as several men unloaded the carriage behind him. He was gesturing toward the suitcases, telling the happy boy about the

433

things he had brought for him.

Flame's eyes took in the charming scene hungrily but then she saw Maria Elena Alvarez approaching from the far side of the carriage. The brunette smiled prettily as she looked up at Joaquin and took his son's hand. Flame froze—she wanted to scream, to cry. Joaquin would bring that woman here, to their home? Had he no shame? Had he so little regard for her feelings that he would humiliate her so brazenly?

When Joaquin turned toward the house he was as appalled as his wife. He had held her memory in his heart and mind; her image had been so clear, but never had he expected her to be pregnant and that sudden realization shocked him badly. The smile left his face as he put down his son and he strode across the yard and swept Flame up into his arms. His face filled with rage as he carried her back into his room and set her down with a force that jarred her teeth and sent a wave of pain up her spine.

"Joaquin! Be careful, you hurt me!" Flame backed away from him, frightened by his menacing expression as well as his thoughtless action.

"My God, what have you done, you adulterous bitch? How many of my men have you had—every damn one of them? Have you any idea whose brat that is? Can you even come close to naming the father?"

"How dare you accuse me of such a vile thing when you have the audacity to bring that woman to my house? This is your child, Joaquin, I have never been with another man!" Flame screamed right back at him, her anger now matching his.

Joaquin stepped closer, forcing Flame back against the edge of his bed. "The hell it is—I know when I last slept with you, I can tell you the exact minute in fact. You expect me to believe you're eight months pregnant? How stupid do you think I am?"

434

Flame was astounded by her husband's lack of logic. Why didn't he believe her, why would he think her unfaithful when she loved him so? "I know I am still too slender and the baby is small but it is your child, Joaquin, I swear it is."

Joaquin continued to curse: "That's a damn lie! Had you been pregnant before I left you would have told me so."

Flame gestured helplessly, not knowing how to explain. "I wasn't certain, I'd been so ill, I didn't want to worry you in case it weren't true."

"Worry me? Christ, are you so stupid you had no idea why I left?"

Flame's eyes searched his face for some clue to the reason for his irrational anger. "A business trip, you said."

Joaquin turned away, too mad to respond for a moment. "When I think how I've worried about you . . . why didn't you write to me, tell me you were pregnant if you're so damn certain that brat is mine?"

Flame had no shortage of taunts to hurl right back at her husband and did so: "And why didn't you tell me good-bye? You left me locked in my room, a prisoner in my own home and you expected me to write to you with news of a child? I wanted to tell you, I wanted you to hold me and kiss me, to love me and I would have told you gladly. But you wouldn't do it, you wouldn't even kiss me good-bye after I had begged you to make love to me." The tears streamed down her face as she let him hear all the anguish she'd kept locked inside herself for six long months.

"Well, if I refused you it was with good reason, but somebody else sure as hell didn't refuse your invitation, did he?" Joaquin grabbed her shoulders and shook her soundly as if she were no more than a rag doll. "Tell me his name, Flame, and you better make no mistake because I don't want to kill the wrong man. Now who was it?''

Flame could not even see his face he had made her so dizzy. ''The baby is yours, Joaquin, yours.''

''Damn your lying tongue! I've a good idea whose baby that is, I'm almost certain in fact. How often has Rafael been here? Is it only a coincidence that he is here with you today?''

''I was ill, Joaquin, sick with loneliness and he came to stay.'' Flame's eyes filled with terror as she prayed silently—not again, please, don't let them fight again because of me.

''When was that, when did he come to stay?''

''In January, the end of January.''

''January! Why didn't you send for me, Flame? I am your husband and I am the one who is supposed to take care of you! Didn't you know I'd come straight home if you needed me?''

''I needed you desperately when you left, Joaquin, I begged you to take me with you but you left me here all alone. Your letters, the few you sent didn't even inquire as to my health, and since you had Maria Elena with you I didn't think you'd want to be bothered by your wife's problems. Why would I have thought you'd want to come home to me? Even if I had died would you have come home?''

''Died? What are you talking about, Flame? You were getting better each day when I left, almost well. Don't be ridiculous—and Maria Elena wasn't with me. Is that what you thought? Is that why you did this to me?''

''I've not done anything to you! This baby is yours!''

As Joaquin stared down at her his eyes turned as cold as ice. ''The child is Rafael's, isn't it? You might as well admit the truth to me now, it will save me beating it out of him before I kill him.'' Joaquin reached out to take her wrist.

Angrily Flame tore herself free from his grasp. ''You touch Rafael and I'll kill you, I'll shoot you down like the mad dog you are! How could you think me unfaithful or that the man who has always been your best friend would betray you? Don't you dare touch Rafael!''

The force of her threat stunned Joaquin, shocked him past all reason. There could be only one reason why she'd defend Rafael so fiercely: she loved him and the baby was his. He knew that Rafael had been with Flame, making love to her all the months he'd been traveling in Mexico nearly dying of loneliness he missed her so badly. That Flame was carrying Rafael's child tore his heart in two and he ran from the room to kill the man who had stolen her love.

Flame struggled against the nausea that filled her throat and followed her husband outside. Rafael had been leaning against the carriage talking with Maria Elena when Joaquin came out of the house; deep in conversation he would never have looked up had Flame not screamed his name. Her warning gave him no more than a second to prepare but it was enough to save his life. He dodged out of Joaquin's way and the larger man's first blow glanced off his shoulder, doing him no harm.

Flame watched in horror as the two men fought. Rafael had been right: when Joaquin was mad with rage he could be beaten, and she was grateful Rafael was not suffering the brutal beating she had feared he would. He avoided Joaquin's punches with agile steps and landed several dreadful blows of his own. The vaqueros were as amused as before by the fistfight and although most bet on Joaquin, several were confident Rafael would be the victor that day. Maria Elena had fled to be violently ill in the nearby bushes while Maria held the little boy's face pressed tightly to her bosom to shield him from the gruesome spectacle taking place in the yard.

Flame knew none of the men would stop the fight when they were enjoying the sport, but when her eyes caught the sight of the buggy whip leaning against the carriage it was in her hand before anyone thought to stop her. She drew it back, then brought it down on her husband's back with a strength born of desperation; and the line of blood which appeared as the whip sliced through his shirt encouraged her to strike him again. This time Joaquin turned, trying to avoid her blow, and the tip of the whip slashed across his face, cutting his right cheek to the bone.

A hush fell over the yard as Flame called to Joaquin. Her voice was soft, taunting as she called his name, exactly as a bull fighter calls to a bull, coaxing him near for the kill. "Come here to me, Joaquin, come kill me. I don't want you to be tired when you come for me. It's me you hate, not Rafael. Come and kill me instead or I will kill you." She held the whip at her side as she continued to taunt him, to dare him to kill her as she spoke in a seductive tone barely more than a whisper.

Without any signal or outward sign Joaquin's vaqueros moved from the edge of the yard to her side. None had forgotten her courage the night she'd freed Juan and none would desert her now. Should Joaquin turn on her he would have to fight every last one of his fierce-willed vaqueros before he could lay a finger on her, and he saw their determination to protect her in their eyes.

Flame waited as Joaquin got to his feet. He took only one step toward her before stopping abruptly. As always she was defying him, daring him to strike her, daring him to vent his anger on her instead of the man who had always been his most trusted friend.

"You will not even try? There is nothing you can do to me that will hurt me any worse than your suspicions, but you could kill me, Joaquin, you could at least try."

Joaquin shook his head as his eyes bored into hers. Her green eyes were glowing with a strange inner light that transfixed him, held him in his place where he could only stand and stare. Her long hair was tossed by the gentle evening breeze which blew the curls around her face in wild disarray. She was so lovely, but her insults were deadly and he knew it. When had his men become so loyal to his wife that they would openly defy him? His torn cheek burned with a fiery pain and blood dripped down his face to stain what was left of his shirt.

Flame waited calmly until she was certain Joaquin had at last regained his senses. "I'm going home, Joaquin, to the only home possible for me now. I can no longer remain here when you still don't trust me. I have waited so patiently for you to come home—I'm sorry you did not know how to greet me. Since you no longer wish me to be your wife, you are no longer my husband." Flame turned then to smile at Rafael, the light in her eyes softening when they touched his face. "Will you come with me now, Rafael, and be the loving husband I have longed to have?" Flame threw down the whip and took her son from Maria's arms as Rafael walked to her side. He held the child as she climbed up into the driver's seat of the carriage, then handed the boy up to her. He leapt up beside her, took the reins from around the brake handle, then flipped them lightly across the horses' backs. The carriage lurched, then rolled slowly across the yard and out the gate, and not a soul moved to stop it.

When at last they were out of sight of the ranch Rafael turned to Flame. "I could have beaten him today, I could have done it. I didn't need your help."

Flame answered slowly: "I know that, but he did."

Rafael frowned as he glanced over at her. "Do you mean that, Flame? You thought I'd kill him? I would not even have tried, but why in God's name did he come after me like that? I have never seen him so angry—he wanted me dead and I do not even know why."

Flame wiped away her tears on her sleeve. "He called me 'an adulterous bitch,' Rafael. He says my baby is yours."

"What? Mother of God, how could he be such a fool? I am sorry, Flame, I had no idea what he'd said to you, I'm so sorry that had to happen. I knew he wouldn't be pleased I hadn't sent for him, hadn't let him know you were pregnant, but that he'd suspect the child wasn't his didn't occur to me."

Flame hugged her little boy more tightly, giving him the warm embrace she had hoped to give his father. "He brought his mistress to our home and accused me of adultery. It would be funny if it didn't hurt so much."

Rafael yanked on the reins to pull the four horse team to a halt. "I will take you back now. I will explain to him how wrong he is if that is your desire, but if not I want you to understand that I mean to be your lover. If you want me to stay with you then adultery will be the right word."

"Words don't concern me, just take me to my house. I am your woman now and you may do with me what you will. I have never had a lover; if you are trying to frighten me into returning to my husband it won't work. Love doesn't frighten me in the least. I have had so little I scarcely know what it is." Then Flame turned toward him and spoke in a more serious tone: "Perhaps *I* can frighten *you*. Did Joaquin ever tell you I'd killed a man?"

"What are you saying?" Rafael's expression was

440

one of complete disbelief, but he realized with a sudden shudder that she was easily capable of murder. She had defied Joaquin with the calm, cool voice of a woman quite capable of being a murderess, but could she possibly have already become one?

"I killed one of Joaquin's vaqueros. He kidnapped me, he meant to kill Joaquin and sell me to a whorehouse in Mexico. They probably would have refused to buy me—what man would pay money for me? Joaquin never wanted my love and I offered it for free. How could I have been such a fool as to hope he would come home and say that he missed me, take me into his arms and say how dearly he loves me. Was that so very much to ask, Rafael, just to hear my husband say that he loves me?"

Rafael pulled Flame into his arms and held her while she wept. "I should never have taken you to his ranch when you first arrived in California. I should have known what he'd do to you. You are so dear and he has been so cruel, he has abused you badly when all you ever asked from him was love."

"You do understand me, don't you, Rafael? You really do know what's in my heart as well as I do." Flame wiped her eyes as she sat back to look at him more closely.

"Perhaps better, my Flame. Now let's go home." Rafael flicked the reins again and the horses continued down the worn trail which led to the Lannier Ranch. Flame lay her head on Rafael's shoulder and closed her eyes but she could not shut out the ghastly scene of her husband's homecoming. It played over and over in her mind with the hurt growing within her heart to an unbearable level. When Rafael began to laugh she could not believe her ears.

"What is so damn funny?"

"I can't help it, Flame, the idea of you being in a

441

Mexican whorehouse is too ludicrous to imagine." He continued to laugh as they rode along toward her newly rebuilt home. He hugged her shoulders affectionately and winked at her son, but he still couldn't seem to control his laughter.

"It's not at all funny, Rafael, and besides, have you ever been in one?"

"Several in fact, but never have I met a woman like you in such an establishment."

"Why not? In spite of the fact my husband doesn't want me, I used to have lots of men who did. Perhaps it would have been a better life for me than this one has been."

"You are not serious!" Rafael was dead serious now. "You understand what whores do, don't you? They fulfill their customers' fantasies, Flame, and not all fantasies are pleasant."

"No fantasy could ever be worse than the reality of my existence, Rafael, for surely whores are not continually betrayed by the men they love."

"Whores are incapable of love, Flame." Rafael spoke matter-of-factly, as if he were an expert on the subject.

"That can't be true, Rafael—they only hide their feelings in order to survive. They have to, they would not be able to live otherwise."

Rafael took in Flame's thoughtful expression and sighed. "You are too sympathetic. Believe me, the whores I have known have no hearts at all, none."

"What is it like then, Rafael? How can you make love to a woman you don't love? What do you think about?"

Rafael grinned as he shook his head. "You expect me to tell you that?"

"Yes. You always answer my questions, that's why I like you so much. You understand I'm a real person,

442

not an empty-headed doll who can't even think for herself."

"I have never made that mistake. I know you have a mind, Flame, and a very keen one. Well, I do not frequent such places all that often, let me just tell you it is not nearly the same as being with a woman I love. That is ever so much better: to hold a woman in my arms all night and know she will smile at me in the morning because she loves me, that is infinitely better."

"You have been in love then, really in love? Why didn't you get married?"

"Is there no end to your curiosity? I have already given you my heart, is it my very soul you're after? You want all my memories, all my dreams laid bare?"

Flame responded immediately: "Yes, I want it all, all you can give I will take for my own. I want to be so close to you I will know what you are thinking before you speak. I want to share everything with you, your happiness as well as your sorrow." She reached for his hand and brought it to her lips, kissing the scraped and bruised knuckles gently. "You are the best friend I have ever had, Rafael, but I want so much more from you now."

Rafael leaned down to kiss her lips lightly. "You will have all I can give, Flame, I promise you that." But when they arrived at her house Rafael was not so cheerful. "We are home. I was not certain how this day would end when Joaquin threw his first punch. While I am still alive and the sun has already begun to set I think we should still be cautious."

"You don't think he'll come after us? He wouldn't!" Flame was terrified by that thought and gripped Rafael's hand tightly.

"He might, but I know he will have to come alone. Did you see what his men did? They would have defended you, Flame. They chose to help you fight

443

against him. I do not envy Joaquin tonight: we will be together but he will be alone with his own evil thoughts."

"No he won't! He'll have Maria Elena to console him—I haven't forgotten her even if you have!" Flame walked toward her front door with a light firm step, leaving Rafael to stare after her in wonder. When had she ceased to limp? The defiant tilt of her pretty chin amused him only a moment before he realized her posture told him everything: she still loved her husband. He called after her angrily: "Flame! I have risked my life for you today, and willingly, but what have you to offer in return? What are you going to promise me?"

Flame's expression was puzzled as she walked back toward him, her son's small hand still held firmly in hers. Her green eyes were clouded as she looked up at him. His face was bruised, cut, his clothes dirty, but the look in his dark eyes was that of the devil, a threatening look she'd never seen him turn upon her. It was a glance that would have struck terror into almost any heart but hers . . . she only smiled. "You did not understand, Rafael? I am yours now. I have given you all that I have—myself, my children, this house, everything it contains, the land upon which we stand. All that I have I will give to you if you will but stay with me." She reached up and caressed his cheek. "I have left my husband for you; I know what people will call me and I do not care."

"You have failed to mention the only thing I have ever wanted from you, Flame. You still cannot say that you love me?"

"What we have is so much better than love, I can not bear the pain of that emotion any longer. I was just a foolish girl when I thought love was all that mattered. I have grown up now, I am finished with love and all its illusions, its dreams of happiness which are no more

444

than imaginative fiction. Joaquin put an end to those ideals, but I will not let him destroy you nor the future we can share.''

At her touch Rafael's expression softened. ''Perhaps you are right, Flame. I will be content to share my life with you, but I do not think you realize how hard it may be.''

''Surely nothing can be worse than today, Rafael. I can never be hurt after what I've suffered today.''

''We will see. You may find me a more difficult husband than Joaquin ever was.''

Flame's teasing smile delighted him. ''That is impossible, Rafael, there never was a worse husband than Joaquin and I will be glad to be rid of him. Now I must take my son inside, he is tired and so am I.'' This time Rafael let her go without an argument.

Maria did her best to clean and bandage the wound on Joaquin's cheek but she was not optimistic. ''It will leave a scar. I have pulled the edges together tightly; I hope it will not be too bad. As for your back, the cuts are too deep, scars are unavoidable.''

''You think I care about a few scars? They mean nothing to me. I am not vain and scars do not trouble me in the least.''

Maria stood back and looked down at him. He had not even flinched as she cleaned his cuts: his mind was obviously elsewhere, occupied with problems far worse than mere physical pain. ''How could you have been so blind? How could you have made such an unfounded accusation? I did as you asked, I locked your wife's door each night but she did not once notice. I am disgusted now that I did it. They were never lovers, never, but if they become so now you have only yourself to blame. Here is the key to your room, I am leaving. I will pack your wife's things and the boy's and go to her.

445

She should not be alone now with the baby due next month."

"Next month, hell! Do you know for a fact that's my child? Have you any proof?"

The housekeeper shook her head sadly. "It never occurred to me to doubt that beautiful child's word. Good-bye, Joaquin, you deserve to be alone. When you would destroy such a lovely young woman by your outrageous jealousy, you deserve to spend the rest of your life alone."

As Maria began to pack Flame's clothes Joaquin came to his bedroom and when he saw the lace dress he'd sent her for her birthday hanging on the wardrobe door he spoke up quickly. "Don't take that one, Maria, I want to keep it. Why did she have it out? If it fit her when I sent it, it can't fit her now."

"No, she has never been able to wear it, Joaquin, but you sent it to her and she loved it so. She wouldn't let me put it away. All she ever talked about was how happy she'd be when you came home. It is a pity she was so badly disappointed. She nearly died of loneliness. I tried to be company for her but we are too different and she grew more and more frail. Had Rafael not stayed here with her you would have lost her in January and returned home a widower."

"Better that she had died then than to disgrace me as she has now."

"You are the one who has committed the disgrace! You meant to flaunt your cousin in your wife's face after what she has suffered for loving you. I am ashamed to know you, you could have been fine and good but you have chosen to be hateful and cruel instead. Well you will bring your own ruin, Joaquin, it is inevitable now."

"The child is not mine, Maria. You wait and see—it will be months before that baby is born, I know it will."

Maria nodded thoughtfully. "Would that it were, Joaquin: Flame might have a chance to live then. Next month she will have so little chance to survive. I will do my very best for her but I have seen women die in childbirth and it is not an easy death. It is slow and horribly painful and the child will be lost as well—your child, Joaquin."

Joaquin's face drained of all color as he listened to Maria's dire prediciton. Her words were too close to Joseph Wainwright's for him not to be alarmed. "Does Flame know that, Maria? Does she suspect what might happen to her?"

"Of course. That is why your dress is hanging up there, so it will not have to be pressed when it comes time to bury her."

Joaquin slumped back against the door. "Dear God, no." What had he done? He was engulfed in remorse and shut his eyes to try and recall how Flame had looked that afternoon, but his face ached so badly he could hardly concentrate and no clear image came to his mind.

"She is a dead woman and she knows it, Joaquin, but she will not let one of you kill the other. You see how pointless it would be, since she has so little time left."

"Just leave my house, woman, I can not stand your ramblings! It is all lies—Flame is well and she won't die because that child will never be born next month! Finish packing her things, but that damn dress stays here. I will pack Rafael's belongings myself, he'll certainly never come back for them, and I want them out of here tonight!"

Rafael fed the horses and turned them out into the pasture since Flame's ranch had no barn. He was just going back into the house when Maria arrived in the

447

buggy. It was filled with luggage but the resourceful housekeeper had been smart enough to bring food along with her as well.

"I told Joaquin what a fool he was, but what did you plan to feed her tonight, Rafael? I fear Flame has little choice between the fools who love her!"

Rafael laughed and helped her to unload the heavily laden buggy. "It looks as though you have brought half the house. Joaquin allowed it?"

"He packed your clothes himself."

"They are probably cut into small pieces then." Rafael wasn't happy at that grim thought.

"No, I think you will be surprised. He took very good care of your things."

When Rafael opened his suitcases he was amazed by the accuracy of her words: no English valet could have packed them so well. Why had Joaquin gone to such trouble? Then he understood and commented softly to himself: "Do not worry, my friend. Your wife will be safe with me."

Twenty-Two

"Come, it is time for bed, Flame. It is very late and this has been too tiring a day for both of us." Rafael extended his hand to help the lovely young woman rise from the sofa. They had been sitting in the parlor for an hour, quietly resting in each other's arms since neither cared to discuss the day's events.

Flame hesitated a moment, then took his hand. "Rafael, I—"

"I know you do not want to make love. I can wait until after the baby is born, but I will share your bed, Flame. I will be happy just to hold you in my arms for tonight. Now come along."

Flame smiled shyly. He had always loved her—and better still he trusted her, believed in her word. She wanted to be with him still, wanted his strength, needed his affection . . . but did she truly love him? "My marriage is over, Rafael. Nothing we can do now will equal the crimes I've committed in Joaquin's imagination. I would love to have your arms around me." Flame relaxed against him and he began to kiss her, gently at first but with growing passion. His kiss was so pleasant, warm and sensuous, she knew then how close they'd come to becoming lovers on her birthday. Had she but kissed him once all would have been lost.

Rafael waited until Flame had gotten into her bed before he came into her room and doused the lamp. He

449

undressed slowly, then got into bed next to her. "Put your head on my shoulder, my love."

Flame did as he asked, but was surprised to find his chest bare. His warm shoulder made a comfortable pillow and she snuggled against him. It had been so long since she had felt so wanted, so dearly loved. The tears began to roll down her cheeks wetting Rafael's smooth bronze skin and he hugged her more tightly.

"I know, querida, I know. It is all right to cry, I do not mind." Rafael held her tenderly and kissed her forehead, then her eyelashes before his mouth found hers. His kiss was light, barely brushing her lips before he drew away but he did not release her. She caressed him shyly, running her fingertips through the fine mat of hair which covered his chest.

Rafael had not kissed Flame since he'd told her goodbye the day after Joaquin's party nearly two years before and he was overwhelmed by the nearness of her now. But he was a man who never lost control of his emotions the way Joaquin did, he was first and always a rational being and took Flame's hand in his and brought it to his lips. "My dearest, I will not be content to just hold you if you do not stop that." He wound his fingers in her thick curls to force her head back down on his shoulder as he spoke. "Just go to sleep, Flame, I want to be with you like this, nothing more."

Flame nestled beside him, complying readily with his request. "I feel so safe with you, Rafael, you are such a wonderful friend, so dear and sweet." She yawned sleepily as she closed her eyes, more tired than she had thought possible and eager for rest.

"I am not in the least bit sweet, Flame." Rafael kissed the top of her head lightly, as if he were bidding a child good night, and closing his eyes was sound asleep before she was.

It was late morning when Flame opened her eyes to

find Rafael sitting up in bed beside her, his smile a rakish grin as he looked down at her. His expression was such a playful one; she thought instantly how very much he resembled Joaquin, how very good looking he was in his own way, almost as handsome as her husband when he smiled. She sat up slowly and leaned forward to hug her knees. "Tell me the truth, Rafael, for you are an attorney and would certainly know. We have spent the night in the same bed . . . is that adultery, or not?"

Rafael could not help but laugh: that Flame was still so innocent a creature struck him as being highly amusing, but he could see she was serious and tried to respond in a like fashion. "No, my dear, the law is quite specific, there is only one act which constitutes adultery and no matter where we choose to sleep you are still a faithful wife. We are no more than friends, close, affectionate companions, but we are not lovers." Rafael's gaze softened as he continued. "At least we are not as yet."

Flame stared at her friend for a long moment and then persisted in her inquiries: "Am I not your mistress then?"

Rafael drew Flame into his arms and gave her a warm hug. "I would never call you that, Flame, for I love you far too dearly to want you for anything other than my wife. Some might call you my mistress, but until your baby is born our relationship will not be that intimate so the term mistress would be an inappropriate one."

Flame laced her fingers in Rafael's as she relaxed against his shoulder. "We are closer than lovers, dear friend, and if people want to refer to me as your mistress I will not be ashamed."

Rafael was touched by the fragile beauty's sweet devotion. "No one will speak to you so rudely, Flame, I

451

will see to that." As he leaned down to give her cheek a light kiss the growth of his beard tickled her tender skin and when she began to giggle he laughed too.

"I love your laugh, Rafael. You do not laugh often enough, and it is such a pleasant sound."

Her curiosity satisfied for the moment Flame went on to a more pressing problem. "Whatever am I going to do, Rafael? If I hadn't built this house where would I be today?"

"On your way to San Francisco with me. You took Joaquin's carriage so we at least had adequate transportation."

Flame jabbed her friend playfully in the ribs. "Can't you be serious for a minute?"

"I thought you just told me I didn't laugh enough? Can I never please you?" Rafael continued to grin at her. His smile was so charming, and so unlike him; he had relaxed completely with her, leaving his serious side behind sometime during the night when she had slept so soundly in his arms.

"Yes, I know what I said, but please, what shall I do?"

"It is your choice. What do you really want to do? I think you know in your own heart what is best for you. Do you have the courage to face that desire and see it through? I think Joaquin will regret his anger at finding you pregnant and realize the baby is his. He may do it soon, Flame. I think he will come for you this week, be prepared for him to arrive with an apology."

"You actually think that he might, after calling me 'an adulterous bitch,' you think he'll just show up here to take me home as if nothing had happened? I can't believe that. He'll never come for me but I'll wait until after the baby is born to divorce him."

"I will stand with you no matter what you decide, Flame. You know I adore you, I want you to marry me

452

as soon as you are free. I want you to understand that now. Don't try and divorce Joaquin just to teach him a lesson. If you divorce him you will marry me the hour your divorce is final.'' Rafael paused for a moment, he hadn't meant to be so stern with her but he wanted to be very certain she understood his terms. ''I would not be too difficult to love, would I?''

''No, my friend, it would be so easy for me to fall in love with you, but please don't ask that of me yet. I don't even want to hear the word. I meant what I said to you yesterday, I am through with love and all its pain. But I want to be with you, to stay with you . . . is that not enough for now?''

''Yes, I will be content to have you by my side whether or not you ever say the words, Flame. Just remember Joaquin already thinks he knows what has happened between us, but you and I know the truth and we owe him no apologies.''

Flame slipped her arm around Rafael's waist, grateful for his wise compassion. She rested quietly while his fingers combed through her tangled curls, slowly separating the strands into bright ribbons of gold. ''Rafael, your friendship has always been such a comfort to me, I do not feel in the least bit ashamed to be here with you now. I hope you don't feel guilty.''

Rafael's handsome features hardened into a grim mask, his disgust plain. ''It is only Joaquin who should be ashamed. He is a great fool, an idiot who does not deserve the love of a woman so fine as you.''

Flame shuddered, as though a cool wind had suddenly filled the bedroom. ''Please, let us talk of anything but him. I can not bear to think of him, my marriage never really existed and now it's over and I never want to see Joaquin Villarreal ever again for as long as I live.'' Yet as she lay relaxed in Rafael's warm embrace the face that filled her mind was her hus-

453

band's, his enchanting smile a taunting reminder of the love she knew she would never forget. Not if she lived a thousand years would she ever forget Joaquin and how dearly she had loved him, for in her heart she knew she loved him still and always would.

Maria shook her head sadly as Rafael left the house. What could Joaquin expect—he'd forced his beautiful young wife to leave his home with a man who adored her. Poor child, her life had not been good with him yet the man was too blind to see the obvious. He didn't understand how cruelly he had treated her. It was clear Flame wanted only her husband's love, so why was he always so unwilling to give it?

Flame was seated in the parlor reading a book of poetry when Maria came rushing into the room. She turned to look over her shoulder and satisfied she had not been followed spoke in a hushed tone. "Señora, your husband is here, Joaquin is here."

Flame glanced up at her housekeeper's anxious expression and smiled wistfully. "Please show him in, Maria." So Rafael had been right, Joaquin had come for her after all and it had taken him only two days to do it. For some reason that thought failed to fill her with either happiness or dread; she felt only a numbing chill. Noticing the worried woman had not moved she hastened to reassure her: "I'm certain Joaquin will behave as a gentleman should, Maria. I'm not afraid to see him. Please ask him to come in now."

Joaquin hesitated as he came through the doorway. He glanced around the room quickly, a puzzled expression creasing his brow. "Rafael is not with you?"

Flame closed her book and laid it aside. "No, he has gone into town. Did you wish to speak with him?"

"No, I wanted only to see you. May I please sit down?"

"Of course." Flame watched the indecision in Joaquin's dark eyes. There were several chairs, and the space next to her on the small sofa; finally he walked over and sat down by her side. He seemed very ill at ease, for a man so confident as he had always been that discomfort was surprising to her. But there was something else too: his eyes were filled with such sadness she reached out to touch his sleeve. "Joaquin, what is it, why have you come?"

"For you. I want you to come home with me, you and Joaquin. I have missed you both terribly these last few months. I was a fool to have left you the way I did, with no explanation and no good-bye." He stopped long enough to take a breath and then plunged on as if he couldn't get the words out fast enough. "What I want to say is that I know everything was really my fault, however it happened, it was my fault. You are an affectionate, loving woman and I never should have left you alone for so long. I know Rafael has always loved you but I don't care whose baby you're carrying . . . I know that the child is yours and I will love him because of that. You're all that's truly important to me, Flame. Please come home with me now and I will accept your child as my own, no one will ever know otherwise, and we need never speak of this again."

Flame's eyes filled with tears as she gazed sadly at her husband. She loved him so very much but he still didn't trust her and she couldn't bear that pain. She reached over and touched the wound which ran across his cheek. "I didn't mean to strike your face, Joaquin, you are so handsome and I never meant to slash your face." She bit her lip then to hold back her tears. Telling him good-bye was going to be the most difficult thing she'd ever done and she scarcely believed she had the strength to do it.

"Flame? Will you come home with me?" Joaquin's

intense gaze searched her face anxiously hoping for acceptance. Her tears always brought him such anguish and he reached out to wipe them away with his fingertips.

"No, I can't go home with you, Joaquin, but that was a wonderful thought. That you would love my child touches me more than you will ever know, but we should never have married when we did and I should not have come back to you last summer. We have caused each other too much pain, far too much, and so few hours of happiness." Flame fought back her tears as she continued. "You don't know me at all and perhaps I've never really known you, you've never let me be your wife as I have longed to be. You always shut me out when I wanted us to be so close."

Joaquin took her hands tenderly in his. "Oh Flame, you have always been my wife, I love you so."

"What value is your love, Joaquin, when you do not understand mine? That you do not trust my devotion breaks my heart, I love you and always will, but I cannot be your wife when you have no faith in me. My child is yours, Joaquin, he will be born soon and then perhaps you will have the proof you seem to continually need to convince you of my faithfulness, but it will be too late. I can't be your wife any longer, Joaquin. I want a divorce so I may marry Rafael."

"Can you tell me that you love him, Flame, love him as dearly as you love me?" Joaquin pressed her for an answer, certain she would see the error in her reasoning.

"Rafael gives me something far better than love, Joaquin, he gives me trust and honest affection. He does not think me unattractive, that I am too slender or have been so long ill matters not at all to him. He loves me, Joaquin, and that is enough for me now. In time I will love him, I know I will."

Flame's words stunned Joaquin, cut him so deeply he cried out in anguish: "No, I'll never give you a divorce. Why have you ever thought I did not find you beautiful?" But he knew why, he had been so clumsy with her, so stupid not to have explained the doctor's warning when the man gave it. Now he couldn't, it would only frighten her and he didn't want that. He nearly strangled on his frustration, but there was no way he could make excuses for any of his behavior now.

Flame looked down at her hand which still lay in his, then she began to remove her wedding ring. "I want you to keep your mother's ring, Joaquin. I pray you will find the woman who can give you the love you need, a woman you can trust for the rest of your life." She placed the gold band in his palm and closed his fingers over it.

Joaquin could no longer contain the bitter anger which filled his throat and shouted angrily as he got to his feet. "I will never give you a divorce, Flame, you will be my wife until the day you die."

"Why? What is it, Joaquin, your pride perhaps? I will file for a divorce as soon as our child is born, you won't be able to stop me."

"The hell I won't! You'll never be able to divorce me, you've no grounds!"

"I think desertion will do for a start. As you said yourself, Joaquin, you left me alone for six months with no good-bye."

Joaquin was furious with himself but turned his rage on her again—that she would not accept his generous offer to acknowledge her child appalled him, that she would accuse him of desertion was outrageous. "Don't try it, Flame, don't even try it."

"There is also the matter of Maria Elena. She is still living quite openly in your home is she not?"

"Don't drag her name into this, Flame, she is no

457

more than a cousin to me, a friend."

"I'm sure she means as much to you as Rafael has always meant to me then." As Flame looked up at him she grew frightened . . . how had she ever been so young as to think making Joaquin Villarreal angry was amusing? That spring was long past and so was any hope for their marriage. "I will ask for a divorce, as soon as our baby is born, I will do it."

"With Rafael serving as your attorney, no doubt?" He yelled at her then, so loudly Maria came running from the kitchen fearful her mistress was being abused.

Flame shook her head and the older woman left the room as quickly as she had entered, too embarrassed to witness any more of their bitter feud.

"Since he handles your legal affairs I think he would be an inappropriate choice for my attorney, Joaquin." She was growing more calm by the minute for she knew he would never hit her, she knew that for certain and she could respond to his insults as long as he wished to make them.

"He's no longer my attorney, and he will never be anyone else's either if you insist upon asking for a divorce."

"Are you threatening his life again?" Flame was too shocked by his words to fear for her own safety.

"Why do you always rush to protect him, Flame? Tell me again he's not the father of your child, go ahead and tell me what a fine, noble friend he is, I love to hear you tell it!"

"With God as my witness, Joaquin, I wish this were Rafael's child, it should be his because he has loved me far more than you ever have. Now I think you better leave my house, our discussion is finished."

"Oh not it's not! We have not even begun to talk yet, Flame I'll go home now but you will be hearing from me again soon. If that child is born next month it will be

458

a miracle and I want to be here to witness it. Send someone for me the minute you go into labor and I want Dr. Wainwright here too, you understand, you send for the doctor and me!'' Joaquin turned on his heel and strode from the house without once looking back.

Flame wanted to scream to Joaquin, to make him come back, to make him understand what his doubts had done to her but it was too late, she was Rafael's woman now and no longer his.

Not five minutes passed before Rafael came into the room and sat down beside Flame. He took her trembling hands and brought them to his lips. ''Was I seeing things or was that Joaquin who just rode out of here as if the devil himself were pursuing him?''

Flame could no longer stifle her tears, she didn't even try. ''You were right, he came for me just as you said he would but he still doesn't believe me. He wants me back but he thinks this is your child, Rafael, he still believes that.'' Flame put her head in her hands and sobbed. ''He will forgive me for having your child but swears he'll never give me a divorce, never.''

Rafael rose slowly to his feet and walked to the window. He stood looking out across the horizon until Flame had at last regained her composure then he addressed her in the serious tone she recognized so well. ''I have had enough of this country living, Flame, it is ridiculous for us to remain here any longer. I think we can make Joaquin change his mind about a divorce but we can't do it here where we have no leverage to use against him. Have Maria help you pack. If Joaquin needs some inducement to give you your freedom then we will damn well give it to him!''

''Where are we going?'' Flame brushed away the last of her tears as she tried to imagine what Rafael had in mind.

"To San Francisco. Do you have dresses you can wear for the theatre, parties? If not I will have some made for you as soon as we arrive."

"Maria brought nearly all my clothes here, and I do have several gowns which fit but they are all grey satin. The last time I was pregnant I was a widow, or at least that's what everyone thought. They still fit me, but surely you don't plan to escort me around town!"

"I most certainly do, Flame, you have nothing of which to be ashamed, and I don't either. People might just as well get used to seeing us together now as later. But we must leave in the morning and I want Maria and the boy to remain here. You will have no time for him in the city and he would have no place to play at my house."

"Oh please, Rafael, I want to take Joaquin with me, please let me take my little boy with me."

"No, he stays here. Do not argue with me, Flame, you are mine now, remember, and you will do as I say." The determined look in his eye warned her not to protest, but she was not at all pleased by his decision.

"May I return home before the baby is born? I want the child to be born here—will you allow that at least?"

Rafael chuckled at her insolent remark. She hadn't argued but she had told him what she thought of him just the same. "Of course, a week or two should be enough time to embarrass Joaquin quite thoroughly. I will bring you home then. I realize we are cutting things very close, but I will do my best to have you back here before your baby comes."

"Is it so important to you to get even with Joaquin? To drag my husband's name through the dirt, is that your intention? It is my name too, Rafael."

"Not any more it isn't. Use your own name again, or mine if you prefer, but you are no longer a Villar-real, you are no longer his wife and I want him to get

460

that message quickly. He started this, Flame, not us, but I will damn well finish it.''

"He has refused to give me a divorce, he just refuses.''

"He won't refuse after the scandal I'll give him, Flame. Now go and tell Maria we are leaving in the morning.''

Rafael was careful not to tire Flame on their journey to San Francisco but once they reached his home she had no time to rest. He had carefully planned exactly where he wanted to take her and when they would go, whom he wished her to meet and precisely what she would say. Wherever they appeared he watched the curiosity sparkle in his friends' eyes but he gave no explanation of his relationship with the stunning young woman to anyone. He was confident that if he never left Flame's side the speculation about them would lead to gossip of the most scandalous sort and to his great satisfaction it soon did.

Flame had never been so tired as she was after spending four days in San Francisco. She had seen every inch of the city and more disapproving faces than she could count. Even Rafael's housekeeper barely kept a civil tongue when she spoke to her. That Rafael would keep her in his home obviously appalled her; that she was pregnant and the wife of his best friend seemed to disgust her completely.

Rafael had already left the house for his office when Mrs. MacLean came into his bedroom to bring Flame her tea. She opened the curtains to let in the warm spring sunshine and began to pick up the clothes which were strewn about the floor. She did not even wish Flame a good morning, she merely moved about her chores as if the room were unoccupied.

Flame sat in the large four-poster bed and sipped her tea. It was very good, spicy and sweet, its warmth very

461

soothing, and she felt like staying in bed all day. "Mrs. MacLean, what time will Rafael be coming home, did he say?"

"Mr. Ramirez will be out until this evening, Mrs. Villarreal." She emphasized the surname as if the disapproval in her facial expression weren't enough.

"There's no reason for you to be so disaggreeable with me, Mrs. MacLean. I know exactly what I'm doing and I don't care what you think of me."

The hostile woman paused at the door. "That is more than obvious, Mrs. Villarreal, or you would not be here. Your husband has been a guest here many times. I hope he does not learn of this disgrace and come here now."

"I have no husband. Now please go—tend to your duties and do not disturb me again until I call for you."

"As you wish, Mrs. Villarreal."

Flame finished her tea, placed the delicate china cup on the nightstand then lay back down among the pillows and stretched out before drawing the soft woolen blanket up to her chin. While she had been busy during the day, Rafael kept her even more busy going out in the evenings . . . and then there were the nights when they were alone together. Flame closed her eyes and hugged her pillow. Rafael never tired of holding her tenderly in his arms until she fell asleep, yet he demanded nothing from her but the joy of her company. Why was she still so wretchedly unhappy? Why couldn't she love him as she loved Joaquin? Why was her heart still filled with affection for a man who had never truly loved her? Was it only a cruel twist of fate that she had recalled his face so fondly and mistaken that for love? If only she not remembered him so well she might have fallen in love with Rafael instead, for he had always been kind to her when Joaquin never had.

She brushed away her tears. She knew what everyone thought of her, she could see the accusations in their eyes and yet she was no 'adulterous bitch' in spite of Joaquin's dreadful suspicions. What was the name for an unfaithful husband? She tried to recall his exact words . . . Maria Elena was only a cousin, a friend, nothing more? Could that possibly be true? Could he have been faithful to her all the months they were apart only to come home and believe the worst of her? The baby would be born soon and then she would have to give herself to Rafael, he would expect her to make love to him in any way he chose and she could not refuse him. It was too late to go back, to stop the drama which continued to unfold, growing more complex each day without her consent. She had now become Rafael's woman, and he understood her far better than Joaquin ever had, better than he ever would now. When she could win a divorce Rafael would insist she marry him, that very day, and she could give him no answer except yes.

Flame struggled to clear her mind, to organize her thoughts, but she could not. She was right back in the middle of the same problem which had plagued her almost from the day she'd arrived in California. She was in love with Joaquin and always would be, but she would spend the rest of her life as Rafael's wife. She could not refuse to marry him after all he had done for her, after all the attention he had lavished upon her when he knew full well she still loved Joaquin.

There was no way out for her, Flame knew that. Her life was not at all what she had hoped it would be, but it was time for her to grow up, to face life as it was, not as she wished it to be. Her features hardened into a determined mask as she lay in Rafael's comfortable bed and tried to make some coherent plans for the future. Wasn't that what Joaquin had always wanted to discuss, her future? She wiped her eyes again. She had no future without Joaquin and she wanted none either. Wouldn't Rafael soon grow bitter if she didn't come to love him as dearly as he loved her? Then he would be as miserable as she was. Joaquin could hardly be content now either. Their lives were so intertwined that their ties would never be severed, and yet they had to be parted somehow. Soon there would be another child to add to the problem, there would be five of them then, five people whose lives were ruined, and why? Flame began to sob in earnest. She had cried more tears than she had thought possible and still the pain persisted. She just didn't want to live without Joaquin and yet nothing was worth the pain of living as his wife when he didn't trust her, did not accept her love as eagerly as she offered it.

A few minutes later when Mrs. MacLean walked down the hall she heard Flame crying pathetically and stopped to listen. Was it possible the girl had some conscience after all? She shook her head and walked on. Rafael was a fool to bring that woman into his home. She was beautiful, but she would bring only trouble, she just knew it, the Villarreal woman would bring only grief and lots of it.

When he returned home late that afternoon, Rafael found Flame still sound asleep in his bed. He leaned down to kiss her flushed cheek then stretched out across the foot of the massive bed. He rubbed his hand over his eyes and sighed. He felt as though he hadn't slept in days. "Joaquin has taken the bait, Flame, he has filed for the divorce himself. He sent the papers to my office this afternoon."

"Is that what you wanted, for him to divorce me?" Flame sat up and pushed her long golden hair away from her face as she came fully awake.

"No, I wanted him to agree to letting you file, not

this mess. I apparently pushed him too far, he must have come up to San Francisco yesterday and gone straight to an attorney.''

"Well then, what did he say? Is he charging adultery or what? What is he asking?''

"He's not asking, he's demanding. He wants custody of Joaquin and the child you're carrying also.''

Flame was too stunned to cry as she fought back her anger. "But that's absurd! Why would he want a child he insists isn't his?''

Rafael considered her question for a moment, then asked thoughtfully, "Flame, do you have any idea who Joaquin really is? I know you've only lived on his ranch, never seen too much of his other business interests. He is an incredibly powerful man, as you well know he has a violent temper and more pride than three men could possibly use. He wants to hurt us as badly as he can. I took a risk in bringing you here, but even knowing him as I do I didn't expect Joaquin to be this vicious.''

Flame moved across the bed and lay her head upon Rafael's shoulder. He put his arms around her and drew her close to his heart. "Why would he want to hurt me when all I've ever given him is love?''

"Who knows? I can't read his mind, but I do not want to see this divorce action come to court as it stands, not like this, Flame.''

"How can we stop it? If he wants to hurt me, to take my children from me—and you say he's powerful enough to do it—how can we stop him?''

Rafael was silent, brooding over the possibilities. "Other than murder I can think of no way.''

Flame sat up, her eyes filled with horror. "No! Oh Rafael, don't even jest about that! I would never want to see Joaquin come to any harm.''

"Nor would I. I have always loved him as though he

465

were my brother, and he has always felt the same about me until now."

"Until I came between you, you mean."

"How can any of this be your fault, Flame?"

"If only I'd told Joaquin that I suspected I was pregnant, he might not have gone to Mexico. Or if he had, he would at least have known the truth before he left and none of this would have happened."

"Until the next time something happened to make him distrust you."

Flame shook her head. "No, please don't say that, that's cruel."

"It's true, Joaquin does not trust women, he never has. It has nothing to do with you, Flame, he has been that way for as long as I can remember. Perhaps because of his mother."

"His mother? But she died so long ago, Rafael."

"She is not dead, Flame. I saw her myself only yesterday."

"What? How could that be? He told me she had died when he was a child. That's how he came to have her ring." Flame looked down at her hand, startled to see the gold band missing.

"I only heard the gossip when I was a child. God only knows what the truth is, but Joaquin believes she left his father for another man. I don't think Joaquin ever recovered from that loss—to have been abandoned with no remorse. The woman has never even contacted him in all these years although she is married to a prominent man and has always had the resources to do so."

"And you know her?" Flame could scarcely believe any of Rafael's fantastic revelation was true.

"No, not really, I know her by sight is all. We do not travel in the same circles, but I did see her pass by in her carriage yesterday as I left my office. It is a public

466

street and I have no say as to who may use it.''

Flame felt weak. Why hadn't Joaquin ever told her that story? If only she'd known what had happened things might have been so different. She would have been prepared for his doubts and been able to reassure him what had happened to his parents' marriage would never happen to theirs. Now it was too late, everything had been ruined and she'd not even known why. She pushed her regret aside and continued to seek Rafael's advice with her current problem. ''Whom can I hire to represent me, Rafael? I will have to fight him in court, there must be someone who would be willing to present my side in the divorce.''

''Since he has named me in the divorce action I can not take your case, our case. How would you pay an attorney, Flame? Did Joaquin ever give you any money?''

''No, he never had reason to, we had everything at the ranch. I didn't need money, never even thought of it. I never shopped in town nor wanted to.''

''Well, how would you pay an attorney then, can you think of some way?''

''I still have the money I saved from the salary I earned from Seth, it isn't much but I could sell the cattle on my land couldn't I? They would bring a good price.''

''They are not your cattle to sell, Flame. Everything there belongs to Joaquin.''

''How can that be? It was my father's ranch, isn't it mine now? Ours?''

''Yes, the land is yours, but the cattle belong to your husband. The stock he has grazing there all have the Villarreal brand, not your father's. His stock was all sold off that spring before you arrived. The horses too, he kept the best, but sold all the rest. When you were married to him, didn't he ever explain any of this to you?''

"No, I never asked about any of that, I didn't even think of it, he just seemed so willing to handle all my problems for me when he was my guardian, I didn't realize I had nothing.''

"You have considerable wealth, Flame, but it is in his hands now and if the divorce goes as he wishes that's where your money will stay.''

Something in his words warned her and she asked hesitantly. "He wants the ranch too doesn't he, my house and everything?''

"Yes, he's asked for your ranch as part of the damages in the suit.''

Flame lay her head back against his shoulder. "I'm surprised he didn't evict me then.''

"He will. You are to leave those premises within a month of the birth of your child.''

"He'd give me a whole month to recover my health? How thoughtful of him.'' Flame was far more than hurt, she was furious. How could the man treat her so meanly? "Rafael, he said something to me, I can't remember exactly what it was, but he threatened you, said you'd not work for anyone as an attorney ever again. Has he done something to hurt you?''

"Yes, of course, I have not escaped his revenge. We were partners in several business ventures. I was a very minor partner but a partner nevertheless. Joaquin has simply withdrawn his support from any project in which I had invested.''

Flame was confused. "What does that do?''

"I cannot fund them alone. I have lost considerable money in the last week—a mere trifle to Joaquin, but a fortune to me.''

"All because of me.'' A wistful smile graced her lips as she looked up at him. Rafael was very handsome, even when he looked dead-tired. He was fine and good, and she would try and love him as much as she could, but she wouldn't let Joaquin ruin his livelihood and his health, not if she could do anything to stop it. "It looks as though I have no real choice then, Rafael. I will have to go to Joaquin and beg him to take me back, 'confess' to whatever fantasies he has fabricated now. It is the only way, I won't let him destroy you."

Rafael chuckled at that solution. "That would be one kind of revenge wouldn't it? For Joaquin to think he was raising my child when all the while it is his own. That is almost justice."

"Yes, it would be a kind of justice, wouldn't it? Oh, I'm sorry, but I simply can't do it. I could never admit something I hadn't done. Maybe I have as much pride as Joaquin, but I won't lie to him. The one time I did everything was ruined because of it. Perhaps that is why he doesn't trust me still, because of that one small lie."

"What do you really want to do, Flame? I still have some money . . . I could get together all the cash I have readily available and we can leave California now. Go as far away as we can, we'll take the boy and Joaquin will never find us."

"Would you really do that for me, leave your beautiful home, everything you've worked so hard to own, leave it all behind for me?"

Rafael leaned down to kiss her lips softly. "Of course, if you will be my wife."

Flame shuddered despite the beauty of his offer. "I can't run away, Rafael, not again, it just made everything so much worse. I'll have to stay and face whatever tortures Joaquin tries to inflict, it's the only way. Besides, I couldn't travel now even if I wanted to. I can scarcely walk. I'm sure the baby will be born soon."

"Do you want me to take you back to your ranch tomorrow?" Rafael reached out to take one of her curls in his fingertips, toying absently with her pretty hair as they tried to decide what to do.

"No, not if Joaquin is here in San Francisco. He wants to be with me when the baby's born and I plan to see he's invited."

"You can't actually want him to be with you!"

"Oh but I do. I want more than anything for my husband to be with me when his child is born."

Rafael did not dismiss her request lightly; her determination was too clear. "Flame, let's be honest with one another for a moment longer. I know you still love Joaquin."

"I won't deny it, but I gave him back his ring and I no longer wish to be his wife."

"Unfortunately, it will not be so easy to divorce the man as that. I think after the baby comes if I go to him, perhaps I can make him understand how greatly he has wronged you. I know he has not been a good husband to you but he can still learn. He can change with your help, Flame."

Flame hadn't dare hope Rafael would be so generous. "When you love me yourself, you would try to achieve a reconciliation between Joaquin and me?"

Rafael took her small hand in his, tracing gentle circles on her palm as he spoke, "It is because I love you so much, Flame. I don't think you'll ever be truly happy with me, not when you still love him. We have no chance for a happy marriage unless you come to love me as dearly as I love you."

Flame shook her head. "You don't understand. I can take no more of Joaquin's love, Rafael, you need never go to him on my behalf. It is over, finished, and I am no longer his wife nor do I wish to be ever again. I am so very tired of the terrible mess I've made of my life. If I were to die when this baby is born I would only be glad."

"Flame, enough! You will not die!" Rafael looked down at her as if seeing her for the first time, and he grew frightened. She was still far too thin, much too frail, her creamy skin now transparent. If she were to simply let go, to give up, she could easily perish. He pulled her into his arms and held her tightly, kissing her tear-streaked cheeks as he pressed her close. "You need never go back, querida, never, not unless that is your choice. We will not speak of this again. After your child is born and you are strong again we will have plenty of time to make all our decisions." He withdrew a small box from his pocket and placed it in her hands. "Here, I bought you a present."

"A present for me?" Flame was delighted, she couldn't remember the last time she'd been so surprised. The velvet box contained a bracelet made of the most delicate of golden chains. Rafael fastened the clasp for her then leaned down to kiss her once again.

"Don't ever take that off, Flame, not ever. I want you to wear it always and remember how dearly I love you. You will live, Flame, you must, and you will always have a man who adores you." Rafael pulled her back into his arms, cradling her head gently upon his chest as she began to cry, weeping so softly she made no sound.

"Thank you, Rafael. You are sweet, you really are." Flame relaxed in his embrace, grateful for his tender compassion which again surrounded her with a loving peace. She knew how desperately he wanted her to love him but the words would not come to her lips. She knew in her heart, even if he did not, that all three of them would be better off if she did not survive her baby's birth. Joaquin would love the baby, she knew he would, just as he had promised, and maybe in time he would come to believe the child was his and recall the brief time they'd spent as husband and wife with fondness rather than regret. That was the only hope she had, that Joaquin would understand her love after she was gone, since she had failed so completely to bring happiness to his life while she was alive.

Twenty-Three

Flame turned slowly in front of the long mirror then smiled prettily at Rafael's reflection as his arms encircled her waist. "Thank you, this dress is so beautiful, but my condition is obvious no matter how I stand. Will I be able to remain seated the entire evening? I certainly won't be able to dance."

"You may do whatever you like, Flame, but we will be there. I don't want Joaquin to believe for an instant that we are frightened by his absurd threats."

Flame wheeled impulsively to face the handsome man. "You don't think he'll be there tonight, do you? I won't go if he'll be there, I refuse!"

"We are leaving now. Do not concern yourself with the other guests, they are of no consequence to our purpose." Rafael adjusted her velvet cape upon her shoulders, tied it securely in a pretty bow at her throat and bent down to kiss her lightly. He had taught her not to argue with him. Unlike Joaquin he did not get angry with her independence, he merely listened calmly to her objections then insisted she do things his way. He smiled to himself as he realized he had again bent her will to his as her husband had never learned to do. He gestured toward the mirror. "We are a striking couple, don't you agree?"

Flame's eyes again met his in the reflection and she had to smile. Rafael's lean build gave his evening clothes an elegance most men lacked and the pride which shone in his eyes could not be mistaken—no prince had ever looked more confident. Her yellow satin gown was exquisite, but she hoped her advanced pregnancy would not be as obvious to others as it was to her. She took her companion's arm, and still smiling hesitantly, was ready to depart.

As usual, Rafael seemed to know everyone at the party for Flame had been introduced so frequently she felt like a puppet as she again nodded in return to a friendly greeting. She had asked to be presented as Linda Lannier but she had overheard more than one person refer to her as 'that outrageous Señora Villar-real' so it appeared her reputation had continued to precede her. Their host, a jovial banker, had spoken to her only briefly but she had sensed his shock as clearly as she had perceived the other guests' disapproval. The gathering was a large one, for the financier lived in one of San Francisco's most magnificent mansions. The rooms were filled with furnishings brought from France and the grounds were as meticulously landscaped as any royal garden. As the evening progressed, the party crowd became increasingly boisterous. A few of the couples wandered out onto the terrace while most remained in the ballroom to dance to the music of the small orchestra which played a succession of enchanting melodies for their entertainment.

"This house is like a palace, Rafael," Flame whispered as she ignored the curious stares which met her at every turn. She followed Rafael's example and held her head high. He had told her so often they had no reason to be ashamed she had come to believe him.

"You think so? This man is not half so wealthy as your husband, Flame. In fact, Joaquin is one of the principal partners in the bank,"

"How could you have forgotten so swiftly that I no

474

longer have a husband?'' Flame tossed her bright curls as she spoke, making the word husband ring with the disdain it deserved.

Rafael chuckled at her defiant outburst. ''Would you like another glass of champagne? Perhaps that will improve your mood.''

''No, thank you, I would much prefer to go home. Haven't we given everyone a sufficient opportunity to stare at me by now?'' Flame smoothed the skirt of her satin dress nervously then crossed her ankles daintily to strike a more comfortable pose. She was the object of a great deal of the conversation that night and knew it. Rafael seemed as always to enjoy the sensation they caused; he was relaxed and smiled easily at his acquaintances. Far from being shunned they had no end of company, as curiosity apparently got the better of whatever moral outrage people felt at their presence. Flame was becoming weary of being a spectacle, however, and longed to go home.

''In a while, Flame. I will bring you another glass of champagne. You will be all right for a moment I trust.'' He turned abruptly and walked away without giving her an opportunity to object to being left alone in the hostile crowd.

Flame tried to appear calm and content but inwardly she was seething. It was difficult enough to be pregnant without having to be on public display. She cared little about the scandal they were causing, all she wanted was a divorce, and a swift one. Then she and Rafael wouldn't have to worry about stares at such elegant parties since they would no longer be invited. She stifled a yawn and glanced over the dance floor wishing they could have danced at least once that evening, for Rafael was a wonderful dancer and she had lost none of her capacity to enjoy beautiful music.

She covered her mouth with no real haste as she

again began to yawn but she was jolted wide awake in the next instant when she saw Joaquin standing on the opposite side of the opulently decorated room. He was staring at her with such open hatred she could not suppress a shudder and grew deathly pale. So he was there after all. She wondered if Rafael had known, brought her there that night to deliberately force another confrontation. She searched the crowd frantically for her escort but he had not returned from his errand and she could not ignore Joaquin's icy gaze as she had the other guests' inquisite stares. He fascinated her as he always had and she could not tear her eyes from his. The energy which flowed between them had an intensity which left her weak and she was filled with sadness at the thought Joaquin had never brought her to San Francisco himself to show her off in front of his friends, had never introduced her to anyone with the pride which filled Rafael's voice when he spoke her name. As she looked at her husband now her expression was soft, surprisingly sweet, as if the pain which threatened to wrench her heart in two were no more than a slight twinge.

Joaquin held Flame's cool gaze locked in his for a long moment, then as quickly as he had captured her eye he looked away as if she no longer interested him and escorted a tall, slender blonde onto the dance floor. If his wife's presence at the gathering embarrassed him he gave no sign of it as he waltzed, easily charming the woman in his arms with his rakish grin and amusing conversation.

Flame could not bear to watch them dance. Joaquin was more than merely handsome; his expertly tailored tuxedo emphasized his height and muscular build and the fair-haired woman in his arms was lovely. Had he found another love so quickly? Flame wiped away the tears which filled her eyes, then slowly rose to her feet, moving unnoticed through the French doors which led to the gardens. She held her skirt above her feet and walked out among the roses. The night was chilly, much too cold for her to be outdoors without her wrap but she could no longer remain in the same room with her husband. Being rejected so coldly was far worse than the angry confrontation she had feared and she could no longer hold back her tears. The garden was dark in contrast to the brilliantly illuminated house and Flame huddled in the shadows lest she be seen by others taking a stroll. Once outside she had no courage to return to the party to find Rafael. She wanted only to avoid Joaquin at all costs and shivered unhappily as she tried to decide what to do.

Flame failed to hear the man's footsteps as he crept up behind her. He threw a heavy cape over her head, stifling her cries as he lifted her into his arms before she had time to struggle against him. He carried her swiftly from the darkened shrubbery to a waiting carriage where his companion grabbed the felon's squirming bundle and thrust it upon the floor of the already moving vehicle. The two men then kept Flame prisoner between their legs as they rode down the driveway and into the night. Flame fought for air but the thick folds of the cape were suffocating her. As she lost consciousness she knew the same terror which had filled her heart when she'd been kidnapped by Miguel and kept in that wretched cave where the freezing cold water of the sea had nearly drowned her at each high tide.

"What's the matter with the bitch?"

Flame gagged as the man dragged her to her feet, forcing her to walk ahead of him by twisting her arm cruelly behind her back. She could smell the sharp salt tang of the sea. She stumbled, sending her captors into another rage; they lifted her to her feet, swearing all the while, and when she cried out in pain she was struck across the face repeatedly by the smaller of the two men. She was too tired and hurt to go on and when she fainted again the men narrowly missed catching her before she hit the damp ground.

When next Flame awoke she was lying in a narrow bunk, her wrists tied securely to a ring at the side of the bed. Her head throbbed painfully and she felt as though she'd been beaten all over. Then she realized she wasn't alone. Voices were coming from the far side of the room, men's voices and angry ones.

"How was I to know who she was? Grab her and bring her here was all he said."

"If we've hurt her there will be the devil to pay, you stupid fool! Now let's get up on deck and leave her be!"

On deck? Flame felt the gentle rocking motion then. She tried to see the cabin more clearly but the light was too dim . . . whatever was she doing in a cabin on some ship? She began to cry and could not stop, she was too badly frightened to think, all she could do was weep until she fell into an exhausted sleep, the last image in her mind that of Joaquin's hostile stare.

The cold draft from the open door awoke her with a start in the next hour, the nightmare continuing as she saw the dim outline of a tall man silhouetted in the doorway. He slammed the door shut and locked it securely but did not light the lamp, leaving the small room still wrapped in gloom. Flame held her breath, praying that if he thought her asleep he'd leave her alone. She lay still and listened as he moved about the cabin, apparently not disoriented by the lack of light. The bunk sagged beneath his weight as he sat down beside her to remove his boots and she could not stifle the gasp of fright which came to lips.

"So you're not asleep after all, my pet. Why didn't you speak up? I don't enjoy undressing in the dark."

"Joaquin! Oh thank goodness you have come, please untie me quickly before those hateful men return, help me to escape them!"

Joaquin chuckled as he placed his hand on her hip. "I am not here to rescue you, Flame. Those were my men who brought you on board. Did you really think I would allow you to continue living openly with Rafael without suffering any consequences?"

"Did you tell your men to beat me too, is that your idea of revenge? I thought you were man enough to beat me yourself if you wanted it done!"

"What?" Joaquin leapt to his feet and returned when he'd lit the lamp. "Good God, what did they do to you?" Flame's pretty face was bruised where they had struck her, her glossy hair tangled, her new dress filthy from the muddy floor of the carriage and her wrists were cut and bleeding from the tightness of the coarse rope which bound her hands. Joaquin set the lamp down at his feet and began to untie her. "No, I did not tell them to treat you so badly, they will be sorry they did. I thought they knew how to treat a lady but obviously they do not."

Flame watched Joaquin's face closely as he cleaned her wrists. The scar where she'd struck his cheek with the whip was going to be with him for the rest of his life and she looked away quickly. It pained her to have hurt him so badly. Even after this awful thing he'd done to her, that she had left his face scarred for life was a great sorrow to her. "I can feel the ship moving. Where are you taking me—or did you simply plan to toss me overboard once we are clear of the harbor?"

"Don't tempt me. Now move over, this cabin has but one bunk and I plan to share it. You'll remember soon enough whose wife you are whether you're willing or not."

"You mean you kidnapped me just to rape me? Let

go of me, let me go!'' Flame tried to scratch his face but he grabbed her hands easily, forcing her back against the pillow as his lips crushed hers in a brutal kiss. Flame became hysterical; she screamed and cursed him, fighting him with all the strength she possessed, surprising him with the sheer terror in her response.

"Flame, damn it, be still, I won't hurt you." He was far too strong and held her down easily so she could no longer struggle so violently. "I only mean to teach you a lesson so there's no need for you to fight me when you know how easily I can win. Tell me, I'm really very curious: how does Rafael do it? I've never made love to a pregnant woman and it must take considerable agility to accomplish. I want you to enjoy this too . . . is there some particular way you prefer?"

"You make me sick! Take your hands off me, you coward! I would die before I'd let you touch me!"

"Oh really, you don't expect me to believe that do you?" Joaquin held her two hands in one of his while he loosened the bodice of her dress, then lowered his lips to her soft, smooth breasts, his mouth caressing her creamy skin tenderly in spite of his taunting words.

Flame tried to move away but Joaquin held her fast. When he moved his mouth up to hers she could not resist his gentle kiss but began to cry in hoarse racking sobs, "Rafael does not make love to me, Joaquin, he never has. He only holds me, kisses me, we have never made love as you and I have so it has never been adultery."

Joaquin leaned back and looked down at his wife's bruised and swollen face. Could what she said be true? "Never? I find that impossible to believe, Flame. If it was not Rafael, then who is the father of this babe?"

Flame turned her head away and continued to cry. She'd no longer fight him, she couldn't, she had no energy left. "Just kill me and get it over with, Joaquin, just kill me now.''

Joaquin got to his feet and moved away. ''Why would I ever wish to harm such a devoted wife, Flame? A wife who gives me such respect and admiration, such undying love. Why? Just because you chose to get pregnant by some other man and then live openly with another shouldn't upset me, should it? My God, what did you think would happen when I came home? Did you think I'd believe your outrageous lies without the slightest suspicion that child was not mine? Is that what you thought? You have been seen all over San Francisco this last week but whom did you think you fooled by calling yourself Linda Lannier? Everyone knows your name is Villarreal, Flame, everyone but you. Are you too ashamed of your behavior to use your husband's name?''

''I have no husband!'' Flame replied with a sudden burst of spirit. ''You have denied your own child so I will continue to deny you! You are not my husband, I have none!''

''That is not my child and you know it!'' Joaquin returned to sit on the side of the bunk and took Flame's shoulders in his hands. ''I want to hear you say your name, Flame. Tell me your last name, say it.''

As long as Flame could still speak she would fight him. ''My name is Lannier.''

''No, it is not. You are my wife, Flame, and you should at least know your own last name, now say it!''

Flame felt faint but her words were still audible. ''My name is Lannier.''

''Do you want me to strangle you, woman? Now say it!''

Flame could only whisper this time, he had hurt her too badly for her to say more. ''Lannier.''

Joaquin gave up in disgust, he released her and stood up once more. Huddled in his bunk Flame looked so small, he threw up his hands in despair. "What am I to do with you, Flame? You would not give me a moment's peace even if I should divorce you. You are too much a part of me to ever cast out. I mean to keep you, but you'll no longer disgrace my name. I'm taking you to Mexico, to a convent where you may have your child then make your choice. You may remain there with the sisters for the rest of your life, or you may come home and be my wife."

"And my baby?" Flame whispered again.

"The child will belong to me regardless of your decision. Your children will always belong to me and so will you, Señora Villarreal!"

"You would allow your wife to reside in a Mexican convent? Isn't that a bit unconventional even for you?" Flame rubbed her hand over her eyes in an attempt to see him more clearly but he had stepped out of the circle of light thrown by the lamp and his features were no more than a blur.

"No, not at all. You were simply too young when we married, not yet aware of your true vocation, but I will make the sacrifice of allowing you to live there and serve God."

"There is no such thing as a married nun!" Flame responded angrily.

"So, you will be the first, the order has been most gracious to accept my donations in your name. They will welcome you with open arms and see that you are looked after for the rest of your days. It will be your choice, Flame, the convent or me, but I will never again allow you to live with another man."

"You are offering a prison sentence either way and I have committed no crime!"

"You obviously need more time to consider the matter. I will trouble you no more. Your meals will be brought to you here. Only the two men who brought

482

you on board know that you are here. It would be pointless to try and escape, the door will be kept locked and no one would ever hear your screams if you were so foolish as to yell. I will escort you to the convent myself, but until then I will spare you my company. Now good night.''

Flame lay trembling on the hard bunk and tried to think . . . would it be possible to escape from a convent? Surely it would be, she could get away and go, but go where? Anywhere away from Joaquin—maybe the sisters would help her when they learned the truth of her situation. It would be difficult to hide in Mexico since her Spanish was so poor but surely she could get away somehow. She smiled to herself. When Joaquin sent her breakfast she'd refuse it—why should she eat? Death itself would be an escape, the ultimate escape.

Flame drifted on the edge of sleep but she could not get comfortable. When the pains began she scarcely noticed them; she shifted her weight and lay back down on the narrow bunk wondering how Joaquin managed to sleep on such a hard bed. She was nearly asleep when the pains in her back became more insistent, demanding to be noticed, too sharp to ignore, and she finally recognized them for what they were. She could not remember Joaquin's birth clearly; hysterical with fright she'd been unaware of anything that was happening to her other than the excruciating pain. She stood up and tried to cross the cabin but couldn't, she couldn't walk, let alone beat on the door for help. Joaquin had said no one would come, had he meant it? Someone would bring food, but would he come in time? Flame lay back down and gripped the edge of the bunk as the next contraction came. Each one was more piercing than the next and she had no hope anyone would come before morning. Dear God, would she have to have the baby all alone? She could think of no punishment more terrible than that, to have to give birth all alone. She didn't think she'd have the strength to do it and knew her baby would die before anyone heard its cry. Joaquin would come too late and his precious baby would be dead. The tears poured down her face as the pains grew more frequent and severe. She called her husband's name with a desperate sob: "Please come to me, Joaquin! Don't leave me now, please, Joaquin, please!"

Joaquin stood at the wheel as dawn approached and tried to make out the California coast line in the fog as they sailed along, smoothly gliding over the calm waters of the Pacific on their journey southward. He tried to keep his mind on the sea. He had taken command of the ship himself so no one would discover his destination but he felt uneasy, apprehensive although he knew the coastal route well. He could not shake the feeling of foreboding which threatened to overwhelm him, crushing in on him as the mist dampened his face and clothes. He was never afraid, never, and the emotion was totally unknown to him when it swept over him now. When he heard Flame call his name he turned quickly but found he was still alone. He was mystified: he'd heard her voice so clearly, he knew he had, she had spoken his voice with an urgent call, and suddenly he was seized with panic and hastily summoned the man on watch to take the wheel before he raced to his cabin. He fumbled with the key, unable to unlock the door as he tried to imagine what terrible thing could have happened to Flame.

Joaquin found his wife lying in his bunk. Her face was drenched with perspiration, she was curled in a ball with her knees drawn up to her chest, her eyes shut tightly, and she was moaning softly into a pillow that was wet from her tears.

Quickly Joaquin knelt down beside her. "Flame, Flame, can you hear me? It is the baby, Flame, is it?"

Flame opened her eyes but could barely see his face through the haze of agony that surrounded her. "Oh Joaquin, you've come at last. I've been praying for you to come and help me. I didn't think I could do it alone but I was so afraid you wouldn't come, that nobody would." She could not stop crying and continued to sob pathetically.

She had been praying for him? Was that how he had heard her voice so clearly, she had simply called out to him in her mind and he had heard her cry? "Flame, is it the baby?"

Flame nodded her head as she fought back the wave of pain which threatened to engulf her. "The baby will be born soon and I've been so frightened I'd be all alone."

Joaquin was horrified as all the dire warnings he'd heard came thundering in his ears. Why did women die in childbirth? He had no idea what the greatest hazard might be—was it their hearts, did they bleed to death— what was likely to kill Flame? He had to do something to help her, to save her, and it had to be done immediately although he had no idea where to begin. "This is all my fault, Flame. I should never have brought you on board. The men were too rough with you, I abused you myself and now the baby will be born too soon."

"No, it is due now, Joaquin, it is time, it is not early."

Joaquin had no desire to debate that point with her any longer. "Can you tell me what to do? How I may help you?" They had medical supplies on board for emergencies but nothing for delivering a child and he searched his mind frantically for what he would need— towels, blankets to keep Flame and the infant warm, scissors, string . . . what else?

Flame gripped his hand tightly. "I'll be Flame Villarreal until I die, Joaquin. You said I'd be your wife until I die.''

"My God, Flame, you won't die, not with me here to help you. I won't let you die. I should never have left you alone like this, I'm so sorry you've been alone but I'm here now and I won't let anything happen to you. Now, can you tell me what to do?''

"No, I can't even remember Joaquin's birth I was so badly frightened. I have no idea what to do.''

As Flame took his hand again the pressure she exerted on his fingers surprised him. She clung to him until the contraction had passed and then relaxed completely, her fingers going limp in his. "I don't even have a nightgown for you to wear, Flame, but we must take off your dress, let me do it.'' Joaquin struggled with the tiny buttons which secured the garment. "Why do you always wear clothes that are so damn difficult to remove, Flame?''

"I'm sorry, Joaquin.'' Her voice was so weak it worried him all the more. She was too frail, far to weak to stand the ordeal which lay ahead. Then he saw the bruises on her shoulders: the outline of his fingers was plain in the ugly purple marks on her silken skin. How could he have been such a stupid fool as to bring her on board a ship where there would be no way to get help for her? It had been lunacy for him to treat her so badly. He had meant to teach her to obey him, he'd had no idea this would happen, he'd not considered the child at all.

All the times he had so lovingly dressed her when she'd been stabbed came back to him so clearly, only nine months before, how dearly he had loved her then. He traced the line of the scar on her thigh. She'd always carry that ugly reminder of that ghastly night, but this child, had the child really been conceived during their love at that time also? He pushed his doubts from his mind, if she said it was true than it was the truth. This

486

baby was his and he had no idea how to deliver him. He'd seen animals give birth hundreds of time, surely human babies couldn't cause so much trouble when animals found birth so routine.

"Flame, try and relax. I know you're more frightened than anything else and you've no reason to be afraid with me here. This baby will be so much easier for you to have, second babies always are, it gets easier every time, I'm certain it does." Joaquin kept on talking to her, filling his voice with a confidence he scarcely felt. He rubbed her back gently and spoke in a soft, soothing voice until he could feel the tension drain from her. The contractions were coming at closer intervals but she could rest between them now without sobbing. He had had no idea having a baby would be so painful for his wife and it was all he could do not to cry with her. If only he hadn't left her alone in his cabin! If he'd stayed with her she wouldn't have become so frightened and he knew it was fear which was making her pain unbearable. Surely having a child shouldn't cause such agony. This was much too hard for her, and he felt so helpless knowing he had caused all her anguish. She was growing weaker with each contraction and he could feel her life slipping away, she could not stand to suffer much more and still survive.

Joaquin pushed Flame's damp curls away from her forehead and she reached for his hand. "Joaquin, if I die, please try and save the baby, please try. You have your knife—you could do it, you must."

Her words were too sad to bear and Joaquin could not accept them. "You will not die tonight, Flame. I have no intention of letting you die. Now stop worrying and try and push when the pain begins. You are strong enough to do this, I know you are. If you could turn a horse whip on me you can damn well have my child."

"Your child? You believe me now, when it's too

late?''

''Yes, I believe you, Flame, and I hope this baby's a girl, one who looks exactly like you. I would love to have a daughter who looks as sweet as you did when you were small. We can have more boys later if you want them.''

''Joaquin, please don't. I'm not your wife anymore, we'll never have another child together, not you and I. It's finished between us.'' The next pain tore through her so violently she could no longer suppress a cry, but she covered her mouth with her hands to stifle the piercing wail.

Joaquin held her shoulders tightly. ''Go ahead and scream if it helps, Flame, scream all you like.''

Flame felt herself falling as the pain washed over her. It didn't stop this time but continued on and on, but she'd never scream, not in front of him. She felt the warm rush of water and Joaquin's hands on her thighs but the pain kept pushing her down into its depths and she couldn't breathe, she was drowning with no way to escape the horrible pain. Joaquin's voice seemed to come from miles away, she could barely hear him as she fainted, but she understood his words clearly. He had his wish, the baby was a girl.

Joaquin stared down at the tiny infant in his hands. She was perfect, as beautiful as her mother in every way. He lay her down next to Flame before tying off the cord. The child's face puckered up as she cried, little cries hardly making a sound as she waved her tiny fists and feet. She was furious with him and Joaquin laughed with the relief of seeing his baby alive and well. ''You're mad at me already, aren't you, sweetheart. Come here, angel.'' He dried her off and wrapped her in a blanket but she continued to cry. Joaquin touched Flame's cheek but she didn't stir. That she had fainted was a blessing and he didn't want to wake her, not when she had earned her rest. He placed the baby at her side and wrapped her arm around the small bundle. As if by magic the baby lay still, blinking her eyes as she peered up at her father. Joaquin patted his daughter's head . . . her few wisps of hair were the brightest red and he swore her eyes were green. "If you're lucky, little girl, you'll be as lovely as your mother, but you'll never be more beautiful to me than you are tonight."

Once the baby was quiet Joaquin turned his attention back to Flame but he had no idea what to do for her, so he covered her to be certain she was warm and then left his cabin to go up on deck to change the ship's course. He would take Flame back to her own house where she would feel safe. They were close to the shore and it wouldn't take long. He would send for the doctor as soon as they dropped anchor in the bay near his ranch.

When he returned to his cabin he realized he had no clothes for his wife and in an open boat it would be cold and the journey through the surf treacherous. He would have to wrap her in blankets and hope that would do, but his hands were shaking—Flame was so pale and he had never expected her to bleed so profusely. Surely she shouldn't still be bleeding, but he had no idea how to stop it. He knelt down beside her and put his arms around her as he began to cry. He had tried his best to save her, God, he had tried but he simply didn't know what to do. He could see her in his mind so clearly, she was so alive in his memory, surely God would not take her from him now. He could do nothing now but pray and that he did as fervently as he had done before, he begged God to save his beautiful Flame one more time.

Joseph Wainwright shook his head in disbelief. "If any man could handle such an emergency I should have

489

known you could, Joaquin. I can understand why you were so frightened but Flame is fine, merely exhausted. You did the right thing by letting her sleep . . . but how did she happen to be aboard your ship? I thought the rumor was you planned to divorce her, or was that only gossip?''

''No, I'm sorry to admit I even considered it but it won't happen now. I was a fool to think I could ever let her go.'' Then his doubts returned, the same nagging questions which had plagued his mind during the last month. ''Doctor, the little girl is so tiny, but is she full term, not premature? Flame was shaken up rather badly—it was my fault. I think perhaps her labor began too early.''

''Premature? Why no, go in and look at her yourself. She's a very lively little thing, so alert and perfectly formed. Your wife is a very petite woman don't forget, she'll never have large babies, but as you know your son is a big, healthy child now. I understand he was small at birth but has certainly grown well. I was very concerned about Flame, I won't deny it. She was so ill less than a year ago . . . when was it she received that severe knife wound, I've forgotten.''

Joaquin shoved his hands into his pockets. ''It was nine months ago, almost to the day.''

''Well, that explains your daughter's size. Flame simply wasn't strong enough to carry a larger child. Now don't worry yourself any longer, they will both be fine.'' The doctor was embarrassed but forced himself to continue: ''I know you were not living here with your wife. Perhaps you would like to go home and rest yourself, when was it that you last slept?''

''I can't remember, but I want to stay here in case Flame needs me.''

''Joaquin, go on home and go to bed. I'll stay here for a while longer and Maria can care for Flame until you return. Although she has plenty to do with your son—she has her hands full with him.''

''Look, I'll take the boy home with me, that will help you all. I've more than enough help at my house to look after him.'' Joaquin was tired, he hadn't slept in two days and the prospect of lying down in his own bed was too inviting to ignore any longer.

''I don't know what to say about that. I'm not sure what Flame would want you to do.''

Joaquin wasn't sure either: she might be furious with him, but he'd take the chance. ''It will be fine with her. I'm sure she wants to have time for the baby. Joaquin's only fourteen months old, he'd be constantly under foot. I'll take him.'' Joaquin walked quietly into Flame's bedroom to kiss her good-bye before he left. She was still sleeping and looked so young, so very young, and when Joaquin leaned down to kiss her forehead he pushed all their problems from his mind. She had to see things his way now, she just had to. He patted their tiny baby and then left the room. He found his son and left quickly before either the doctor or Maria had time to realize that would never had been Flame's wish.

Flame stretched her arms as she awoke, languidly testing her cramped muscles as she opened her eyes. She recognized her own bedroom immediately and woke with a start. How had she gotten home, and when? Then it all came back to her and she called for Joaquin, her voice rousing Dr. Wainwright from his momentary afternoon nap.

''He's gone home for a little while, Flame. I sent him home to rest but he'll be back soon. I let him take the boy . . . I hope that's all right with you.''

''He took my little boy? Oh no, you didn't let him, please say you didn't! I want my little boy here with me!'' Flame was terrified—Joaquin was going to do it,

491

he'd take her children and send her to the convent where she could never see them again, dear God he was going to do it!

The kindly doctor grew alarmed. "Flame, he only meant to help you. He is so worried about you and the little girl. I assured him you were both fine. He was very concerned he'd caused the child to be born prematurely."

Rather than having a calming effect, his words broke her heart. "He didn't say that, did he? He didn't ask if she were premature?"

"He was only concerned because of her size, Flame, but I doubt he has seen many newborn infants. The question was a natural one, the little girl is petite but very healthy."

Flame shut her eyes but the tears still rolled down her cheeks. He hadn't believed her at all, he'd never trust her, no matter what he'd said. Deep down she knew if they were married a hundred years he'd never really believe their little girl was his.

The physician stared down at his patient with increasing concern. "Flame, what is the matter? Joaquin will be back soon, don't worry. He was so tired I convinced him to go home and rest but he'll return soon."

Flame shook her head. "No, don't let him in, I won't see him. Don't you understand, he's got my little boy and now he'll try and get my baby and I have no way to stop him." Flame cried on and on so pathetically the doctor sat down beside her and took her hands in his. When he turned them over the rope burns on her wrists were unmistakable.

"Good Lord, Flame, did Joaquin have you tied up? Is that what he did?"

Flame pulled her hands away as she cried out. "Yes, now do you believe me? He wants my children, don't let him in!"

"If you do not want to see him then I will tell him you are still sleeping and send him back home. Don't worry yourself anymore, just go back to sleep and I'll take care of everything."

"I can't sleep. Joaquin will come and take the baby."

"Flame, you must calm down and rest. you're still not strong, you'll make yourself ill, now just shut your eyes and go back to sleep." The doctor frowned as he paced the room. What in heaven's name had been going on between those two? It had obviously been a terrible mistake to send little Joaquin home with his father, but that couldn't be undone now. He crossed to the window and looked down the road but there was no sign of Joaquin returning.

Joaquin slipped on his coat as he left his room. All the way home his son had talked to him, the cheerful ramblings of a child learning more new words each day. He had been enthralled by the carriage and horses as well as his father, a man he did not recognize without help. Joaquin had slept longer than he'd wanted to and he was afraid he was going to be late getting back to Flame. He hoped with all his heart she hadn't meant what she'd said—that their marriage was over, finished. He couldn't accept that, not now when they had such a beautiful baby daughter.

As soon as Joaquin saw Dr. Wainwright's serious expression he knew something was wrong. "Doctor, my wife—"

The portly physician gestured toward a chair in the parlor. "Please sit down for just a minute. Your wife is sleeping quite soundly again."

"Did she awaken while I was gone? Did she ask for me?"

"Well, I don't know exactly how to explain what

happened. Flame did call your name, seemed to want to see you, but when I said you'd taken your son home with you she became hysterical. Is there some reason she'd believe you'd not return the child to her care?''

Joaquin slumped back in his chair, his disappointment obvious in his posture. "Yes, I've asked for custody of both children in the divorce suit but I'll not go through with it. I'd hoped the divorce would be the last thing on her mind. I'm sorry to see it isn't.''

"One other thing. I remarked that you were concerned about the baby's size, worrying that you might have caused the child to be born prematurely and—''

"Dear God, you didn't say that to her did you?'' Joaquin cried out in alarm.

"Well yes, but I was only trying to reassure your wife the babe is normal and healthy in every way.''

Joaquin drew in a deep breath and got to his feet. "Thank you for all your help, Dr. Wainwright. I'm sure we'll get along fine now, you may leave and let me know your fee and I'll see you're paid promptly.''

"I can't charge you any fee, Joaquin. You delivered the child yourself. I don't deserve any fee.'' The doctor rushed on quickly, the next part of his message too unpleasant to dwell upon for any great length. "I think maybe you better leave now too, Joaquin. Your wife insists she won't see you now. She's terrified you'll take her baby.''

"Her baby? The child is mine also, and Flame is my wife. I'll stay right here until she awakens and we can discuss this ourselves. Good-bye, doctor.''

Joseph shrugged helplessly. He'd not argue with Joaquin—the man could break him in two so easily nothing was worth provoking him. Still, he had to try. "Joaquin, be patient with her. She had a difficult time, didn't she? Don't expect her to be thinking all that clearly tonight. Give her a few days to rest . . . please

494

don't upset her.''

"I won't upset her, I just want to make her understand how much I love her, something which is always damn near impossible to do!''

"Joaquin, you're tired yourself, don't start any arguments you'll both regret. I'll stop by again tomorrow to check on Flame and the baby. You did a fine job delivering your daughter; you can be proud of yourself. What will you name her?''

"I hadn't thought of any names. I'll let Flame select one.'' Not only had he not thought of a name, he hadn't thought of the baby at all. The child had never seemed real to him, not until she'd lain in his hands. If only he hadn't left—Flame had wanted to see him, she had, only to be told what she interpreted as another denial of his parenthood and a threat to her son. Why did things never go right for them, not ever.

Joaquin closed the bedroom door softly and walked to Flame's bedside. The doctor had placed the baby in a cradle and the child was sleeping as peacefully as her mother. Joaquin wondered where Flame had gotten the cradle, it was old from the looks of it, then he bent down to touch the wood and saw the carving at the end. It was his cradle, one that had been in the family for generations. His grandfather had made it for his first son. Maria must have brought it over when he was away. He smiled as he touched the wood; it was worn smooth by countless gentle touches and he had no doubt the baby was his and she belonged in the cradle . . . it was part of her birthright.

Joaquin moved a chair close to the bed and tried to make himself comfortable. When Flame awoke this time he wanted her to find him at her side so he could tell her how much he loved her before the doubts could creep into her mind again. She was so lovely, and she looked so sweet as she slept. He leaned down to kiss her

495

and touched her cheek. How could he ever have thought he could send her away as he had threatened, send her so far away he'd never see her again? He could not bear to be away from her side now. How could he ever have imagined that he could have taken her to Mexico and left her there?

The sun had just begun to send golden streaks across the morning sky as Flame began to stir. Joaquin touched her shoulder tenderly. "I'm here, Flame." His voice woke her abruptly, bringing her eyes open wide as she stared up at him.

"What are you doing here?"

Though her harsh tone hurt him he ignored it. "I wanted to stay here with you, Flame. I'm sorry I wasn't here when you woke up yesterday afternoon."

"Why did you take my little boy? Couldn't you have waited? You know I have no way to fight you, none, but couldn't you have at least let me keep him a little while longer? I had no chance to tell him good-bye, and I love him so." Flame began to cry again with her tears running down her cheeks, dampening the pillow slip beneath her head.

"Flame, I'll not keep the boy from you. Don't worry another minute, you've not lost him. I want you to come home with me and be my wife again. Things will be so much better for us this time if you'll just let them be. It's all up to you."

Flame looked up at her husband. His dark eyes were so warm, they drew her into their depths, but the promise of his love was too painful to endure. "I'm not going home with you, Joaquin, not ever. This is my home now."

Joaquin reached for her hand and brought it to his lips. "Don't ruin all our lives, Flame, you'll ruin everything if you won't even try. Please, let's at least give our marriage another try."

Flame closed her eyes, unable to speak. She tried to remember what their life together had been. The pain and tears so far outweighed the joy she had no courage to place her heart in his hands again. She could take no more of his violent temper, his moods, his drive which took him away from her for months at a time—she could take no more of what he called love. It just wasn't worth the price she'd have to pay in pain.

"Joaquin, I love you with all my heart, truly I do, but I can't be your wife. Please let me go now, just let me go. Let me live here and you can see your children whenever you wish, but please don't make me take any more of your love. I can't bear any more of it."

Joaquin sat back in his chair too numb to respond. He couldn't lose her like this, not with her so fearful and hurt, not when he wanted so desperately to love her again. But he didn't understand the depth of her anguish, not in any way did he understand how badly his doubts had hurt her. "Flame, I know the little girl is mine. Is that your fear, that I'll not love her as I do my son?"

"Oh Joaquin, if only you had believed me when you first came home, if only you'd believed me then, just me, just believed my word because I love you so, but you didn't then and you still don't. You had to ask Dr. Wainwright, didn't you? Don't bother to deny it, because he told me you did."

Joaquin clenched his teeth and swore. "Damn it, Flame, how many times must I tell you I'm sorry? I am so sick of apologizing to you! Can't things ever be right between us? Just tell me what to do and I'll do it, I don't care what it is you want, I want you to be my wife and I'll do anything to keep you."

The sadness in Flame's eyes told him everything. "I only want to be free. I want a divorce."

Joaquin's frustration was more than he could bear.

Why wouldn't Flame accept him as he was, why? Maybe the doctor had been right: she was too tired, too weak to know what she wanted. He decided to change the subject: maybe if they spoke only of their new baby it would help her to see how much he cared. He leaned closer and took her hand again. "What name have you chosen for our daughter? Did you have one picked out?"

Flame's green eyes flashed as she looked up. She wanted only to hurt him as badly as he'd hurt her. "I thought maybe I'd call her Maria Elena."

Joaquin drew back, astonished by her bitter mood as much as her words. Then he began to get angry, really angry with her. She was so totally unreasonable he was incensed. "That's it, Flame, I won't take any more from you, you were a spoiled brat when I married you, but at sixteen what could I expect? Unfortunately, you're no better now, no more of an adult after almost two whole years of marriage and bearing two of my children. I know that I hurt you, really hurt you badly by accusing you of being unfaithful, I should have known better, it was just plain stupid of me, but I was just so shocked to find you eight months pregnant when you'd never even bothered to let me know you were expecting a child. Do you think I have no feelings? Didn't you know I'd come straight home, that I'd be happy to be a father again? Why did you ask Rafael to stay with you instead of summoning me? I came to the conclusion you'd hide your condition from me for only one reason. So I was wrong, dreadfully wrong, but I've begged you to forgive me, to come home and you won't even give me a chance."

Flame stared up at her husband. He was furious with her as usual, he was always mad, she thought sadly, but she couldn't think clearly with him so close. She wanted him still in spite of what she'd said. She'd always love him, but why did it have to hurt so much?

"Since you insist upon acting like a child I will treat you as one. You have one month to recover your strength, then I'm coming to take you home. You'll be my wife from now on, Flame. You've accused me of not trusting you, well it's obvious you don't trust me either. There's nothing between Maria Elena and me, nothing more than the regard one cousin would naturally have for another. I've never loved any woman but you, Flame, but you're not really a woman yet. You're still a child, no more able to think than your daughter. You don't even believe that I love you, do you? I've been with no others since the day you came to my home. I haven't even wanted anyone else, but that devotion means nothing to you, does it?"

Flame turned her face away from him, too hurt and ashamed to listen any longer, but Joaquin put his hands on her shoulders and made her turn back to face him.

"Don't try and leave me again, Flame. I'm posting three guards on this house and they'll stop you if you set foot out of the yard. In one month's time you'd better be ready to be my wife, and I think you know exactly what I want, Flame."

Flame shook her head. "Yes, you mean rape and I'll never go back to you!"

"Then I'll drag you home screaming if I have to but you'll be home with me in one month's time. I'll keep Joaquin with me too. You'll have enough to do with our baby—call her Maria Elena if you like, my cousin will be honored regardless of your motive. Don't hold any hopes that Rafael will come to your rescue either. He thinks you left the party that night with me willingly so he will never come down here to see you. He took a gamble taking you to San Francisco and he thinks he lost. It would be funny if it weren't so far from the truth. I'll give you this one last chance, Flame, and you better make the most of it. You're going to spend the rest of your life with me and it can be heaven or hell depending on what you want to make it!'' He slammed the door as he went out, too furious to stay a minute longer in her presence.

The sound of the door woke the sleeping infant who began to wail in her high-pitched squeaky cry. Flame tried to push back the covers to get up and go to the baby, but she was too weak. She felt dizzy and sick to her stomach and lay back as she closed her eyes and clenched her fists. How dare Joaquin threaten her when she couldn't even stand, how dare he!

Maria came through the door hurriedly and lifted the crying child into her arms. "Señora, your husband was angry again, even today?"

"My husband is always angry, Maria, you must know that. Now please bring me my daughter so I may see her." Flame unwrapped the soft blanket which covered the child and inspected her thoroughly. Though small the girl was perfection, exquisite as a rosebud, from her tiny fingernails to her wisps of golden hair. Her skin was the same creamy ivory tone that made Flame so lovely and she stopped crying the moment she was in her mother's arms. She peered up at her parent's face with a concentration that made Flame laugh. "Maria, I think she knows me already. Could that be true?"

"I'm sure of it, Señora. She is a beautiful child, what is her name?"

Flame frowned wistfully. "She has no name, not yet at least. I had wanted Joaquin to name her, but now—"

"Señora, I have known Joaquin all his life, I have been with the Villarreals since I was a child, I have known them all. Joaquin can be such a good man—

500

very strict, but just and fair. I cannot believe he is otherwise as a husband. I told him myself he was wrong about you and now he knows it. I could not help but overhear—can't you forgive him and return to his home?''

Flame looked up at her faithful servant's hopeful expression. The woman meant no harm, but Flame could not agree with her. ''Maria, is he right, am I no more than a spoiled child? Not old enough, not woman enough to be his wife at all?''

''You are young, Señora, do not worry, you will grow as your children do, you will make him a fine wife some day.''

That's it then, Flame thought sadly, even Maria thought her a child, but that wasn't true, not at all. Her childhood had ended forever the night she'd married Joaquin and found how little his promise of love was worth. No, her childhood was definitely long behind her, but what would any other woman do, any real woman do in her place? Flame bit her lip as she choked back her tears. ''Come baby, are you hungry? Could she be hungry already, Maria?''

''She seems wide awake. Let her try.''

Flame unbuttoned the top buttons on her nightgown and instantly the memory of Joaquin's easy touch flood over her—tiny buttons bothered him so and yet he could do them handily. Would she never be free of him? His face, his strong lean body, the gentle caress of his hand . . . he could be so tender when he wanted to be . . . every glance, every gesture he made was imprinted upon her heart. There was no way to leave him when he'd always fill her heart so completely. She lifted her daughter to her breast and the infant began to suck contendedly, not realizing her mother as yet had no milk to give. Flame laughed; this child was no different than her brother, she thought—always famished. ''How

501

strange it is that I can see nothing of myself in my son and nothing of my husband in our daughter. I wish you a happy life, little one, a very happy life, filled with love.'' Flame sat and hugged her child as she cried the tears she could no longer hold back.

Embarrassed, Maria left them alone, but she shook her head as she went. Someone should speak to Joaquin: he should be ashamed for tormenting his wife so. She was so young and foolish but he was a grown man and should know better.

Twenty-Four

By the time her daughter was two weeks old Flame was completely well, feeling better than she had in almost a year. Motherhood agreed with her. Her creamy skin glowed, her golden hair sparkled with radiant highlights in the sun and her slim figure became more rounded. She was as attractive as she had ever been and at last she knew it. She shut out all thoughts of her husband, closed her mind to him entirely as she enjoyed her tiny daughter's sweet company. The petite child was growing rapidly, her frail cry was now robust and her appetite voracious. Flame could not nurse the baby without laughing. The girl was always so hungry but slept soundly between feedings, content and happy. The June weather was warm and mild; only the three guards who kept a diligent vigil at the house marred the atmosphere of contentment which pervaded the home.

Flame still had no name for the child, called her only babe or sweetheart. She would have named her for Joaquin's mother but since she had learned the woman had deserted her family such a tribute seemed totally inappropriate. She hoped some name would occur to her soon, yet she still clung to her original hope Joaquin would name his child. But at that thought his memory flooded her being, overwhelmed her spirit so completely that she wept pathetically, frightening her housekeeper badly.

"Señora, you must not carry on so, things cannot be so desperate as you fear. Joaquin loves you, you know that he does." Flame continued to weep unconsolably in the older woman's arms, and Maria worried her mistress was becoming as melancholy as she had been when Joaquin had first brought her back home the previous summer. She waited until the pretty young woman was resting that afternoon and took the buggy to call upon Joaquin, for she could not allow things to continue as they were.

Frightened by the sight of the approaching buggy, Joaquin ran to meet the housekeeper. "Is something wrong? Is Flame ill, or the babe?"

Maria gestured impatiently as he helped her down from the high wooden seat. "I can stay only a moment. Your wife and child are fine, Joaquin, they are strong and well but I can no longer bear to hear that dear woman cry. I should have come to you before this."

Joaquin took Maria's arm as they walked into the house but he did not speak until he had closed the door of his study behind them. He did not look pleased as he turned to face her. "Did Flame send you here today? Is this some idea of hers?"

"No, she would be furious if she knew I'd come." Maria rushed on, her time too precious to waste. "You should never have gotten so angry with her after your daughter was born. You should be ashamed of what you have done to that lovely young woman, Joaquin. She has had so little happiness in your home and you cannot understand why she hesitates to return to you?"

Joaquin leaned back against the door. He still appeared exhausted; if Flame had recuperated fully from her ordeal at sea it was obvious he had not. "I know what I've done, but it's no use, Maria. Perhaps it is our fate never to find happiness—it eludes us so often, so completely. But I can do no more than I already have. I was willing to promise Flame anything and she refused to give me the slightest consideration. I will come for her when the girl is one month old and not a day sooner or later.''

"You will not come simply to visit your wife now? To reassure her of your love?''

"No, she knows when I'm coming for her and I'm sick of telling her I love her when she values my feelings so little.''

Maria frowned sadly. "I thought you were a wiser man than your father, but I see I was wrong. You are as great a fool as he was. Perhaps worse because you have not learned anything from the lessons of the past which should have been so clear.''

Joaquin snarled angrily, "You have overstepped your place, old woman, my father was no fool.''

"Oh but he was, he drove your mother from this house with jealousy and accusations which were totally unfounded. Drove her into the arms of a man who offered the love and trust he withheld out of foolish pride. I thought he'd hurt only himself but I see now what he did was far worse on you. I tried, but I was not the mother to you your own mother would have been. If you had only known her, Joaquin, if you were to seek her out even today, you would be a far different man, and a better one.''

Joaquin continued to stare at the housekeeper, his mood unyielding still. "I cannot change the way I am now, Maria, is is too late. I am the man I am and no other.''

"It is not too late! Come with me now, Joaquin, tell your wife you are sorry. She will choose to return to you but she must make the choice herself. Your threats have broken her heart and she will never find happiness with you now.''

"No! I will not go to her again! Go back to her

505

house, Maria, leave me in peace. Flame knows when I'm coming for her and she'd better be all packed and ready to come here. See that she is.''

Maria hurried away. She had done her best, perhaps it was time to retire, to return to Sonora. The Villarreal household held no promise for the future and she could bear no more of Flame's tears or Joaquin's sullen temper. He was a fool, he would lose everything and not even understand why.

Maria Elena moved out of the shadows and returned to her room. She had overheard enough of the conversation to agree that Joaquin was indeed a fool, but she had been an even greater one. Perhaps if she tried, she could accomplish what Maria could not: maybe she could undo all the harm she'd caused Flame while there was still time. Yes, there would be time—Joaquin would not go for his wife for another two weeks and that would have to be enough time. Maria Elena rushed to her room to think, to devise a plan, some solution to the torment which threatened to destroy them all, Joaquin, Flame and Rafael. A sob escaped her lips as she thought of Rafael. Yes, she could help, she would think and pray and with God's help she would make everything right again.

Joaquin sat morosely considering Maria's words long after she had gone. He could not even remember his mother, his father had kept nothing of hers other than her wedding ring. When she left the ranch she had simply ceased to exist, he could not even recall her presence in his home. She couldn't have loved him and left him alone as she had with no word, no visits while he was growing up. As he sat and tried to remember he found only a void where the memories of his mother should have been. Could what Maria had said possibly have been true? He knew his father had held women in low regard and had taught him to do the same, but had the man actually driven his wife from his home because of groundless suspicions?

The similarity of circumstance was too close for Joaquin to ignore. He saw himself becoming the embittered man his father had been, and it appalled him. That wasn't the life he wanted for himself, he wanted so desperately to make Flame happy, he wanted her to fall in love with him again and be content to be his wife . . . but that prospect seemed impossible now.

He left the room quickly and went to tell José he was leaving. There was only one way to discover the truth and he had to know it. If his father had raised him on lies then he had poisoned his own son's chances to find love from the beginning and Joaquin could not leave any approach untried in his quest to regain his wife's love. Any risk would be worth the taking if he could win back his dear wife and little children.

Joaquin knew San Francisco well and had no trouble locating his mother's home. The house was large, its owner very prosperous, a man he had seen only once years before and had avoided ever since. His mother's husband would not allow him to speak to her until he was certain of the reason for the visit. Joaquin sat opposite him now and tried to fight his anger. He hated the man—everything about David Caldwell revolted him. As if it weren't horrible enough that his mother had deserted him, she had had to do it for this blue-eyed bastard from the East who'd made his fortune in the railroads. That the villain was still so handsome and trim was just another point against him.

"I must say I was amazed to receive your message after all this time, Mr. Villarreal. Your mother expected you to come to see her years ago. It has been the one great heartbreak of her life that you have never sought her out."

It took all of Joaquin's self-control, and he knew he possessed very little, not to strike David Caldwell across his smug face for his rudeness. "Well, I have come now and I would like to speak with my mother, please."

"But of course, I will not prevent you from seeing her. All I want is your assurance that you are not here to reopen old wounds, to revive the pain your father so loved to inflict upon Marissa."

"I only want the truth, Mr. Caldwell. I have no wish to find fault; my father is long dead and I would appreciate it if you did not ever speak his name to me ever again."

"Exactly, the man is long dead, but why have you waited so many years to come to see your mother?" David leaned back in his chair and watched Joaquin's reaction closely. He knew all about Joaquin Villarreal; that his wife's son was such a wealthy and powerful man had always annoyed him tremendously. They had disliked each other on sight and after talking for several minutes neither had any sympathy for the other.

"I had forgotten I even had a mother, forgotten her so completely I never felt any need to find her before now."

"Why should today be so different from all the days in years past?"

Joaquin could not help but recall his conversation with Seth Randall. Lord, had that been only a year ago? He decided to be honest—he had nothing to lose, he cared little what Caldwell thought of him and pride no longer mattered to him where Flame was concerned. "I have married a woman who means the world to me and have succeeded in making her life miserable. I want only to find the cause for my own faults, not to blame my mother for hers. I just want to see my mother. I need her to help me."

Joaquin's plea was too sincere to be ignored and

David was suddenly ashamed he had been so rude to the man he knew his wife loved dearly. He touched Joaquin's shoulder as he stood to leave. "I'm sorry, I should not have spoken to you so rudely, Joaquin. I will tell your mother you are here."

"Will she see me, do you think?"

"Of course. She knew you would come someday . . . she will be very happy you are finally here." David strode out of the room and left Joaquin to sit and wait wondering what sort of woman he would find his mother to be. He was very curious but terribly afraid she would be the hateful shrew his father had always described.

At fifty-one, Marissa Caldwell was as slender and graceful as she had been as a bride. Her black hair was only lightly touched with grey and her smooth olive-toned skin unlined. Her features were delicate and sweet, she was nearly always smiling and she was smiling radiantly as she came into the room to greet the son whom she had not seen for more than twenty-five years.

Joaquin stood quickly as his mother approached, but he could only stare in disbelief. He remembered her instantly—her tender touch, her lilting laughter, her sweet love—it all came back to him in the second their eyes met. How could he have forgotten her so completely when he had loved her so? Except for her coloring and age she was so like Flame he was astonished. He swept her up into his arms and hugged her so tightly she began to laugh as she kissed his cheek warmly.

"I think you are as happy to see me as I am to see you, Joaquin, but I have seen you many times before today although I did not let you see me. You are so tall and handsome, I have always been so very proud of you. Now come sit down with me and tell me how I may help you."

Joaquin held her small hands tightly in his as he spoke. Without realizing it he addressed her in Spanish, the only language they had ever spoken together. "I want to know the truth about you and my father, I want to know how he lost you. I am so afraid I am going to lose my wife and she is so dear to me. I may have already lost her love, Mother, and I don't know what to do."

Marissa sighed and frowned slightly. "There was gossip, you must have heard it also. She was here in San Francisco recently, supposedly living with the attorney, Rafael Ramirez. Was any of that true?"

"Yes, every last word of it, but I will tell you everything later if you will first tell me what happened to you. Please tell me what happened, I must know."

Marissa smiled wistfully as she squeezed his hands. "It was so very long ago, Joaquin. I have been so happy with David—we have three beautiful daughters. Did you know you had three sisters? They all look a little like you except their eyes are blue. I hardly know where to begin, I've pushed all that sorrow from my mind for so long, but let me try and tell you what I can remember."

Joaquin listened attentively as his mother spoke and her story was as Maria had told him. His father's insane jealousy had ruined their marriage, and his mother had been blameless.

"I stayed with him as long as I could take his abuse, Joaquin, I stayed for your sake, but when our arguments began to become more violent I became frightened. When one night he became so incensed he struck me I left him. I had nowhere to go except to David; he was my only friend and he was kind enough to take me in. We were not lovers—which was Miguel's accusation in court—but there was no way to prove that. I thought I would never want to be married again, but

David was very patient, and so loving that in time I came to love him as dearly as he loved me. We were married two years after your father divorced me. We have had a happy life together, but I never forgot you, Joaquin. Maria and your Aunt Teresa have sent me word over the years to let me know how you were. I knew your father would not beat you, that he would treat you well, and you loved the ranch so, I knew you would be happy there even without me." But as Marissa looked at her handsome son his eyes were so filled with pain she knew he had not been happy for a long while. "But how does knowing what happened to me so many years ago help you now?"

Joaquin released his mother's hands and stood up. Too nervous to remain seated he began to pace up and down in front of her as he replied. "No, he never beat me, not once. It might have been better if he had. What he did do was much worse. He raised me to believe men should be cold, unfeeling, that any feelings of tenderness or love were a weakness. He gave me all his suspicions and hatreds. He raised me to use women for pleasure, as one would play a game of cards or race a horse, for a momentary diversion and nothing more. When I think how many women I've known it makes me sick and the worst part is I never cared for one, not even one until I met Flame and then I had no idea how to make her happy, how to truly love her and trust the love she had for me. I have been so mean to her and she was always so loving and sweet to me."

Marissa was alarmed by Joaquin's mood—he seemed to be skirting the borderline of madness and she was afraid for him. "Joaquin, my love, come and sit beside me again and tell me about your wife." Her voice was soft, lilting, enticing him back to her side.

"I cannot believe I had forgotten you, Mother. Flame is so like you and I must have seen that somehow, known when I first saw her why I wanted her so badly.''

"Many women are my size, Joaquin; it is a coincidence only. Now tell me about her. I hear she is a great beauty.''

"She is far more than beautiful, Mother, she is so charming and bright . . . but she thought I didn't love her, didn't want her anymore.''

"Joaquin, you must begin at the beginning. Tell me how you met, about your wedding, your children . . . tell me everything, but start with your earliest memories of her. I cannot help you unless you do.'' She nodded and made sympathetic comments wherever she could but she was stunned by Joaquin's tale, it was far worse than anything she'd imagined and she could not keep from crying as she listened to him recount the last three years of his life. In so many ways Flame's story was her own and as she looked at her son she could see his father so clearly and she remembered all too well the pain his love had caused her. "When was your daughter born, Joaquin?''

"Three weeks ago. She is a beautiful baby, so like her mother, she has her golden hair and green eyes . . . at least I think she does.''

Marissa had listened calmly, hoping to be able to compose some sort of an answer to Joaquin's anguished plea for help, but she could see no simple solution for the problems he had compounded over the years. "Your wife sounds like a truly remarkable woman, and she is just eighteen?''

"Yes, at least I think so. I think her birthday is in March but I'm not certain of the day. She was more of a child than a woman when we married—she was my child, Mother, only sixteen and—''

"Joaquin, stop it this instant! It does not seem to me as if Flame were ever a child. At least she was an ex-

512

tremely independent one and that is undoubtedly what has helped her to survive these last few years. You have obviously done her a great wrong and she loves you still, doesn't she? I think I can see why. Let us try and think what to do. You have spent only three months with your bride in all your marriage, is that correct?" Marissa wanted Joaquin to analyze his problems, see them in some sort of perspective, that was the only way she could think of to help him.

"Yes, but when she came home to me last summer she was so distraught, so distant, then she nearly died and was so terribly ill. We have never had any kind of a life together. As soon as she began to recover I went to Mexico and left her. I thought it was the only thing I could do at the time but the trip was pointless when she was already pregnant." Joaquin put his head in his hands and cursed. Every decision he had made had been the wrong one, time and again: the mistakes were always his.

Marissa placed her hand on her son's shoulder and patted him gently. "But what of Rafael? You two will not fight again over Flame? Don't you need to settle this issue with him soon?"

Joaquin sat up, straightening his shoulders proudly as he looked at her. "Do you know him, Mother? Have you ever met?"

"I know who he is by reputation alone. I have not seen him more than once or twice since he was a child and his family were our neighbors. From what I've heard he is not a man to be regarded lightly, but then neither are you."

"I went to see him yesterday, to explain everything. He and Flame are so close, so dear to each other I may never win her back. He has a drawing she made for him, a scene near our ranch which he has hanging in his office. I never even knew Flame could draw and he has her sketches framed and hanging in his office!" Joaquin got angry again just thinking of it.

"Well what did he say? I cannot imagine any good coming out of such a meeting. It frightens me to think you would even consider speaking with him."

"I am not afraid of Rafael, Mother." Joaquin scoffed at that notion. "He is furious at me for what I did, for kidnapping Flame, and rightly so. He wants me to let her choose between us. He thinks she can make up her own mind, that it would be pointless for us to fight over her again."

"I see. He'd set her free, let her decide for herself even though she left you and went to live with him? She was living quite openly with him from what I heard."

"Yes, but what their relationship was I don't know. Flame says he never made love to her because of her pregnancy but I find that difficult to believe. She is only using too narrow a definition of making love in order to placate me. Rafael will say nothing of what happened between them, but he cannot speak her name without smiling. All I know is that I want her back. I don't care what went on between them, I don't care if he made love to her a thousand times or how he did it, I just want her back home with me."

"Oh Joaquin, I'm sorry to say this but it's true. You are going to have to win your wife's trust: she has no reason to trust you now after the things you've done to her. You've treated her dreadfully and it may take a long time to win back her love. You will have to be a friend to your wife this time, Joaquin, a true friend as Rafael has been. Tell her your dreams and listen to hers. It will take time and it will not be easy, but it will be worth all your time if you succeed." Marissa took her son's hand in hers. "Love is like a flame, Joaquin, it burns where it will and like fire it cannot be held in your clenched fist. If you reach out for it, try and capture it, you will hold nothing but pain. Rafael is right, Joaquin. Let Flame go, let her make her own choice, and you will be surprised how easy it will be to hold your wife's love when your hand is open.''

Joaquin shook his head. ''No, I can't do that. I mean to bring her home next week. I'll go for her exactly as I said I would.''

''Force her to be your wife? Don't be a greater fool than you have been already, Joaquin.''

''Flame is mine and I'll never let her go. But I will try and treat her so gently and love her so dearly she will never again want to leave me. I can't bear to lose her and I will not risk giving her a choice when I am not certain she would choose me. I will keep her with me this time with whatever means it takes.''

Marissa began to argue, then stopped. He didn't see her point and she was afraid he never would. Love couldn't be forced, demanded from a woman, brought forth with threats. Would he never learn? ''We have talked for hours, Joaquin. It is getting late, and I know you must leave, but would you like to meet one of your sisters before you go? She was so excited to hear you were here, but I will not tell her what you have told me. I will tell no one, Joaquin, it will be our secret. Come to see me again, as often as you like, and I will always be happy to try and help you.''

Joaquin hugged his mother again before they left the room. ''You'll like Flame, Mother, I know you will. I'll bring her and the children with me the next time I come to San Francisco so you can meet them. I hope it will be soon.''

Marissa smiled as best she could and took his hand. ''Yes, I'm sure we will like each other, Joaquin. I will love her as you do, I know we all will.''

After Joaquin had left David Caldwell walked up behind his wife and hugged her slender waist, kissing her throat as he had loved to do for so many years. "Well, what was your impression of your son? Is he all you'd hoped he be? He is quite a man from all I hear, very shrewd in his business dealings—he can spot a poor investment in an instant and never makes any mistakes where his money is concerned."

Marissa shuddered as she relaxed against her husband. "No, he is nothing like I had hoped he would be. His deeds make his father's sins pale by comparison. I cannot believe he could have been so cruel to a woman he swears he loves. He does not even know what love is."

"Really? And yet he expected your advice?"

"Yes, but what could I tell him? He wants so badly to make his wife happy and he has not the vaguest idea how to do it. He has no concept of love at all, David, not in any way does he understand the beauty of love."

"Then his wife will have to teach him, Marissa, as I taught you." David again lowered his mouth to caress her silken skin. His kiss was playful, teasing as he hugged her.

Marissa closed her eyes as she covered his hands with hers. "Oh David, you were such a joy as a teacher but I am so afraid it is too late for Joaquin to learn. He is too old and has lived without love too long."

"Perhaps not, we will have to wait and see. What happened to his cheek? That scar is new—has he taken up fencing, or fighting duels with swords?"

"No, his wife hit him with a buggy whip."

David chuckled at that thought. "Well, she has an unusual approach but I'd say she should be able to teach him whatever she wants!"

"It's not funny, David, it's incredibly sad. They love each other so and they are tearing each other to bits. I'm frightened for my son, truly frightened."

David held his wife more closely and stroked her soft

shiny hair. "He is your son, Marissa, and if he wants his wife back do not doubt for an instant that he will succeed. Believe me, my dearest, from all I hear of Joaquin Villarreal he wins in whatever game he plays. He will be back to see you soon and the next time he will bring his wife and your grandchildren with him."

"You cannot think of them as your grandchildren too?"

"Marissa, Joaquin was never my son."

"No, but he could be."

David smiled at her words. "That will take some getting used to, my love, but I will try."

"Yes, I knew you would." Marissa kissed her husband and thought how dearly she loved him. But she had lived happily when she had thought her son was happy too. Now her life would never be so carefree until she knew Joaquin had solved his problems as happily as she had solved hers, with the joy of love.

Twenty-Five

Maria Elena was ecstatic when Joaquin announced he was going to San Francisco and would be gone for more than a week. Now she could visit Flame without having to worry about her mission being discovered. She had not forgotten Joaquin's threats and if he ever found out she'd gone to see his wife there would be hell to pay. But with him gone, it would be easy. The guards might tell, but not if she told them what she meant to do—no, the men would keep her secret then.

As she rode to the Lannier ranch her fears began to mount. What if Flame refused to see her, as well she might? After all she had treated Flame horribly every time they'd been together. She could not recall saying even one pleasant thing to Joaquin's wife in all the time she'd known her. Oh, she had been hateful, and look at the mischief she had caused. She worried as she rode along, all her hopes evaporating as she approached the new house, dreading what was surely to be Flame's refusal to admit her. But to her surprise Maria returned almost immediately and ushered her into the parlor where Flame sat sewing some tiny garment made of pink linen and lace.

"Thank you for seeing me, I was so afraid I would be turned away."

"And yet you came anyway? My curiosity would not allow me to miss this opportunity, Maria Elena. Sit

518

down here beside me and tell me why you have come."

"Oh Flame, I have done such terrible things to you, I can no longer bear to have them on my conscience."

Flame's eyes were cold as she looked up from her sewing. "Your conscience? Why Maria Elena, I was unaware you even had one."

"Say whatever you wish to me, Flame, I know you must hate me. I could not expect otherwise after what I've done to you. The awful things I've said, what I tried to make you believe."

Flame set her needlework aside and folded her hands in her lap. "If it's absolution you want I suggest you visit Father León. My nature is not a forgiving one in spite of what you may have heard."

"No, I don't care if you forgive me or not, Flame, that's unimportant. I only want to make you understand about Joaquin and me, I—"

Flame got to her feet quickly. "Please go, I don't want to hear it, not a word of it. Just go."

"No! You must listen. There has never been anything between Joaquin and me. He is my cousin, no more. He has never even liked me, Flame, he only tolerates my presence because I am related to him."

"Oh really? And yet he took you to Mexico with him, and not me, not his wife?" Flame crossed her arms over her chest and tapped her foot impatiently as her anger grew.

Maria Elena rushed on with her story, anxious to finish while Flame would still listen. "He couldn't bear to see you so ill, it was tearing him apart. I begged him to take me with him because I wanted to get away, anywhere away from Monterey. I could stand being at home no longer. My father wished me to marry a man I didn't love, I was going to run away until Joaquin agreed to take me with him. He stopped at our house on his way to San Francisco to tell my mother he was going to Mexico and I convinced him to take me along. We weren't together once we reached there: I went to Taxco to stay with my father's aunt while Joaquin went on to the capital.''

Flame frowned. Was that the truth? "It matters little now, Maria Elena. It is too late for explanations now.''

"No it isn't! Don't you see? Joaquin was wrong in what he thought about you but you were just as wrong in what you assumed about him. He adores you, Flame, you are his whole life. We were only together on board his ship but he talked of nothing but you and his son. He missed you so much—he didn't want to leave you at all, not even for one minute, but he just couldn't stay.''

"You must forgive me if I don't believe you. He has given me no choice but to return to him and we have no chance for happiness when he would keep me with him out of fear rather than love.''

"It could be different, Flame, it could be as you want it to be. There is a way.''

Flame turned away. She walked to the window and pulled aside the white lace curtains. "Do you see that man out there? How am I to change anything when my husband, whom you say adores me, keeps me as a prisoner in my own home?''

"Come back and sit down, Flame, I will explain. I have thought of a plan.''

Flame stared at the young woman who had caused her so much misery in the past and shook her head. "I cannot imagine myself using any plan which you have devised, Maria Elena.''

"You must listen, Flame, you must! You will not be Joaquin's prisoner if you go home to him. The guards will not stop you from returning to your husband.''

Flame was intrigued. "Just what do you mean?''

"If you go back, by yourself, you will take away the

520

only weapon he had to use against you, Flame. He cannot threaten a willing woman, a loving wife."

As Flame sank back down on the sofa her mind was a confusion of thoughts, hopes, memories and dreams. She had loved Joaquin all her life: his was the face she had remembered, and he'd waited for her. She'd come to him as soon as she could—perhaps sixteen had been too young but she could have waited no longer to find him. She was miserable without him, to live the rest of her life without his love was unthinkable. Would Maria Elena's plan work? All she'd need to do would be to return one day early, one hour early and Joaquin's angry threats would be useless. She began to smile. "It is a charming idea, Maria Elena, it would disarm Joaquin completely . . . but why have you suddenly decided to help me? I have always thought that you wanted Joaquin for yourself. You no longer love him?"

"Yes, I do love Joaquin, but as a sister loves an older brother. I was jealous of you, Flame, even hated you, but it was never because of Joaquin. It was always because I love Rafael."

"Rafael!" Flame's eyes widened in surprise she was so shocked by Maria Elena's disclosure.

"Oh, he has not even noticed me since he met you, Flame. I know he wanted to marry you; he still does. I have no hope that he will ever come to love me."

Flame was stunned, but of course, Rafael and Joaquin were together so often, she'd not understood Maria Elena's interest was in one and not the other. "You're wrong, Maria Elena. He told me one time that he thought you were very pretty, but I don't think he had any idea how you felt about him. Have you ever told him?"

The dark-haired young woman struggled to blink back her tears. "No, he has no idea. We are acquaintances only, he has never wanted more although we

521

have known each other all our lives.''

"Well, it shouldn't be too difficult to change his mind.''

Maria Elena could not help but smile at Flame's determined expression. "Oh Flame, I have none of your beauty, your charming ways. He would never choose me after loving you.''

"Nonsense, you are a beauty yourself, you know that. That Rafael has known you for so long and hasn't realized he's attracted to you is only a minor problem. Once he knows I've gone back to Joaquin, and willingly, he will doubtless be sad and need consoling.'' Flame looked down at the gold bracelet on her arm . . . sad was too slight a word for the way she knew he would feel. "I don't want you to think I'm saying this lightly, Maria Elena. If Joaquin is my heart, then Rafael is my very soul, truly he is, and I cannot give him up lightly. His friendship means so much to me, and if this is only a whim of yours then forget it now. Rafael has so much love to give and I could not bear to see him hurt if you were only going to lead him on, if you were not really serious about wanting his love.''

"My feelings for him are very real, Flame, I love him so much. Joaquin's temper always frightened me, but Rafael is so strong and good, he was always so pleasant and kind to me. I couldn't help but fall in love with him, even when I knew he cared nothing for me.''

Convinced of her former adversary's sincerity, Flame smiled warmly. "I do not think it will be too difficult for you to travel to San Francisco, will it?''

"No, I have friends with whom I stay when I want to go. I have my dresses made there and—''

Flame had no time for details, and interrupted. "Perfect, I'm sure you need lots of new clothes so your stay will be an extended one. I will write Rafael a letter which you will deliver. You will of course be sympa-

thetic, tell him I insisted that he read it in your presence
. . . the rest should be easy.''

''You would help me after what I've done to you,
how I've hurt you?'' the brunette asked incredulously.

''Maria Elena, if Joaquin and I can find happiness I
will be so grateful, so delighted I will help anyone! Now
help me to think of something to say to Rafael. He
knows I've always loved Joaquin, it will come as no surprise to him that I have chosen to return to him now. I
want to give Rafael absolutely no hope that I'll ever
leave Joaquin again, no hope that I'll ever turn to him
again for comfort or love.'' But as Flame spoke her eyes
filled with tears. At night when she lay alone in her bed
she could still feel his arms around her, still hear his
voice. Her memories of happiness with Joaquin were so
few, but all her thoughts of Rafael were pleasant ones.
She brushed away her tears quickly as she went to get
paper and pen. Her decision had been made for her
long ago: she was Joaquin's wife and she would go
home to him, but she would never forget Rafael.

When Maria looked in later she was amazed to see
the two young women busy writing a letter, their heads
close together. They were talking and smiling as if they
were the closest of friends. She threw up her hands and
went back to the kitchen; never had she ever expected
to see Flame and Maria Elena become friends.

After her caller departed Flame could not stop
smiling. Joaquin would be gone a week at least, she'd
need that much time to get ready. She'd go back to him
as soon as he returned home—that would be only two
days early, but all the time she'd need to show him how
much she loved him. She had been foolish to refuse him
when the baby was born. Why had she been so afraid
when he had promised so much, tried so hard to convince her of his love? He was right, everything was
going to be perfect this time. She rushed outside to

speak with one of the guards. The startled man got to his feet and removed his hat as she approached.

"I'm sorry, I've forgotten your name, was it Luis?"

"It is Luis, Señora, Luis Sandoval."

"Luis, you must come and tell me the minute my husband comes home. It's very important, will you do that for me?"

"If that is your wish, Señora."

"Good, but don't tell him I asked you, just let me know. You won't forget?"

"I promise you, Señora, you will know when he returns."

"Thank you, Luis. Are you thirsty? Hungry? You men have been bored to death out here, haven't you? Come into the kitchen and bring the others, Maria and I will fix your lunch. Well, come on, I can't escape if you're all with me, now can I?"

Maria had not had such enthusiastic guests to feed in weeks. Had Joaquin come by that afternoon he would have been astonished to see his pretty young wife entertaining her guards as happily as if they had been visiting royalty. The men laughed and joked amongst themselves for the remainder of their duty and they thought their boss a most fortunate man indeed.

Luis Sandoval was a man of his word and as soon as Joaquin arrived home he rode over to the Lannier ranch to inform Flame. Early the next morning she and Maria loaded all their things into the buggy, wrapped the baby up snugly in a crocheted baby blanket Flame had made herself and started off home with their three guards as an escort. They had been easy to convince it was permissible to let her go home, for they understood that was what Joaquin had wanted all along.

As they came within sight of the Villarreal home Maria reined in the horse. "Señora, look, there are several carriages. What could your husband be doing now?"

"I don't care who's visiting, Maria, I'm going home today and that's it, now let's go." But as they drove around to the barn Flame's heart sank. One of the carriages bore the seal of the state of California on the doors: the governor was visiting. "Oh Maria, look at that, the governor of all people!" As if on cue, Newton Booth appeared walking across the yard.

"Good morning, Mrs. Villarreal, how are you? You've certainly been out early this morning. Here, let me help you down. I forgot my briefcase in my carriage last night and was on my way to fetch it. What a beautiful daughter you have. Your husband is so proud of her, as well he should be." The governor continued to chat for several minutes before retrieving his briefcase and returning to the house.

Flame turned quickly to Maria. "Do you think he'll tell Joaquin we're here?"

"He might, I don't know. Do you want me to go and get Joaquin for you myself?"

"No, let's wait. I'll just get my things put away and speak to Joaquin when he has the time, but first I want to see my little boy." Flame walked into the house with a light springy step, the limp which had saddened her husband now completely gone. She was once again the bright, beautiful young woman he had loved so dearly, once again the happy girl he had never been able to resist.

It was not until the men had been served lunch that Governor Booth had a chance to speak informally with Joaquin. "I thought your wife would join us for lunch."

"My wife? Well, no, that's really not possible." Joaquin refilled the governor's wine glass and tried to think of some way to change the subject before he had to admit Flame didn't reside under his roof.

"I understand—she is busy with your daughter no

525

doubt. Such a pretty child, looks exactly like your wife, even has her peaches-and-cream complexion."

"What? When did you see the baby?" Joaquin sat forward, intent upon hearing the governor's response.

"This morning early, when I went out to get my briefcase, she and her maid were outside with the baby. I must say motherhood has not harmed her looks: she is even more lovely than she was when I first met her. That was just after she'd come here to stay with you I believe."

"Yes, that was when it was." Joaquin couldn't believe his ears—Flame was home? She had come home? "Excuse me a moment, gentlemen, please finish your lunch without me, there's something I neglected to tell my wife this morning and I must go and mention it to her now." He left the table with what he hoped was a dignified walk but when he'd left the dining room he broke into a run. He looked first in son's room, then Flame's bedroom, but they were both empty so he went on to his own room where he found Flame seated in a rocking chair nursing their daughter.

"Hello, Joaquin." Flame's happy smile lit her whole face with a radiant glow.

"You have come back to me, by yourself?" His expression could not have been more confused. He was ecstatic to see her, overjoyed to find her in his room, and he sat down on the edge of his bed to be near her. "I was going to come for you the day after tomorrow."

Flame's luminous green eyes sparkled brightly as she smiled. "I couldn't wait any longer to come home to you, Joaquin. I have missed you so terribly, I simply couldn't wait another day to see you. I would have come home last week but you were gone. I'm so sorry I didn't come home with you right after our daughter was born, I should have come home then, when you first asked me to. I'm sorry I was so foolish but I was just so tired I couldn't think straight. I know I hurt you, I was so miserable without you, I'm sorry to have made you suffer the way I did."

Joaquin shook his head in disbelief—he had always been lucky, but such good fortune as this amazed him. To have Flame back, really back, and happy to be with him was something for which he'd not even dared hope. He leaned over to kiss her, his mouth lingering upon hers until she began to giggle.

"Joaquin, wait! The baby is nearly asleep, then I will put her in her cradle and kiss you as much as you like. What do you think of your daughter now?"

"She has grown so much in only one month." He reached down and touched her tiny hand and she gripped his finger tightly. "What is her name?"

"She still has none; I wanted you to name her. What would you like to call her?" Flame found her heart beating rapidly and knew her cheeks were flushed—she was delighted to be home with her husband. She would never tire of looking at him, he was so handsome and when he smiled as he was now she thought the world of him.

"Could we call her Marissa? That's my mother's name, and I think she would be very pleased if we named our daughter for her."

Flame tried to hide her surprise from her husband, but she was appalled by his suggestion. "You told me your mother was dead, Joaquin."

"No, that was merely a convenient lie, one I've told far too long. I was too young to understand what had happened between my parents. I went up to see her this week. That's why I went to San Francisco, but had I know you wanted to come home I wouldn't have gone." Joaquin couldn't resist kissing Flame again in spite of her promise to put the baby to bed soon.

"Joaquin, just tell me about your mother!" Flame

laughed but she was only pretending, she wasn't at all angered by his affectionate kisses.

"I hope to take you up to meet her soon, Flame, I have been so wrong about her all these years. I'm too happy to tell you what she told me about my father now, but it made me see a lot of things differently, I hope more clearly. I'll tell you everything someday soon. You will like my mother and I know she'll love you—and wait until you meet my sisters. Do you believe I have blue-eyed sisters?" Joaquin smiled at his wife as he wondered if a man should feel as he did . . . was the sight of his wife nursing their baby supposed to be such an erotic one? "Ah, Flame, you look so well, how are you feeling?"

Flame needed only one glance at his expression to read his thoughts. "I am quite well, thank you, but I had very good care. I will insist you attend me at each of our children's births."

Joaquin shuddered, his memories not nearly so pleasant as hers. "You are not afraid to have another child, Flame?"

"Not if you'll stay with me, Joaquin, I won't be afraid at all the next time. You were right, you know. I was simply terrified and that made everything more difficult for me. Next time I won't be such a coward."

"Oh Flame, I would never call you a coward, and no wonder you were frightened after the way I treated you. No, things will be much better for you the next time, I promise they will." Joaquin looked away, trying to think of some tactful way to ask his next question. "Flame, is it too soon now? What I mean is, when could we—"

Flame was touched by his concern. "You lock the door and I will put Marissa to bed, she's asleep."

Joaquin leaned back against the door and watched in fascination as his wife approached him. "You can walk

528

without limping?''

''Why yes, my leg is completely healed, it bothers me no more. I can dance as well as I used to also, even if you have never been gentleman enough to invite me to dance yourself.'' She placed her hands on his chest, unbuttoning his shirt and running her fingertips over his chest as she did so.

''I will never miss another opportunity to dance with you, Flame, but that is not what I want to do now.'' As he reached for her waist he broke into a wide grin. ''Well for once your dress is already unbuttoned!'' He pulled her into his arms, covering her face with light kisses as he slipped off her dress and lace undergarments. He carried her to his bed and then began to peel off his own clothing as quickly as he could.

Flame propped her head on her hand and smiled sweetly. ''I hope you don't mind my putting my things here in your room, Joaquin.''

''No, this is where you belong, Flame. I won't make the same mistake again. Now come here.'' Joaquin stretched out beside his wife, caressing her softly rounded figure slowly as he kissed her. It had been so long since he'd kissed her and he couldn't get enough of her sweet mouth now. He held her tightly in his arms and kissed her until she clung to him, as hungry for his loving as he was to give it. He kissed the length of her silken throat then moved his mouth slowly to the soft tip of her breast, but stopped to look up. ''What will happen if I kiss you here as I always have?''

Flame tousled his shiny hair and whispered, ''What do you think? Go ahead, your daughter leaves little milk left.''

Joaquin's mouth closed over the rosy crest of her breast and he tasted the rich sweet milk his daughter loved so well and smiled as he looked at Flame once again. ''I was wrong to call you a child, Flame. I seem to be yours." He lowered his head and his tongue again flicked over her tender flesh with a warm caress which sent a tremor of desire through her long slender limbs and she drew him nearer still, hugging him close to her heart. The rapture of his loving kisses filled her with such pleasure she closed her eyes to dreamily drink in the delicious sensation his mere presence brought. His touch was like magic, sweet and slow and she responded readily to his affection, for it was filled with the promise of perfection he'd given. Their life would be overflowing with this ecstasy forever, for in his arms she'd truly found all that exists of paradise upon earth. She wound her fingers in his dark, glossy hair, intent upon capturing his elusive spirit, but he slipped away, lost in magnificent dreams of his own.

Joaquin's passion for Flame burned clear to his soul. Her name sang in his heart, her exquisite smile shone in his mind and her lithe body filled his arms with love, erasing the pain of their bitter separation with a surrender so entrancing he was captivated by the beauty of her love. It had always been the same for him, from the very first moment their lips met her affection wove an electrifying spell he could not resist and he was consumed by his need to possess her. Making love was no longer a foolish game but the natural solution to the unbearable longing she created within his heart. He closed his mind to all conscious thought, feeling only the ecstasy she gave and the joy he wanted so desperately to return to her in full measure. No man had ever given any woman more loving devotion than he lavished upon his dear wife that sunlit afternoon and yet he knew they had barely begun to share the joy he hoped would be theirs.

Joaquin shifted his weight and held Flame against his broad chest. He would never have enough of her and kissed her lips once more with the same undisguised passion he'd shown before. "How I have missed you. I love you so, Flame." He kissed her long thick eyelashes, the tip of her pretty nose; his lips clung to hers as he took her again. She was so loving, so delightfully playful and eager for his love that he lost all track of time in his passion for her. She aroused him so easily and satisfied him so completely he would never tire of her enchanting kiss, her soft slender body that welcomed his again and again that lazy afternoon.

"How long does the baby sleep, my love?"

Flame stretched her body against the length of his, pressing her supple form into his arms. "Not much longer, but she'll sleep all night without waking before dawn."

Joaquin nuzzled her neck affectionately as he hugged her again. "How was I ever so lucky as to find a woman like you? No man has ever had greater pleasure in a woman's arms, of that I'm sure."

"And you would certainly know, wouldn't you!" Flame made no attempt to stifle her happy giggle.

"Flame!"

"I love teasing you. I'd forgotten how much fun it is to tease you, Joaquin."

"Tease me and you know what you'll get!"

"Again?" Flame purred softly as she moved closer to him. She touched the silver hair at his temples and kissed his throat as hungrily as she had an hour earlier.

"Yes, you little vixen, again!" Joaquin rolled over on his back, pulling Flame up on top of him. They were both laughing now, so happy to be together nothing mattered but the delight of each other's loving touch.

"What has the governor been doing all afternoon, Joaquin?"

"The hell with the governor, come here." Joaquin's mouth captured hers again in a luscious kiss and they lay entwined in each other's arms until Marissa began

531

to stir, the baby making soft little noises to remind them of her presence.

Joaquin groaned with disappointment. "Well, it looks like I'll have to go now and see what the men have been discussing all afternoon . . . probably nothing of any importance. I despise the intrigues of politics: these men talk for months and still nothing is decided. I can't live that way."

Flame propped herself across the pillows as she watched her husband dress. "Do you suppose anyone will inquire as to where you have been all afternoon?"

Joaquin turned back as he unlocked the door. "I'll simply say I was making love to you."

"You wouldn't!" Flame cried out in horror.

"Yes, I would. You see, I enjoy teasing you too! I almost forgot, I have something for you." Joaquin crossed to his dresser and opened the top drawer to withdraw a small leather box. He sat down on the bed beside her to open it. "Here is your ring. After only two years I finally remembered to buy it. I hope you'll like it, I thought you would." He slipped the ring on her finger and Flame gasped in delighted surprise.

"Oh Joaquin, it's magnificent!" The wide gold band was set with emeralds and diamonds which sparkled in the afternoon sunlight, giving off rainbows of color against the stark white walls of the room.

"Do you like it?"

"I love it, thank you so much." Flame's sweet smile let him see how much she did indeed appreciate the exquisite ring.

"You're welcome. Now I have given you one horse, one dress and one ring. I'm not a very generous husband, am I?"

"You have forgotten the most important gifts, Joaquin. You have given me two beautiful children and best of all, yourself. I shall never need any other gifts

532

when I have so much already.''

''Oh Flame, why did things go wrong for us when we love each other so?''

Flame reached out to touch his cheek and he kissed her palm softly. ''She sleeps all night, you say?''

''All night.'' Flame smiled so seductively he leaned down to kiss her again before rejoining his guests. ''Come and eat dinner with us. Governor Booth expected to see you at lunch.''

''All right, I'll be ready, come and get me.''

''Until later then.'' Joaquin shut the door quietly and Flame rose from the bed to pick up Melissa and lay her on the foot of the bed.

''I love your daddy, sweetheart, I've always loved your daddy.'' Her smile faded as she recalled Joaquin's question. Didn't he know what had happened, why things had gone wrong? He had ruined everything, he himself, didn't he know that? Flame closed her eyes and said a prayer that this time everything would be perfect, just as her husband had promised, but still she was afraid.

Joaquin's wide smile left no doubt in his visitors' minds as to how he'd been spending his time. They joked amongst themselves but none made any untoward remarks to Joaquin, for none dared. When he returned to his room to dress for dinner Flame was wearing the beautiful lace gown he'd sent her from Mexico. ''You are as lovely in that dress as I knew you'd be, Flame. When I had it made for you I hoped it would fit.''

''Thank you, your memory is very good, for the fit is excellent. Who is here with the governor, Joaquin, anyone I might know?''

''Two of his advisors, three state senators . . . they are a dull group but an influential one, but thankfully they will be gone tomorrow. Then I will have nothing to distract me from you, my love." He pulled her to him and kissed her with such longing Flame couldn't bear to draw away. Finally Joaquin lifted his head and grinned at her. "Let's go in for dinner now while we still can." He took her hand in his as they entered the parlor but leaned down when Flame gripped his hand with a frantic tug. "What's wrong?"

"Senator Collins—I know him. He was a friend of Seth's!" Flame explained in a frightened whisper.

Joaquin drew her to his side and replied in a firm but quiet tone, "We have nothing to hide, Flame, no apologies to make to anyone. You and I understand each other and that is all that matters. Now come, let me introduce you. Perhaps Collins will not recognize you." Joaquin patted her hand warmly. Seth Randall was the least of their problems. Good Lord, what gossip was still circulating in San Francisco he could only guess, but these men had come from Sacramento and must not have heard about his wife's exploits, yet. But they would soon, he was positive of that.

Joaquin introduced his guests to his wife and those who had not met her before as the governor had were delighted to meet her. That he had a wife who was both beautiful and intelligent was a definite asset to their plans; that she was also so young and poised amazed them. They smiled knowingly at one another; they were pleased to meet her, very pleased indeed. Only Senator Collins frowned slightly. Instantly he had recalled that he'd met Flame before: her prettiness was unmistakable, but her name was wrong . . . where had he met her and when? He hardly followed the conversation at dinner as he racked his brain. Finally it came to him in a flash. He stared at Flame intently, then leaned forward. "Excuse me, Mrs. Villarreal, but I'm certain we've met. Was it by some chance in San Francisco at

Seth Randall's home?''

It took all of Flame's concentration to replace her wine goblet carefully on the table without spilling its entire contents on the white linen cloth as she replied. "Yes, we did. I was employed as his governess."

The conversation at the long table stopped abruptly. Only Joaquin appeared calm as he smiled at his wife. He winked at her and grinned. He loved her and nothing else mattered in the least to him, and his attitude was plain to her in his rakish smile.

"But wasn't your name Linda then? Linda—"

"Lannier." Joaquin supplied the missing surname in a casual drawl.

"Yes, that was it. Mrs. Lannier, then you have just recently married Joaquin?" Then he remembered the governor's comments on her baby and hastened to add, "I realize you must have been married a year or so."

"Joaquin and I have been married nearly two years, Senator, our anniversary is next week in fact. In addition to our baby girl we also have a fifteen-month-old son." Flame replied with far more confidence that she felt, but Joaquin's ready smile gave her all the courage she needed to speak the truth.

The senator frowned, obviously perplexed. "I'd swear you worked for Seth more recently than that. Weren't you there at his home a year ago last Easter?"

"Yes, your memory is very good, Senator. I left his employ last summer."

"What? Why on earth would you have been working for him if you were married to Joaquin!" the man blurted excitedly.

Joaquin responded for his wife: "Flame and I were separated for a time. We are together now, quite happily married as you can see."

The senator was flustered and stammered an apology: "I'm sorry, Mrs. Villarreal, if I've embarrassed you. I only recalled that you were a widow."

Now the governor leaned forward to enter the discussion. "Joaquin is your second husband, Flame?"

"No, he is my only husband. We were married when I was sixteen, he was my guardian before that."

That announcement met with a series of explosive comments but Joaquin only chuckled and continued to grin at his wife. He thought her flushed cheeks extremely attractive and couldn't wait to be alone with her as soon as he could get rid of his tiresome guests.

Senator Ridgeway waited for a lull in the conversation, then turned to Flame. "What do you think of your husband as a prospect for the next governor of California, Mrs. Villarreal?"

"Have you forgotten women are not permitted to vote in this state, Senator?" Flame couldn't resist making that retort, she hadn't lost any of her liberated views.

"Joaquin, you really must speak to your wife, unless of course you support woman's suffrage too," the senator scoffed at Flame's reply.

"As a matter of fact I do. My wife is the equal to any man I know and I can see no valid reason why she shouldn't be given a say in who is elected to office."

Flame was astonished but very pleased by her husband's words. "Thank you, Joaquin, but is this true? Are you planning to run for governor?" Flame held her breath. That is all we need, she thought. She could just imagine what the men at the table thought of her now.

"No." Joaquin grew serious as he replied. "I've no wish to run. That is Senator Ridgeway's hope, not mine."

Senator Collins coughed nervously. "Just a minute, gentlemen, let's not change the subject so abruptly. If I remember Mrs. Villarreal surely others will too. How could we explain that your wife was another man's governess?''

Joaquin looked down at his wine glass, seeing his reflection mirrored in the clear red liquid. Just wait until this group got to San Francisco and had to find a way to explain his wife had been another man's mistress and so damn recently too. ''I have nothing to explain and neither does my wife.''

Joseph McCall, one of the governor's advisors spoke up then: ''I wasn't going to mention this, but I did hear a rumor, several rumors actually, something about a divorce, but since your wife was here I thought I must have been mistaken. What is the truth?''

''A suit was filed, I have withdrawn it.'' Joaquin's expression was now subdued, his earlier good humor gone. He could see what was coming and didn't want Flame to have to hear it. The whole mess was his fault and although he knew she was blameless she was going to be hurt again.

Senator Collins lost his temper completely then: ''Joaquin, you really should have told us about your troubles with your wife when we first approached you about running for the office. The newspapers will have a field day with this divorce story. That you were separated for a time is bad enough but if you filed for the divorce people will jump to only one conclusion. This could cause a terrible scandal.''

Joaquin's stare sent a shiver down Senator Collins's spine: If ever a look were murderous, his was now. ''I have told you repeatedly that I have no interest in running for the office. I have been most consistent in my lack of enthusiasm for your proposal, but if anyone should dare to insinuate my marriage is of such a scandalous nature as to have kept me from seeking public office they will be extremely sorry. Where my wife lives and for whom she choses to work is her own business and I'm more than willing to fight any man who maligns her reputation. Shall I begin with you, Senator Collins?''

The senator turned pale. ''Mr. Villarreal, forgive me, I didn't mean—''

''I know exactly what you meant, Senator.'' Joaquin turned to smile again at Flame. ''Nothing is more important to me than my wife and children. I love them all dearly and have no wish to leave them ever again. I certainly would not leave them for so frivolous a pursuit as campaigning for governor.''

In spite of Joaquin's forceful reassurance and tender gaze Flame felt sick, appalled that he was being considered for so important an office and would refuse it because of her. Scandal? My God, their two-year marriage was one continuous scandal and if his name were seriously proposed people were bound to talk. There would be too many people who could tell what they knew and ruin Joaquin's reputation in the telling, all because of her . . . to say nothing of his terrible temper and unreasonable jealousy and the problems those faults had caused. Could Alex's death be called a problem? And dear God, what sort of reputation did she have left—she had met so many people when she'd been in San Francisco with Rafael, that was enough of a scandal in itself. It was surprising none of the men at the table had heard about that. When she looked up she realized all the men were staring at her, waiting for her to respond in some reassuring manner, but there was no way for her to salvage either her own or her husband's reputation. ''I'm very sorry, gentlemen, if I've proved to be a disappointment to you.''

Senator Ridgeway wasn't ready to admit defeat. ''I'm sure we can make up some plausible reason that will satisfy everyone should the fact you were employed as a governess become public knowledge, Mrs. Villarreal. After all, it is a respectable profession for a woman.''

Flame could barely see as she rose unsteadily to her feet. She gripped the back of her chair as she faced them. ''That I was a governess will not present your greatest problem.'' There was no way to tell these men Rafael was her dearest friend but nothing more, and the gossip they'd soon hear would brand her as the most wanton of whores. ''Excuse me, I think I hear my baby crying. Good night.''

Joaquin stared after Flame but let her go. He knew exactly what she was thinking, how dreadfully embarrassed she must be—but, hell, he was the one who'd forced her to seek Rafael's company when he'd been so damn stupid as to withhold his own. He would have more than enough time later that evening to reassure her just how highly he prized her devotion, and that's what he'd do.

Ridgeway shrugged. ''If Flame remains here on the ranch perhaps no one will realize you're married, Joaquin. We might get through the entire compaign without anyone mentioning your wife.''

''That idea is too absurd to merit comment for I won't leave this ranch ever again without taking Flame with me. Let us understand each other right now, gentlemen: I do not wish your support for the office. Is that finally clear? Good, now let's finish our dinner. I am surprisingly hungry tonight.''

When Joaquin bid his guests good night they were as relieved to see him go as he was to leave them. To his great despair, however, he found Flame crying as though her heart were broken and gathered her up into his arms. ''Flame, stop it. There's no reason for you to weep over this, none at all. I'd make the worst governor this state could ever have. I'd never be elected in the first place with my views!''

''Because of me you mean, just because of me,''

Flame wailed.

"No, not because of you, my pet." Joaquin stroked her soft curls gently.

"Oh Joaquin, you were right. I've been an awful bother for you—I've ruined your whole life now. You never should have married me."

Joaquin couldn't help but laugh. "Flame, that's ridiculous. Look at me, my life was absolutely nothing before I met you. I was so arrogant and self-centered and—"

"And so handsome all the women you met fell in love with you immediately!"

"Well, yes, that's true, they usually did. All except for you, Flame—you've given me the devil of a time. How could I have called you a child when I've behaved like a spoiled brat all my life?" He leaned down to kiss her damp eyelashes sweetly, brushing away her tears. "Please, don't cry, my love."

Flame sniffed as she tried to dry her eyes. "You really don't want to be governor? You really and truly don't?"

"Lord no! Never! They only asked me because my name is well known as an opponent of the railroad interests and I can well afford to finance a campaign—but believe me, I'd never be elected and I certainly don't want to serve. I mean it, Flame, I don't ever want to leave you again. Now have you fed Marissa?"

"No, not yet." Flame sat up and tried to compose herself for that task. "What will happen when those men hear about Rafael and me?"

"All of San Francisco must know about you two; our guests will hear the story soon enough. But you needn't worry about gossip, Flame. That episode is better forgotten. Now please get undressed and I'll bring Marissa to you."

Flame removed her lace dress as Joaquin cuddled his

little girl. She hung the pretty gown in the wardrobe, then removed the rest of her clothing before climbing into Joaquin's bed.

"Don't you want a nightgown?"

"Why? You'd just take it off me, wouldn't you?"

"Yes, but I always liked that lace one . . . where is it? I'll get it out for you."

Flame looked down at her new ring, unable to meet Joaquin's inquisitive glance. "I took it with me to San Francisco. I guess Rafael still has my things at his house."

Joaquin turned away as he began to swear softly. "It doesn't matter, I'll buy you a dozen more just like it." He hadn't meant to remind her of Rafael but it seemed unavoidable: every topic of conversation led right back to the man.

"Please bring Marissa to me and come get in bed with me, Joaquin." As always Flame found the little girl eager to nurse.

Flame's alluring expression was too inviting to resist and Joaquin sat down on the edge of the bed to unbutton his shirt. "I'll bet Joaquin was glad to see you, wasn't he?"

"Yes, we played together most of the day. But I can't say he's thrilled as yet to have a baby sister."

"It's only natural for him to be a little jealous. He'll get used to her before long."

Flame watched her husband undress with unabashed admiration—he was so handsome, so strong and fit— but as he turned away she saw the two long scars which ran down the length of his back, and she winced. "I'm so sorry I had to strike you with that whip, Joaquin. You'll have those scars for the rest of your life because of me."

"The scars are nothing to fret over, Flame, of no consequence to me. I'm afraid to think how far I might have gone that day had you not stopped me. You saved my life then. Whether you realized it or not, I did."

Flame bit her lip nervously, dreading to ask her next question, but she had to know how things stood. "Joaquin, what has happened to Rafael?"

"What do you mean?" He lifted the covers to get into bed beside her but his tone wasn't reassuring.

"Are you still mad at him? I know you made things extremely difficult for him and now that you and I are so happy I wonder if you would try and make things up with Rafael. Everything that happened was my doing. You heard me yourself, I asked him to come with me. I'd hate to think he had been ruined all because of me and now—"

"Flame, I have settled everything with Rafael. I spoke with him this week, but I had already made up all his financial losses. I did that right after Marissa was born."

"Are you two friends again then? Is that even possible now?"

"Yes, we have known each other far too long, and we both love you too much to part company now. But I told him to find his own wife and soon—I can't worry constantly about your leaving me for him, and I'm sick to death of fighting him for you. That reminds me, I have another present for you." Joaquin got up from the bed, went over to his dresser and quickly returned to her side. "Give me your hand a moment, the one with the bracelet."

Flame shifted Marissa to comply with his request. So he'd noticed the new bracelet. She had no story prepared; if he asked about it she would tell him the truth. Her eyes widened as he fastened another gold bracelet to her wrist, identical to the first. Both golden chains gleamed in the dim light.

"Now I want you to wear that and never take it off,

not ever. I want you to always wear it and know that I love you and you will always have a man who adores you. Will you try and remember that? I hope I got the words right.''

For the second time that evening Flame was certain she was going to faint, simply pass out right there. Why had Rafael told him about the bracelet? It had been such a sweet gift, his promise of love so important to her . . . what had possessed him to repeat that tender vow to Joaquin? She closed her eyes and turned away but she couldn't stop the tears which rolled down her brightly flushed cheeks. She wasn't ashamed of the time she'd spent with Rafael, his company had been so precious to her, but how could he have betrayed her trust so completely? How many of their conversations had he repeated to Joaquin?

''Flame?'' Joaquin put his fingertips under her chin to turn her head back to his, then leaned down and kissed her lips softly. ''Rafael didn't tell me a damn thing, Flame, not one thing about what happened between you two and I don't want to hear it from you either. But I won't share you with him ever again: he knows that and I want you to believe it too. Rafael told me about the bracelet because he didn't want me to force you to take it off and I'd never do that. He told me exactly what he thought of me for the way I've treated you and he's right about everything as usual. If I had half the sense that man has I never would have come so close to losing you.''

Flame looked down. There was no way they could avoid talking about Rafael or the time she'd spent with him: if she did it would always be a barrier between them. It was best to have it done with now, in spite of the pain. Yet she dreaded his every word.

''I told him to stay away from you, Flame, and he knows I mean it. Keep this bracelet and anything else

543

he gave you. I know you'll never forget him and I know he still loves you, he's told me often enough. But I won't let him anywhere near you ever again until he has a wife of his own. He's my age and it's high time he had a wife and family of his own."

"Joaquin, I wanted to come home to you. Rafael always knew I'd come back to you, he knew it all along, even when I didn't see any hope for our reconciliation. He would have brought me home to you whenever I'd asked him to."

Joaquin's features hardened and his voice rose in volume as he made his point: "Well, he is still my best friend, and my attorney, but by God, Flame, he will never be your lover ever again!"

Flame wiped her eyes in a vain attempt to stem the flood of tears which poured down her cheeks. "Please don't call him my lover, Joaquin, it wasn't like that at all, not some cheap affair based on nothing but lust. Rafael is my best friend too, perhaps the only true friend I've ever really had. He came here and stayed with me when you would not. He did more than merely keep me company when I was lonely: he filled my days with happiness and helped me to raise our son. He gave me hope for the future when I thought I'd have no future to live. I would have died without his attention, Joaquin, and there has never been anything between us but the deepest of friendships. I should not have asked him to go with me to my ranch that afternoon you arrived home from Mexico but I was just shattered by the way you left me. I knew you'd be angry I hadn't told you about the baby but I never dreamed you'd not accept the child as your own. That was the final humiliation, and it was too much for me to bear alone. I had never so much as kissed Rafael until that night we went to my house, but I was never unfaithful to you, never, I told you that the night Marissa was born."

Joaquin reached out to wipe away his wife's tears, his touch soft and sweet. "Oh Flame, why would you have remained faithful to a man who'd refused to be your husband? You needn't make any denials, nor confessions either."

"No." Flame sighed unhappily. "I keep telling you there's nothing to confess. Rafael was my friend, a true and dear one, but not my lover no matter what you choose to think. He gave me the attention I craved but only after you had refused to see how desperately I needed your love. I can never repay him for all he has done for me. I owe him my life and I gave him so very little in return." Flame could not help but weep now: she was so very grateful for Rafael's loving attention and she had never told him that she loved him and now she knew she did—not the way she loved Joaquin, but she loved him all the same, and now he would never know.

As Joaquin watched his wife weep he knew that what his mother had said was true. Rafael had known it, and Maria too. Everyone seemed to understand love better than he did. In one tender moment he knew her happiness was far more important than his own and that he'd have to let her go. He didn't deserve to have such a wonderful woman when all he'd given her was sorrow. "Flame, let me put Marissa to bed. Give her to me." He took his daughter in his arms, held her for a few moments, and her eyes closed in a contended sleep as he laid her in her cradle. "I know you told me you wanted to come home to me, and maybe you thought you really did, Flame, but that is not enough for me. Rafael has been the man for you all along. I'm sorry you didn't marry him two years ago, it would have saved us all so much pain. I was a terrible guardian and a worse husband but perhaps I can do something right for you now. It isn't too late for me to take you back to Rafael.

We'll leave in the morning. You file for the divorce; use any grounds you wish and I won't fight it. I just want you to be happy, Flame. After all the grief I've given you let me do this for you now. We can work out some agreement so that I can see my children frequently. The ranch will go to my son and I will provide well for Marissa too—you'll never have to worry about their futures."

Flame dried her eyes on the silken sheet which covered her, but when she spoke her voice was still hoarse with tears. "Then I am free to go where I choose, you will not threaten to banish me to Mexico or to take my babies from me?"

"I am ashamed I ever made such vile threats, Flame. You are free now, just as you have always wanted to be free. You may choose your own husband and live your own life. I'll not stand in your way any longer."

A slow smile spread across Flame's lips until it grew to an impish grin. "Why are you always wrong, Joaquin? Why is that?"

Joaquin sighed sadly as he hurriedly began to dress so he could leave the room. "You have broken my heart, Flame, must you tease me too? Good night, I will see you in the morning."

"No, wait! I want to thank you for so generously giving me my freedom, but there is one thing you have forgotten."

"Oh Flame, what is it I've done wrong now?" Joaquin inquired regretfully.

"You seem to have forgotten that I am so in love with you that I do not want to leave, that you are my choice and always have been. It's you I want for my husband. I love you so dearly, Joaquin, now please come back here to bed with me."

Joaquin approached his wife slowly, too shocked to speak, for he had lost her and won her back in the space of a few minutes and could not comprehend his good fortune. He still didn't really believe her, not even when he lay back down by her side. She came into his arms eagerly, her small hands moving over his powerful body with an enchanting caress. He had been too thrilled by her affection that afternoon to think at all, but now that he had come so close to losing her all his jealousy returned, flooding his mind with all the dreadful suspicions he had tried so hard to forget. He knew Rafael, knew his close friend's passions as well as his virtues and could not accept his wife's words as the truth, for surely no man alive could resist Flame's seductive caress. His hand closed over her wrist and he pulled her down across his chest. "Show me what he taught you, Flame. Will you not give me the same pleasure you gave to Rafael?"

Flame froze, her heart caught in her throat and choked her reply, "Joaquin—"

"Do it, Flame, show me what you did with Rafael."

It was his voice which frightened her, the same tone he had used to order her about, the same tyrannical tone against which she'd always rebelled. But Rafael had indeed taught her a great many things, not the least of which was to think before she spoke. Flame remembered that valuable lesson now and fought back the anger which welled up inside her. Coming home to Joaquin was going to be far more difficult than she had hoped, but his happiness meant everything to her now. Was there no way to convince him she had not been unfaithful? Then she began to smile: perhaps the best way to reassure him was simply with her love, and as always she was eager to offer him that. When finally she replied her voice was as sweet and lilting as a contented cat's purr: "Rafael taught me his fantasies, Joaquin. Perhaps they are not yours."

"It doesn't matter whether they are or not, just show

me.'' His hold on her wrist had not slackened. He held her in a strong firm grip but she did not struggle, only relaxed against him. He was daring her to love him, to convince him he was really her choice and she saw then how desperately he needed her. His anger was really pain. Truly they were far more alike than different: he needed her love as greatly as she needed to give it, perhaps more.

Flame's fingertips traced the outline of his lips before she leaned down to kiss him. ''Do not ask me to remember him when I am so happy to be with you. Tell me what it is you want me to do and I will gladly do it, but because I love you, Joaquin. There will be no other reason.''

Joaquin was explicit in his request. He described what he was certain she'd done with Rafael and waited for her to refuse. Flame, however, only smiled more broadly, trying not to let her surprise show in her expression. She had not known such a thing was even possible, let alone had the benefit of Rafael's instruction. Joaquin was coldly making a request—surely that was the way a man treated a whore, not a beloved wife . . . but she understood him now, knew his doubts were so ingrained it would be a long while before he would trust her as she hoped he would. She wasn't angry at what he was doing, perhaps he didn't even realize what he had done to her, but she had no intention of letting him treat her in such a fashion. If he didn't understand he had hurt her, then she would have to teach him how to behave toward her in the manner she desired. The idea occurred to her instantly, an idea too delicious to ignore: he could make whatever demands he wished, she would simply seduce him, drive him so mad with desire that what he had asked would be the last thing on his mind. Joaquin had always been so affectionate, she knew he would be a joy to love no matter how he wanted her to do it, and her smile grew more teasing as she looked down at him now.

"Are you certain you're not too tired, Joaquin? I don't want to tire you."

"I have seldom felt more awake and fit, Flame. I assure you I won't fall asleep."

"All right, but I warned you . . . now first of all you have to promise not to touch me."

"What?" Joaquin didn't believe her request.

"Do you want me to do this or not? This was your idea and not mine, so you must allow me to do this my way."

"Just get on with it, Flame." Joaquin released her arm and made no further move to touch her. He held his breath and waited for her to begin. It seemed completely unreal to him that she'd comply with his request with no argument and he lay in a stunned silence, not really knowing what to expect.

"Good, now just leave your hands at your sides, my love." Flame wound her arms around his neck and lowered her lips to his but she kissed him only lightly, her tongue flicking over his lips, then moving on to caress his cheeks, his ears, then down his throat. She kissed him very slowly, as if she had the entire night to spend just caressing him with her lips as her slender body moved slowly down the length of his. She spoke to him in the most seductive of whispers, telling him again and again how she had missed his sweet touch and longed to make him happy now. She poured out her love for him in the most beautiful words which came to her mind, and had her tantalizing touch not driven him past the limits of his endurance, her enchanting promises alone would have. She felt his breath quicken as her fingernails stroked his ribs and she smiled to herself, for if he had thought to teach her a lesson he was not going to succeed. Her long nails traced patterns lightly on the inside of his thigh while her lips moved down the taut muscles of his stomach and a low moan escaped his lips.

Joaquin could stand no more; he grabbed for her, pulling her luscious body close to his as he rolled over, pinning her beneath him in a loving embrace.

Flame reached up to draw his mouth down to hers. "I did not please you, Joaquin? You don't want me to finish?" Her green eyes were soft and glowing as they looked into his.

Joaquin's voice was hoarse with desire, and as he found himself being pulled into the beauty of her deep green eyes he shut his own to block her spell. "Yes, you please me far too much but I want you this way, only this way." His hands moved over her as he deepened his kisses, gently arousing her until her passion matched his own before he took her again, holding her tightly in his arms as if he were afraid she would slip from his grasp, disappear as if her love had been only a wonderful dream. But Flame was real, so very real, and her love enveloped him in the most delightful way. She made him feel alive as no other woman ever had and he wanted to please her now, to make her forget she'd ever known Rafael. She was his wife, only his, and he buried his face in her golden curls and clung to her, his passion spent but his heart too full of love to release her yet. He realized then what she had done: he had demanded something from her just to test her love, but she had overwhelmed him with the depth of her devotion. Her love had no limit and he had been foolish not to know that all along. She had been telling him the truth, she had never been Rafael's mistress no matter how lurid his imagination might have been, no matter what erotic pictures his jealousy had painted in his mind. He leaned back as he began to laugh, his good-natured chuckle bringing a lovely smile to his wife's lips. "You tricked me just now, didn't you, Flame? I can see it all so clearly now, and I understand how Rafael could have been no more than an attentive friend even if I have never had the strength to resist your charming ways myself. I'm sorry, I should never have made such a demand of you, it was neither fair nor polite. Please forgive me.''

Flame hugged Joaquin tightly as she purred in his ear: ''Did you really think I would refuse to make love to you? Being with you is my fantasy, my love, and I will always want to fulfill yours.''

Joaquin began to smile with the engaging grin she had always remembered. He loved caressing her soft slender body, kissing her warm, delicious lips, holding her once again and he would never have his fill of her, for the more he made love to her the more he wanted to love her again. ''Stay with me this time, Flame, promise you'll stay with me forever this time.''

''As long as I live I will be yours, Joaquin, and I hope I live forever.''

''I think you might just do that, Flame, and each day I will love you more.''

''Oh Joaquin, I don't think it's possible for me to love you more than I do now, I love you so much already. I've adored you my whole life, you know that don't you?''

Joaquin propped his head on his elbow and smiled down at her. He longed to tell her everything he'd hidden in the past but hardly knew where to begin. ''Yes, and I'm sorry I didn't let myself love you for such a long time. I swear I had no emotions at all until I met you, and I had no idea how to deal with them other than to deny them. I know now my need for you is as natural as yours for me—we are a better-matched pair than any of my thoroughbreds, Flame, and we can be so close now. Do you know the night Marissa was born I heard your voice calling me so clearly? That's why I came to you when I did, I knew you needed me and I couldn't reach you fast enough. That I didn't understand how desperately you needed me last summer was just my own stupidity, for you were always so honest with me about your feelings. If I had but told you I couldn't stand to spend another night in this house without making love to you then you would have told me about the baby and I would never have gone away."

"Yes, I would have been so happy to tell you, but I didn't want you to stay with me out of pity, Joaquin, only out of love."

"Do you understand now how much I love you, Flame? Do you believe me now? You'll never need Rafael ever again because I plan to be the husband you deserve. I can be your best friend as he has been. I didn't even know that you could draw, Flame, nor am I sure of the exact date of your birthday . . . there is so much about you I have to learn, but I do want to learn, Flame, I really do. I want to be everything to you if you'll just let me."

Flame reached up to kiss him, then smiled. She didn't want to discuss Rafael, for the time she'd spent with him no longer mattered. It was part of the past, over, closed like a beloved book which would never again be read. "Joaquin, I am so very happy to be your wife. Now please do not mention Rafael's name to me ever again or I will begin to think I have made the wrong choice! Whether he marries or not does not matter to me for I will not see him again—it would too difficult for all of us for Rafael and I ever to meet again. I sent him a letter and told him good-bye, he knows it's finished between us, but I can't believe you'd recommend marriage to him after all the troubles we've had."

"They are over, Flame, and I'd recommend marriage to anyone who would listen.'' He leaned down to kiss her again, slowly and sweetly as he twisted her golden hair between his fingers. "I know you do not like Maria Elena, and with good reason, but do you suppose there is any way we could get her interested in Rafael? I've always thought that he rather liked her, and if she'd only give him some encouragement I think he would fall in love with her swiftly.''

"I don't know how we could help, Joaquin.'' Flame could not help herself and began to giggle.

"What's so damn funny?''

"You are! I can't believe you'd want to play match-maker, Joaquin.''

"Well it does seem like a good match, doesn't it? It would solve all our problems to have those two occupied with each other.''

"Yes it would, but let's see if they don't come to the same conclusion on their own.'' Suddenly Flame was curious. "Who was that pretty blonde woman you were dancing with that night at the party?''

"I'm not sure. When I saw you with Rafael I was so angry I just turned to the closest woman and asked her to dance. I have no idea who she was. I just wanted to make you jealous so you'd know the wretched unhappiness I felt.''

"You'll admit that to me?'' Flame was surprised by his candor, he really had changed.

"Yes, did it work?''

"Of course, but don't do that to me ever again, Joaquin.''

"I'm certain I'll never have reason to, my pet. Would you like to go to San Francisco with me on my next trip? I know Rafael took you everywhere but it is a marvelous city and—''

Flame's expression saddened as she declined his invitation: "Oh Joaquin, how can you even want to be seen in that town with me after the scandal we caused?''

"I've told you repeatedly you have nothing of which to be ashamed, Flame. How you live your life is your own business and no one else's. I'll be proud to introduce you as my wife . . . it might be amusing to watch people's faces when I do.''

"Joaquin, that's awful! If you like scandals so much shall I cause a few more?'' Flame's eyes shone with a wicked gleam.

"Don't even consider it, Flame. I plan to keep you with me all the time from now on. I will never leave this ranch again without taking you with me. That's a promise—you'll have no time on your hands in which to cause scandals.''

"Will you take me to Mexico? Will you take me aboard your ship when next you sail?''

"Yes, but I will have a larger bunk installed before we travel together again, we were really much too crowded. I've always hated the sea, but if you were to share my cabin—''

"Was that your cabin where Marissa was born?''

"Yes, but don't remind me. I still don't believe I actually kidnapped you. That was the stupidest thing I have ever done.''

Flame frowned thoughtfully. "I don't know, Joaquin, that would be difficult to decide.''

"Flame! Must you rub it in? I know only too well what horrible mistakes I've made, if only—''

Flame interrupted him quickly with a lengthy kiss. "Joaquin, we only waste time on regrets. We can't undo the past, you taught me that. We could sit here all night recounting the mistakes we've made, or we could make up for the love we've missed. I know which I'd rather do.'' As Flame leaned over him her soft breasts brushed his chest lightly and he began to laugh.

"God, you just deliberately drive me wild, don't

you?'' Joaquin pulled her into his arms, kissing her as only he knew how, with both tenderness and passion.

Flame gazed down at her husband with eyes filled with love. "Joaquin, I'll always be your wife and I do so want to please you . . . teach me all about love. You teach me yourself this time.''

"Why Flame, all that I know of love I learned from you.''

When his mouth found hers again she understood: she was his only love. He had never loved another woman and now he never would, for she would stay with him for as long as he wished, she would be his forever.

Joaquin held Flame in his arms for hours, talking to her in the low, mellow voice she loved. She was totally his once more, soft, yielding, adoring. No man had ever had a finer wife and he knew it. "I'll never leave you again, my golden-haired beauty, I will never ever leave you again.''

"I'm going to insist you keep that promise, Joaquin.''

"I will. You know, I used to think once I married, began to raise a family, my life would be routine, placid to the point of dullness. That was, of course, long before I met you, Flame. If anything, our life grows more exciting each day. I never expected our marriage to be such an adventure.''

"But you like adventure, don't you, Joaquin?''

"That all depends . . . what did you have in mind?''

Flame snuggled against her husband's warm chest, her smile most alluring and playful. "Come here, my dear, and I'll give you another adventure.''

"Yes, my Flame, I'm certain you will.'' Joaquin needed no encouragement to make love to his precious wife once again, and his lips sought hers eagerly. Her affection was always new, always exciting. She was so right: their love was the ultimate adventure.

MORE RAPTUROUS READING

WINDSWEPT PASSION   (1484, $3.75)
By Sonya T. Pelton
The wild, wordly pirate swept young, innocent Cathelen into an
endless wave of ecstasy, then left with the morning tide. Though
bound to another, the lovely blonde would turn one night of love
into a lifetime of raging WINDSWEPT PASSION.

BITTERSWEET BONDAGE   (1368, $3.75)
by Sonya T. Pelton
In sultry, tropical Morocco, Rosette would forget the man who
had broken her heart. And forget she did in the tantalizing embrace of mysterious, magnetic Mark — who knew he'd always
keep her in BITTERSWEET BONDAGE.

AWAKE SAVAGE HEART   (1279, $3.75)
by Sonya T. Pelton
Though Daniel craved tantalizing Tammi, marriage was the
farthest thing from his mind. But only Tammi could match the
flames of his desire when she seductively whispered, AWAKE
SAVAGE HEART.

THE CAPTAIN'S VIXEN   (1257, $3.50)
by Wanda Owen
No one had ever resisted Captain Lance Edward's masculine mag-
netism — no one but the luscious, jet-haired Elise. He vowed to
possess her, for she had bewitched him, forever destining him to
be entranced by THE CAPTAIN'S VIXEN!

TEXAS WILDFIRE   (1337, $3.75)
by Wanda Owen
When Amanda's innocent blue eyes began haunting Tony's days,
and her full, sensuous lips taunting his nights, he knew he had to
take her and satisfy his desire. He would show her what happened
when she teased a Texas man — never dreaming he'd be caught in
the flames of her love!

*Available wherever paperbacks are sold, or order direct from the
Publisher. Send cover price plus 50¢ per copy for mailing and
handling to Zebra Books, 475 Park Avenue South, New York,
N.Y. 10016. DO NOT SEND CASH.*

RAPTUROUS ROMANCE BY CONSTANCE O'BANYON

SAVAGE AUTUMN (1457, $3.50)
The white woman Joanna gave a cry of terror when the tall young leader of the Blackfoot tribe carried her away from all she held dear. But when he took her in his arms in his tepee, her soft moans were as rapturous and her kisses as urgent as his own. He knew the heights of passion awaited them in the . . . SAVAGE AUTUMN.

ENCHANTED ECSTASY (1386, $3.75)
Fearless and independent, the Indian princess Maleaha was the most sought-after woman in the New Mexico territory. No man had ever claimed her supple body, but Major Benedict knew she couldn't refuse him, and then he couldn't let her go!

SAVAGE SPLENDOR (1292, $3.50)
Married to the mighty King of the Lagonda tribe, beautiful Mara was respected and admired, but was she truly happy? By day she quesioned whether to remain in her husband's world or with her people. But by night, crushed in the muscular arms of the King, taken to the peaks of rapture, she knew she could never live without him, never let him go . . .

ECSTASY'S PROMISE (978, $3.50)
At seventeen, beautiful Victoria burned the family plantation to keep Sherman's Yankee troops from having it. Fleeing to Texas, meeting handsome, wealthy ranch owner, Edward Hanover, Victoria's passion burst into a raging blaze as his fingers brushed her silky skin. But Hanover had fought for the Union—was an enemy—and the only man she would ever love!

Available wherever paperbacks are sold, or order direct from the Publisher. Send cover price plus 50¢ per copy for mailing and handling to Zebra Books, 475 Park Avenue South, New York, N.Y. 10016. DO NOT SEND CASH.

THE BEST IN HISTORICAL ROMANCE
by Penelope Neri

HEARTS ENCHANTED   (1432, $3.75)
When Lord Brian Fitzwarren saw the saucy, slender wench bathing in the river, her fresh, sun-warmed skin beckoned for his touch. That she was his enemy's daughter no longer mattered. The masterful lord vowed that somehow he would claim the irresistible beauty as his own . . .

BELOVED SCOUNDREL   (1259, $3.75)
When the handsome sea captain James Mallory was robbed by the scruffy street urchin, his fury flared into hot-blooded desire upon discovering the thief was really curvaceous Christianne. The golden-haired beauty fought off her captor with all of her strength — until her blows became caresses and her struggles an embrace . . .

PASSION'S RAPTURE   (1433, $3.75)
Through a series of misfortunes, an English beauty becomes the captive of the very man who ruined her life. By day she rages against her imprisonment — but by night, she's in passion's thrall!

JASMINE PARADISE   (1170, $3.75)
When Heath sets his eyes on the lovely Sarah, the beauty of the tropics pales in comparison. And he's soon intoxicated with the honeyed nectar of her full lips. Together, they explore the paradise . . . of love.

Available wherever paperbacks are sold, or order direct from the Publisher. Send cover price plus 50¢ per copy for mailing and handling to Zebra Books, 475 Park Avenue South, New York, N.Y. 10016. DO NOT SEND CASH.

CAPTIVATING ROMANCE FROM ZEBRA

MIDNIGHT DESIRE (1573, $3.50)
by Linda Benjamin
Looking into the handsome gunslinger's blazing blue eyes, innocent Kate felt dizzy. His husky voice, so warm and inviting, sent a river of fire cascading through her flesh. But she knew she'd never willingly give her heart to the arrogant rogue!

PASSION'S GAMBLE (1477, $3.50)
by Linda Benjamin
Jade-eyed Jessica was too shocked to protest when the riverboat cardsharp offered *her* as the stakes in a poker game. Then she met the smouldering glance of his opponent as he stared at her satiny cheeks and the tantalizing fullness of her bodice—and she found herself hoping he would hold the winning hand!

FORBIDDEN FIRES (1295, $3.50)
by Bobbi Smith
When Ellyn Douglas rescued the handsome Union officer from the raging river, she had no choice but to surrender to the sensuous stranger as he pulled her against his hard muscular body. Forgetting they were enemies in a senseless war, they were destined to share a life of unbridled ecstasy and glorious love!

WANTON SPLENDOR (1461, $3.50)
by Bobbi Smith
Kathleen had every intention of keeping her distance from Christopher Fletcher. But in the midst of a devastating hurricane, she crept into his arms. As she felt the heat of his lean body pressed against hers, she wondered breathlessly what it would be like to kiss those cynical lips—to turn that cool arrogance to fiery passion!

Available wherever paperbacks are sold, or order direct from the Publisher. Send cover price plus 50¢ per copy for mailing and handling to Zebra Books, 475 Park Avenue South, New York, N.Y. 10016. DO NOT SEND CASH.